HID FROM
OUR EYES

HID FROM OUR EYES

A Clare Fergusson/Russ Van Alstyne Mystery

~

JULIA SPENCER-FLEMING

MINOTAUR BOOKS
NEW YORK

First published in the United States by Minotaur Books, an imprint of St. Martin's Publishing Group

HID FROM OUR EYES. Copyright © 2020 by Julia Spencer-Fleming. All rights reserved. Printed in the United States of America. For information, address St. Martin's Publishing Group, 120 Broadway, New York, NY 10271.

www.minotaurbooks.com

Library of Congress Cataloging-in-Publication Data

Names: Spencer-Fleming, Julia, author.
Title: Hid from our eyes / Julia Spencer-Fleming.
Description: First edition. | New York: Minotaur Books, 2020. | Series: A Fergusson/Van Alstyne mystery; 9
Identifiers: LCCN 2019049217 | ISBN 9780312606855 (hardcover) | ISBN 9781250022660 (ebook)
Subjects: LCSH: Fergusson, Clare (Fictitious character)—Fiction. | Van Alstyne, Russ (Fictitious character)—Fiction. | Murder—Investigation—Fiction. | GSAFD: Mystery fiction.
Classification: LCC PS3619.P467 H53 2020 | DDC 813/.6—dc23
LC record available at https://lccn.loc.gov/2019049217

ISBN 978-0-312-60685-5 (hardcover)
ISBN 978-1-250-02266-0 (ebook)

Our books may be purchased in bulk for promotional, educational, or business use. Please contact your local bookseller or the Macmillan Corporate and Premium Sales Department at 1-800-221-7945, extension 5442, or by email at MacmillanSpecialMarkets@macmillan.com.

First Edition: April 2020

10 9 8 7 6 5 4 3 2 1

To the three people who are my past, present, and future:
Victoria Hugo-Vidal, Spencer Hugo-Vidal, and
Virginia Hugo-Vidal

Immortal, invisible, God only wise,

In light inaccessible hid from our eyes,

Most blessed, most glorious, the Ancient of Days,

Almighty, victorious, Thy great Name we praise.

Unresting, unhasting, and silent as light,

Nor wanting, nor wasting, Thou rulest in might;

Thy justice, like mountains, high soaring above

Thy clouds, which are fountains of goodness and love.

To all, life Thou givest, to both great and small;

In all life Thou livest, the true life of all;

We blossom and flourish as leaves on the tree,

Then wither and perish; but nought changeth Thee.

Great Father of glory, pure Father of light,

Thine angels adore Thee, all veiling their sight;

All land we would render; O help us to see

'Tis only the splendor of light hideth Thee!

—WALTER CHALMERS SMITH (1842–1908)
THE HYMNAL, 1982, THE CHURCH PENSION FUND

HID FROM
OUR EYES

AUGUST 1952

1.   He had parked his cruiser in the muddy verge of the county highway, a little way from the circus that was going on up the road. The thunderstorms that had crested over the mountains and crashed over the valleys had paused; the night's pounding rain had lightened to a drizzle. The Millers Kill chief of police splashed into a puddle as he exited the car, twisting and cracking his back and flexing his knees. He felt every one of his fifty-odd years after being hauled out of bed at 4 A.M. He never could have survived being a dairy farmer, that was for damn sure.

He checked around to make sure no one had seen his display and settled his broad-brimmed rain cap in place. His own, not his MKPD flat. He was here on courtesy, not on right, and he had tried to parse the difference with his clothing: his uniform blouse and departmental rain jacket over his own twill pants and rubber boots.

The state police had cordoned off the road coming and going and had two enormous lamps illuminating the crime scene. The dull roar of the generator sounded like a jet engine. He splashed up the side of the road, past the other cop cars and the mortuary van, wondering why none of the bad ones ever happened on a clear, temperate afternoon. Or maybe some had, and his memory was playing tricks on him, turning everything bright into darkness and heavy weather.

He ducked beneath the tape and approached the scene. Two evidence officers: one the camera man, the other bent over searching for anything that might prove useful in the investigation. Which, even when a battering rain hadn't washed everything away, wasn't ever much. Ninety-nine out of a hundred crimes were solved by knocking

1

on doors until someone talked, in Harry's experience. Two detectives in trench coats that made them look like they were headed for the executive offices at General Electric, smoking and talking. One uniform, almost anonymous in rain cap and full sou'wester, the first man on the scene.

"Hey!" A detective spotted him. He recognized the man; Stan Carruthers, a hotshot from downstate who was disgruntled by his exile, as he saw it, to the hinterlands of Troop G. "What're you doing here?" Carruthers glared at the uniform, whose charge was securing the scene and who should have stopped anyone from crossing the line. The trooper tried to appear innocent, and mostly got it right, since he was so young he looked as if he ought to be home sleeping in his mother's house, not guarding a corpse.

"Who's this?" the second detective asked.

"Harry McNeil, Millers Kill chief of police." Harry held out his hand and the other man shook it automatically. "Pleasure to meet you."

"There's no need for you to be here, McNeil." Carruthers sounded more bored than upset. "We're almost finished up."

Harry got his first good look at the body. A young woman, barely more than a girl, sprawled face-forward in a tangle of wet limbs and hair. Night-black hair shone slick in the state police lights. She was wearing a fancy dress, a party dress in pale green, with petticoats plastered over her legs and back, the flattened ruffles like waves frothing around her knees. Bare feet. No stockings. His mother had had a picture book of famous ballets she would read to him as a child; the name *Ondine, or The Water Nymph* surfaced after a fifty-year sleep.

"Any idea as to the cause of death?" Harry directed his question to the evidence officer.

The man shook his head. "No signs of violence from here, although the rain could have washed any blood away. We're about to move her, though, so maybe we'll see something from the front."

"It's obvious," Carruthers said. "Some good-time girl, got liquored up and passed out and died of exposure. I've seen it before."

"In August?" Harry looked around. "In the middle of McEachron Hill Road?" On either side of the two-lane road, wide fields disappeared into the mist. To the west, the first Adirondack hills that would gather and crest a hundred miles away in the High Peaks were shrouded kettledrums, echoing distant thunder. Not a single farmhouse light relieved the gloom.

Carruthers waved his cigarette. "Maybe her john wouldn't pay up. They had a fight, she stumbled out of the car to show him what's what, he took off."

"In the pouring rain. Without her shoes and stockings. Or wrap."

Carruthers frowned. "Drunks do stupid things, McNeil."

The mortuary men had left the cover of their wagon and were placing their stretcher next to the body. "Okay, boys," the evidence officer said. "Nice and easy."

They rolled the corpse over, depositing her neatly on her back. Everyone moved closer to get a look. Pretty, despite the mascara that had run across her cheeks. Her lipstick was still vividly red. No blood, no bruises, no scratches or ripped fabric or anything to indicate she might have been attacked. A detailed crucifix still hung from a delicate chain around her neck. Carruthers's partner pointed to it. "Catholic." He took out his handkerchief and turned the figure over, shining his flashlight on the silver. "Nothing engraved. No mark." He straightened. "She sure ain't Polish. Maybe Italian." He pronounced it *Eye-talian*. "Maybe French?"

"Not from around here, anyway." Carruthers took a last drag and flicked his stub away, a sure sign that he no longer considered this a crime scene. If he ever had. "She passed out and died of exposure. Or maybe alcohol poisoning. She could have thrown up a couple fifths of Four Roses and we wouldn't find a trace after all the rain."

Harry looked at the evidence man again. "Have you found anything? Shoes and stockings? Handbag?"

The officer shook his head. "Nothing. And I did a thorough search, up and down the road." His tone was bland, but his eyes shifted to the detectives for a moment. Harry could picture Carruthers yelling at the man to stop wasting his time and for God's sake just get the body bagged already. "Either side of the road as well, although we ought to go back over it in daylight to make sure."

"Oh, for Christ's sake. Can one of you geniuses give me any *other* reason she'd be here like this?"

There was a pause as Harry turned the picture over in his head.

"Murdered and dumped." Everyone turned toward the speaker. It was the responding trooper.

"Oh, great," Carruthers said. "Now even the traffic cops are detectives. What's your theory of the crime, Sherlock?"

"She could have been poisoned by chloroform or ether. Suffocated after she passed out from drinking. There might be an injury not visible yet." The officer was young, but his voice was firm.

Harry nodded. "Why do you think so, son?"

"First off, if she were drunk, where'd she get the liquor? Here and Millers Kill are dry towns. The nearest bar's in Fort Henry, thirty minutes away. Second, if she's a prostitute, where's her purse? Working girls carry rubbers and lipstick and powder and lots of cash. Maybe she was drunk enough to get out of a car in the middle of a storm without her shoes, but without her purse? Finally, why would a john bring her here unless it was to get rid of her body? There's not a hotel or motor inn within thirty miles of this spot. Any farmer out for a good time would've headed for Glens Falls or Lake George and taken care of business there."

Harry tilted his head toward the trooper. Exactly his reasoning, laid out cleanly and logically.

"Never attribute to malice what you can pin on stupidity, kid." Carruthers gestured to the mortuary men. The pair lifted the stretcher and began a swaying march back to their van. "A couple drunks going from point A to point B, they screw in the backseat, they fight, or maybe she just stumbles away to pee in the bushes, he skips out without paying and here we all are. Death by misadventure." He nodded toward his partner. "Let's go."

"Detective—" Harry began.

"It's not your case, McNeil. Cossayuharie is Troop G's concern, not yours." He shot a look at the young officer. "Keep that in mind the next time you're tempted to call in the locals, Trooper Liddle."

The evidence officer and the cameraman began to break down the lights. Harry waited until he heard the slamming of the detectives' car doors before he spoke. "Thanks for letting me know, Jack."

The trooper shook his head. "I'm sorry I wasted your time. It's just . . ." He glanced toward where Carruthers was pulling out. "It gets so frustrating. He doesn't take anything that happens up here seriously. He thinks it's all tipping over outhouses and hiding illegal stills because we're in the hills." He looked back at Harry. "What do you think, sir?"

Harry studied the young man. Jack Liddle's people had lived in this area for more than two hundred years. Harry had never dealt with Jack personally—he'd been a good kid, not the sort who drew police attention—but he knew his parents. Jack favored his mother's Dutch blood: blond and square-set, with bright blue eyes that stood out even beneath the shade of his trooper's lid.

"I think I agree with your reasoning, son. I'd sure like to see any evidence reports they come up with, if there's any way you can lay hands on them for me. And I think you should stop with the 'sir.'" He smiled a bit. "Call me Chief."

AUGUST 20, 1972

2.   "We've got the perp in custody."

"Hmm?" The Millers Kill chief of police was so intent on the body sprawled in the road, he didn't quite hear his sergeant. He had been awake—barely—when the phone rang with the news from the dispatcher. He had taken just enough time to shim into his uniform before climbing into his Fairlane and barreling up the hills into Cossayuharie, praying the whole time that this was different. A hit-and-run, or a gunshot victim. Route 137, not McEachron Hill Road. His prayers had gone unanswered.

He squatted next to the pretty girl in her lacy white minidress. Long, dark hair in a braid as thick as a rope. No shoes. No pantyhose and no bag. He could see one side of her face; her lips, pale in death, made even paler by her frosted lipstick. It changed, women's makeup.

You wouldn't think that, since faces didn't change. Two eyes, one nose, a mouth. Nowadays, it was all blue eye shadow and lipstick like this. The other woman had worn a deep red. Someone had told him it was called Cherries in the Snow. He couldn't remember if he had paid his phone bill this week or not, but he remembered that.

He stood abruptly, stepping out of the way of the coroner and his assistant. "Okay. Turn her over." He wanted to see a gunshot wound. The marks of a car grille. A slit throat. Anything except more of the lacy dress and pale skin, untouched and inexplicable. *Control yourself,* he thought. *Control yourself, control the situation.*

They maneuvered the body onto a stretcher. No necklace on this one; instead, a pair of plastic hoop earrings. One set of false eyelashes had slipped, and lay half across her cheek. Other than that, there were no signs of anything amiss.

"Huh." The coroner frowned. "If that don't beat all. You ever seen anything like this?"

"Yes," Jack Liddle said. "I have."

"Chief," his sergeant said again. "We've got the perp in custody. Some drifter on a motorcycle banged on the MacLarens' door before daybreak asking to use the phone. Claimed he found her here." The sergeant lowered his voice. "Vietnam soldier. Probably high. You know what those boys come back like. Stone killers."

Jack sighed. "Any other reason to suspect him? Other than the fact he's a soldier?"

"MacLaren held him on the porch with his shotgun while his missus called us. This guy pulled out a knife the size of your arm and threatened to gut MacLaren with it."

"That may be, but he didn't use it on this girl." At the expression on his sergeant's face Jack held up a hand. "Okay. I'll talk to him." He looked up at the circus that had assembled itself up and down the sides of McEachron Hill Road. The ambulance and the meat wagon and police prowlers and, oh joy, a Karmann Ghia he recognized as belonging to a reporter for the *Post-Star.* "Is he in a car?"

"Davidson took him down to the station house. We got the impound truck coming for his bike."

"Okay. I want the men walking quarter turns across these fields looking for evidence. Tire tracks, footprints, anything that doesn't belong."

His sergeant looked at him as if he were crazy. "For a hit-and-run?"

Jack swung back to the coroner. "Does this look like a hit-and-run to you?"

The coroner didn't glance up from where he was bending over the body. "Doesn't look like anything to me. Which makes me think maybe an overdose." He ran his hand up her arm, bunching the lacy sleeve and revealing more blue-white skin. "No needle tracks. Huh."

"She might have been shooting up between her toes or near her groin if she wanted to keep it hidden," Jack said.

The coroner looked up at him. "Don't worry. The pathologist'll give her a good going-over once she's on the table."

The sergeant snickered. Jack turned to him. "Did you find any paraphernalia on the soldier? Or on the bike?"

"No, but—"

"So we're looking for evidence. Get them out in those fields and I don't want to find anyone's doing a half-assed job of it. Finding the perp is only half the case. Finding—"

"Finding the evidence for the prosecutor is the other half. You got it, Chief."

Jack considered stopping at his house for a shave on his way to the station, but weighing a scratchy face against getting a cup while the first pot of coffee of the day was still fresh decided him on the latter. He barely managed the cup of joe—he had to call out his request to the dispatcher while Davidson, who had more enthusiasm than brains, herded him to the interrogation room. "We got that knife off him, Chief." Davidson handed him a manila folder with his preliminary notes and the tape recorder. "No track marks on his arm, but he's definitely on something."

The *something* was Old Grand-Dad, by the smell that greeted Jack when he entered the room. The kid was folded over the table, head buried in his arms. He was wearing a wrinkled olive drab army jacket over blue jeans so new they still had fold marks in them. Army boots

7

on his feet. Not just another 'Nam vet, then. This boy looked to be straight off the plane from Saigon, or wherever they flew them from these days.

Jack laid the manila case folder and the tape recorder on the table. "You're in a spot of trouble, son. Why don't you tell me what happened up there in Cossayuharie."

The soldier lifted his head. Sandy hair growing out of a military cut, bleary blue eyes. A bruise starting to purple up on his temple.

Holy Mary, Mother of God. It was Margy Van Alstyne's boy.

SATURDAY, AUGUST 19, PRESENT DAY

3. The chief of police of Millers Kill had experience with hostile fire. There had been the war, of course, and that infantryman in Panama who had snapped and started sniping passersby on base. Those had been places he had expected trouble, though, not the colonial-cute meeting room of the Millers Kill Free Library. His small Adirondack town wasn't without its dangers—just a few years back, a couple gang members had decided he'd look better with a few bullet holes in him. That had been bad. Scary bad.

But nothing had prepared him for the League of Concerned Voters, Washington County Chapter.

"Chief Van Alstyne, in the comprehensive accounting from the town's aldermen," the elderly man said, shaking a fistful of papers, "we can see that dissolving our police department and relying on the state police instead will save taxpayers eight hundred thousand a year. That's a hundred dollars a year for every man, woman, and child in the three towns! What do you offer to me and my wife that's worth paying an extra two hundred dollars a year for?"

The twenty-odd senior citizens crammed into the high-ceilinged room nodded along with the tirade. Russ briefly considered offering them a hundred sixty bucks each for their votes and then crawling back home to get some more sleep. Eight o'clock in the morning was too damn early to field questions from a bunch of Tea Party types.

"Having law enforcement in Millers Kill, patrolling here and Fort Henry and Cossayuharie, is a lot like having insurance, Mr. Bain." Russ tightened his jaw against a yawn. Since she was nursing, his wife took most of the night duty with their four-month-old, but even at her most quiet he woke when she did, and, more often than not, wound up changing at least one diaper in the wee hours. "We're there for you when things go wrong."

"Yeah?" Another geezer stood up. "Only time I ever seen your cops was getting ticketed for driving my farm vehicle on the road."

"You're out of order, Teddy. Hank has the floor." This morning's moderator was Michael Penrod, the library director. Supposedly, he was chairing the meeting because the library was hosting a series of public events around the upcoming vote. The real reason, Russ suspected, was that the Concerned Voters were so ornery, they couldn't agree on a leader. Too many generals and not enough soldiers.

"Thank you, Mr. Penrod." Hank Bain glared at the interloping questioner before redirecting his ire at Russ. "Are you saying the state police won't be here once a crime's been committed? Or that they can't handle an investigation better'n you can? Or at least as good?"

"I have no doubt the state police can handle any investigation. We already use their crime lab technicians. But your police department"—he had to remember to keep framing it like that. *Your police department* was one of his talking points—"is here for a lot more than solving crimes. Think of our community as a car. You don't wait until the oil's turned to sludge and the engine throws a rod to get it checked out. You take it to the mechanic for regular tune-ups. You get the tires rotated and the liquids topped off." Even the ferociously frowning men in the audience nodded. Russ's deputy chief, Lyle MacAuley, had come up with the car analogy. So far, so good.

"Your police force is the mechanic. We stop petty vandalism before it becomes ugly damage that lowers the property values. We stop the local small-time dealer before his business becomes profitable enough to attract the big guys. We stop speeders before they cause accidents. And yes, when a crime's been committed, we're right there. I can't say we're better than the state police, but I can guarantee we care more. Because this is our town, too, where we live and shop and bring up our kids." Next time, he thought in a flush of inspiration, he'd bring the baby along. There would definitely be a next time. Russ planned on addressing every voters' group, book club, civic organization, and congregation in Millers Kill between now and the vote in November.

Before Penrod could recognize one of the many hands waving in the air, Russ's phone vibrated. He checked the text display. **MKPD: 10-80.** He wasn't sure if he was annoyed or relieved by the interruption. "I'm sorry, everyone, but duty calls."

Someone in the group muttered, "Cheap theater."

"Thanks, Chief Van Alstyne." Michael Penrod raised his voice. "If anyone wants to help themselves to coffee or banana bread, go right ahead, and we can continue the discussion in a minute." He gestured toward the entrance, and Russ followed. Since the library had been built in 1909 and was largely unchanged since Russ was a boy, he figured Penrod wasn't worried about him getting lost. The director paused by the front desk. "I just wanted to let you know the entire library is behind you, Chief."

Russ raised his brows. "I thought *you* were the entire library, Michael."

"There are the volunteers and the friends' organization, thankfully. We'll do what we can." Penrod sighed. "If the board of aldermen is willing to put the police department on the chopping block, God knows what could be next. Taxpayers complain about libraries all the time."

Russ shook his hand. "I appreciate the support." The little bell on the door tinged as he exited, just as it had when he had been a kid.

The long walkway through the immaculate front lawn gave him time to call his dispatcher. She answered on the first ring. "What took you so long?"

Russ glanced at his watch. It had been all of five minutes since she'd texted him, but Harlene had her own standards for police conduct. "I was listening to a message of support. We need all of those we can get, these days. What's up?"

"We've had a nine-one-one call." Harlene's voice sounded oddly subdued. "Reporting a body in the middle of McEachron Hill Road in Cossayuharie. A young woman. Wearing a party dress."

His lungs seemed to seize up. He swallowed. "It can't be the same."

"Oh, no?"

"For God's sake, Harlene, it's been . . ." He couldn't calculate how long. More than half his lifetime. "Who's on the scene?"

"Knox."

"Okay. I'm headed over. Let her know."

"Lyle's on the way as well. Do you want me to—" She hesitated. Harlene never hesitated. "Pull the old files?"

"Yes. Maybe." Russ pinched the bridge of his nose. "No. We need to go in clean, not making assumptions based on—"

"But if it is—"

"No." He was definitive. "It's not. At least not until proven otherwise to my satisfaction."

Her deference was exaggerated. "You're the chief."

"At least for now." He hung up the call.

4.   Clare Fergusson had chosen her pediatrician based on the fact that the practice had weekend hours, which gave her some much-needed flexibility with her oddball schedule. The downside? It seemed she never saw the same physician twice. She liked this one well enough so far. He reminded her of Master Sergeant "Hardball" Wright, her air force survival trainer; tall, lean, bald. Dr. Underkirk did not, fortunately, look as if he could kill you with his bare hands.

"I agree with Dr. Mason," he was saying. "It's simply too soon for a diagnosis of fetal alcohol effect. Difficulty sleeping, a high startle reaction, fussiness—it's all within the normal developmental parameters so far."

"At four months?"

"At four months." He glanced to the carrier on the examination

11

table where her little bundle of joy was watching the colorful mobile overhead like a tiny, placid Buddha. *Sure, now you calm down.*

"I don't want to minimize your concerns." The doctor flipped open the file again. "You were binge drinking throughout the first three months of your pregnancy, correct? As well as using . . ." He thumbed over to another page. *My faults are too many to list.* "Amphetamines and hydrocodone."

Clare clenched her teeth against the urge to justify herself and nodded. "But I stopped the moment I found out. I saw an addiction counselor until last March."

"And now?"

"I'm in group therapy. Well, more of a support group. It's a veterans' group, actually, but we deal with a lot of the issues that were involved with my drinking—" She stopped herself.

Dr. Underkirk gave her a look of kindly understanding that had undoubtedly never appeared on Hardball Wright's face in his lifetime. "I meant the drinking. Are you still . . . ?"

"Sober? Yes. I'm nursing."

"How about the pills?"

"No pills."

"Do you ever want one? Or a drink?"

Every day. Sometimes she could feel the glass in her hand, a little condensation wetting the surface, that feeling right before she took a swallow. Or the slow pulse of warmth spreading through her veins as the Percodan kicked in, not getting high, not feeling fuzzy, just making life a tiny bit easier.

"Sure," she said. "Of course I do. But believe me, after screwing up so badly at the beginning, I'm not passing on any *more* drugs or alcohol in my milk."

"Glad to hear it." Dr. Underkirk crossed his legs. "I'm going to suggest that part of your baby's behavior might be environmental rather than innate. That means—"

"It's a reaction to my behavior? I'm causing it?"

The doctor held up a hand. "I'm talking about the total environment, not just you."

But I'm included. She wondered when she would stop feeling like the worst mother ever.

"It sounds like you have erratic work hours, and your husband's a police officer, right?"

"Chief of police."

"Nine-to-five job?"

She snorted a laugh. "No. I mean, he tries, but it's a small force and when he's needed, he goes."

"What do you do for childcare?"

"My mother-in-law helps out several days a week, morning or afternoon as I need her. And we've hired my husband's oldest niece as a mother's helper. At the church offices, it's just me and the secretary and the deacon, so it's a very baby-friendly environment. You know, unless I'm doing counseling. Or holding a meeting. Or taking a service." She shut up again.

"So you and your husband have irregular schedules, with childcare plugged in here and there when you need it. I don't know about the life of a minister, but I'm guessing your husband's job is pretty difficult."

She nodded. "There's a town measure coming up for vote this fall. Whether or not to replace the police force with state troopers. It's incredibly stressful—everyone's livelihood is on the line."

"I read about that in the *Post-Star*." Dr. Underkirk flipped open the file and jotted something down. "And in your case, in addition to the usual strains on a new mother—lack of sleep, hormones, that scary weight of having a human being entirely dependent on you"—he flashed her a brief smile—"you're dealing with fairly new sobriety and some issues with your military service. Do you have any PTSD symptoms?"

Clare had been about to say *I'm not an alcoholic, for heaven's sake* but was diverted. "Symptoms? Yes. Sometimes."

The doctor sat up straight. "You and your husband are living with a great deal of stress right now, Mrs. Fergusson. Babies can be very affected by adult stress, irregular schedules, and too many transitions—going from home to your office to grandma's house to back home, say. It may eventually turn out to be fetal alcohol effect.

You may also simply have a sensitive child. My suggestion? Find some good, consistent childcare and use it. Being able to work, uninterrupted, having time to exercise and not having to be constantly thinking about who has to be where each day of the week will do more to bring down your stress levels than any pill. Or drink. In the meantime, I suggest some calming meditation. It doesn't take long out of your day for some mindful breathing and a positive suggestion, like 'I am at peace' or 'Be still.'"

"Mindful breathing. Right. But my issue is that I don't want to hand my child off to strangers." She took a deep breath. Mindfully. "I feel like . . . I already failed at my first job as a mother. Keeping my baby safe. I want to do better, now."

Dr. Underkirk gave her his kind-and-understanding look. She would have preferred Hardball Wright staring her down. "Obviously, it's entirely up to what you and your husband think is best. But—and this is as a dad as well as a doctor—I subscribe to the airplane emergency rule in life."

"Um . . . always sight your horizon before attempting a powerless landing?"

He laughed. "No. Always secure your oxygen mask *first* before attending to your child."

5.   Hadley had done a good job as first responder. By the time Russ turned his truck onto the county road, the fire and rescue guys were already in place with cones and blinkers, ready to reroute any morning traffic that might come through. The scene—an isolated stretch of road with pastures running away on either side—was ringed round with yellow tape fluttering from flex poles. Hadley's unit blocked the road on the Cossayuharie side, its lights looking almost dim in the brilliant August sunshine.

It had been a beautiful day back in 1972, hadn't it?

He heard the whoop-whoop-whoop of a siren as he climbed out of his truck. He waited while the squad car crested the rise, slowed, and pulled in behind his pickup. Lyle MacAuley, his deputy chief, flipped off the light bar and got out, stretching and snapping his back. "Heard we have a traffic fatality."

God, maybe that was it. Russ had been so overwhelmed by the news, he hadn't thought to ask Harlene to patch him through to Hadley for the details. "I hope so," he said.

Lyle's bushy gray eyebrows shot up.

"Not that way." Russ headed for the yellow tape. Lyle fell in beside him. "Just . . . I hope it's not a homicide."

"Person dead in the road? Vehicular manslaughter and fleeing the scene. Probably some damn fool jogger not watching where she was going meeting up with another damn fool texting and driving. What have you got here, Knox?" Lyle held the tape up so Russ could duck through.

Hadley Knox, three years at the department, was their junior-most officer, and the only woman sworn as a peacekeeper. Despite taking the job as a last resort—she had two kids and an infirm granddad to support—Russ thought she had the potential to be an excellent cop. If he could keep her on the force. If he could make sure there would be a force for her to work at.

"White female, looks to be in her early twenties. No ID I could see in the first pass." She stood next to a blue Tyvek tarp spread over the body. Whoever it was beneath there, she was so slight she barely lifted the plastic shroud.

"This where you found her?" Lyle looked around at the verge of the road as if expecting to see signs of the body being dragged. A scattering of gravel marked the line between asphalt and the field beyond. No blood. No crushed grass or broken wildflowers.

"Right here in the middle of the lane, Dep. I wouldn't move her." Hadley sounded defensive.

"We know that, Knox." Russ pulled his purple silicone gloves from his pocket and tugged them on. Lyle did the same. "Let's take a look." He peeled the tarp away from the body.

Young. Pretty. Dressed up like one of the girls he saw outside St. Alban's a week ago, guests at a wedding. He glanced at her feet. No shoes.

"Anything that might be hers along the side of the road? Purse, backpack?" *Please say yes. A flip-flop. A water bottle. Anything.*

"I didn't find anything in my first sweep, Chief. Maybe the crime scene techs will get better results."

No. They won't.

"If she was a hit-and-run, where's the injury?" MacAuley got down on one knee. "No scrapes. No torn clothing." He stretched himself flat on the roadway next to the body. "Doesn't look like there's any blood underneath her."

"Dr. Scheeler's on the way," Hadley said. The Washington County ME. "And the state crime scene lab."

"Good job," Russ said automatically.

MacAuley got back up onto one knee. "Damndest thing I've ever seen." He glanced up at Russ. "You think she was shot at real close range with something small caliber? We might not see that with all her hair."

"I thought maybe she was a medical," Hadley said. "Her heart or a fatal allergy attack."

"Hell of a place to drop dead, in the middle of McEachron Hill Road in a prom dress." Lyle braced his knee and stood. "No witnesses, I suppose."

Hadley shook her head. "No one else reported seeing a body. I haven't been able to canvass the neighborhood yet." She looked around at the pastures rolling away from the highway, their only inhabitants grazing cows and buzzing insects.

"Who called it in?" Saying anything felt like pounding through concrete. Russ tightened his fist and took a deep breath. In. Out. *Control yourself, control the situation.*

Hadley flipped open her notebook. "Mrs. Laura Cunningham of 23 McEachron Hill Road. She was on her way to an eight o'clock vet appointment with her dog. She thinks it was about seven forty when she saw the body."

"Did she see anything else? Another vehicle in either direction?"

Hadley shook her head. "No. She was pretty shook up, but she insisted her car'd been the only one on the road."

"ATV," Lyle said.

That word sliced through the web Russ's memories were winding around his brain. An all-terrain vehicle. Of course.

"Chief?" Hadley was looking at him strangely.

"Sorry. Sorry, Knox. This is just . . ." He stopped himself. He had told Harlene he had wanted the others to go in without assumptions, but he was pulling theories out of thin air. They hadn't done a large-scale area search for evidence yet. They knew nothing about the cause of death. They had no identity on the victim, no points of contact, no possible motives. He was having a hard enough time focusing on other scenarios that might explain this girl's death. He didn't need the rest of his team sucked into his blind spot. "Nothing," he said. "I'm a little sleep deprived. Let's get—" The sound of an approaching vehicle cut Russ off.

Hadley headed toward the sound, ready to turn around whoever had gotten past the fire and rescue guys. She stopped as the medical examiner's car came into view.

Daniel Scheeler's day job was pathologist at the Glens Falls hospital. When the previous ME had retired, Scheeler took the very part-time position. At every call, he complained about getting dragged away from his life to some godforsaken spot at some inconvenient hour. Russ used to apologize until he realized Scheeler loved working crime scenes as much or more than any of the cops there.

Scheeler ducked under the tape, his bag beneath his arm. "Lovely day, gentlemen, Officer Knox." He was wearing an expensive, rumpled suit and bright blue shirt, neither of which looked as if it had been fresh that morning. As he bent over and slipped paper booties over his highly shined dress shoes, Russ caught a whiff of a very feminine perfume. "What have you got for me this fine morning?"

Lyle hummed a bar of "Bow Chicka Wow Wow."

"You tell us." Russ gestured toward the body.

Scheeler set his bag down and gently unfolded the tarp. "When do you expect the photographer? I'm not going to get much until I can move the body."

Russ looked to Hadley. "Harlene confirmed the staties the same time she told me she'd reached the doctor," she said.

That could mean anywhere from twenty minutes to an hour, depending on where the CS unit had been and what they were doing. "Just your preliminary impressions, please." Russ nodded toward his officers. "Knox, I want you to start searching the shoulder and the verge of the road over here. Lyle, you take the other side." The deputy chief grunted in agreement. In larger shops, an officer of his rank wouldn't be caught dead doing shoe-leather investigative work. But in the MKPD, down to six men and one woman since their youngest had been hired away by Syracuse a half year ago, everybody pitched in. Including the chief. "I'll start looking for tracks in the field."

"That's a lot of space to cover thoroughly," Lyle said. "You wanna call in everybody who's not on patrol?"

"Not until we have a better idea of what we're dealing with. You and Knox said it yourselves; she could be a medical."

The sound of Lyle's doubtful "Hmm" followed him as he crossed to the far side of the road. Russ pulled out his phone and snapped a few pictures of the edge of the highway, the field, and the horizon so he could remember where he had started. He picked a spot at a right angle from where Scheeler was kneeling next to the dead girl, and struck out from there.

They had been two weeks without rain this August, and the ground beneath his boots was unyielding. The bad news was there wouldn't be any convenient muddy ruts leading him to a suspect's garage. The good news was the field hadn't been used for grazing this season—no fence running alongside the highway—so any vehicle would have left clear marks through the high, thick grass. Russ walked slowly, looking ahead and to each side for anywhere the hip-high seed heads might be broken or bent. Bindweed and running myrtle caught around his ankles while thistle and dock scratched his pant legs.

The sun was well and truly up now, beating down with the unrelenting force of late summer in Upstate New York. Russ could feel the sweat begin to trickle down his back as he waded through the field, crossing and recrossing his own path in a self-imposed grid. He flushed a few red-winged blackbirds, sent grasshoppers and field mice rustling out of his path, but he couldn't find any trace of another person, let alone an ATV.

The rumble and growl of a heavy vehicle approaching made Russ turn toward the road. The NYSP mobile crime lab rolled into view. Only—he glanced at his watch—fifty minutes after Hadley had called it in. He'd have to mention that at the next stop on his local law enforcement goodwill tour.

He took a few more pictures with his phone so later searchers could map out past where he had already been. Then he retraced his path back to the highway.

The NYSP photographer had just finished with the body and was now headed up the road to confer with Knox. Scheeler stood to one side as the other two technicians carefully transferred the body into a transport bag. Russ could see a slice of the girl before they zipped her up; she had on the kind of makeup women used for a big night out. Over her death-pale face, it looked obscene.

"She hasn't been here long enough for hypostasis to set in," Scheeler said. The postmortem bruises where blood had settled in the body. "At least not where I can see any."

"So you can't tell if she was killed here, or elsewhere and then moved?"

"When I can get her clothes off back at the lab, I might see something." He waved toward where the two techs were inching over the patch of asphalt where her body had lain, searching for any tiny bits of physical evidence that might help tell them all what had happened. "As you can see, there's nothing biological here to indicate her death. No blood, no feces, no vomit, nothing."

"Any thoughts as to cause of death?" Russ asked.

Scheeler shook his head. "Nothing readily apparent. No visible signs of strangulation, no bullet or knife wounds, no visible signs of blunt force trauma—"

"But you might find something in the lab, right?"

Scheeler looked at Russ. "Of course I'll find something in the lab. Death doesn't just happen without leaving evidence of its passage. Not in a healthy young adult."

Russ hesitated. "What if I told you I had seen a case like this, a long time ago? And that no one had found a cause for the woman's death?"

Scheeler looked skeptical. "If it was a long time ago, I would say the technology must not have existed to properly diagnose cause of death. That's not the case today. We have MRIs and CTs and nuclear microscopes. We can decode the human genome, for God's sake." He stripped off his jacket, releasing another delicate tendril of ladies' perfume. "Trust me, I'll have a cause of death for that girl. Two weeks tops."

"Good," Russ said, but what he meant was *Please.*

◆ ◆ ◆

Margy Van Alstyne was loading her gardening tools into her Camry when her son pulled into her dooryard. Her first thought was *Two minutes too late*—she had just heaved a forty-pound bag of mulch in the trunk and was feeling it in every muscle. Her second thought was *What's wrong?* Russell wasn't one to stop by in the middle of his shift. She set the pruning hook and secateurs on the backseat and walked down the dusty drive to meet him.

Russell unfolded from his police cruiser like a Macy's balloon, going up and up and up. Fifty-three years on it still shocked her, at times, that she had made this tall, broad-shouldered man out of her own small body. He enveloped her in a hug. "Hi, Mom."

Her arms went around to the middle of his back. "Hello yourself, sweetie. What're you doing here? I don't have the baby today."

"I know." He straightened. "Where are you off to?"

She gestured to her ratty old denim shirt and baseball hat. "Garden club. We're working on native plant restoration at the old Haudeno-saunee estate."

"Native plants. That's nice." He looked toward her side yard, where a fence overgrown with flowering shrubs separated her property from a sharp downward slide into the shallow, rocky Hudson River. "I should tear out that old fence and rebuild it. It's got to be pretty punky by now."

"Just don't disturb my weed. I keep it planted underneath the spirea."

"No, I wouldn't—" His eyes sharpened and his attention snapped back to her. "What?"

"How 'bout you tell me what you came for?"

He frowned. "You don't really have any pot plants on the premises, do you?"

"Be pretty foolish of me, with my son the chief of police, now, wouldn't it?"

"Mom . . ."

She relented. "No, I'm not growing any marijuana. No promises if the state makes it legal, though. Tell me why you're here."

His face settled into uneasy lines. "We've had a suspicious death this morning. We're investigating."

She raised her eyebrows. Why on earth he was sharing one of his cases with her she couldn't imagine. Well, yes, she could. But it wasn't for any nice reason. "Yes?"

He shifted his feet. "The body was found on McEachron Hill Road. It's a young woman. In a party dress."

Margy felt her mouth go dry. "It surely can't be . . ." She lost her thread for a moment. "The same. It can't be the same."

"I know. I can't see how. But it looks the same. I've got three officers canvassing the area, talking to everyone in the hopes of turning up some sort of witness. So far, nothing."

"Do you know who she is?"

"Not yet." He anticipated her next question. "No obvious cause of death. The medical examiner promises a preliminary report within twenty-four hours."

She pressed her fingers to her lips in thought. "You know, some of the folks up in Cossayuharie are bound to remember what happened back then."

"Oh, yeah. I'm sure there are plenty of geezers left in Millers Kill who still have opinions about it, too."

She shot him a look. "Watch it, junior. You're practically a geezer yourself these days."

He laughed a little.

"I hate to be political—"

"Don't lie, Mom. You love to be political."

"Okay, yes. But if you can't get this case solved quickly, and it starts to bring up all the old stories and gossip, it's not going to do the 'No' campaign any favors." She brushed an invisible piece of dust off his uniform shirt.

He smiled down at her. "Can I bring you in as a consultant if necessary?"

She smacked his arm lightly. "If you'll listen to me, yes." She sobered. "That poor girl. Somewhere, someone is missing her. Solve your case for that person, if you can, son."

Russell kissed her on the cheek. "I'll do my best, Mom."

She stood in the dooryard and watched him drive away. She stood for a long time, waiting for the August heat to chase away the chill of the ice water cooling in the back of her brain. *Trouble coming to town. Trouble.* She shook her head to get the foolishness out of it. She was being an old lady. The last time she'd been thinking that way was early April, when her newest grandchild had been born. Of course, there were reasons she'd been worried back then. First there was the kerfuffle over her son and his bride tying the knot while already three months pregnant—not an issue for most of the world these days, but Margy's daughter-in-law was an Episcopal priest, so that particular bit of timing had been . . . inconvenient. Then it fell out Clare had been drinking during those first months. Not that Margy blamed her, not at all. Clare wasn't the first soldier whose head had gotten screwed up in Iraq, and she wouldn't be the last. But Margy had spent way too many years dealing with alcoholics not to know about the dangers to mother and child, and she worried, for the baby and for Clare, who seemed to find it way too easy to stop drinking while pregnant. In Margy's experience, easy sobriety was not lasting sobriety.

So it shouldn't have been a surprise when the child decided to make its appearance two weeks early, catching them all off guard. Maybe she should have tweaked to it when she called Clare Tuesday morning to ask her where to drop off the leftovers from the previous day's baby shower. "Bring them by the church," Clare said. "I've got so much heartburn, I don't even want to think about eating. Might as well set it out for the rest of the staff and the vestry to enjoy."

"Oh, the heartburn can be awful. When I was expecting Russell, I went through a box of Alka-Seltzer a day by the end. How are you elsewise?"

"I've been having Braxton-Hicks contractions all morning." Clare laughed. "My office is littered with scraps of paper with time and duration jotted on them."

"Maybe you ought to go home and put your feet up, sweetie."

"I'd love to, but Holy Week starts on Monday and the diocesan retreat is this Friday. I'm just too busy."

"Hmm. What does Russell say?"

Clare laughed again. "About what you'd expect. Look, I'm telling everybody, and you can hold me to it, that as soon as I've taken the last service on Easter Sunday, I'm out of here." Someone said something away from the phone. Clare laughed. "Lois doesn't believe me. She's threatening to lock the doors."

"You listen to your secretary. She's a smart woman. Try to have a sit-down until I get there. Don't make me call Russell."

When Margy walked into the offices of St. Alban's an hour later, toting half a sheet cake and a bag of Tupperware containers full of hors d'oeuvres, someone was already trying to call Russell.

"I understand," the church secretary was saying, her normally smooth voice fraying around the edges. "But you need to listen to me. His *wife* is in *labor*. You've got to get a message to him. That's all. Just take him a god—" She bit herself off. "No. No. I'll call back in five minutes to see." She hung up the phone. "Oh, Mrs. Van Alstyne. Thank God. Can you drive Clare to the hospital?"

Margy dumped the containers on Lois's desk. "I was just talking to her on the phone! What on earth happened?"

"Her water broke. She's in her office with Deacon de Groot. She says she'll have *hours* yet, so there's no *rush* to get to the hospital, for heaven's sake." Margy could hear her daughter-in-law's Southern cadences in Lois's recounting. "Maybe *you* can talk some sense into her."

"How often are her pains coming?"

"Every four minutes."

"What!"

"I know, I know! I'm trying to reach Russ, but he's testifying in court today, and I'm having a hard time persuading this idiot deputy to interrupt while they're in session."

"You keep trying. I'll take care of her." *Braxton-Hicks, my aunt Fanny.*

In her office, Clare was leaning over her cluttered desk, braced on her hands, panting. The Reverend Elizabeth de Groot, her deacon, was pushing against the small of Clare's back with one hand and holding a watch with the other. "Hello, Mrs. Van Alstyne," she said, no differently than if Margy had arrived for Bible study. Clare let out a moan. "Keep doing your breathing, Clare."

Finally Margy's daughter-in-law let out a long exhale and straightened up. "Forty seconds," Elizabeth announced.

"Oh, Margy." Clare was hot-cheeked. Her enormous black blouse, complete with white clerical collar, was creased and damp around the edges.

Margy gave her as much of a hug as she could. "You're coming with me to the hospital, and you're not going to argue about it."

"But the first stage of labor takes eight to twelve hours! They said so in Lamaze class!"

Margy and Elizabeth exchanged glances. "Clare, sweetie." Margy used the same tone of voice she would have talking to a not-very-bright child. "That's the average. Some women take more time. Some women take less. It looks like you're in the less camp."

"A lot less," Elizabeth said.

"But Russ isn't here! I don't have my bag packed. I haven't got my music for labor!"

"Clare, if you don't get going right now, this baby's going to arrive in less time than it takes to play the doxology."

"Elizabeth's right, sweetie. Russell will meet us at the hospital. Let's go. There's a good girl."

Clare had two more contractions before they got her in the car and another two by the time Margy had reached the Washington County

ER. While an attendant was helping Clare into a wheelchair—over her protests that she didn't need one—Margy called the church.

"I got ahold of him," Lois said. "He's on his way."

"Thank heavens. What did he say?"

"That the first stage of labor lasts eight to twelve hours, so Clare shouldn't be this far along yet."

"Good grief. What do they teach them in those birthing classes nowadays?"

"Not statistical analysis, I'm guessing."

Margy followed Clare up to Labor and Delivery. Her birthing room was in soothing shades of cream and gold, with a comfortable rocker and a bed that folded up like a piece of origami if you wanted to sit, or lean, or turn around while laboring. She helped Clare change into a johnny robe. No shaving, no enema—a lot different from Margy's day. A lot better.

A nurse bustled in to take Clare's vitals and to give her her first internal check. "Reverend Clare. We finally get to see you as a patient instead of as a chaplain." She glanced at her tablet. "And I see you've reported contractions every four minutes, right?"

Instead of answering, Clare nodded and began to pant.

"And here's one now. I'm just going to strap this monitor over you and get the baby's pulse rate. Do you know what you're expecting?"

Clare shook her head and pawed at Margy. Margy gave her hand to squeeze. Clare lost her blowing rhythm and began growling, "Ow, ow, ow, ow, shit, shit, *shit*!" At the end of the contraction she fell back against her pillow, scowling. "That really *hurts*!"

"What did they tell you in class?" Margy said.

"That there would be discomfort. And that I should visualize my birth canal as a tunnel of golden light."

The nurse pushed away from the rolling stool where she'd been giving Clare an internal examination. "Well! You weren't kidding about those contractions. You're already eight centimeters dilated."

"Visualize your birth canal as an express elevator," Margy said.

Clare laughed, then grimaced. "Oh. Damn. Damn, damn, damn,

damn." She rode out the contraction, clutching Margy's hand. When it was over, she said, "Where's Russ? I want Russ."

"He'll be here any moment, sweetie. I promise." She was worried he'd make a liar of her, though. Under normal circumstances, there'd be no problem, but this baby was in one all-fired hurry to come out and meet the world. Then she heard, far away and floating, the sound of a police siren. "Listen!" She wiped Clare's face with a damp washcloth. "Can you hear the siren? That'll be Russell."

"Everything looks fine," the nurse said. "I'm going to put in a call and make sure your doctor's on the way. Grandma, you can just press this button if she needs anything."

"I need my husband," Clare snarled. "God! Damn!" She panted and blew her way through the remaining contraction before sagging back, damp and wilted. "I'm sorry," she said in an entirely different tone. "I thought this was going to feel a lot more spiritual. Taking part in creation and all that. Can you fix it so I'm sitting up more?"

"You swear all you want, sweetie." Margy pressed on the bed's control. "We like to think we're different and better'n the other animals, with our big brains and our religion. Giving birth takes us down a peg or two, that's for sure."

There was a thud of heavy footsteps from the hall. "Clare? Clare?" The door, closed by the nurse when she exited, burst open. Russ had taken the time to divest himself of his duty belt and gun, but otherwise he was still in uniform, his khakis slightly rumpled as always, his chief's badge and thick-soled shoes polished to a high shine. Margy scooted out of his way as he crossed to Clare's side. "Oh, darlin'." He took her hand. "Are you all right? God, I'm sorry I took so long. I'm so sorry I wasn't there for you." He held out his other hand to Margy. "Mom, thank you. Thanks for staying with her." He dropped a quick kiss on her hair.

"'Course I stayed with her." She picked up her purse from the bedside table. "I'll be in the waiting room now."

"No," Clare said. "Margy, please don't leave. I want you here. Please?"

Margy glanced up at her son. "Whatever Clare wants," he said.

"Smart boy," Margy said. "I'll stand on that side of her, near the machine, and you take this side." *This side* was Clare's dominant hand.

Margy supposed it was a husband's privilege to have his knuckles ground into dust during his wife's contractions.

He looked around the room. "Do you want me to get you a chair, Mom? Some kind of stool?"

She smiled at Clare. "I don't think this baby is going to keep me standing long enough for my feet to get tired."

She was right. Clare labored on for less than half an hour before the doctor, who had performed another internal exam as soon as she arrived, announced it was time to push. And a good thing, too, since Clare's obvious pain and wrenching contractions had turned Russ pale. Or maybe it was her prodigious vocabulary of obscenities, none of which she used in her day-to-day life as a priest.

"Okay, Clare," the doctor said. "When you feel the urge, go ahead and bear down. Keep pushing for as long as you can. Dad, Grandma, you help keep her in position."

Clare pushed with a guttural growling sound, as if a wild animal were trying to escape her body. Margy could see her stomach bunching, the powerful muscle of her uterus working to bring her child into the world. It was so amazing to see it from this angle, without the haze of drugs and pain of her own children's birth. She glanced at her son. He was leaning over his wife, supporting her back, holding her hand with his free hand. His eyes were wide and wild, looking at Clare with such a fierce intensity Margy had to turn away again.

"I can see the head!" the doctor said. "Lots of hair. Just a few more, and your baby will be here."

Russ pressed his lips against Clare's sweaty temple. "You can do it, darlin'."

Clare nodded, and pushed again, red-faced, open-mouthed, curling up over the bulk of her stomach.

"Okay, the head's out! I want you to breathe instead of push for the next one, Clare, while I ease the shoulders out." Clare nodded, panting. The doctor bent between Clare's legs, then beckoned to the nurse, who grabbed a receiving blanket. "All right, Clare. This one should do it."

Clare pushed one last time. Margy saw a long wet body slither into the doctor's hands. "It's a boy! And he's a big one." The doctor held him up, his legs kicking, his mouth working in outrage. "You want to cut the cord, Dad?"

Margy had never seen that expression on her son's face. He nodded, never taking his eyes off the baby. "Come on over here, then. See? I've tied off here and here and all you have to do is snip right there." As if the final separation from its mother was the last straw, the baby began crying angrily. "You can follow Mary over to the station while she cleans your little guy up," the doctor told Russ. "Clare, I'm afraid you still have a little work left to do."

Clare groaned. Margy looked at the clock. Three hours since she had arrived at St. Alban's. She couldn't believe it. "Ten pounds!" the nurse announced from the other side of the room. Almost the same size Russell had been at birth. "Eight on the Apgar. Here you go, Dad. You can bring him over to Mom."

Russ turned toward them, the tightly wrapped baby cradled against his chest. He looked so utterly struck with wonder it brought tears to Margy's eyes. She had never thought to see her son have a child of his own, but here he was, over halfway through his life, made a father.

He crossed to Clare's side and laid the baby in her arms. "Oh, Clare." His voice was almost broken. "We have a son." They bent over the tiny, wrinkled face, their heads together.

"Hello, Ethan," Clare said softly. "Hello, little boy."

Hours later, standing outside the nursery, looking at the Perspex bassinet containing Ethan James Van Alstyne, Russell put his arm around Margy and hugged her close. "I'm glad you were there, Mom."

"Me, too."

"It makes me think . . ."

"What?"

"I wish Dad could have been here, too."

She felt a hot sting beneath her breastbone. The night Russell had been born, his father had been at a bar getting drunk. He hadn't seen his son until the next afternoon. She had spent a lifetime cultivating her children's good memories and downplaying the bad, tying herself in knots to create moments with their father and shouldering the burdens on the many, many times Walter had been absent. In the end, after he'd passed, she had been oddly grateful. When trouble came to her house, she was well able to deal with it. She glanced up at her son, so grown and still so worrisome.

"Me, too, sweetie. Me, too."

AUGUST 1972

6.   Jack Liddle stared at the boy sitting in his interrogation room. "Russell?"

"The prodigal returns." Fatigue, yes, and also anger in the boy's voice, and barely leashed violence. He smelled of liquor, but whatever he had drunk the night before had burned off him. He dropped his head back onto his arms, as if the weight of all it carried was too much to bear.

Jack stopped himself from saying the first thing that came to his mind, and the second, and the third. Just because he knew this boy, had known him since birth, didn't mean he wasn't involved in the young woman's death. The fact she had been dumped on McEachron Hill Road, the missing shoes and stockings—he couldn't let himself get caught up in the similarities between this death and the one he had been witness to so many years ago. He knew damn well Russell couldn't have been responsible for that debacle. He also knew Russell had been a good-natured kid. But he had been a hell-raiser, no doubt about it, and God alone knew what two tours of combat duty in Vietnam had done to him.

So. He was going to approach this very carefully. Jack pulled out the chair opposite the boy and sat. "It's good to see you again, son."

"Oh, yeah." Russell didn't bother lifting his head this time. "It's like having a parade. Except I was handcuffed in the back of a cop car instead of waving to the crowd."

"Well, it's a hell of a welcome home for you, that's a fact. I'll tell you what. We'll get some coffee in here, and you tell me how you came to be banging on the MacLarens' door."

"I didn't have anything to do with that girl. I just found her. I didn't do anything to her."

"Okay. Tell me how you found her."

There was a rap on the door. "C'mon in," Jack said.

The dispatcher entered, balancing a tray with two mugs, a bowl of sugar, and some packets of creamer. Two large doughnuts sat on two white napkins. "I thought you both might like some." She smiled nervously.

"Thanks, Harlene." Jack refrained from pointing out they didn't, as a rule, treat suspects in the interrogation room as guests. Harlene was new—the first woman ever at the MKPD—and she was desperately anxious to prove her worth. Most of the officers openly speculated she'd leave as soon as she fell pregnant, and Jack wasn't sure they were wrong.

Harlene closed the door behind her. Jack tore open a creamer and watched as Russell spooned sugar into his mug. He let the boy take a few swallows before continuing. "Okay. So you met up with the girl . . ."

"I didn't meet up with her." Russ set his mug down. "I was coming home from Saratoga when I found her lying there in the middle of the road."

"What were you doing in Saratoga?"

The boy looked at him incredulously. "Drinking. Trying to meet chicks."

"All night?"

The boy shrugged.

"How long have you been home?"

"Three days."

"Pretty quick work. Saratoga can be a rough town."

Russell's eyes went flat and dead. "Really? Thanks for the warning."

Jack shook his head. "I'm sorry. That was a damn fool thing to say to a soldier, wasn't it? Where did you go in Saratoga?"

"Bennie's. The Paddock. The Flying Dutchman."

"That's up by the college."

"I told you, I was trying to meet girls. I struck out." He paused. "I left the Dutchman and headed for the Golden Banana."

Jack raised his eyebrows at the mention of the notorious strip club.

"Decided to try for a different kind of girl, did you? Did anything happen at the place by Skidmore?"

Russell scrubbed at his face. "I got into a fight with some rich asshole who thought the war was my fault." He flashed a wolfish grin. "I flattened him. They threw me out."

"Did you pull a knife on him, too?"

"Hey, that farmer had a 12-gauge pointed straight at my gut! I was just defending myself. He's lucky I didn't take the gun away from him and break it over his head."

Jack took a drink of his coffee. "Is that what you wanted to do to Mr. MacLaren?"

"I was *trying* to do the right thing. Jesus. Look. I'll plead guilty to hauling my knife out if you want. Resisting arrest, punching that jerk in Saratoga, whatever. I don't care. I did those. But I didn't have anything to do with that girl in the road, and I wish to hell I'd'a just swerved my bike around her and kept going."

"Tell me about finding her."

"I was swinging down from Route 137. It was just getting light in the sky. I spotted something in the road—I thought maybe it was garbage fallen off a truck. I went wide to avoid it. Her. It was as I was passing I realized it was a body." He paused for a moment. "I wasn't sure I was really seeing it, you know? I thought maybe . . ."

"Did you touch her?"

"Of course I did. I turned her over to check if she was breathing."

"What did she feel like? Was she warm? Cold?"

Russell thought for a moment. "Cool. Like the way your skin is after swimming. I'd guess she'd been dead a couple hours by then."

Jack just managed to stop himself from asking how Russell would know that. The boy might have dealt with more dead bodies than he had at this point. "Did you see anyone else on the road? Any other vehicles?"

"No. There wasn't any other traffic after I turned off Route 9."

Some of the tension he'd been holding in his shoulders eased. Nobody under suspicion would pass up the chance to point to a vehicle or two to throw the scent off himself. Unless he was stupid, and Jack was confident that, whatever other changes Vietnam had wrought in Russell, he was still smart as a whip.

There was a quick rap, but before Jack could say anything, the door burst open. Harlene looked frazzled. It was only eight thirty, and she had already chewed the lipstick off her bottom lip. "Chief, Mrs. Van Alstyne is here. She's demanding to see her son." Her voice dropped, as if Russell couldn't hear her if she whispered. "One of the men at the impound garage is her cousin, and he called her. I didn't know what to do."

The boy stood.

"Sit down, Russell. You're not going anywhere yet." Jack stood up. "I'll talk with Mrs. Van Alstyne."

She was waiting for him at the front desk. "Where is he? What has he done? Is he hurt?" Her dark hair was in loose, unruly curls and she was wearing jeans and a wrinkled shirt that did nothing to hide her figure. Her narrow feet were thrust into unlaced tennis shoes.

"Come into my office, Margy." He ushered her down the hall, not actually touching her back. "Russell's okay. I'm not sure what he's done, but I don't think he's hurt anybody." He spoke with more certainty than he felt. Seeing Margy, he realized he didn't *want* her son to be guilty. Which was a hell of a dangerous mind-set to take into an investigation.

"You don't *think*—?" She turned back to him. She clutched at his arm, hard, then let go instantly.

Jack closed the door behind them. "A young woman's died. He claims he found her body on the road when he was coming home early this morning."

Margy stared. "You can't imagine Russell had anything to do with that."

"He says he was out all night roistering in Saratoga. We'll have to check out the places he's said he'd been to to firm up his alibi."

Margy looked up at him. "He was drinking."

Jack nodded. "He was drinking."

Margy had the clear, fair skin of the Cossayuharie farm girl she had been, the kind of complexion that showed her every emotion. He watched as her cheeks flushed with a dull red color. "God*damn* it!"

He blinked. Margy Van Alstyne never swore.

"I'm sorry." She pressed her hands against her cheeks.

"I know you worry about him and alcohol."

"Apparently, I have good cause." She let out a brief laugh tinged with hysteria. He moved toward her, but she held up one hand. "It's all right. I'm all right." She hugged her arms around herself. "It's just—I thought everything would be okay again once he came home. But he's not really home. I mean, he's *there*, at the table or in front of the television or in his room. But the rest of him is somewhere else. He has no idea what to do with his life now he's out of the army. And he certainly doesn't want to listen to me. I'm a middle-aged mother who's lived in the North Country her whole life, and he's spent the last two years shooting people in Southeast Asia. We have nothing in common anymore."

"Really." Jack leaned against his desk. "Seems to me you know all about fighting a war you can't win."

Her cupid's-bow mouth curved into a sad smile. "You'd think watching his father drink himself to death would have taught him something, wouldn't you?"

"Some things can't be taught. You just have to learn them through experience." Jack pushed himself away from the desk. "I need to go over his account of events some more. How about I call you in an hour or so and then I'll release him to your custody."

"How about I call a lawyer and he doesn't answer any more questions until he's got some legal advice?"

Now she sounded more like the tart apple he was used to. "He hasn't asked for representation yet. And he's an adult now."

"We'll see about that. I'm not going to let the system roll over my son." She glanced at his desk. "May I use your phone?"

Jack couldn't help himself. He laughed. "Help yourself. When you're done, you can wait for your attorney at the front desk."

"You're going back to interrogate him, aren't you?"

"Margy." He put his hands on her shoulders, squaring her, squaring himself to her. "I've got a job to do. But you can absolutely rely on me to deal fairly with your boy. If he honestly had nothing to do with the girl's death, he'll be fine."

Her brown eyes brightened with tears. "But what if he did?"

He thought about the girl, about her fancy dress and her shoeless feet and the sprawl of her limbs in the road. He thought about this time. He thought about the last time. "I don't know, Margy. I don't know."

SATURDAY, AUGUST 19, PRESENT DAY

7.   Clare's car was in the narrow rectory driveway, but neither she nor Ethan were downstairs. Russ walked carefully up to the second floor, but his wife and son weren't taking a much-needed nap. The jogging stroller was still gathering dust in the dining room, so they hadn't gone out for a run, which was a damn shame, because lately, when she wasn't falling over from lack of sleep, she was wound tighter than a stock car's coil spring. Running had always been her way to decompress. Well, that and having a couple drinks. He sighed.

In the kitchen, he opened the fridge for a bottle of water and spotted a dinner salad waiting in a large ceramic bowl; something with lots of veggies and what looked like ground-up nuts. Clare was very into whole grains this summer. He suspected she'd been talking to his mother, who had expanded her quest to save the world at large into an effort to save everyone around her by dint of serving nothing but healthy, organic shredded cardboard.

Six thirty on a Saturday evening . . . he thought for a minute. Obsessive rewriting of the sermon she'd composed on Wednesday. He replaced the water in the fridge and went back out toward the church next door.

He let himself into the St. Alban's kitchen like a neighbor borrowing sugar. It was closer than walking the length of the whole parish hall. A dingy little hallway, two flights of stairs, and he was by the offices. He heard a soft *woof* from a few steps down the hall and then

Oscar, their Lab mix, poked his nose out the door. "Hey, good dog. It's me." He gave Oscar's head a scratch and followed him into Clare's office. "Hi there."

Oscar, seeing no more scratches were coming, collapsed back onto his bed. Clare looked up from where she was writing at her desk. She smiled. "Hey. I didn't expect to see you until later."

"I am trying to keep it down to sixty hours a week."

"Or less."

"Ha."

Clare's office was a hodgepodge of her two careers, military aviation and the church. Aeronautical charts mixed with carved wooden saints and crosses on the walls, and her visitors could pick either military surplus armchairs or a lumpy love seat left over from a long-ago St. Alban's white elephant sale. Mirrors reflected the end-of-the-day sunlight streaming rose gold from the room's original diamond-paned windows.

Ethan's carrier was resting on the threadbare oriental carpet, within Clare's reach. Russ bent over his son. "How's he been today?"

"So-so. Quiet this morning, screaming around lunchtime, and he had one of his fussy fits this afternoon, but I strapped him on when I took Oscar for a walk, and that settled him back down. I just nursed him a little while ago. Please God, he'll sleep until eight."

Russ touched Ethan's tiny hand before straightening. "And how are *you*? How did the doctor's appointment go?" The baby was still nursing every night at nine, eleven, and four. Clare hadn't gotten more than five straight hours of sleep since he had been born, and it showed in the deep violet smudges beneath her eyes.

"I'm doing okay. The doctor said it was still too early to tell if he has FAE symptoms, or if he's just a sensitive, highly reactive kid. Or who knows? Maybe he's got ADHD. Or sensory integration dysfunction. Or—"

Russ squeezed her shoulders and dropped a kiss on her hair. He dug his fingers into the muscles bunched in her upper back and began to knead. "Anything else? Any suggestions?"

Her head dropped back against his stomach. "Oh, God, that feels good. Mmm. Yeah, he told me I ought to try to calm down and stop winding him up."

"Really?"

"Well, not in so many words. He suggested putting Ethan in regular day care. He said fewer transitions and a more regular schedule might be good for both of us."

"You know I have no problem with that."

She sighed. "I know. It's me. And maybe it would be the best thing for him. But the expense—"

"We can afford it."

"And how could I keep nursing?"

"You pump when he's over at Mom's."

"That's for one feeding!"

"So we don't put him in all day. We could try mornings. Or the after-school slot, two till six. That would help a lot with your counseling sessions and meetings."

Her eyes had closed as he continued to massage her neck and shoulders. "Mmm. Maybe. I still think coming in for the afternoons will be doable, at least for a while. I feel like if I could just get one full night's sleep, I could handle anything. Your mother swears you were sleeping through the night by your second month, but she was feeding you some god-awful concoction of Karo syrup and condensed milk. That's got to be enough calories to stun an ox, let alone an eight-week-old."

"I've seen pictures. I looked like a prize porker headed for the Washington County Fair." She laughed. He released her shoulders. "Feel better?" She nodded. "You done with your sermon?"

"I guess so. Yes." Clare leaned forward and hit the PRINT button. In the main office down the hall, he could hear a faint whirring noise as the printer came to life.

He tugged her away from her desk and the two of them dropped into the love seat. Ignoring a spring poking his lower back, Russ bent over and hefted Ethan's carrier onto his lap.

Clare scooted in close. "Now how about you? You look stressed."

"I always look stressed."

She flipped a hand open. *Go on.*

He sighed. "We found a body on McEachron Hill Road this morning. A girl—a young woman. No idea who she is or where she came from."

"Oh, Russ. How awful. Was it a hit-and-run?"

"No. I don't think so. I think it's foul play, but there's not a mark on her to indicate how she died."

"Is Dan Scheeler doing an autopsy?"

"Oh, yeah. And Lyle's running down missing persons and Hadley's following up on the ViCAP reports of similar cases. Not that there're many of those."

"Do you have to go back in tonight?"

"Sixty hours a week, remember?"

"Ha."

He grinned a little. "I don't think so. Maybe. I hope not. Eric will take over from Lyle and we called in Duane to cover Eric's patrol." He pinched the bridge of his nose beneath his glasses. "God, I wish we could replace Kevin. We're hurting for manpower."

She turned toward him, her knees bumping Ethan's carrier. She reached up and ran her fingers through his hair, stroking the nape of his neck and rubbing his scalp. "I know being shorthanded is frustrating."

He sighed into her touch. "Tourist season's the busiest damn time of the year. We've had three traffic accidents, two lost kids, and an idiot who fell into the river and needed the boat rescue over the weekend. The Sacandaga Road project *still* isn't finished, despite what Jock MacEarnon's been promising me, and that sucks up one officer's shift every day. I have to waste my time doing high school debate team with people who'd rather save twenty cents a day than have a police force keeping the peace and I've got a dead girl in the road and the only damn thing I know about her is that it's not my fault."

Russ's voice, rising with his temper, broke through Ethan's milk dream. His eyes and mouth popped open, and he began to squall. "Oh, hell." Russ scooped him up, letting the plastic carrier drop to the floor. He cradled his son against his chest, rubbing the baby's cotton-clad back. "I'm sorry, darlin'. I'm sorry. Daddy isn't mad at you."

Clare snagged a blanket and draped it over Russ's shoulder. "It's not your fault?"

"I didn't mean to wake him up." He leaned back, tugging the blanket over as much of his uniform blouse as he could. Good thing the shirts were nigh-on indestructible, because his boy showed a real talent for upchucking when Russ was wearing one.

"That's not what I meant." She braced her arm against the love seat's back and propped her face in her hand. "You said you've got a dead girl in the road and it's not your fault. Can you tell me what you meant by that?"

"Are you *counseling* me?"

She flicked his shoulder. "Everything else you were complaining about is old news. You've been dealing with tourists and roadwork and not having enough officers for months now. What's really going on?"

Ethan's angry sobs were quieting to irregular whimpers. He began gumming his fingers. Russ kissed his wispy blond hair. "This case. If it is a case. There was a murder a lot like it back in . . ." He thought for a moment, counting the events of his life. "In '72. I was just back from Vietnam."

"Where?"

"Here." He shifted in the love seat. "'A lot like it' isn't quite the right description. It's more like exactly the same. So far. Unknown victim. Pretty, young, all dressed up, with no shoes or pantyhose. No visible cause of death."

"That's not the easiest set of circumstances you've ever had to work with, but it doesn't seem unsolvable . . . It's awfully hard to hide an identity forever these days. And if the pathology is too much for Dr. Scheeler, you can always kick it upstairs to the state crime lab."

He opened his mouth.

"Yeah, I know you don't want to ask the state police for any more help than you have to."

He couldn't help it; he smiled. "Think you know me pretty well, do you?"

"I do." She laid her free hand over his, where he was clasping Ethan's back. Their hands rose and fell together with the light movement of the baby's breathing. "What did you mean by 'it isn't my fault'?"

He shook his head. "It's stupid. It's just . . . when the other girl was found, back in '72? I was a suspect in her death."

Clare's hand spasmed over his. "You're kidding me."

"Nope."

"Why?"

"I found the body. I had— There were some things that didn't look good."

"Why am I just finding out about this now?"

He gave her the best smile he could muster. She kept frowning. He dropped the attempt. "I was just back from the war and my head was pretty messed up. It's not a time of my life I like to revisit."

She scooted forward, freeing her arm to wrap it across his shoulders. "Okay. I can understand that, for sure."

He laughed a little. "I'm okay now. But, Christ, Clare, when I got out to the scene on McEachron Hill Road and it was exactly like what I had seen thirty-four years ago . . ."

"You were suddenly back in your younger, messed-up head?"

He sighed. "It felt like getting stuck in time. I like who I am now. I don't care about my creaky knees and my spine going snap-crackle-pop when I get out of bed. You couldn't pay me to be twenty again."

"Are you worried your memories of the old case are going to color the way you approach this new one?"

"Hell, yes. I didn't tell Lyle or Hadley anything other than the town had seen a similar death before. If the initial investigators buy into a theory too early, they can wind up slanting the rest of the investigation to fit. Evidence gets overlooked or misinterpreted. Facts get shoved around to fit the theory. I've seen it happen."

He heard the *urp* and felt the wet, warm liquid spreading over his chest before he had a chance to get the blanket on it. "Damn." He wiped the spit-up off, but the damage had been done. "I'm going to change the undress uniforms to camo."

"I don't think they make baby-barf camo."

Russ cleaned off his son's face. The baby yawned and closed his eyes. "It's a good thing Ethan can't vote. Clearly, he doesn't have much respect for the uniform."

Clare smiled. "You don't think he's destined to be a soldier or a cop?"

"God, I hope not." He cradled his boy close. "I'd like him to avoid making all the same mistakes I did."

8.   The Millers Kill Police Department was small enough so no one needed lockers to hold their stuff. Desk drawers in the squad room, a row of hooks for coats and umbrellas and bags, one small refrigerator where you kept your lunch and took a chance that no one would eat it. So whoever wanted to send Hadley a message didn't have to exert himself to break a combination. He could just slip a note beneath her laptop or hang something off her hook.

This morning it was a pair of lacy thong panties, tucked inside her windbreaker. She held them for a moment—they appeared to be brand-new and unworn, thank God—debating whether to go to the chief again. He had already spoken to every man in the department, including the part-time guys, individually. He had read them the riot act about sexual harassment and respect for the uniform. It hadn't made much of a difference.

Hadley hadn't been in the station house the afternoon her ex-husband's little gift for the MKPD had arrived. A box full of fifteen-year-old tapes. If the chief had been there, she liked to think, no one would have put one of them into the VHS player. Or if they had, he would have pulled the plug as soon as he saw what it was. But the chief had been with the board of aldermen, getting the news that all their jobs might be gone come Election Day, and half the force saw her in the flesh, writhing with her co-stars in *College Girls Go Down*. The box had been full of movies, all starring her, and by the time she had gotten back to the station house from her afternoon shift, every one of her co-workers knew the one and only female officer on the force had been in porn when she was twenty. Practically half a lifetime ago, not that it mattered. When it came to what people thought of you, it was never far enough in the past.

She stuffed the panties in her pocket.

"Knox? Good, you're here." The chief beckoned to her from the squad room doorway. "Are you familiar with the state CCRF?"

"Yeah. I mean, familiar enough. I've used it four or five times."

"Thank God. Lyle and I could use some help from someone a little more computer literate than we are."

The chief wasn't all that bad on a database interface, just slow. The dep, on the other hand, approached computers like they might explode at any moment. Kevin Flynn had actually written down step-by-step directions so MacAuley could attach files to an e-mail. Of course, he was gone now. Off to the Syracuse PD. Couldn't help any of them anymore. The self-righteous lying bastard.

"Knox?"

"Absolutely, Chief." She followed him into the squad room, an overly modern name for the high-ceilinged, high-windowed area furnished with old metal desks and a battered pine table the chief liked to sit on while he thought. Bulletin boards and maps hung on the walls and a slightly wobbly whiteboard stood at the front, along with a scattering of chairs from the morning briefing.

"Oh, good." MacAuley got up from the laptop he'd been staring at. "A young person."

Hadley plopped down in the vacant seat. "I'm thirty-five, Dep."

"Like I said, a young person. I messed something up and now I can't get the damn machine to do anything. You better try it again."

Hadley logged MacAuley out and logged herself in. The state Cold Case Referral File was supposed to be the end repository of all the unsolved cases that had piled up in various law enforcement agencies across New York State. In theory. In actuality, its database was limited to cases someone had had the time to scan and enter in, which left a lot of potential gaps. Every police department in the country would swear, when asked, that cold cases weren't lower priority than those on the front burner. But when push came to shove, closing cases talked and PR walked.

Hadley looked up at the chief as the interface loaded. "Did the crime scene guys find anything yet?" The chief had asked the staties to help search the site yesterday, while MacAuley and Eric McCrea focused on ID'ing the decedent.

"Nothing," the dep said.

"Did Dr. Scheeler confirm she wasn't a medical?"

"Nope," the dep said. "And no, we haven't gotten any info on who she was yet." He glanced toward the chief with something in his eyes Hadley couldn't read.

"We've got a request in with the federal ViCAP database." The chief's voice was firm. "They'll send us any open cases that resemble ours. Following up on the cold cases just makes sense."

Hadley realized she had walked in at the back end of an argument that had been going on for a while.

"Throwing everything we've got into an investigation when we're not even sure a crime's been committed is *not* good sense," MacAuley said. "Especially when we're short-handed. I'm on overtime right now."

"She didn't just walk down that road by herself and have a heart attack."

"You don't know that. She could have dumped her date in a huff and had a stroke before he had a chance to pick her up again. She could have had alcohol poisoning." MacAuley waved his arms. "Hell, she could have gotten a mosquito bite and died of West Nile fever!"

The chief gave him a look.

"Okay, okay, maybe not West Nile fever. But my point is still good." MacAuley dropped his voice. "We can't afford to be seen running up OT and calling in the staties at every turn when this might be a case of unlicensed disposal of a body."

The chief rapped his pine table. "What we can't afford is letting the Golden Hours slip away doing the bare minimum and then find out we've let someone get away with murder. Trust me, that's going to look a hell of a lot worse to the voters than Tim and Duane getting time-and-a-half for flagging road repairs. Knox."

Hadley jumped in her seat. She had thought they'd forgotten about her.

"You know how to enter the parameters of the search, right? Unsub, no visible cause of death, rural location—no, change that; the important thing is that the body is dumped—"

"If the body is dumped," MacAuley said.

"Between midnight and dawn," the chief continued, ignoring the dep. "Party dress, makeup, and don't forget the missing shoes and purse."

Hadley glanced up from where she was typing. "The dress? You think that was a component?"

"I do."

She shrugged and continued entering the search terms, slotting them in order of possible importance, adding every synonym she could think of.

"Not every girl carries a purse nowadays," MacAuley said.

"Yeah, but have you ever known one to go anywhere without her cell phone? They carry them on these little dangly things . . ." The chief stopped. "Oh, hell." He thumped himself on the forehead. "I'm an idiot. Cell phone towers. We need to get a list of the calls relayed through the area cell phone towers."

"I'm on it." MacAuley headed toward his office, a space that had once been a cloakroom when the MKPD had had a lot more officers on hand.

The chief was making little noises of frustration. "This is what happens when you think too much about past cases." He leaned against the table, frowning ferociously at the county map on the opposite wall. Hadley didn't think he was talking to her. "Cell phones. *Cell* phones!"

She finished outlining the search request and entered it. "Okay, Chief, it's all set. It'll probably take awhile—" She cut herself off as a short list of cases popped up in a window. "Damn, that's fast." She clicked OPEN ALL, and an array of scanned records spilled across her screen. She blinked at what she saw. "Chief?" She turned to him. Van Alstyne looked . . . guilty. "The top match is from right here. It's a cold case from the MKPD."

He frowned at his boots. "Is there anything from any other locations?"

43

"It's still searching. It'll return more hits in descending order of matches." She turned back to the screen. A line of blue words beneath the law enforcement agency names and case file numbers indicated how many search terms the document contained. The previous MKPD record had them all. She hit the PRINT key. "Chief." She chose her tone carefully. "This isn't just a close match. It's identical."

The printer, located just inside the door where the dispatcher could reach it as well, chunked away.

Van Alstyne sighed. "I know, Knox." He glanced at the printer. "Better make copies for everyone."

"Okay, the good news is, we don't need to apply for a warrant to get the cell transmission records." MacAuley emerged from his office waving a slip of notepaper. "The company doesn't require one unless we're going after somebody's individual number."

He slapped the note on the desk next to Hadley. "Thank God for the Patriot Act." He pointed to where he had scribbled an address. "We have to file a request on one of those online pdf things. That's where you'll find it, Knox." He paused, as if he had finally noticed the strained air in the room. "What's up? You find something?" He put on his reading glasses and bent over Hadley's shoulder to look at the screen. "What the hell?"

The printer stopped. Hadley crossed behind the big pine table and began collating the documents into separate batches, partly to be a good worker bee—if she was going to be thrust into the role of secretary, she might as well try to shine—and partly to keep out of the way of the dep and the chief.

MacAuley snatched one of the stacks of papers off the table and began reading. "What the hell?" he repeated. He flipped a page. "What the ever-loving *hell*?" He looked at the chief. "There wasn't another Russell Van Alstyne waltzing around here in 1972, was there? A cousin, maybe? An uncle?"

The chief shook his head. "No."

"You were the prime suspect."

The chief nodded.

"In a death that was," the dep glanced at the pages in his hand again, "exactly the same as this one."

"Yeah."

MacAuley looked toward Hadley. He had the expression of someone watching an alien spaceship land, or maybe pigs flying. She shrugged.

"I didn't tell you right off the bat because I didn't want anyone's approach to the case tainted by the events of the past. Anyone else's, I should say." Van Alstyne tilted his head back, cracking his neck. "My head's so stuffed with the '72 case, I'm having a hard time objectively seeing the facts on the ground."

His mutterings about cell phones suddenly fell into place.

"For chrissakes, Russ. Give the rest of us a little credit." MacAuley flipped through the papers. "They had a couple leads that didn't pan out." He paused and read more closely. "You weren't exactly cleared, were you? They just couldn't link you up to the vic." Hadley could hear a faint thread of suspicion in the dep's voice.

Evidently, the chief could, too. "Really, Lyle? You want to put me up on the board as a person of interest?" He crossed his arms. "Go right ahead."

"Don't be ridiculous. I'm just saying—"

"Could this be a copycat crime?" Hadley said. Both men stopped their antler-clashing and looked at her. "I mean, obviously, the previous case wasn't so very long ago that it couldn't be the same person. Only . . . doesn't it have a kind of ritualistic feel to it? With the clothing and the makeup and the missing shoes and all exactly the same?"

MacAuley nodded. "It does, yeah." Inadvertently or not, he looked at Van Alstyne. "But that makes it *more* likely it was the same perp."

"Like me, you mean?" The chief glared at the dep.

"Except the gap in time argues this isn't the same killer." Both men's attention swung back to her again. "Murderers who kill for ritualistic or sexual purposes usually don't stop cold for—" She did the math in her head. "—thirty-four years. Not unless they're dead or have been put away for an unrelated crime."

"Or have relocated." The chief pointed to the laptop, where the CCRF program was still searching the old records. "This is just the New York State cold case database. There could be identical killings somewhere else in the country."

"Are we agreeing to call it murder?" MacAuley said.

"What do you think?"

MacAuley nodded. "One woman walking down the road and dropping dead, I can see. Two is pushing it."

The chief took a deep breath. "How about a third?"

AUGUST 1952

9.   The squawk box on his desk lit up and Harry McNeil pressed the button. "I've got a call from the county coroner," his secretary said. "He didn't tell me what case it's about, though. Said you'd know."

"Thanks, Cloris. Give me a minute to grab a file and then put him through." Harry circled his desk and crossed to the three file cabinets on the far wall, so new their coated metal surfaces still gleamed. The drawer slid open noiselessly. Good-bye to out-of-warp wood dating back to the Coolidge administration. Hello, steel ball bearings.

He found the folder and closed the drawer. His whole office had been redone, and he didn't miss the old oak desk with its stains and snags. He especially didn't miss the wooden chair snapping and creaking whenever he leaned back. He said a silent prayer of thanks to the mayor and the aldermen as he sat in his quiet, comfortable desk chair. It had only taken them twenty-five years to find the money.

He picked up the phone and pressed the button. "Dr. Outwin? Thank you for calling me back."

"Well, Chief McNeil, I do owe you a couple favors." The coroner had a laugh like Santa Claus and a taste for jollity to match. Harry's men had helped him safely home several times when he'd had a few too many cocktails.

"What did you find out?"

"Not much, I'm afraid. The young lady was between twenty-one and twenty-five, going by her teeth, and in good health, heart, lungs, and liver."

"So what was the cause of death?"

"I don't know."

Harry looked out his window, where only a single plume of smoke from the Allan Mill broke the clear blue sky. "You don't know?"

"It wasn't a heart attack. She didn't have any indications of a fatal allergic reaction. No signs she was assaulted."

"Had she been interfered with?"

"I did find traces of male emission, yes. But there were no marks of violence on her body, so there's no way to tell if she was willing or not."

"Do you have a theory?"

"I have a possibility. If she had an aneurysm—that's when a blood clot breaks off and is carried through the circulatory system to the brain—it could have killed her, then dissolved naturally. To anyone she was with, it would have looked like a brief seizure, followed by death. If she were with a married man or a customer . . ."

"He could have panicked and dumped her body." Harry sat back in his chair, pleased with its smooth tilt. "Is there any way you can see her death being a homicide?"

Dr. Outwin sighed. "Poisons almost always leave their mark, although I suppose there could be something so exotic I didn't catch any sign. Blowfish from the Japanese islands, that sort of thing. It could have been a drug overdose, but there's a problem in that any amount of, say, heroin great enough to kill would register in her blood even after death. The liver doesn't have enough time to flush all of the drug out of the system before it shuts down for good."

"And you didn't find any drugs."

"She had alcohol before she died. Oh, and she was a smoker."

"Well, that might have given her a cough, but it didn't kill her." Harry tried pulling out his lower drawer and putting his feet up. Very nice. "What's going to happen with the body?"

"I've released it to the morgue. The state police will keep her as long as possible while trying to identify her. The detective with whom I spoke didn't sound especially encouraging on that front."

"I can guarantee you pinning a name on a girl who may have been a prostitute who died of natural causes is very low on Detective Carruthers's to-do list."

"That's a shame."

"I agree." Harry swung his feet off the drawer and stood up, cracking his back. "Fortunately, my to-do list is a lot shorter."

"I thought this case was under state police jurisdiction."

"Oh, it is." Harry grinned. "Fortunately, I have an in. It's always wise to cultivate cross-jurisdictional friendships."

SUNDAY, AUGUST 20, PRESENT DAY

10. At six o'clock the heat was still rolling off the driveway as Hadley climbed out of her car. No AC— she couldn't afford to have it replaced—meant she looked like an over-baked potato, even after the short drive from the station. Her never-iron khaki and brown uniform was crumpled and damp, and the fringes of her boy-short hair stuck to her temple and to the nape of her neck.

Good God, she was glad to get home. It had been a fruitless, fretful day. No progress on the dead girl's killing had made Van Alstyne and MacAuley snappish, and for officers like her, assigned to patrol, dealing with angry tourists and disgruntled townies in the swamplike heat set everyone's teeth on edge.

The enclosed porch at the back of the house wasn't any cooler than the outside, but she got sweet relief when she stepped into the kitchen. The sudden drop in temperature made her feel twenty pounds lighter, even before taking her duty belt off. "Genny? Hudson? I'm home." Granddad's big old boat of a Lincoln wasn't in the drive, but the only thing he and the kids had planned was church in the morning followed by a visit to Supercuts to take care of Granddad's and Hudson's hair.

Silence, except for the rattle and chuff of the window air conditioner unit in the family room. There was a note on the kitchen table, scribbled on the back of an envelope. *Honey, I'm taking the kids to the lake to cool off. Don't worry, I'll get them dinner.*

She sighed. That meant a stop at McDonald's or Burger King, where the kids would eat their junior meals and Granddad would put away enough fat and salt to give himself another heart attack. Not to mention what his customary large milkshake would do to his blood sugar levels.

Her yellow and green kitchen was fairly neat, which meant the kids must have just run after getting their haircuts, grabbed their swimming things and run out again, touching nothing. She shuffled through yesterday's mail, still piled on the counter. Bill, bill, credit card application—like *that* was going to happen, with the amount of debt she was carrying—Red Cross blood drive and a fat envelope addressed to Granddad from Medicare that promised hours of work for her sorting out his treatment and benefits.

She tossed it back onto the counter—her careless mother's voice in her head saying, *There's always time for bad news*—and headed upstairs. In her room, she deposited her gun and duty belt in her lockbox and replaced it on the top shelf of her closet. She gratefully stripped off her poly shirt and slacks and tossed them in the hamper. In the winter, she could get three or four wearings out of one uniform, but in heat like this, she'd go to work in her undies before wearing a set twice. More laundry for her, but at least she didn't feel like she might be breeding mold in her pockets.

She considered a shower, then decided she'd rather eat. She tugged on a pair of cool cotton pajama pants and opened a drawer to dig into her crumpled jumble of T-shirts. Her hand closed around a neck and she pulled, only to discover it wasn't her T-shirt at all. It was large, long enough to fit a slim guy of over six feet, and the faded lettering on the front read MILLERS KILL MINUTEMEN BASKETBALL.

She felt a sting, as if she were holding a scorpion instead of a limp piece of clothing. She wanted to fling it away, and because that was her first instinct, she kept it clenched in her fist. Pain from a misbegotten love affair wasn't real pain. It hadn't really been love, anyway, had it? Just gratitude and proximity and the loneliness of being a single mother who hadn't slept with a man in God knows how long.

She had been shivering, she remembered, when Kevin Flynn had given her the T-shirt that had been hanging over the foot of his bed. It was January, and the cold leaked in around the edges of his apartment and pooled in his bathroom. He had laughed about her delicate California sensibilities and tossed her the shirt, and when she'd gotten back to the bedroom he was already pulling on his uniform, because he was on duty in fifteen minutes. She was going to be late getting home to Granddad and the kids. An hour and a half stolen out of the day, because they had been so love-struck with the raw newness of it all they couldn't wait for their Friday date, which, as it turned out, never happened.

Well. Hadley laid the T-shirt on her bed and smoothed it out. She had thought they were both love-struck. She had been mistaken. Nothing surprising about that—she had a history going back to high school of picking the exact wrong guy and falling for him. She had probably had a crush on the worst girl-hater in kindergarten. She folded the T-shirt neatly.

She pulled a sleeveless shirt from her closet and buttoned it on, then picked up the Minuteman T-shirt and crossed the hall to Genny's room. She had a box half-filled with kids' clothes destined for Goodwill, and she dropped the folded T-shirt into it and left it there. She opened all the bedroom doors wide to share the cool air coming from Granddad's room—he had the sole air conditioner upstairs.

Downstairs, she debated making some pasta or just having a sandwich for dinner. She decided on the sandwich. The initial thrill of cooler air had faded, and the kitchen felt a lot warmer than it had when she first came through the door. The thought of boiling water made her want to fan herself. She was laying out the lettuce and cheese and bologna on the counter when the front doorbell rang.

It was a Washington County sheriff's deputy. She knew the guy; they had met at a seminar on policing and the mentally ill. Jason? Justin? Joshua. "Josh. Hi. What can I help you with?" She couldn't imagine why he'd be at her door on a Sunday evening instead of contacting her at the station.

He looked embarrassed. "Hey, Hadley." He handed her a thick manila envelope. "Sorry to do this, but you've been served."

She stared at the envelope stupidly. She couldn't seem to get her head off the guest-at-the-door track, and she found herself saying, "Um. Would you like to come in? Can I get you a soda?" Good God.

Thankfully, the deputy shook his head. "Nah. I'm working." He took a step backward, then paused. "Maybe we could get together for a drink sometime, though?"

"Mmm. Yeah. Give me a call." She shut the door, still staring at the envelope, Josh and his invitation already on their way to the circular file in her brain. She ripped the envelope open and pulled out a sheaf of papers. Some from a California law firm, some from a lawyer with an Albany address.

Oh, Christ. Her ex was suing for custody. The fear nearly blacked her out, dimming the room, bleeding the ink across the page, setting her swaying on her feet. She closed her eyes and forced herself to breathe slowly. Once, twice, three times. Okay. She would start by reading the papers. Carefully.

She turned on the overhead light and spread everything across the dining room table. She braced her hands against the smooth wooden surface and began going over the document. *Criminal proceedings. Alleged false imprisonment. Alleged tampering with evidence. Methamphetamines.*

She jerked her head up. *Methamphetamines?* Oh, thank you sweet Jesus, these weren't about custody. They weren't about her kids at all. This was about her ex-husband being charged with possession. She was summonsed as a witness for the defense.

She sat down with a thud, her momentary elation gone. Witness for the defense. She looked at the second set of papers, from the California office. *Civil suit. Unlawful restraint. Interference with custodial visitation. False evidence. Slander. Damage to reputation.*

What the hell? Did her ex think he was going to get money out of her by suing her? Could you even bring a civil suit when you were facing criminal charges? Hadley read on. *Required to appear for deposition.* She realized she was once more being summonsed as a witness. She flipped back to the beginning, all the way back, and realized she had missed the very first page.

DYLAN KNOX v. KEVIN FLYNN and MILLERS KILL
POLICE DEPARTMENT

Oh, hell, no.

Her phone was on the kitchen counter, next to the mail. She hadn't deleted his number, any more than she had tossed his T-shirt. Well, at least this bit of idiocy would prove helpful. His phone went straight to voice mail. "Flynn, it's Hadley." She took a breath. "I need you to call me as soon as you get this. We have to talk." She clicked off and set the phone back down by the bills.

Hadley's mom had been right. It didn't matter how safe you felt, how well things were going.

There's always time for bad news.

11. Russ closed the folder with the legal papers inside and slid it across the table to the mayor. This was not the way he had planned to spend Monday morning. Jim Cameron took a drink from a bottle of water. "Keep it. We've got plenty of copies." Russ retrieved the folder with one finger. He thought of Ethan sleeping in his crib this morning, the first long rays of the sun brightening his silk-shot hair, the light making his skin seem lit from within. It was a nice thought.

Harold Collins's voice burst his bubble. "Well? When were you going to tell us about this?"

Russ resisted the urge to pinch the bridge of his nose. Absolutely nothing had broken in the unsub case, both his part-time officers were unavailable, lunch was going to be a candy bar from the vending machine, and he had the mother of all headaches brewing. "As soon as I found out about it. Which was five minutes after I stepped into this meeting."

The board of aldermen didn't look as if they'd been given any more notice than he had when he got the urgent message from the town clerk. Ron Tucker was in his garage overalls and Ed Palmer, who owned the Italian Bakery—his mother had been an exotic beauty named Giadella Tremoni—smelled powerfully of flour and butter. Bob Miles, the county's public works engineer, hadn't even made it yet. Probably hung up on another one of the never-ending road repair projects blighting Russ's life.

"I don't mean the lawsuit," Harold snapped. "I mean the cause of it. You've got one officer accused of tampering with evidence and false imprisonment and another one who appears to have been hanging around cheering him on while he broke the law!"

Russ laid his hands flat on the table, a once-perfect slab of cherry wood that had been scratched and dinged and marred by the coffee cups of forty years of meetings. He felt just like it this morning. "At this point, you know as much as I do, Harold. The incident described in those papers, whatever the truth of it is, wasn't part of any MKPD action. I won't know any more until I've spoken with my officers. Officer, I mean. Kevin Flynn has gone to the Syracuse Police Department."

"And isn't that convenient? He quits and moves halfway across the state within a week of assaulting this"—Harold glanced down at his copy of the document—"Dylan Knox."

"*Alleged* assault," the mayor said. "Let's not make the plaintiff's case for them, hmm, Harold?" Harold drew in a breath, but Jim raised his hand. "It's entirely possible this is a nuisance suit. It wouldn't be the first time a disgruntled ex-spouse adopts a scorched-earth policy." Jim, who had met his gloriously Swedish second wife before severing the bonds of matrimony with his first, had personal knowledge of the topic. He turned to Russ. "What do you know about the relationship between Officer Knox and her ex-husband? Is it bad enough for him to try to punish her by lashing out at the entire department?"

Russ thought about the box of old porn tapes that had arrived at the station house last January, courtesy of Dylan Knox and his "production company." Tapes that had made it explicitly clear how Hadley Knox had earned her living as a twenty-year-old. Tapes that had set up walls of embarrassment and sly speculation between her and the rest of the force.

"Yes," he said. "Yes, I think it is."

"So you think there's no basis for this suit? That your officers did nothing wrong?" Ron Tucker sounded hopeful.

Russ was going to have to walk the knife edge with this one. "I have no knowledge of the incident alleged in the suit."

Alderman Garry Greuling, who had so far sat silently, raised a hand. "No offense, Russ, but that sounds like legalistic weaseling."

"Let me finish. I don't have any knowledge of the events described in these papers. But I do know my officers. And I'd stake my reputation on their good conduct. I can't believe that either of them is in any way at fault here."

Harold snorted. "Like the good conduct of that feller of yours who put somebody in the hospital."

"That was a year ago, Harold." Jim Cameron sounded annoyed. "The investigation justified Sergeant McCrea's use of force."

"We're lucky we didn't get sued then, that's all I'm saying. And I'm going to point out *again* that one of the advantages of going with the state police instead of a pricey local department is that the town'll be immune from this sort of nonsense."

Garry Greuling rolled his eyes. "Oh, for God's sake, Harold, it's not as simple as that—" And they were off and running. The board had split three to three on dissolving the police department and the topic had become a permanent point of contention among them.

Jim Cameron looked at Russ, tilted his head toward the door, and stood up. Russ followed. They exited the office and Jim shut the door on the wrangling voices.

"I'll talk to both my officers," Russ said. "I mean, Officers Knox and Flynn."

"Do. And let me know what they say. One thing I don't want is to be blindsided by the plaintiff's attorneys."

"Understood." Russ turned to go.

"Russ."

He turned back.

"I also hope you understand that I didn't vote *against* the police department. I voted to put the question on the ballot, because I think this is something only the residents of the three towns can decide." He hesitated. "If it weren't for the budget . . ."

The budget. Russ knew all about the goddamned budget. "Yeah."

"Don't give Harold and the folks who think like him any more reason to want to do away with your jobs, Russ. Get this thing sorted out. Quickly."

"I will." Russ paused, his hand on the doorknob. "I hope *you* understand I'm not fighting the ballot measure to save jobs. I believe in community policing. I believe having local law enforcement right here, responding to peoples' needs, is the right thing for the town."

"I know you do." Jim pointed to the folder in Russ's hand. "Just make sure that message doesn't get lost in a nasty legal fight." He smiled a little. "And it wouldn't hurt if you got all your cases closed before Election Day."

"Right." Russ smiled weakly. He hadn't updated the mayor's office on the situation with the dead girl yet. "Get those cases cleared. No problem."

12. Clare had tumbled into love helplessly and unexpectedly three times in her life. It never got any easier, and she never landed anywhere near her starting point. The first time was when her ordinary, understandable—she thought—relationship with God became something that tugged and pushed and pulled her until she had abandoned her military career and entered the priesthood. The second was when she had looked over the top of a squad car at the Millers Kill chief of police, frowning and frustrated, snow

spangling his hair, and a key fit into a lock she hadn't known was there and everything changed. The third time was when the nurse had laid her flannel-wrapped son in her arms, and it hadn't felt like love, it had felt like a fortress, with Ethan the center and Clare the wall.

Just once, she'd like to have a soft, simple love. Puppies, maybe. She glanced down at Oscar, who had literally taken a bullet for her last winter. Even her dog came with baggage.

Oscar at least had the virtue of being easy to bring to work. He dozed in her office, went for a walk a couple times a day, and was sober and polite to everyone. Ethan . . .

Ethan was screaming. "Maybe something's wrong with his tummy." Lois stayed just outside Clare's door, presumably for protection if Ethan should begin to projectile vomit.

"It could be colic." Elizabeth de Groot, a braver woman than the secretary, frowned by the bookcase. "One of my nieces' children cried for three months straight. They couldn't do anything."

Clare, jiggling Ethan against her shoulder, closed her eyes against the prospect. "It's not colic."

"Comes on like *that*." Elizabeth snapped her fingers.

"What's this, here?" From over Lois's shoulder, Clare could see the sexton, Glenn Hadley, peering in through the door. The old man was wearing his summer uniform, a twill shirt and pants that had faded to the same indeterminate color and had permanent cigarette-carton-shaped creases on all the pockets. "Little guy giving you trouble, Father?"

"Mr. Hadley, you really don't have to call me—" Clare stopped herself. "Yes. Yes, he is." Her uniform didn't look any better than the sexton's—her black skirt was damp and creased and despite draping herself with a rag, she had a streak of spit-up across her sleeveless black blouse. "Lois, the Dale-Yeager nuptials will be here in five minutes." And she had a lunch meeting with the financial committee after that. "Could you . . . ?" She shifted Ethan toward the secretary, who backed away. "It would just be until I could call . . ." She didn't know who she could call. Margy was off getting her hair done in Glens Falls and Russ's niece was at Lake George with a bunch of friends and Someone

Special. Maybe Russ's sister? Her friend Karen Burns? If only Ethan would stop screaming for a moment so she could *think,* she could—

"Lemme take him, Father." Mr. Hadley brushed past Lois and held his hands out. "I'll walk him downstairs until you figger out who can sit for him." He scooped the wailing, red-faced baby out of Clare's arms, held him up high, and took a sniff. "Don't smell like he needs changing."

"Uh, no. I checked."

"Clare." Elizabeth gave her a quelling look. "I'm sure we don't want to trouble Mr. Hadley, who, after all, has lots of mopping and scrubbing to do."

"Don't worry none, Deacon, I'll keep him well away from anything bad for him. He already do his burp, Father?"

Clare touched her blouse. "Oh, yes."

"Okaydie-dadie. Maybe he just needs a change of view." Mr. Hadley lifted Ethan up airplane-style and settled the infant atop his bald head, stomach to scalp.

"Oh, I don't think—" Clare began.

Ethan stopped screaming. His eyes went wide and his tiny mouth opened in astonishment. Mr. Hadley bounced up and down a few times and Ethan flung his arms and legs out. He bubbled a breathless laugh.

"Baby hat," Mr. Hadley said. "Works every time." Bobbing up and down, he left the office. Clare could hear him talking to Ethan as they made their way down the hall.

"My," Elizabeth observed.

"Baby hat," Lois said. "Baby hat."

Clare dropped into her desk chair and reached for her phone. "I'm going to see if Karen Burns is home with Cody today. If she is, she can probably take Ethan, too."

Elizabeth brushed an invisible speck from her immaculate black clericals. "Clare, I hate to be the one to puncture any balloons—"

Oh, really?

"—but you've got to see that having Ethan here for any stretch of time isn't going to work out. I mean, if you had a sitter in the rectory next door, or if you were only here part time—"

"I can't do part time. I won't." Clare clamped down on her temper. "I've already had maternity leave, I've got Guard duty one weekend a month, and this fall I'll be gone for two weeks' annual training. I'm not going to take any *more* time away from my parish." She flipped open her address book and speared Karen's number with one finger.

"I think you should consider—"

Voices in the hallway kept Clare from having to hear what her deacon thought she ought to consider. Resignation, probably. Or full-time day care. How many people had to sing that tune before she'd finally sit up and listen? Was it really the best thing for Ethan, or just temptingly convenient? God, if she could just get her mind to settle and be still for twenty minutes, she might be able to sort her life out, but the way things were going, she wasn't going to have a second of calm until Ethan left for college. She breathed in deeply, trying to be mindful. What had the pediatrician suggested? *I am at peace.* Too aspirational. *I have a calm mind. I have a quiet mind.*

The engaged couple entered the office. Elizabeth let herself out with only a flashing look to indicate their conversation wasn't over. "Hi, you two," Clare said. "Why don't you grab some coffee or tea from the parish hall. My little boy didn't want to settle for his nap, so I have to take just a minute to line up a sitter."

"Sure thing." The bride-to-be bent down and scratched Oscar behind his ears. "You get to bring your dog *and* your baby to work?" She sighed. "Oh, Reverend Clare, I envy you."

13. **R**uss dropped into the chair opposite the medical examiner's desk with a graceless thud. "I hope to God you've got good news for me."

"Well, good afternoon to you, too, sunshine." Dan Scheeler turned away from the Keurig machine hissing and foaming atop the credenza. "Can I offer you anything? Coffee? Xanax?"

"A solution to the unsub killing. Or a quick and merciful death.

They both feel about equal at this point." Russ took off his glasses and rubbed his face.

Scheeler waited.

"Okay, coffee and a couple aspirin, if you got 'em." Scheeler held up one of the tiny containers and Russ squinted to read FRENCH HAZELNUT. "Sure. Fine. Anything's better than the stuff they used to have in the vending machine."

Scheeler slid a cup beneath the spout and punched a few buttons. "When the county asked me to take over from Dr. Dvorak, I had three stipulations. High-speed Internet, some office furniture that didn't look like it was featured in a 1950s Sears catalog, and to take that vending machine out to the dump and shoot it."

Russ glanced around at the steel-case bookshelves and the ponderous metal desk with paint chipped away at its edges. Only Scheeler's desk chair, with its smooth mesh and ergonomic curves, looked like it came from this century.

"Yeah, I bought the chair myself," Scheeler said. "Sometimes, you have to pick your battles."

"Amen to that."

Scheeler handed Russ his coffee before seating himself. He opened his desk drawer and pulled out a bottle of pills, which he tossed to Russ.

"You had that right handy."

Scheeler grinned, his teeth white against his close-trimmed black beard. "Trust me, you're not the only one who has headaches." He flopped open a file. "Speaking of which . . ."

Russ sighed. "Let me guess. You didn't find anything."

"I always find something." The medical examiner slid a few sheets across the desktop. "The unknown woman was between the ages of twenty-one and thirty. She had no fillings, which you'd expect from a young person who'd been treated with dental sealant. I e-mailed the X-rays and file to your office."

"Dental records never help."

"Maybe not, but at least we know she had access to decent insurance and went to the dentist's regularly. She broke her right arm above the wrist. Sometime after she stopped growing so, say, sixteen at the earliest. Not recently, it was well healed. Her stomach was empty. She hadn't eaten in at least six hours before her death, which I estimate was between three and six hours before she was found. She had a small amount of alcohol in her bloodstream. Maybe two drinks' worth."

Russ lifted his head from the paper Scheeler had given him, which presented exactly the same facts as he was hearing now. "Okay. She was a normal, healthy girl who drank responsibly and didn't eat between meals. Can you give me anything helpful? Can you tell me how she died?"

Scheeler leaned back in his fancy ergonomic chair. "No."

"Oh, hell."

"I can tell you how she *didn't* die." The medical examiner started ticking off reasons on his fingers. "She didn't die of alcohol poisoning. She didn't have a heart attack or stroke. She wasn't shot, knifed, or killed by blunt force trauma. I examined her entire epidermis under a magnifying glass and found no puncture wounds which might indicate she'd been injected with something. I can only conclude the culprit will be some sort of agent that will only show up in the tox screen."

"By 'agent,' do you mean poison?"

Scheeler juggled his open hands as if tossing an invisible ball between them. "'Poison' isn't a word I like to use lightly. There are a lot of perfectly natural chemicals around that can kill us if taken in excess. You can die from drinking too much water, for instance."

"How soon—"

"I prepped the slides and sent them off to the state lab this morning. I stressed time was of the essence so . . . maybe three weeks?"

Russ uncapped the bottle and shook out three aspirin, which he chased down with a mouthful of coffee. "You remember, I told you there had been another case like this in '72? What if I got you the medical records for that victim?"

"I'd take a look at them. Honestly, though, we have so many diagnostic tools they didn't have then. I doubt there's anything they did that we can't do better." He swept the loose papers back into the file and handed it to Russ. "Are you thinking it might be the same perpetrator?"

"I'd be a fool not to consider it." Russ shrugged. "I don't know. There was a third incident very much like this one back in '52. The county coroner couldn't find any signs of foul play so it was labeled natural death, unknown causes. It was never officially investigated as a homicide, just a Jane Doe. If we're looking for the same perp between '72 and now, don't we have to consider the same perp for all three deaths?" He cut himself off. "Sorry. It's been running round and round in my head like a hamster on a wheel." He drained his coffee cup and rose.

Scheeler got up to walk him to the door. "A particularly vigorous seventy-something? Maybe. Psychological models of serial killers suggest they don't change. They'll only stop when they die or are incarcerated."

"Huh . . ."

"What?"

"Oh, I've heard that, too. Went to a symposium on repeat killers down in Kingston last year. It just never really struck me before— how can they not change? I mean, I can barely recognize the kid I was at twenty."

Scheeler shrugged. "Pathological, unresolved psychology. You probably weren't killing cats and setting fires when you were twenty."

"No, but I was closer to that than to a civilized human being. Stupid, careless—I was strung out with PTSD, although nobody recognized it back then. And I was angry. So angry, all the time." He pushed his chair back and stood. "Believe me, if you'd known me back then, it wouldn't be a stretch to think I could have committed murder."

AUGUST 1972

14. "**R**uss Van Alstyne." Detective Arlo Simpson held up Russ's mug shot, taken the morning they had brought him in for questioning. Looking at the boy's disheveled, angry face, Jack Liddle realized he should have gotten a better photo from Margy. Anyone would agree Russ was guilty of something, going by that picture.

"We confirmed positive identification from the bartenders at the Paddock and the Flying Dutchman."

"What about Bennie's?" Jack shifted his position on the heavy maple worktable at the head of the officers' desks. He had taken to sitting on it during their meetings when, assuming the chief's badge, he had discovered the wooden briefing podium was just over-tall enough to make him look like a junior high schooler giving a report on Civics Day.

"The barkeep at Bennie's said business was heavy last night. He didn't remember the face in the photo. However, since Van Alstyne places himself at Bennie's first, with the two other establishments coming after, I don't think the lack of corroboration is significant."

Sergeant George Gifford rolled his eyes. Arlo did have a tendency to talk like a dictionary'd been shoved up his ass.

"What about the Flying Dutchman? Did his story hold up?" Jack tried not to sound hopeful. The last thing he needed was his men thinking he'd lost his objectivity.

Arlo nodded. "Oh, yes. The bartender remembered the fight very well. He said Van Alstyne was clearly the aggressor, and claims he threatened to call the police on our boy." He held up his notebook. "The young man Van Alstyne fought with is a regular. David Reyniers. I'm attempting to find his address so we can follow up with him."

"Did anyone recognize the girl?"

"No. But the barkeep at the Flying Dutchman was quite certain of the time Van Alstyne left. Eleven thirty."

62

Jack nodded. "And he went to the Golden Banana." There were some snickers from the rest of the investigating team.

"No."

"What?" Jack stared at Arlo. "Are you sure?"

"Because of the nature of the establishment, the Golden Banana has three bouncers on duty each night, as well as the bartender and a girl who takes the cover charge. None of them recognized Van Alstyne's photo. I can find no record of his whereabouts between the time he left the Flying Dutchman and the time he appeared on the MacLarens' porch."

Lieutenant Calvin Ogilvie, Jack's second-in-command, whistled. "That's six hours unaccounted for." He nodded toward Arlo. "This guy starts to look better and better."

"Maybe we should retry with a better photograph," Jack said.

George and Cal looked at him as if he'd cracked his skull. "If you think it would help, I can go back," Arlo said doubtfully.

"Chief, this kid's been trained by the army to be a cold-blooded killer." Cal stood up and walked to the case board, where pictures of the still-unknown dead girl were pinned like macabre souvenirs. "We know some of these guys in Vietnam had ways of offing the enemy without making a sound, with just sticks and ropes." He rapped his knuckle against a photo of the girl's unblemished skin. "Who else would know how to kill without leaving a mark? And he can't account for his whereabouts for six whole hours around the time of death?" He jerked his thumb to the mug shot still in Arlo's hand. "I say we bring him in and sweat him good. Five bucks says we'll have a signed confession before we finish the first pot of coffee."

Jack pressed his lips together. He had recruited Cal Ogilvie out of the Albany force precisely because the man was smart and dogged. "Okay. I'll go to his house and question him again. George, what have we got on the dead girl? Any leads?"

Arlo cleared his throat. "Excuse me, Chief, but don't you want to bring Van Alstyne in to the station?"

"No." Everyone looked at him. "I want him relaxed. Not feeling like he's a person of interest. If he's going to trip up on his story and let something drop, it'll be at home, where he's comfortable." Arlo frowned and Cal screwed up his face. As well they might. It was a bullshit reason. But at least it wasn't *I'm sure he's innocent.* "George? The victim?"

"Oh. Yes." George flipped open his notepad. "The ME can't find any cause of death. Autopsy is scheduled for tomorrow or the day after, depending on the pathologist's schedule."

"We know that part," Cal said.

"Oh. Yeah. Sorry." George had only recently moved up from supervising the patrol officers to investigations, and he hadn't yet gotten the hang of the more informal give-and-take of the team. He bent over his notes again. "Description sent out on the wire and we're following up with mailing her photo to other area law enforcement. No hits have come back yet. One of the uniforms and I canvassed homes within a five-mile radius, no one recognized the picture."

"And we already know the bartenders at the places Van Alstyne went to didn't see her." Cal peeked over George's shoulder. "Anything from open-case missing persons?"

"Nothing that fits her age range."

"Did you apply to Troop G for that old case file I told you about?" Jack asked.

"The one from '52?" George leafed through his file folder and pulled out several mimeographed papers stapled together. "Officer Durant drove down and picked it up. There's not much there, Chief. Based on the evidence, the medical examiner—"

"Coroner," Jack said.

"Excuse me?"

"It was a coroner back then." Jack waved a hand. "Sorry. Go on."

"Okay. The coroner ruled the death natural from unknown causes." George flipped to the second page. "There's a note from his office stating it could possibly have been a drug overdose." George looked up. "They couldn't tell? Didn't they do blood work?"

"Sure. But the science twenty years ago wasn't half what it is today." Just saying it made Jack feel old. "And don't forget, drugs were a lot rarer up here back then. I didn't make my first bust for possession until almost a decade later."

"Those were the days." Cal took the papers from George. "You think the two deaths are connected?"

Jack gestured toward the mimeographs. "You can see for yourself. Summer, young woman, party dress, McEachron Hill Road—all the same."

Cal flipped through the pages. "You were the responding officer, Chief."

"That I was. Twenty-four years old and green as a field of clover."

Cal handed the pages on to Arlo. "Are you suggesting this might be a copycat killing? Or are you thinking the same person might be responsible for both deaths?"

"I have a hard time making it a copycat. The case was never a homicide investigation. There wasn't much in the news about it, just a short article about a girl found dead on McEachron Hill Road. None of the details about her clothing were released. The chief here at the time put a 'do you know this girl' picture in the paper. That's not enough information for anyone to re-create the death exactly."

"Unless they heard all the details at the time," George said. "People love to talk."

"Or unless it was someone with access to police records," Cal pointed out. They all paused for a moment.

"On the other hand," Arlo said, "we could be seeing a coincidence."

Jack shook his head. "I don't believe in coincidence."

Arlo rattled the papers in his hand. "The coroner found evidence that the girl in '52 had had sex sometime before her death. Then and now, a young woman in fancy clothes could be a prostitute, or a taxi dancer, or even a coed out for a thrill. All vulnerable populations. Let's say she's with a man. As part of the deal, he gives her drugs. She takes off everything under her dress and they have sex. Then she dies, he panics, dumps the body, and leaves with everything else she had on."

Cal nodded. "If I wanted to dump a body quick, that stretch of

McEachron Hill Road'd be one of my top choices. Very little traffic, but well paved with a straight shot to Route 57 and from there, the Northway."

"I agree with your reasoning for the '52 case," Jack said. "Everyone working it assumed she'd been dumped from a car. But unless our victim was a contortionist with Barnum and Bailey, she wasn't having sex on that motorcycle."

Cal pointed to George. "We need to canvass area motels right away." George nodded.

"Canvass at the carnival," Arlo said.

Jack stared. "Are you trying to make a *joke*, Arlo?"

"No, no, no, no, no. The Washington County Fair. The agricultural and craft exhibits are local, but the rides, the freak show, the music hall—all that is a traveling carnival. Which has been here since they began setting up at least thirty-six hours ago."

"Check it out," Jack said. "Both of those are good starting points. But we still have the issue of getting her to where the body was dumped. Let's say Van Alstyne picked her up—at the fair, or at a bar—and took her to a motel. Let's say he gave her something that caused her to OD. Then what? How does he drive to McEachron Hill Road with a corpse on his motorcycle?"

"They didn't engage a room," Arlo said. "They enjoyed themselves *en plein air*."

Cal gave him a look. "English, please?"

Arlo sighed. "They did it outdoors."

"No pro is going to turn her trick in a field," Cal said. "Not with so many motels around."

"But a free-spirited coed might. Or an amateur carnival girl who doesn't know the area."

"The pathologist may find evidence of that," George said. "A little grass or pollen in her hair."

"We've got twenty-four to forty-eight hours before Dr. Roberts reports to me." Jack slid off the table, the thud of his feet emphasizing his words. "I want to have her identity by the time we have the autopsy results. And I want every possibility on the board. The same perp in '52 and now, a copycat killer, or"—he made a face—"a coincidence based on the fact the girl might have been a pro."

Arlo stood and handed the mimeographed papers back to George. "Van Alstyne is still our best lead."

"I know." Jack hoped he sounded tired, rather than depressed at the thought. "If anything in his story is off, we'll do what Cal suggested. Bring him in and sweat the truth out of him."

MONDAY, AUGUST 21, PRESENT DAY

15. Hadley was headed toward the squad room to get her notes in order for the investigation team's end-of-shift briefing, when the chief beckoned her into his office. He closed the door behind her—actually closed it, which he never did—and pointed at the chairs opposite his desk. Since one was stacked with magazines, papers, and what appeared to be crushed brown lunch bags, she took the other, feeling sick to her stomach.

The chief sat opposite her. He pulled a sheaf of papers off his desk and held it up to her. "Have you seen this?"

DYLAN KNOX v. KEVIN FLYNN and MILLERS KILL
POLICE DEPARTMENT

She swallowed. "Yes. I was served last night."

He gave her a look. "I got my copy this morning, at the mayor's office. I wasn't happy to be sandbagged."

"I'm sorry, Chief, I didn't think—"

He held up his hand. "Before you go on, I need to let you know you're entitled to have a union rep here for this discussion. Do you want to reschedule for when you can get someone?"

"What? No!" Her sick stomach yawed open, as if she were standing on the edge of a long and fatal fall. "Am I being fired? Oh, God. I didn't know— What do you want me to do? Tell me, I'll do it. I need this job, Chief. Please don't let me go."

He jerked back at her last words. Opened his mouth. Closed it. Set the summons flat on his desk. When he finally spoke, his voice was gentle. "You're not getting fired, Knox. I'm not even putting you on administrative leave. Yet. I just want to figure out what we're dealing with here. Your ex"—he tapped the papers with a couple of fingers—"alleges you and Kevin conspired to plant meth in his luggage."

"That's not true."

"What part? The conspiracy? Planting the meth?"

Hadley shook her head, less a denial than to dispel the questions coiling like smoke inside her head. "This is what happened. Dylan had taken my kids to the Algonquin Waters while Flynn and I were in Albany working an investigation. He didn't have my permission to remove them from my house and I was afraid he might be making a run with them back to California. We drove from Albany to the hotel, we talked our way past the desk clerk, and we got Hudson and Genny out of there."

"Did you flash your badge to get it?"

"No, Chief. We didn't identify ourselves as cops, and we were in our civvies."

He tapped the papers again. "Your ex alleges you two roughed him up."

"I never touched him. He started to get scary and out of control, and Flynn got him into a hold. Just long enough for me and the kids to get out into the hall."

"What about the meth allegation?"

She spread her hands to give herself a moment. "The case we were working on involved meth. Maybe I mentioned it? I know I didn't have anything on me that I could have snuck into Dylan's stuff. And as far as I know, Flynn didn't either." That was true. She had suspicions, but she didn't know.

"Were you and Kevin ever separated from each other? Did either of you have any time alone with your ex?"

"I left the room with the kids while Flynn had Dylan restrained. They had, I don't know, maybe fifteen, twenty seconds before Flynn followed me into the hall? But he'd been near the door, and was dealing with a really pissed-off guy. I honestly can't see how he could've planted anything on Dylan."

"In the luggage. The notice claims the packets were in the luggage."

"That's less probable than slipping it into Dylan's pocket, then."

"Did you or Kevin see your ex after that night? Before he left for the Albany airport?"

"No."

The chief paused, pressing two fingers against his lips. "I don't want to get into your personal life—"

Hadley couldn't help it, she barked out a laugh. "Chief, my personal life's been smeared from one end of this department to the other."

He flipped open a hand, conceding the point. "How would you characterize your relationship with your ex-husband?"

"Poor."

"Hostile?"

"For me? I feel less hostile toward him than . . . I just wish he'd go away and leave me and the kids alone."

The chief's eyes sharpened. "Go away as in, to jail on possession charges?"

"No!"

"He sent those tapes deliberately, Knox, to sabotage your job. He wanted everyone to know you used to . . ." He trailed off with a noncommittal gesture that might have meant anything from *skip out on parking fines* to *run a dog-fighting ring*. "The lawyers are going to see that as pretty compelling motivation for you to try to stick it to him."

She'd been trying to sit up straight like a good student, but she found herself slumping against the seat, folding like she was going to toss in her hand. "I don't know what to say. Except that I didn't do it. All I wanted that night was to take my children out of there. I didn't conspire or entrap Dylan or, or hit him or anything. I just got my kids and left." If the chief didn't have her back on this, she would be totally alone.

"I believe you, Knox."

She jerked her head up. "You do?"

He smiled a little. "I do. Hopefully, we'll be able to take care of this early, in the deposition stage, before it costs the town too much money." He fixed her with one of his *I'm counting on you* looks. "I'd rather this doesn't get around, either in the shop or in town."

"Oh, I'm right there with you, Chief."

"Okay." He slapped his hands on his desk and rose. "Let's get into the briefing and find out how much we still don't know about our unsub killing."

16.   Clare had turned her computer off for the night and was putting her thermos into her tote bag when she heard footsteps in the hall. As far as she knew, she was completely alone—even Oscar was at the Burnses' house, waiting to be picked up along with Ethan. There was a rap on the door and without waiting, the archdeacon of the Albany Diocese stepped inside.

"Father Aberforth." Clare glanced pointedly toward the clock. The Venerable Willard Aberforth was her spiritual adviser, and in that capacity he wielded truth like a paint scraper, scorned pretense and self-pity, and had a sense of humor as sharp as a paper's edge. She was quite fond of the old horror. She was not fond of him showing up unexpectedly five minutes before she was out the door. "What are you doing here?"

Aberforth arched one overgrown eyebrow. "And to think Virginia is said to be the cradle of manners in this country."

"I'm a New Yorker now. I'm practicing being rude."

"All the better to fit in, no doubt."

"I repeat; what are you doing here? If you have some bomb from the bishop to set off, I'd think it could wait till tomorrow. I'm on my way to pick up Ethan."

"It is about Ethan that I have come."

"Oh, for God's sake." Clare dropped her tote bag on the desk and turned to Aberforth. "Did Elizabeth come crying to the bishop again? Why doesn't she just bug the place and have everything transmitted directly to the diocesan offices?"

"I take it your plans to have the boy here went awry?"

"I don't care what she said, Father, it's not going to be a problem. I'm just . . . it's early days yet. I'm still putting Ethan's schedule in place." She turned to him. "I made it for the renewal of vows in Holy Week seven days after he was born. I can handle work and motherhood."

"My dear Ms. Fergusson. I have no doubt you can handle almost anything." He gestured to the chairs and she plopped down sullenly. Aberforth followed her, folding his lanky limbs like an old-fashioned locking ruler. "Let me clarify my original statement. *You* are presently having a problem meeting all your childcare needs. *I* have a staffing problem. I believe we can help one another."

"Staffing problem?"

"I am attempting to find an internship for a seminary student."

"In August? Won't he have to be back in school within the month?"

Aberforth inclined his head. "He's attending Union, and, if this should work out, he intends to commute for two days of classes each week."

"That's a heck of a commute." Union Theological Seminary was on the west side of Manhattan. "What's the catch? Why isn't he already two months into his internship?"

The archdeacon steepled his fingers. "Mr. Langevoort lives in the diocese of New York, but his family has summered in the Adirondacks for decades. He wanted to intern here, and has, in fact, been at his parents' camp for much of the summer." Clare wasn't fooled by the word "camp." With an old Dutch name and a family that could escape from the city for months at a time, she'd bet good money it was a rambling compound on its own lake. "The Langevoorts have been good and faithful summer supporters of the diocese of Albany for many, many years," Aberforth went on. "Since they plan to retire here, soon they will be year-round residents."

"Giving year-round money. Sounds like a catch for the diocese."

The archdeacon frowned at her. "The bishop, naturally, wished to help to find a place for their son. This has, however, proved difficult."

"What's wrong with him?"

"He's . . . well, you shall see. His theology as well as his lifestyle is decidedly nonorthodox. His views, which may be described as *exceedingly* progressive, do not fit well with most of the congregations in our diocese."

Clare laughed. "He's a flaming liberal. So you're giving him to me."

"One devil knows another, as the saying goes."

"Sure. Fine. But how is this going to help me with Ethan? Does your Mr. Langevoort do babysitting?"

"I was thinking more along the lines of having another backup in addition to Deacon de Groot. Giving you more flexibility and enabling you to spend more time with the baby, as necessary."

"If I recall my own internship, I spent a lot more time following the rector around asking questions than I did taking work off his hands."

"If this were a usual internship of ten to fifteen hours a week, you would be correct. However, Mr. Langevoort intends to have what I understand to be significant surgery near the end of the year; he then plans to take the next semester off."

"Surgery? Is he ill? Disabled? I mean, that's not a bar, but—"

"No. His health is fine. He's only in his thirties; he was with his father's investment firm before receiving his call. However, if he wishes to complete an internship before he temporarily suspends his march to ordination, he will need to put in twenty to thirty hours a week. Leaving plenty of time to be a much-needed extra pair of hands for you." Aberforth sat back in his chair. "I know you're not eager to park your son in some institutionalized day care—"

"There is nothing wrong with using day care—"

He raised one hand. "Spare me your feminist platitudes, Ms. Fergusson. Regardless of its social utility, I don't see you rushing to enroll the boy in Polly's Play Palace."

"You are a *horrible* snob. You give my mother a run for her money." Clare twisted her hair and resecured it with a bobby pin. "Is the bishop really okay with this? If I ease up a little?"

"He is. The solution is a neat one, after all; Mr. Langevoort will be finishing with the internship at a time when you may expect your son to be more regular in his habits. You may even be drinking caffeine again, which will certainly put you in a better mood."

It's not the caffeine I'm missing. Her hand twitched around an invisible glass. *Let it go, let it go.* "Why do I have the feeling this internship is more for my benefit than his? You thought this up, didn't you?"

"I thought to kill two heterodox birds with one stone." Aberforth gave her a look. "And if you suit, perhaps his parents will start being good and faithful supporters of *your* parish."

17.   "Are you pregnant?"

"What the hell? Really?" Hadley had seen it was Flynn on her cell phone, of course. "No hello, no 'How are you,' no 'Gee, Hadley, good to hear your voice again'?"

"You said we needed to talk. I was thinking about it today and . . ."

"You thought I was *pregnant*?" She remembered to drop her voice at the last minute. She had stepped out onto their tiny front porch before she had answered the phone. Genny and Hudson were safely inside, glued to the television, and Granddad was off at the VFW, but not everyone on Burgoyne Avenue had air-conditioning, and there would be more than a few neighbors' windows open to catch a night breeze.

She dropped into the two-seater porch swing. "You do realize, if I had been pregnant, I'd be seven months along by now. What'd you think, I was calling to invite you to the baby shower?"

"I don't know." His voice was frustrated. "I don't know what I thought." He stopped. She let the pause lengthen. Finally, he said, "So you're not pregnant, then."

"I had my tubes tied after I had Genny. So, no."

He let out a sigh—she couldn't tell if it was relief or disappointment. "All right. You asked me to call. I'm calling. You tell me what's on the agenda."

She braced her foot against the porch rail and rocked the swing back. "I take it you haven't gotten the summons, yet?"

"Summons? Like . . . a legal summons? No. I'm kind of hard to get ahold of just now."

She frowned. "Don't tell me they put you on the dog shift?"

He huffed a laugh. "No. I'm working undercover."

"Undercover?" She had pictured him in uniform all this time, doing the same sort of work she and he had done together. Traffic. Accidents. Investigating under the weathered eyes of their superiors.

"It's complicated. I'm traveling around a lot. They needed someone who looked young and impressionable."

"You *are* young and impressionable." Her routine jab at his age didn't have any heat.

"I'm twenty-seven, Hadley." There was no force behind his comeback, either.

She watched the lights of a car grow large and flash past her on the street. "It's not dangerous, is it?"

"No."

She snorted. "You sound like the chief. Not quite as convincing, though."

"What can I say? I learned from the best."

She was starting to feel comfortable talking with him, comfortable and soft and stupid. "The summons. You'll be getting one as soon as they can track you down. The town and I have already been served." Across the way, someone was walking their dog, a flashlight picking out the sidewalk. "It's Dylan. My ex. He's suing you, and me, and the town for false imprisonment, and damaging his reputation and a whole laundry list of charges. One of which is tampering with evidence." This part she could quote by heart. "To wit: secreting meth-amphetamines on his person or in his personal effects."

The silence from the other end was vast.

"Flynn? You there?"

She heard him exhale. "Yeah."

"Flynn. That night when we got the kids away from him—I wasn't exactly at my best so I don't know if I'm remembering things right. But if I am—"

"I don't want to talk about this over the phone."

"What? Flynn—"

"Just give me a minute to think, will you? Just give me a minute."

She could hear him breathing. Something rasped, like his hand over his hair. It sounded short again.

"Okay," he said. "I'm going to come there."

"What do you mean? Here? Granddad's house?" She twisted her head to where she could see the family room window out of the corner of her eye.

"No. Someplace public. Where an out-of-towner might go."

"Uh . . ." She could think of lots of places tourists went. None of them were good for a private conversation. "What about the library? Or St. Alban's?"

"That's it. I'll meet you at St. Alban's. I can't get away tomorrow, but Wednesday or Thursday should be good."

"Wednesday or Thursday *when?*"

"It'll be evening, that's the best time for me to get away. I'll text you. Don't talk to anyone until you and I have gotten a chance to . . . go over things."

"Flynn." She was whispering again. "What did you *do?*"

"Don't worry. I'll take care of everything. None of this is going to touch you."

"That doesn't actually reassure—"

"Gotta go. Bye." The connection was broken before she had a chance to respond.

She pressed her phone against her stomach and let herself swing. Here, next to her, is where he had sat, and there, on the steps, he had told her he loved her, and out there in the soft darkness they had sat trading kisses in his car until she had tumbled out, afraid the kids would see something through the windows. She had thought he was one of the good guys and she had been wrong.

Hudson burst through the front door. "Mom? Can we watch *Jaws*?"

"No."

"What if I watch it after Genny goes to bed?"

"That's not fair!" his sister whined. Hadley creaked out of the swing and went inside to settle the fight. All the while hearing her own whisper in her ear.

Flynn. What did you do?

AUGUST 1972

18.   The morgue attendant hit the buzzer that unlocked the interior door before Jack reached the glassed-off reception desk. Jack gave him a wave, but the kid was already face-down in what looked like a hefty medical book.

Behind the windowless door, the temperature dropped ten degrees. The reception room was prettied up in an attempt to make visitors comfortable—fuzzy upholstered chairs and paintings of sunsets and flowers on the paneled walls. Back here, there was no pretense, just easy-to-mop linoleum floors and industrial green paint beneath fluorescent lights. He passed the medical examiner's office and the records room and shouldered through the swinging double doors that opened to the meat locker, as the refrigerated body storage unit was unofficially named. Probably been called that back when the corpses had been kept on literal blocks of ice.

"Chief Liddle. Good timing." Dr. Roberts gestured toward the autopsy area while snapping on her gloves. "I've got her on the slab and ready to go." The county's lady medical examiner was such a novelty, the Glens Falls *Post-Star* had done a story on her when she'd arrived last year. Jack had waffled back and forth on what to bring her when he made his first courtesy call, finally settling on the traditional gift from police chief to ME: a bottle of Scotch. Fortunately, Suzanne Roberts drank like a man. She had confided in him once—after they'd shared a few glasses—that she had wanted to be a surgeon. "Which meant I got shunted into pathology. You know why? Because dead patients can't complain about having a woman doctor."

Truth to tell, Jack thought she did a better job than the last guy, who would check his watch ostentatiously while testifying in court and who pitched a hissy fit every single time Jack wanted to sit in on an autopsy. Like now.

"There were some hairs on her dress," Dr. Roberts said as she folded down the cloth covering the body. "I'm pretty sure they're hers, but I've saved them all in an evidence bag."

76

"Thanks." Jack took a moment to look at the nameless girl's face. *The last thing we can give to the dead is justice. I hope we find it for you.* "Do you have an idea of her age?"

"Between twenty and twenty-two. Her wisdom teeth are partially erupted, so that gives us a pretty narrow time frame."

So young. So heartbreakingly young. Of course, the other one had been about the same age. But back when he was twenty-four, he hadn't seen the tragedy of it. Jack stifled a sigh and took her arm, turning it to see the inside of her elbow.

"No needle tracks," Dr. Roberts said. "I checked. Nothing between her toes, either."

"She's awfully thin, though."

"Could be on a diet. The Twiggy look is still going strong."

"Speaking of strong." Jack bent the girl's arm. "Look at those muscles." He felt her bicep and shoulder, solid and well-shaped even in death, then shifted to her hand. There were hard calluses ringing her palm and fingerpads.

Roberts bent over the girl's other hand. "Huh. You don't get these being a hooker."

"My hands looked the same when I worked on my dad's farm. Same tan, too." He traced the line along her shoulder where her skin changed color from golden brown to white. He flipped the cloth up, uncovering her legs to the upper thigh. "See there? She was doing outdoor work in a sleeveless T-shirt and shorts."

"If she's a local farm girl, how come there's no missing persons report out on her?"

"That's the question, isn't it?" Jack gripped the girl's heel to squeeze the muscles in her calf and was struck by the texture of the skin in his hand. It felt like he was holding a baseball glove. "Come take a look at her feet, will you?"

Dr. Roberts gently bent the girl's knee, pausing to tug the cloth into place to preserve her modesty. She examined the bottom of the girl's foot, running a gloved finger down and pinching the sole between her fingers. "I'd say she must have spent a great deal of time barefoot to build up calluses like this. Look." She pointed to grimy patches on the ball and heel. "That's dirt so ground-in it didn't come out in the shower."

"How do you know she showered?"

Roberts lowered the girl's leg and pointed to her shin. "No hair. On her legs nor armpits. No stubble to speak of, which means she shaved within twelve hours or less of the time of death."

"Barefoot. Huh." He shot a look at the doctor. "Barefoot and pregnant?"

The doctor's voice was dry. "The two states don't necessarily correspond, in my experience. Let me take a quick look at her cervix." She reached for a speculum and Jack turned away. "No bruises or signs of roughness on her inner thighs," Roberts said. He heard the rattle of paper tearing off something and then the faint clunk of glass set on the instrument table. "It doesn't look like she was assaulted."

"Any semen?"

"Maybe. I'm taking an internal swab. I'll have to look at it under the microscope to let you know for sure." There was another clunk and the sound of a lid snapping in place. "No change of color or enlargement of the cervix. I'll see when I do the internal, but my opinion at this point is that she wasn't pregnant."

Young. Working outdoors. Barefoot. Not local.

Jack blinked. "I have an idea where she might have come from."

"You can turn around if you like." Dr. Roberts didn't hide the amusement in her voice. "Where?"

He shook his head. "I don't want to influence your thinking. I'll let you know after you do the autopsy."

"You're not staying?"

"I want to move on this possibility now. Any chance to ID her . . ." He had told the doctor before about the Golden Hours, that investigative rule of thumb that said most homicides were broken, if they could be cracked at all, within the first day or two. They were already past the initial twenty-four hours, and the sun was sweeping relentlessly through the sky, an unstoppable watch hand.

"Understood." The doctor waved him on. "I'll let your office know when I have the results."

AUGUST 1952

19. In civvies, the kid looked even younger. Harry had suggested the Liddle boy—and boy howdy, he bet the kid would hate to hear that—meet him at his office, but Jack was worried someone might notice and word would come back to his bosses at the state troopers' barracks. Harry didn't blame him, really. Millers Kill was a small town in a county full—or not full—of small towns, and if everybody didn't know everybody else's business, it wasn't from lack of trying.

Which is why he was sitting on a wooden bench near the fence of the draft horses' ring, watching farmers compete their teams in pulling contests. They were mostly for show nowadays, harnessed up for hay rides and sleigh rides, their tails and manes brushed and braided by little 4-H girls. The Washington County Fair was the only place they could show what they were meant to do: haul the immensely heavy loads no lighter horse could have managed. Harry remembered helping his father log out their forested land back in the twenties, Gil and Gay maneuvering four or five cut trees at a time through the woods as neatly as you'd please. Can't get a machine to do that.

"Chief McNeil?"

He could hear the kid before he saw him, and then Jack emerged from around a cluster of youngsters and crossed to the bench. He was in light pants cinched up with suspenders, tie knot halfway down his open-necked shirt, jacket over his arm, and what looked like his daddy's hat on his head.

Jack snatched it off and fanned himself with it as he plopped down next to Harry. "Oh, gosh, this shade feels good. I can't believe the heat today."

"It's a scorcher, all right. I'll be glad to see September." Harry reached for the bag Jack had set at his feet. "Is this it?"

The kid nudged it toward Harry. "Yeah. One of the secretaries likes me. She slipped me the third carbon."

Harry opened the bag, and the faint scent of ink drifted into the air and was gone, washed into the odors of sweat and horseflesh and popcorn. He pulled out the onionskin papers: detective's report, coroner's report, Jack's report, and best of all, pictures. Harry shuffled through photos of the dead girl, in situ on McEachron Hill Road and in the morgue, a close-up of her face, and one of her dress, showing the design and the label at the neck. "You didn't get these from a secretary."

"I swapped a favor with the guy who does the developing."

"Must have been some favor." Making unauthorized copies of crime scene photos could get a chemist fired, mostly to discourage them from getting a second paycheck from the scandal sheets.

"You don't want to know." Jack grinned. With his shirt undone and his yellow hair flopping to one side, he looked like a Dutch pirate.

Harry sighed. "Tell me about this one." He held up the photo of the dress.

"That was my idea. I mean, I suggested it to the guy who took the morgue shots. I thought it looked expensive, like something that might have come from a fancy store." Jack pointed at the label. "You can't see it too well without a magnifying glass, but that says 'Celeste of Paris.'"

"Yeah, that sounds fancy. Good thought, there, getting the photo." Jack's cheeks pinked up. Harry slid the photos and papers into the bag and stood up. "C'mon, let's go."

"Where?"

"There's an expensive ladies' shop in Glens Falls. They might be able to give us an idea where Celeste of Paris is sold. If not, I've got a friend in New York City, but that would take some time."

"What if it comes from France?"

Harry tried to bite down on his grin. "In my experience, son, the more a ladies' hat or bag or shoes tries to sound French, the more likely it is they come from a factory in Hackensack."

◆ ◆ ◆

You would have thought storekeepers were giving the goods away, there were so many autos on the streets. Harry was driving his own car, which meant he couldn't just wedge it in an official-vehicle-only spot and be done with it. He finally found space to park a couple blocks away. It was even hotter on the city sidewalk than it had been at the fair, but Jack dutifully put on his jacket.

The kid jerked his head toward a pair of ladies crossing the street in broad-brimmed sunhats and airy, cap-sleeved dresses. "It's the only time of the year I wish I was a woman."

Harry, sliding the photos from the bag into a manila folder, laughed. "C'mon, Jacqueline." He slammed the door shut.

"It'd probably be Joan," the kid said as they started toward Broadway. "My Christian name's John. I started calling myself Jack right after I started school."

"Your father's a John, too?"

"Oh, no, he's Matthew." Jack made a face. "But can you imagine what it's like when you're six years old and the teacher says 'Liddle, John' at roll call? It took me *years* to get past the Robin Hood jokes."

Harry laughed.

When they reached La Belle Dame—Harry pointed out the French name and nodded—it was empty of customers. He could understand why; even with the casement windows cranked and fans whirring, it was uncomfortably warm, and every rack near the door was filled with plaid and tweed meant for much colder weather than they'd been having this August. A saleswoman came out from the back, drawn by the tinkle of the doorbell. "Can I help you, gentlemen?"

Harry pulled out his badge and flapped it. "I'm Harry McNeil, of the Millers Kill Police Department. I'd like to see if you can identify a dress for me."

Her eyebrows went up, but to her credit, the saleswoman didn't lose her poise. "Do you have it with you?"

Harry placed the manila folder on the glass-topped counter and opened it. "Just a picture, I'm afraid."

She frowned. "I can tell you right now, it didn't come from here."

"We thought it looked like an expensive dress," Jack said. "We thought it might be a name you recognize. The label says 'Celeste of Paris.'"

"Hmm." The saleswoman retrieved a delicate magnifying glass from a shelf holding measuring tapes, pin puffs, chalk, and ribbon. She bent over the photograph. "It's not a knockoff. That's a genuine Celeste label. You can see the double stitching around the capital letters."

"You mean there are counterfeit dresses?" Jack sounded astounded.

"Oh, yes. Fashion is a cutthroat business." The woman tapped at the picture with a lacquered nail. "Can you tell me what color it was?"

"I only saw it the one time," Harry said. "It was green."

"Um . . . this main part was kind of a light green?" Jack pointed to the bodice. "And these lines here—"

"Cording," the woman said.

"The cording was a darker green. You can sort of see in the picture, the fabric was shiny. But not silk shiny."

The saleswoman stepped away from the counter toward a rack of clothing. She pulled out a brown dress. "Like this?"

"Yes, that's it."

"Polished cotton. Hang on a second." She walked to the back and returned with a couple of summer dresses with SALE tags dangling from the hangers. "Was the dress more this shade of green? Or this one?"

Jack pointed to the one in her left hand. "More like that."

"Good." She returned the dresses to the back of the store and then joined them at the counter. "Celeste of Paris has two lines with the same tags, one of which is aimed at the more mature lady, and the other, a bit less expensive, for the younger woman. Your piece here comes from this spring's Celeste junior line. That shade of ice green was shown at the Paris shows last year, and was everywhere in the American manufacturers' mid-priced clothes this year."

"What does it mean if Celeste of Paris is mid-priced?" Harry asked.

"They generally retail for between fifty to a hundred dollars."

Jack's mouth dropped. "A hundred bucks? For a *dress*? What the heck do the top-priced ones go for?"

The saleswoman laughed. "I take it you're not married, Detective."

"No, I'm not. But if I was, my wife would make her own dresses, like my mom does."

"Mmm. We'll see."

"How about where the dress was sold?" Harry said. "Is there some-place local we could try?"

She shook her head. "I know exactly where that dress was sold, but I'm afraid it's not local. Celeste of Paris is one of Bonwit-Teller's exclusive labels. The only place you can buy it is in New York City."

TUESDAY, AUGUST 22, PRESENT DAY

20. Russ tried to remain positive while handing out assignments at the end of the morning shift briefing. "Noble, you're going to hit the motels and the bars again, and this time, add in any of the area attractions along Route 9 and the Northway. Rodeos, amusement parks, stuff like that. You're asking if they recognize her as a guest or as an employee. Plenty of college kids come up to the area for summer jobs; maybe that was her gig."

"Right, Chief."

"Knox, you get the sex offenders list."

She groaned.

"I know, I know, but we've got to either alibi them or mark 'em as persons of interest."

"Can I cut it down to offenders who would have been old enough to do the scene in '72?"

Russ shook his head. "No, but you can limit it to the ones who like 'em eighteen and above."

Lyle snorted.

"Just shoot me in the ass," Knox said.

Russ elected not to hear. "Lyle, you pursue those cell phone record warrants. We know there were calls made within that area, and we've got a list of numbers. I want to find out the owners' names and where they were calling. Once we have those, we can scratch anybody local we've already cleared and start to follow up on the rest."

"You do realize Judge Ryswick is gonna want a separate application for each and every number, right?"

"I'm sure your work will be up to its usual meticulous standard." He turned to the other side of the room. "Paul."

Paul Urquhart started, his mouth half-open in a yawn. Lyle had moved him off the night shift to help with their manpower shortage during the investigation.

"Tim and Duane will be splitting the road construction shifts. You're going to be on traffic, and our swing responder."

"Ticketing tourists. Yay."

"Think of them as paying guests. We want them coming back, so use your company manners."

Paul sketched him a salute. Russ wasn't happy with leaving Paul as the public face of the MKPD, but he'd be worse on the investigation. Russ supported the police union, but sometimes he wished it didn't make it so hard to fire guys like Paul. Being lackadaisical on the job and aggressive with motorists wasn't enough. Of course, with the budget the way it was, even if he *could* get rid of Urquhart, the aldermen wouldn't pay for a replacement. And then he'd be even more shorthanded than he was right now.

"Okay," he said. "Dismissed. Noble, Knox, let me know immediately you find anything." The group rose, gathering their notebooks and laptops before leaving. He noticed Knox went out of her way to avoid Urquhart, which probably meant Russ was going to have to drag the man into his office for another lecture on respecting his fellow officers.

"Trouble there." Lyle nodded toward the now-empty doorway.

"You noticed it, too?"

"Ayah. She's been a lot less chatty, more businesslike with all of us since, you know. The tapes. But she's ducking and weaving to keep away from Paul."

Russ shook his head. "Christ on a crutch. I must be the only police chief in history who has to deal with one of his people being a former porn star."

Lyle picked up the cell phone numbers printout. "You could cut her loose, you know. Morals charge."

"I don't want to cut her loose. She's a good cop. Better than Urquhart, for sure. Plus, she needs the job."

"So, doesn't Paul? He's paying child support for three kids."

"And Noble won't be able to find a position anywhere else, and Tim and Duane need the health insurance, and being a cop is the only stable thing Eric's got in his life right now. Everybody needs these jobs."

Lyle grinned. "Excepting maybe us."

"Retirement's looking better all the time." Russ sighed. "I'm going to have Harlene call a press conference this afternoon. In time for the five o'clock news."

Lyle squinted up toward the ceiling, looking like a farmer worried about rain. Russ knew it signaled his deputy chief's brain whirring furiously. "Not a bad idea. We've got a lot going on. We ought to get out in front of the latest goodie instead of being hit from behind. You want me to contact the mayor—no, better would be Garry Greuling. He's in our corner."

"We don't need anyone from the board of aldermen. Or the mayor's office. I intend to lay out more of the facts on the case—what little we have of 'em—and ask for the public's assistance."

"Huh. Really?" Lyle leaned against the whiteboard, somehow managing to avoid getting smudges on his summer uniform sleeve. "I mean, it's true the 'possible hit-and-run' story is getting pretty thin. I've been fielding calls from the *Post-Star* and the TV stations. But asking for help from civilians? We'll have to assign someone full time just to answer the phone. For credible tips, mind you. I'm not even talking about the psychics and crazies and false confessions. Don't you think we'd be better off using what manpower we have on the investigation itself?"

"We've got nothing, Lyle." Russ gathered up his briefing folders and slid off the table. "It's been seventy-two hours and we've got no ID, no evidence, no cause of death, no suspects. We've got to shake things loose. I need the girl's face out there. I need people seeing her dress, and hearing some of the details, and calling in with tips, even if they do flood the switchboard. We need to get a"—he twisted his hand in the air—"a handle on something. One thing we can pull on to crack open the rest of what we don't know." He started for the door.

Lyle fell in step. "Let me take the press conference, then. I'm the department liaison. And I happen to know you hate answering reporters' questions only a little less than you hate not having any leads on a case."

"I want you there, absolutely. But as soon as we release any details, the old story is going to surface. Like you said, I need to be out there in front of it, from the start, so no one can say I've got something to hide."

Lyle looked at him dubiously. "How 'bout I whip you up a statement you can read. Just in case." He headed for his minuscule office. "Make sure you've got your dress uniform. Half the work of being a press flack is looking the part."

TUESDAY, AUGUST 22, PRESENT DAY

21. "Hello? Reverend Fergusson?" The mellow voice came from outside the sacristy, where Clare was stowing the altar cloth and silver from this morning's seven-thirty service. She had had ten communicants, a bumper number for a weekday at any time of the year, but especially in August. Tourists all, up for the river and the hiking and the amusement parks that stretched farther and farther south from Lake George every year. She wondered if, by the time Ethan was a man grown, there'd be nothing to Millers Kill but vacationers and those who served them.

She gave herself a twitch. "In here."

"Your secretary told me I could find you here." The woman who entered the sacristy was handsome rather than pretty, tall, with an enviably thick fall of dark red hair. "Oh, wow. This is just lovely." She gestured to the well-waxed mahogany cupboards and marble counters running along two sides of the small room. Diamond-paned windows, opened in the vain hope of catching a breeze, allowed natural light to gleam along the brass candlesticks and reflect through a row of crystal vases awaiting the flower guild.

"It is, isn't it?" Clare couldn't keep from smiling. "I have no cause to take such pride of place in St. Alban's, but I do. Can you open that armoire for me?"

The woman did, and Clare stepped past her to slide the long muslin-wrapped cylinder of altar cloth in its place. Clare turned, still smiling. The woman was even taller than she had thought, broad shouldered and boyishly slim. Boyishly. The penny dropped. Clare kept smiling. "You must be Ms. Langevoort. Welcome to St. Alban's." She extended her hand.

"Thank you. It's Joni."

"And I'm Clare." Joni shook—Clare tried not to think *like a man*—and grinned with visible relief. "And thank you for taking me on. It's been . . . difficult, finding a place in the diocese."

"Mmm. Let's grab some coffee and sit down—do you like coffee?"

"I live on it."

"Good! I like you already. Let's sit down and talk about your internship and what you and St. Alban's can do for one another."

◆ ◆ ◆

They spent a few hours talking and filling out paperwork for Joni's home church, seminary, and the diocese, so it wasn't until Clare asked Joni to run to Corsetti's and pick up the lunch platter for the noon vestry meeting that she had enough privacy to call Willard Aberforth.

"You told me Joni Langevoort was a *guy*," she began.

"And hello to you, too, Ms. Fergusson. Yes, I did."

"She's not a man. She's a transgender woman. You could at least have given me a heads-up. No wonder no one else would take her." Not every congregation or even diocese was open to transgender clergy. Certainly not Albany, which would probably get around to it at the same time they gave the thumbs-up to gay marriage, i.e., the twelfth of Never.

"I assure you, if you look under his skirts, you'll find he's still all male."

"That is, bar none, the most revolting thing you've ever said to me." She forced herself to breathe in deeply. *Calm mind. Quiet mind.* "For God's sake, Father, gender isn't a matter of what's between your legs. It's what's between your ears."

"As comfortably smug and modern as I expected. Good. I take it you'll keep him?"

"Her. She's a her. And yes, I will."

"I'll notify Union Seminary. You'll be getting some paperwork from them. Try not to encourage him, will you? I received the strong impression his father is hoping this is just a phase."

Clare pressed two fingers against her lips and reminded herself that Aberforth was a seventy-five-year-old ex-marine who still hadn't recovered from Yale going coed. "I'm surprised you've gone out of your way to find her an internship. I would have thought you'd be opposed to her ordination."

"*We* are not ordaining him, New York is. And my dear Ms. Fergusson, if you read your scripture, you'll notice God has called all sorts of confused people to His service." *Like you* went unsaid. "If the Almighty wants young Langevoort, who am I to stand in the way?"

◆ ◆ ◆

Clare decided she might as well beard all her lions in one den and introduce her new intern to the vestry at the beginning of the monthly meeting.

Despite the widespread Episcopalian stance that God would understand missing church during the summer, some groups and committees continued on through the hot months. Altar guild and flower guild, whose weekly work, like Clare's, went on year-round. The grounds committee, for whom summer was the busy season. And the vestry, the governing body of St. Alban's, which gathered for lunch every month in the meeting room, with its linen-fold paneling and ornate plaster ceiling, its wheezing, inadequate radiator and sluggish summertime fans. Clare was grateful to them all, and she tried very hard to love each member of the vestry. Sometimes she succeeded.

"Everyone, I'd like you to meet Joni Langevoort. Joni is a divinity student at Union Theological Seminary and a candidate for ordination in her home diocese of New York. She's going to be interning with us this fall."

Clare thought she could hear the crickets chirping outside. She smiled brightly. "Joni, this is our senior warden, Robert Corlew." The real estate developer paused a moment before nodding his almost-certainly-toupee-covered head. "Our junior warden, Geoff Burns." The lawyer's eyes lit with an unholy glee as he reached across the antique black oak table to shake Joni's hand. "Terry McKellan, vice president of AllBanc and our finance chair." Terry assumed a genial expression—with his round face and walrus mustache, he did it well—and murmured a polite greeting.

"This is Sterling Sumner, our distinguished professor emeritus and architect." It never hurt to butter Sterling up. He sniffed at Joni, which was his usual greeting to anyone he didn't know. "And Mrs. Henry Marshall and her very good friend, Norm Madsen."

The elderly lawyer gallantly rose and pulled out the empty high-backed chair next to him. "Why don't you sit right here, young lady."

The rest of the men stared at him. Mrs. Marshall gave them all a quelling look. Joni made her last *how do you do* and the group began to work their way through the agenda.

The meeting went surprisingly quickly. With a stranger sitting in, the usual bickering, in-jokes, and long, rambling digressions were absent. Clare ticked item after item off her sheet, until they came to the last.

"A voters' meeting." Robert Corlew peered at her over his reading glasses. "Here. At the church."

"In the parish hall," Clare said. "I realize no one's going to think I'm an objective party—"

Sterling snorted.

"—but the question of defunding the police department is the biggest issue to come before the town since the Algonquin Waters was permitted."

"Very true," Mrs. Marshall said.

Terry McKellan looked at Clare. "What were you thinking of? Having Chief Van Alstyne come in and speak to the congregation?"

She shook her head. "It needs to be open to the public. Like when we have a guest speaker or a concert. And I thought we should invite someone from both sides to present. Otherwise, we'd be promoting a political viewpoint."

"We may be doing that anyway." Geoff Burns templed his fingers. "If we sponsor the program, as we do with a guest speaker or a concert, we're engaged in obvious political speech. We don't even have the fig leaf of you preaching in the pulpit." Clare opened her mouth to object. Geoff went on, "If we *don't* sponsor the program, we're making our parish hall a public accommodation, which leaves us open to a suit if, say, the Christian Dominionists and the U.S. Communist Party want to hold a debate here."

"That would at least have the virtue of being interesting," Sterling said under his breath.

Clare knuckled her eyes. "Is there some way we can get this to work, Geoff? There are ten people employed by the police department, one of whom is a member of our congregation—I mean Hadley Knox and her kids, Sterling, not Russ—and if the ballot question passes, every one of those people will be thrown out of work."

"Including your husband," Robert said.

"Including my husband. We can handle it financially, but others, including Hadley, won't be able to. I'm not saying we ought to go out and knock on doors, but I do think an open forum to educate people is entirely appropriate."

"Let me do some research and get back to you." Geoff gestured toward his fellow vestry members. "If there's no legal impediment, will anyone here object to such a meeting?"

"I guess not," Corlew said. "I'm pushing for them to keep the department." At Clare's obvious surprise, he continued, "I'm selling homes. Mostly to folks who want to get away from the big, bad city. Safety's a big selling point."

"*If* both sides of the question are weighted equally." Sterling Sumner looked suspiciously at Clare and Corlew. "I'd want there to be a fair and equal hearing of the budget-minded point of view."

Mrs. Marshall shook her head. "I'm sure everything will be on the up-and-up, Sterling. I'm think a voters' forum is an excellent idea."

"Okay, are we good? Great." Clare bowed her head and said the shortest prayer she could manage before anyone else decided to object. The echo of Amen still hung in the air when she said, "Meeting adjourned. Terry, we're going to go over the loan payouts in my office?"

"Let me visit the little boys' room and make a few calls and I'll meet you there."

"Thanks, Terry. Thanks, everybody," Clare called to the departing vestry members. She turned to Mrs. Marshall. "And thank *you*."

Mrs. Marshall patted her hand. "The more voters know about the issues, the better." She turned to Joni. "I wanted to ask you, are you related to the Kent Langevoorts?"

"I am, yes. My parents."

"I've met them several times at fundraisers for Senator Gillebrand. It's nice to see summer people who care about the local government."

Joni smiled a bit. "My parents are nothing if not political."

"I approve."

Clare cut in. "Mrs. Marshall is the former president of the League of Women Voters."

"Since you raised the issue, Clare, I have to tell you the pro–police department side needs some sort of decent, easy-to-remember name, like the Committee for Public Safety."

Joni touched her neck as if feeling for the guillotine cut. Clare refused to smile.

"Also, we need to start gathering opinion makers and money. I think the Langevoorts would be the perfect people to host a campaign opener."

"We?"

"My parents?" Joni and Clare spoke at the same time. Clare recovered first. "Mrs. Marshall, it's not electing a congressperson. It's a town referendum. I'm sure Russ and his men can represent their side more than any *opinion makers*." She hoped. She had told the truth when she said she and Russ weren't under financial pressure. What she was afraid of was more subtle—what if Russ got another job in another town, and she had to choose between following him and leaving St. Alban's?

91

"It's been—" Joni paused as if searching for the least harmful word. "—difficult for my parents these past months. I've only been living as a woman since last Christmas."

The interruption of her education at the end of the year suddenly made sense. Clare was pretty sure many doctors treating transgender patients wanted a year's wait before committing to gender reassignment surgery.

Mrs. Marshall tilted her head to look up at the seminarian. "What better than a project they can throw themselves into as a distraction, then?"

Joni looked helplessly at Clare.

"Mrs. Marshall, Joni's been an intern here for"—Clare checked her watch—"three and a half hours. We don't want to impose on the Langevoorts. Besides, what do we need money for?"

Mrs. Marshall shook her head in a way that reminded Clare of her mother-in-law, who also thought the younger generation hopelessly naïve when it came to politicking. "For TV and radio ads. For voter education handouts." She frowned at a speck of dust floating in the air. "I wonder if there's time to get something over to the League of Women Voters' booth at the county fair. They always get big numbers the final weekend."

"You really think we need TV and radio ads for a town referendum? Russ and Deputy Chief MacAuley have been speaking with groups of voters when they can." She realized she had been concerned before, but not really *afraid* the ballot question would pass. But Mrs. Marshall and Margy were right, she was a political neophyte. What if it was going to be more difficult to reach the public than she had assumed? There had been no surveying, no opinion polls—she had no idea what the people of the three towns actually thought of the referendum.

"The combined population of Millers Kill, Cossayuharie, and Fort Henry is over eight thousand. You can't reach them all face-to-face, not in the next twelve weeks. Not to mention an ever-increasing number of vacation home owners, who have as much to lose as the regular residents. After all, I don't think the state police are going to be making snowbird visits to houses shuttered over the winter."

"That's a good point," Joni said. Clare wasn't sure if she realized she was nodding along. "Okay, what if the Reverend Fergusson—"

"Clare."

"Clare and I meet with my parents." She turned to Clare. "They'll be relieved to see I've landed a good internship. We could have you over to dinner. And your husband, of course."

"Umm . . . okay?"

"With conviction, Clare." Mrs. Marshall pierced her with a birdlike eye. "Politics are like pregnancies. You can't go in halfway."

"Oh, I believe that." Clare picked her agenda off the black oak table. "It's just that I'm learning the pregnancy isn't the hard part. It's how to deal with the actual, individual child taking over your life that's difficult."

AUGUST 1972

22. He planned to swing by the station, get the necessary information, and take off again, so Jack was unpleasantly surprised to find Russell Van Alstyne waiting for him in his office. Margy had made it very clear she didn't want him talking to her boy without a lawyer, and he didn't want to get any further onto her bad side.

"What are you doing here?"

The boy scowled at him. "You said I should tell you if I remembered anything else."

Today, he was wearing fatigues and a MKHS T-shirt. Still in army boots. Was the boy deliberately trying to be provocative? Surely, some of his civvies must still fit him. Jack rubbed his forehead. "You didn't have to—you could have just *called*, Russell."

Russell surged to his feet. "I didn't know! I thought I was supposed to report in person!"

It wasn't lost on Jack that the kid's temper fired faster than a moon rocket on a short countdown. He may not have killed the Jane Doe in Dr. Roberts's care, but he was headed for some serious trouble if he didn't learn to control himself. Jack gestured him back to his seat. "What was it you remembered?"

"The name of the girl I talked to. At the Paddock. She was Cyndi Bradford."

"This is the one who shot you down?"

Russell looked at his boots. "Yeah."

"And you're sure about her name."

"Yeah. I was lying in bed and all of a sudden it popped into my head."

"Okay. Stay here." Jack half-closed his office door and strode into the bull pen. No one from the investigating team was in, of course, so he grabbed Andy Carruthers, on his way out for traffic patrol, and sent him off to connect "Cyndi Bradford" to an address and phone number. Then he hustled to the dispatch board, where he found Harlene poring over a ten-code list as long as her arm.

"Harlene, I need an all-call for our guys. I know someone mentioned a hippie commune somewhere around here, and I want to know where it is."

"Um." Harlene looked up from her switchboard. "I know that."

Jack's eyebrows shot up. He made a *go on* gesture.

"I heard Sergeant Gifford talking about them. They're part of the back-to-nature movement—you know, chop your own firewood, can your home-grown produce, that sort of thing."

"That's a movement? Half the farmers around here do that."

"Well, the commune also has a no-private-property rule and free love." Harlene's voice went down on the last phrase, as if just speaking the words might conjure a writhing mass of undressed hippies. "Or so Sergeant Gifford said. I don't know *personally*."

"Where are they?"

"Cossayuharie, at the old Stevenson farm. I guess they're going to try to bring the orchard back."

He pictured the house and barn, left mouldering since Roscoe Stevenson died with no descendants willing to work the land. It was a straight shot from that property, across Route 17, and then onto McEachron Hill Road. Far enough away in miles that his men hadn't gotten to it in the first round of knock-and-ask, but less than a ten-minute drive by car. Or motorcycle.

"Okay. I'm headed out there."

"Are you all done with the Van Alstyne boy?"

"Yeah, he can—" The thought stopped him. Margy wasn't going to want him to interview her boy. He'd bet she didn't even know Russell was here right now. He turned it over in his head for a second. If he took the boy along, he'd have a chance to talk with him. More importantly, he'd have a chance to see how Russell reacted, if the hippies knew their dead girl's name. "I'm going to take him with me."

• • •

"This is stupid." Russell was slumped down in the passenger seat, his knees hitting the glove box and his chin tucked into his chest. Jack figured he was hoping none of the shoppers along Main Street would recognize him riding shotgun in a squad car.

"The folks out at the commune are going to be your age. I'd like your impression of them." That was true, as far as it went.

"You really think I've got anything in common with a bunch of hippies?" Russell ran his hand over his bottle-brush hair. "Besides, I've got stuff to do."

"Like what?"

There was a long pause. Finally he said, "My mother wants me to help paint the new house."

"That's good. That'll be less work she has to do." Jack slowed to a stop for the red light on Route 17. "Free her up to cook for you, do your laundry . . ."

"What do you want? I've only been out for a couple weeks!"

"Fair enough." The light turned, and Jack took the right toward Cossayuharie. "But you ought to have some plans. Are you going to start looking for a job?"

"Yeah. I guess. I don't know."

"Well, that's definitive."

Russell jerked upright. "What the hell kind of job am I supposed to get? Go back to bagging groceries? You know what my skills are? I can strip and reassemble an M-14 rifle in the dark. I can dig a foxhole and plot my location on a map. I can slap a bandage over a man with a gaping hole in his gut and toss flare canisters in the hopes that maybe there's a chopper near enough to evac him before he bleeds out. I can hump through a rain forest in ninety-degree weather carrying sixty pounds on my back. And I can kill people. Tell me what sort of job that's going to get me in Millers Kill."

Jack found himself noticing the granite plinths on Veterans' Bridge as they crossed over the river. "Have you ever thought about law enforcement?"

Russell looked at him as if he'd suggested cannibalism. "Be a *cop*?" He shifted his focus to the radio and baton rack by his thigh. "No."

"Why not? You're bright, inquisitive, you notice things"—at least that described the boy he had been before he left for Vietnam—"I assume you can keep your cool in a tense situation."

Russell huffed a laugh. "Yeah. That's one way to put it."

Jack pressed the accelerator as the car began to climb the first of the rolling Cossayuharie hills that would eventually top out at the colonial-era Muster Field. "We've got a Jane Doe. In all likelihood, we won't be able to break the case if we can't figure out her identity. How would you go about finding who she was?"

"How would I know?"

"Give it a shot." Jack kept his voice light. Casual.

"Unh . . . fingerprints? Or, um, a missing person report?"

"Already tried those. No dice."

"Then I'd take her picture around to bars and discotheques and schools and places like that. See if anyone recognized her."

"Good. What else? Remember, we only know what was on her when you found her."

"Maybe . . . where her dress came from? Or . . ." He turned to face Jack for the first time. "Was there anything unique about her, herself? A birthmark or something?" He looked at his own hand. "Like, I have calluses on these two fingers, from the M-14. So even if I couldn't tell you, you'd know I'd been a soldier."

Jack repressed a satisfied smile. "Why not an avid hunter?"

"Hunting season's been over too long. Any calluses I'd have built up would be gone by now."

"Good thinking." Jack turned off Route 17. The road to the old Stevenson place wound through fields sliced with rivulets and pinned down by granite boulders. They topped a rise and were greeted by row upon row of apple trees, twisted with growth left too long unattended, crowded with saplings and thornbushes and grass gone to seed. As they neared the farm, a good quarter mile downslope, Jack could see signs of industry: branches pruned, junk plants uprooted, grass mown.

He had expected a VW van or a repurposed school bus in the dooryard—cliché, really—but instead he parked next to an aging European car he couldn't ID and a '52 Chevy pickup that looked to have been used for hauling manure not too far in the past. The large barn doors were rolled back; inside Jack could see a spreader and a disc harrow, as ancient as the truck outside.

"What are we doing here?"

"Listen and learn." Jack opened his door and stepped out into the sunshine. "Hello! Anyone home?"

AUGUST 1972

23. He caught a glimpse of movement behind a window, and a moment later, the front door inched open. A narrow-faced young woman stuck her head out. "Hi!" She smiled as if Jack was there to give her the Publisher's Clearing House grand prize. "Just a sec, I need to get decent!" The door slammed shut behind her.

Russell had gotten out of the squad car. "What do you think that was all about?" Jack quizzed.

"Probably hiding her stash." Russell was looking at the roofline of the many-gabled house, at the barn loft, at the tall maples growing along the edge of the dooryard. His fingers flexed, once, as if closing around an invisible rifle.

The door opened again and the narrow-faced girl came out, a spangly gypsy-fabric skirt whisking around her bare ankles and feet. A young man emerged on her heels, wearing boots and overalls and more beard and hair than Jesus Christ. His smile was a good twenty degrees cooler than the girl's had been. "Can I help you, Officer?" His eyes flicked toward Russell. He took in the army boots and the brush cut, frowning slightly.

Recognition? Jack motioned for Russell to stay put and advanced across the dusty drive toward the couple. "Jack Liddle, Millers Kill chief of police." He smiled, let his voice drop to a quieter conversational tone. "You know my young friend back there?"

The hippie farmer shook his head. "Is he plainclothes?" The girl's smile bent a little.

Jack made a mental note to come back here sometime when he wasn't trying to get information from these people. If he could borrow a drug-sniffing dog from Albany, he had a feeling he'd turn up a whole bunch of interesting stuff. Not today, however. "No, Russell there's helping me out." He beckoned the boy forward. "I'm looking for a missing girl." The team was using the first picture taken on-site, with the sun on her face and her hair falling around. She looked, if not alive, at least less dead. He pulled it out of his jacket and handed it to the couple.

"That's Natalie," the girl said. "Isn't it?"

The man frowned. "Maybe. I've never seen her with makeup on. And I've never seen her hair in a braid."

Given both of them had hair that was tangled and none too clean, Jack thought the difference might have been shampoo and a comb. He glanced at Russell, who was craning a bit, trying to see the picture in their hands. He seemed indifferent to the hippie pair, and Jack would have said he was relaxed until the door slammed. Russell flinched and jerked backward.

The girl had already turned toward the house, but the bearded guy caught the movement. "Are you okay, man?"

Russell's mouth tightened. He nodded, once.

"Isaac, Fran, what's going on?" A shorter bearded kid ambled across the dooryard. His brown hair was held back in a ponytail and

he was barefoot beneath a pair of rolled-up pants that could have been sewn out of old flour sacks.

"The chief of police here is trying to find this girl." Isaac handed the picture to the new guy. "Does she look like Natalie to you?"

Ponytail studied the photo. "Yeah, that's Nat. See? She looks pissed off even when she's—" His brows quirked. He lifted his head to stare at Jack. "What is this? Where did you get this?"

"I'm sorry. If that's your friend Natalie, she was found dead yesterday."

Isaac stepped forward. "What the hell?" Behind him, the girl started to cry.

The ponytailed kid continued to stare at the photo. "How . . . who . . ."

"She was found in Cossayuharie." Jack glanced at Russell, who shifted uncomfortably. "We're not sure what happened yet. Can you tell me about her? What's her full name?"

Isaac and the other kid looked at Fran. "*I* don't know," she said.

"We don't use last names," the ponytailed boy said. He sounded as if he was just realizing why that might not be such a great idea.

"It implies ownership," Isaac said. "A commune is a new kind of family, where everyone belongs to himself."

"Right." Jack didn't bother to keep the skepticism out of his voice. "I take it she was living here?"

"Yeah." Isaac nodded. "Until, um, four days ago."

"Last Saturday? What happened?"

"She got tired of the work, man. When we started the collective, everybody knew they'd have to put in long hours. Living off the land isn't just braiding flowers and rolling around in the hayloft."

"How long had Natalie been living here?"

The girl—Fran—rubbed her forearm across her eyes. "Since March. We met the guys on spring break and just . . . didn't go back."

"She was going to college?"

Fran nodded. "Vassar."

"But you don't know her name?"

"She went to Vassar. I went to Barnard."

Russell snorted.

Isaac glared at him. "College is bullshit, man. We're out here living in the real world."

"Oh, the *real* world." Russell crossed his arms. "Living on a farm you're renting with your parents' money."

Isaac's eyes narrowed. "I suppose you think putting on a uniform and going overseas to kill people is a better use of your time."

Jack's fist hit Russell's chest before the boy could respond. "Enough." He nodded toward the girl. "You were here since March. When did Natalie start talking about leaving?"

Fran glanced from Russell to Isaac and back again before addressing Jack. "She started complaining a couple months ago. When we first got here, there wasn't much for us to do, but once the weather got nice, we were outside all day, working in the orchard or hoeing. Nat really hated hoeing. And she didn't like"—her eyes shifted to the boy with the ponytail—"sharing. We had some . . . fights about that."

Harlene had said it was a free-love commune. Jack wondered if Natalie had discovered she wasn't as free-thinking as all that. "How many of you are there?"

"Me and Terry"—Isaac thumbed toward Ponytail—"Natalie, before she left, and Fran, Susie, and Wind."

"Wind?"

"Her real name's Wanda," Fran said. "She didn't think it suited her."

Jack could swear he heard Russell's eyes rolling. "And how did you all come to be renting the Stevenson place?"

The ponytailed guy—Terry—raised his hand. "I knew about it."

"You from around here, son?" The kid nodded. "What's your name?"

"McKellan. Terry McKellan."

"I know you," Russell said. "From high school. You were a senior when I was a sophomore." The older boy looked at him doubtfully. "I played basketball? Forward?"

Terry's eyes lit up. He pointed his finger. "Russ."

"Yeah."

"Weren't you drafted, man?"

Russell shrugged. "I'm back."

Jack stepped in and gestured to the girl. "So. She took off on Saturday. What happened?"

"Friday night, we all went to the opening of the fair. For fun, you know? There was . . . things had been tense, we all needed a break."

"Did anything happen at the fairgrounds?"

"No. We wandered around. Went on rides. The usual stuff."

"Did you all stick together?"

Fran rolled her eyes. "The guys went to the agricultural tents."

"You can learn a lot of good stuff," Isaac snapped. "Farming is more than just sticking seeds in the dirt, you know."

Jack steered them back on track. "How about you girls?"

"Not all the time, no. Wind and I went to get our fortunes told. Nat took off." She looked sideways at Isaac. "I think she might have gone for an Italian sausage."

"We're vegetarians." Isaac's voice was dry.

"Did she meet anyone?"

Fran shook her head. "No. We all caught up again and came home. For me, I don't know, it was a nice break, and I was happy to get back to work the next day."

"But not for Natalie."

"Maybe it reminded her of what she was missing? All I know is, she said she was going to leave and she did."

"Did she take anything with her?"

"She had a backpack. Some books and clothes, toothbrush, things like that. She didn't have much. None of us do."

"We're living simply," Isaac corrected.

Jack plucked the photo from Terry's hand and held it in front of Fran. "How about this outfit? Did she leave here with this?"

"No. She didn't have anything dressy like that. Jeans, a couple miniskirts. You know."

"How did she get off the farm?"

"I drove her to the bus station in Glens Falls," Isaac said. "We got there at half past three. Gave her her share of the money and wished her luck. And that's the last I saw of her."

Jack looked at the girl. "Did Natalie tell you what her plans were?"

"Not where she was going," Fran said. "Just that she really wanted to take a shower. The water pressure from our well's no good." Isaac glared at Fran and she raised her hands. "*I* don't mind, but Nat did. She wanted a shower and a hamburger and a couple of drinks."

"Fran, can you show me whatever she left behind? And if you have a photo of her, that would be real helpful. Russell, you stay here." Jack figured that would split up the group, and sure enough, Isaac stayed in the dooryard while Fran and the ponytailed boy led him to the house. What was his name again? "Terry." The kid turned back toward him. "I need the VIN numbers of your farm machinery. Could you copy them down for me?"

The kid screwed up his face. "What? Why?"

Jack motioned him closer. "I don't want to say, but you're a smart man. I'm sure you can imagine why."

Bafflement was writ large on the boy's face. "Okay. Right. Sure." Bless his heart, he took the bait and ambled off, casting backward glances as Jack and Fran climbed the steps and went inside without him.

The house, surprisingly, wasn't much different from other working farmhouses Jack had known. Bare floors—easier to clean—sturdy wooden furniture, no clutter or mess in the kitchen. A heavy black phone sat next to the calling bench in the hall. The Indian-print fabrics and poorly thrown pottery were unique, and where other farmhouse mudrooms would have a row of rubber boots against the wall, here there was a pile of ugly sandals. "Our room's upstairs," Fran said.

Jack followed her to the second floor. "You two were roommates?"

"There are four bedrooms, so we girls shared two and the guys each got one." She gestured toward an open door. "Here it is."

Jack looked around the plain, white-plastered room. Two ascetic twin beds, layered in more Indian fabric. A single dresser. A shelf holding a row of paperbacks including Herman Hesse's *Siddhartha*, some poetry. Not exactly what Harlene would have imagined. "Did Natalie leave anything behind? That you know of?"

Fran opened the narrow closet door. A pair of winter coats and

some woolen jumpers were shoved to one side, making way for summer-weight shirts and skirts. "The black coat and some of the winter clothes are hers." She pulled a shoebox off the shelf, opening it to show photographs, a journal, and some girlish trinkets.

"Hers?" Jack said hopefully.

"No, these are mine." Fran handed him a Polaroid. "Here's a bunch from when we were in Daytona." Jack shuffled through the pictures until he came to one that showed Natalie alone. She was smiling toward the camera, one arm shielding her face from the sun, bright blue Florida waters visible behind her.

"May I keep this one?"

Fran nodded. "I wish I had paid more attention when she started talking about leaving. I didn't think she'd really go."

Jack squatted so he could look beneath the beds. Nothing there. He tipped a book off the shelf, riffled through it, then repeated the process with several other volumes. Nothing there, either. He delved into the pocket of the coat Fran indicated belonged to Natalie, but only came up with a crumpled tissue and a peppermint.

He turned to Fran. "You said Natalie had trouble sharing."

The girl nodded.

"You weren't talking about sharing clothes or food, were you?"

She shook her head.

"Was she involved with one of the boys?"

Fran twisted a part of her gypsy skirt between her hands. "We're not supposed to be exclusive. We're breaking beyond traditional bourgeois morality."

Jack waited for her to continue.

"She and Terry had been together. He was the guy she met at spring break, he was why she came here, I think. At least at first. But then Isaac started leaning on them, saying they'd ruin the whole thing if they paired off like geese. So . . ."

"They broke up?"

Fran blew out a breath. "One night after dinner, Isaac took her up to his room. We didn't see her again until breakfast."

"And Terry? How did he react?"

"He tried with Wind. I mean, she was perfectly cool with it and all, but I'm not sure anything really happened."

"Was he angry at Natalie?"

"No. But she was angry with him. I think she thought he should have . . ." Fran looked out the old window. Its wavering glass panes were propped open by a simple screen. "He should have come after her. She liked it when boys wanted her. Not that I'm judging," she added quickly. "I think . . . I got the feeling she would have been happy if Isaac and Terry fought over her, you know? But Isaac didn't treat her any different after they, you know, and Terry was trying so hard to be okay with it he practically ignored her. That was when she started talking about splitting."

"How soon after that did she leave?"

"Maybe two weeks?"

"Did Terry and Isaac—" Jack's question was cut off by a shout from outside. He pressed against the window, but the porch roof below kept him from seeing what was happening.

There was another yell. He swung out of the bedroom and thudded down the stairs, reaching the door in two strides and loping out into the front yard.

Russell and Isaac were wrestling on the grass, throwing punches and clawing at each other. Terry stood nearby, a hand clapped over his jaw, shouting unheeded commands to "Quit it! Stop it!"

Behind him, Jack heard Fran's terrified "Oh, no!" He struck out across the lawn, wishing like hell he had slid his baton into its slot on his duty belt. Before he could reach the boys, Russell rolled Isaac onto his stomach and straddled his back, pinning his hips and legs. Russell slammed the other boy's head into the dirt, then, while Isaac was stunned, twisted his arms back in a brutally efficient hold.

"What the hell, boy? Get off him!" Jack fisted Russell's collar and hauled him bodily off the other young man. "I brought you along for your point of view, not so you could start World War—"

As he railed at Russell, Isaac collected himself, surged off the ground, and head-butted Russell. Jack barely escaped going down himself. The two boys rolled in the dirt, fists flying, teeth bared, eyes wide and wild.

"You!" Jack pointed to the ponytailed guy. "You got a garden hose hooked up?"

The boy tore his gaze away from the brawl and nodded.

"Turn it on and bring it over here!" Jack pelted back to his squad car, popped the door, and grabbed his baton. By the time he got back to the still-fighting combatants, Terry had unspooled the hose and was standing by.

"Hose 'em down," Jack ordered. "Get 'em right in their faces, if you can." A nose full of ice-cold well water ought to cool them down some. Jack stepped in and began applying the baton freely, bashing an arm here, whacking a leg there. Terry sprayed the boys enthusiastically, apparently feeling no qualms about half-drowning the leader of the commune.

Within seconds they had ceased hitting each other, turning their energies to escaping. They coughed and choked and crawled, reduced to animal brains fleeing pain and wetness. When Russell staggered to his feet, Jack grabbed him and propelled him toward the car. He slammed the kid over the hood, one hand on the back of his neck, one between his shoulder blades. "Stay here."

He turned back to discover Isaac still under aquatic assault. "Terry! Put the damn hose away!"

"Oh." The boy looked at the hose in his hand as if he didn't recognize it. "Sure."

Isaac had lurched to his feet by the time Jack reached him. The boy was bent over, clutching his midsection with one hand and wiping away the water streaming out of his hair with the other. "He's fucking crazy!" The boy's voice was almost gone. "You oughta put him away!"

"What happened?"

Isaac wheezed. "I asked him about being a soldier, that's all." He wrung out his beard, still bent over. "He freaked out on me. They come back, they're not fit to be with the rest of us, man. They're trained killers, like some kind of goddamn Doberman." He pressed a hand against his side and gritted his teeth. "Christ, I think he broke a fucking rib."

"Were you talking about Natalie before you started throwing punches?"

"Natalie? Hell, no. Why would we be talking about Natalie?"

"I understand you took her away from Terry over there." Jack tilted his head toward the house, where the boy in question was re-looping the hose over its hook. "I understand there were some bad feelings, after."

Isaac railed and rattled and spat on the lawn. Not blood, fortunately. "You don't understand much. I didn't *take* Nat from anybody. She doesn't—she didn't belong to Terry. None of us belong to anyone else. We're not doing that jealous caveman shit."

Terry, having rolled the hose neatly enough to satisfy the fussiest Dutch farmer, had rejoined them. He gave Isaac a sideways look at the leader's pronouncement, but didn't contradict him. Jack wondered how many times, throughout history, ideologues convinced themselves they could change human nature just by saying it was so. "Do you want somebody to take a look at that? I can drop you at the hospital."

"No, thanks. Just leash your dog and get him the hell out of here."

"One more thing. Where were you two between Friday when you left Natalie at the bus station in Glens Falls and Sunday morning?"

"The hell?" Isaac tried to bellow, but the pummeling had left his voice thready. "You think we had something to do with it? You're crazy." Jack waited. Isaac finally sighed. "I had a couple beers at the Green Diner after I took her to the bus station. I came back home, we worked the rest of Saturday, then Wind and Susie and I went to hear a band at SPAC. Terry and Fran stayed home."

"That's how you remember it, Terry?"

The boy nodded. "Yeah. Except I was gone part of the day on Saturday, meeting with some local grocery stores to see if we could expand the market for our produce."

Jack kept his face neutral, but mentally, he was kicking rocks across the drive. A concert at the Saratoga Performing Arts Center, with its open-air seating, couldn't be more anonymous. There'd be no way of proving Isaac's alibi. And "at home with another person" was the second-least-likely-to-crack story, after "in the confessional booth."

"Okay. Thank you for your help." Jack nodded toward Isaac's chest. "Get that looked at if it starts to hurt worse or if you have trouble breathing." Jack turned to go.

"Umm. Officer?" Terry stopped him. "Will you let us know? What you find out about Natalie, I mean."

"I will, son, yes." Jack might be doing it at the end of a warrant, but he would let them know.

TUESDAY, AUGUST 22, PRESENT DAY

24. Russ wasn't surprised that two of the other men who had been persons of interest back in '72 were still living in the area. After all, he had come home from a lifetime in the army, twenty-odd years after he'd sworn he'd never set foot in Millers Kill again. It was a little uncanny that Isaac Nevinson was living on the same farm where Russ had met him all those years ago, though. Driving through Cossayuharie's fields of grass-green corn and pastures going straw-gold in the August heat, he felt he could crest the next hill and be back in the land of his youth. What was the song they had sung last Sunday at St. Alban's? *Time, like an ever-rolling stream, bears all its sons away.*

The road still wound down past the orchard, but where the one he remembered was overgrown with branches and brush, this orchard was rank on rank of perfect trees, glossy green leaves, and barely blushing apples as far as the eye could see.

He pulled into the neatly graveled drive and parked. The original house and barn had been joined by several outbuildings and a little farm shop. Russ could see jars and jellies stacked behind the counter, and a glass-fronted refrigerator crammed with jugs and egg cartons. NEVINSON ORGANIC FARM, the sign over the shop read. CIDER—APPLE BUTTER—FREE-RANGE EGGS—HONEY.

He got out of the car, cracking his back and letting the heat of the sun soak in for a moment. He was headed toward the house when the slam of the screen door stopped him. A young woman raced down the steps barefoot, her gypsy skirt swirling around her legs as she ran toward the farm stand.

The hairs on Russ's arms stood up. The girl stopped at the corner of the stand, flipped her long dark hair over her shoulder, and smiled at him. "Sorry. I'm trying to keep an eye on the store and help Isaac with the baby. What can I help you with, Officer?"

It took him two tries to find his voice. "I'd like to speak to Isaac Nevinson."

Her mouth and eyes both went round. "Ohhh." In a whirl of skirts she was gone, back to the house. The screen door slammed before Russ could say anything else.

Russ walked to the farm stand. Its roof was built out over the counter, offering a couple feet of welcome shade for customers. The strings of dried apple slices and crafty little dolls did nothing for him, but the sight of cinnamon-dark apple butter and golden honey made his stomach growl. He sighed. Lunch was likely to be a heart attack in a sack again today.

The slamming door turned him around. The man coming toward him—barrel-chested, balding—could have been anyone until he opened his mouth.

"This is bullshit. Now they're sending cops? Well, go ahead!" His arms windmilled. "Search the whole damn place! You're not going to find anything, because I got rid of every scrap of equipment, which, they probably didn't tell you, I paid over a thousand bucks for! A man tries to make an honest goddamn living in this country and this is what he gets! A friggin' nanny state propped up by the fascist police!" He poked his finger toward Russ's chest, and suddenly Russ could see the young wild-haired Isaac inside this middle-aged farmer. "Ask yourself why they're setting the law on me. Hmm? You know why? Because I said I was going to sue them. You take one step toward threatening some pencil-pushing bureaucrat's authority and this is what you get." He held out his hands, wrists together. "Go ahead. Arrest me. I'll sue the goddamn police department, too."

Russ was pretty sure, but he had to ask. "Mr. Nevinson?"

The man looked at him as if Russ were a particularly stupid five-year-old. "Who *else* would I be?"

"What is it you think I'm here for, Mr. Nevinson?"

The farmer frowned. His eyebrows had grown as full and thick as his mustache had been in '72. "The Liquor Licensing Authority?"

"Ah." Russ nodded. "They catch you making illegal apple jack, did they?"

"It wasn't *apple jack*. It was French-style apple brandy." Nevinson rolled his eyes. "You can't call it Calvados unless it comes from Normandy. Friggin trademark protection." He squinted at Russ, as if trying to place his face. "The Licensing Authority didn't sic you on me?"

"No." Russ tugged at his collar. "Mr. Nevinson, can we go inside? This heat is just about killing me."

"Oh. Well. Yeah. Okay. Sure." The farmer turned back toward the house, Russ trailing after. If necessary, Russ could stand outside the whole day long, but he wanted to get a glimpse of what was going on in Isaac Nevinson's life. He may have lost his hair and gained a gut, but the man's hair-trigger temper was just the same.

The temperature was twenty degrees cooler once they had passed through the screen door. A long waterproof runner ran up the middle of the wide front hall, with rows of hooks for raincoats, jackets, leashes, and hats on either side. One archway led into a front room crowded with plastic baby toys and a playpen. Another opened onto the kitchen.

"Glass of water?"

"Thanks, yeah." Russ took a seat at the checker-cloth-covered table. Nevinson filled two glasses and handed one to Russ before sitting down. His change of manner made Russ uneasy. Nobody was that casual when the cops dropped by wanting to chat.

Nevinson braced his elbows on the table and leaned in. "Look, I gotta be honest, I'm probably going to be voting for the state police option. I've been in business over thirty years, and I've never had any need for law enforcement. I mean, I'm glad you guys are there on the Fourth, directing traffic, but there's no reason that couldn't be done by the fire and rescue team. The sheriff's department has said they can budget for a deputy at the high school. What else do we need?"

Okay, that explained Nevinson's relaxed air. "I'm not here about the referendum, either." Russ took the unsub's photo out of his pocket and laid it in front of the farmer. "Have you ever seen this girl before?"

Nevinson picked the picture up. His face changed, stilled, closed in on itself. His eyes shifted to Russ. "This is a dead person."

Russ nodded. "Do you know her?"

Nevinson put the picture down. "No. Why should I?"

"Her body was found in the middle of McEachron Hill Road. She was wearing a fancy dress, but had no shoes and no purse. No signs of violence. We can't tell how she was killed. Yet."

The farmer folded his hands and was silent for a long moment. "Okay," he finally said. "You obviously know about the '72 investigation. I'm sure it was in the record or whatever you guys keep. If you have that, you know I wasn't ever charged with anything."

Russ tipped his head toward the man, a not-quite assent. "I'm not saying you had anything to do with either death, Mr. Nevinson. I'm just trying to find some connections. We have two identical . . . incidents separated by thirty-four years. Not a lot of people who were involved then are still around today."

"Bullshit. Terry McKellan still lives here. That carnival company the cops were interested in last time are still around. Have you checked with them? And there was that guy who found the body, what about him?"

Russ shifted in his seat. Nevinson blinked, leaned forward, and peered over the table. His mouth opened in an O. "Holy shit. That's you. You're that guy." He waved his hand at Russ. "It is you, isn't it? The glasses and the hair threw me off." He made a sound that could have been a laugh. "Jesus, buddy, you must be the only guy in the county whose hair is longer now than it was then." He scraped his chair back and stood. "You're barking up the wrong tree. I had nothing to do with Natalie's death, and I sure as hell don't have anything to do with this one."

"You won't mind letting me know where you were Friday evening into Saturday night, then."

Isaac grinned. "I was at my daughter and son-in-law's house in Saratoga all weekend. Brooke and Dan Shaftsbury. I brought my grandson home on Monday so they could have a few days' vacation. They'll be back tomorrow to pick him up."

He stopped at the slap-slap-slap of small bare feet on wooden floors. A toddler raced into the kitchen, the dark-haired girl close behind. "Sorry, Isaac. He got away from me."

"Aw, that's okay." He scooped up the boy. "What's up, bud? You ready for your tractor ride?"

"Twacta!" the boy yelled.

"I've got him, Steffie. You go ahead and get the rest of the stuff unpacked in the store."

The girl swished out of the room, leaving a glowing smile hanging in her wake. "Your, um . . . ?" Russ invited.

"Apprentice. I've got four agronomy majors from SUNY Adirondack learning the ropes." He snorted. "I left academia for the simple life, and here I am, teaching college kids." The boy in his arms wiggled and Isaac put him down. "Go find your hat if you want your tractor ride, buddy." The toddler ran into the wide hallway, circled once, then tore back upstairs.

Isaac ripped a sheet of paper from a notepad and bent over it. "This is my daughter's address and number. I'd take it kindly if you'd speak to her, clear me, and then leave me the hell alone."

Russ tucked the paper into his pocket.

Isaac looked at him and shook his head. "I can't believe you kept all your hair."

Russ shrugged. "Maybe I'm not that old yet."

Isaac crossed his arms over his broad chest. "In which case, there's gotta be any number of guys who aren't too old to have killed this new girl. Lotta people who've spent their whole lives in this area."

"I know." Russ sighed. "I've got to go talk to one of them now."

25. Clare had almost finished her meeting with Terry McKellan when she heard the knock on her office door. Terry was the best finance officer she could imagine, patiently going through the complex web of loans, pledges, income, and endowments that kept St. Alban's afloat, but words like "cash flow" and "accounts payable" and "adjustable interest option" made her want to cross her eyes and sink into a coma, so she called, "Come in!" with a tone of desperate relief.

"Hi." Her husband filled the doorway. He wasn't smiling.

Clare looked at her watch. "What are you doing here so early? Oh, my God, is it Ethan? Is everything okay?"

Russ held up his hands. "I haven't heard anything from Mom, so I assume they're both doing fine." He nodded toward Terry. "I'm here to see Mr. McKellan. Your office told me you'd be here."

Terry looked around as if there might be another McKellan hiding in the corner.

"No bad news. I just need to ask you a few questions."

"Me?"

Clare was as surprised as Terry. The AllBanc vice president's life was as orderly as his spreadsheets: work, church, golfing at Saratoga National and the occasional trip to visit his oldest daughter in New York City. His only vice, as far as she knew, was sneaking food when his wife, who was eternally trying to get his blood pressure and cholesterol down, wasn't around.

"Is this about the bank? Someone has an account there?"

"Maybe we could talk privately, Mr. McKellan?" Russ glanced toward Clare.

"This is *my* office!"

"Hmm." Russ gestured toward the door. "How about the parish hall?"

Terry folded his hands over his rounded belly. "Unless it involves client confidentiality, I can't think of anything I wouldn't say in front of Clare."

"Why, *thank* you, Terry." She put a little extra Southern into it.

"Oh, for chrissakes." Russ dropped onto the ancient love seat. "Look, Mr. McKellan—"

"Russ, he was a guest at our wedding. I think you can call him Terry." Russ glared at her.

"No, no, he's just trying to keep things professional. I understand." Terry dropped his voice a bit. "I wish I could do the same thing when I have friends applying for a commercial loan. It would be useful to remind clients that having dinner together doesn't mean I won't do due diligence."

"Thank you." Russ's voice was strained. "Mr. McKellan. Terry. Can you tell me where you were from the evening of Friday the eighteenth to the morning of Saturday the nineteenth?"

"Huh." Terry stroked his luxurious mustache. "What *was* I doing? Were we in Lake George?" He leaned to one side and reached into his coat pocket. Clare saw Russ tense for a second.

Terry pulled out his phone. "Let me see. Yep, Lake George. We have a boat there. I went home after work, got changed, and headed up to the lake."

"What about your wife?"

"Deborah joined me Saturday afternoon. I needed to process the chemical head and do some other dirty chores." His cheeks plumped up when he smiled. "Not her favorite part of boat ownership."

"Where did you stay the night?"

"Right on the *Spare Change*. She sleeps six."

Russ frowned. "Anyone see you? Do you have to check in with security to get access to your boat?"

"No, every slip has its own gate and key. I just let myself in." Terry smiled again and leaned back in his chair. "Now. I've been very cooperative. How about you tell me what's going on?"

"Did you make any stops at all? Anything that might confirm you were in Lake George? Did you fill up at a gas station?"

Terry spread his hands. "There'll be a record of me using the pumping station. And lots of folks were at the marina Saturday morning."

"Before that morning. Friday night."

Terry shifted in his chair. "Well . . ."

"Oh, Terry," Clare said.

"I got takeout from Harborside Burgers."

"That place where they have the deep-fried Oreos?" Clare asked.

"Oh, they're so good." His eyes closed for a moment before he shot a glance at Clare. "Don't tell my wife."

"That stuff is going to kill you, you know."

"But what a way to go." Terry's eyes sharpened. "So, Russ, are you going to let me know why my itinerary is of such interest?"

Russ looked at Clare, then back to Terry. "Early Saturday morning, we found the body of a young woman dumped on McEachron Hill Road. She was wearing a party dress, no shoes, no purse or cell phone. The ME can't find a cause of death."

Terry's mouth made an O as he let out a silent breath. "Like Natalie."

"Like Natalie," Russ agreed. Clare noticed he didn't mention the other, earlier case. He went on. "You were never actually cleared in that investigation."

Terry gave him a look. "Were you?"

"No."

Clare had to press her fingers to her lips to keep a torrent of questions from spilling out.

"You know, Isaac Nevinson's still—"

"I know," Russ said. "I spoke with him earlier today. Are you two still friends?"

"I'm not sure we were friends back then. Isaac was . . . like a planet. The rest of us were orbiting around him. Is Saturn friendly with its rings? I don't know." Terry tapped the chair arm. "I've bumped into him a few times over the years. Said hello, how's the family. That was about it."

"Are you still angry with him for taking Natalie away from you?"

"Good God, no. She wasn't interested in being anybody's girl-friend. I'm lucky the only thing we had to worry about in those days was pregnancy." Terry glanced at Clare, his cheeks pinking over his brown moustache. "Sorry."

Clare refrained from pointing out she didn't expect all her congregants to have been virgins when they married.

"In some ways, Natalie's death set me straight. I thought free love and communal farming was going to save us all. When she was killed, I realized the world was harder to change than that. I went back to college and finished my degree and got a decent job. Met Deborah." He smiled.

"You ever miss the excitement?" Russ asked.

"What excitement? Getting up at dawn to hand-weed fields? In bare feet, so we could be at one with Mother Earth? No, thank you."

"The women?"

"The ratio of naughty fun to endless discussions and slamming doors was extremely low. If I want tears, shrieking, and drama, I still have a high schooler at home."

Russ smiled at that. "Okay. Thanks, Terry. I may be in touch."

"You know where to find me." Terry stood and gathered up the financial papers from Clare's desk. "Clare, I'll see you on Sunday. Russ—" He paused at the door. "I hope you catch whoever did this. The fact no one was ever brought to justice for Natalie's death . . ."

"I know. I'll do the best I can."

Clare waited a few seconds until she heard Terry's footsteps recede down the hall. Then she moved to sit next to Russ. "Terry McKellan in a free love commune. I did not see that coming." She glanced at Russ. "How about you?"

"I was not in a free love commune. More's the pity."

"I mean, what were you doing during the investigation in '72? You didn't tell me if you were arrested at any point, or what the cops thought at the time, or anything. Were you living at home with your mom?"

He frowned. "Clare, it was so long ago. That summer wasn't my finest hour, not by a long shot. I'd just as soon leave it all in the past."

She tried not to feel stung. "Vietnam was a long time in the past, and you've told me about things that were, well—"

"I know. I have." He took her hand. "There was stuff I needed to let out, and you were there for me, and I thank you for that." He squeezed her knuckles. "The summer of '72 isn't like that. It's not a half-healed wound, it's an embarrassment. I was a little shit to everyone around me, and I made a lot of poor choices, and I really, really don't want to hash it out with you. I have to deal with it enough as part of the ongoing investigation."

"Okay." Lord knows she had had any number of folks she'd been counseling refuse to dig deeper on a subject. It just didn't hurt like it did when the person sitting in her office was Russ.

"Thank you." He put his arm around her shoulders. "I don't need to remind you that everything discussed here is confidential, do I?"

"You mean about Terry? Of course not. He's cleared, though, right?"

Russ frowned. "I'll have Noble check Harborside Burgers to see if we can confirm Terry's story. It's a pretty thin alibi, though."

"Terry McKellan some sort of serial killer? The guy who looks like President Garfield?"

"*Somebody* out there killed that girl, and another girl in 1972, and another girl twenty years before that. *If* the cases are connected. I don't know."

"Terry's your age. He couldn't be involved in the 1952 death."

"Nor could Isaac Nevinson." Russ pinched the bridge of his nose. "Which is one of the reasons I'm giving a press conference at the end of the day. Nothing like standing up in public and admitting failure to get the voters thinking about drop-kicking our department."

Clare felt her stomach drop. He was right, that wasn't going to look good. "I was going to wait till tonight to tell you this, but Mrs. Marshall has some very sharp ideas about educating voters on the referendum. We're going to do some strategic planning, and some fundraising, and we're getting your mother on board. I think they'll make a formidable team."

"God save us all." He groaned as he levered himself up from the love seat. "I better get back to the station before you ladies take charge of it, too. Don't bother to turn on the TV. I suck at press conferences."

"Are you kidding? You'll be fantastic."

26. The last time the MKPD had held a press conference, back when Hadley was still working her way through the police academy, she had done all in her power to duck and weave her way out of sight of the cameras. So it was—ironic? Annoying?—that MacAuley wanted her to take part in this afternoon's assembly. Like the movie where Death comes back for each of the students who had escaped him the first time.

The dep had said it "gave better optics" for her to be standing with him and the chief. Part of her was amused that the otherwise technophobic MacAuley slung around media-speak like a thirty-something PR rep, and part of her was horrified at the thought that anyone watching a news clip might recognize her. She'd been avoiding attention since before she'd left California—not that it had done her much good in the end.

"Look, Hadley, I know you feel embarrassed about the . . . thing." MacAuley kept one eye on her while talking and the other on his reflection in the hall mirror as he adjusted his dress hat. Lid. She was never going to get used to the uniform jargon. "We all feel embarrassed about the . . ."

"Thing."

"Right. The only way through is through. Nobody not in this department knows what happened that afternoon—"

Hadley was pretty sure that wasn't true, but she knew MacAuley and the chief liked to push the party line.

"—so I want you to square your shoulders, stick your chin out, and if anyone asks you about it, just look 'em straight in the eye and lie your head off."

"Lying? That's my fallback position?"

The chief strode out of his office. Like the dep, he had changed into his summer dress uniform; the knife-creased khaki and brown looked sharp but was sticky-hot. The chief looked like his temperature was already rising. "You ready?" He glanced at Hadley. "What's she doing here?"

"She's coming with us."

The chief stared. "Isn't that a little risky? I mean, no offense, Knox—"

"None taken, Chief."

"—but the last thing we need is for anyone to raise questions about the, uh . . ."

"Thing," Hadley said.

"Right. Not that anyone outside the department knows anything." Hadley wondered what would happen if she started to scream and didn't stop. The chief went on. "But what about the lawsuit? It's bad enough we're going public with two—or *three*—unsolved cases. If word gets out the town's getting sued for police misconduct, we might as well give up on the vote right now and hand the keys to the building over to the staties."

"Chief, the suit *is* going to get out sooner or later," Hadley said. "All legal filings are a matter of public record."

MacAuley shook his head. "Oh, my sweet summer children. You don't think Harold Collins hasn't already leaked that info to the press? Am I the only person on the force who understands how politics works?"

"Yes," the chief said.

"That's the other reason Hadley has to be standing there with us by the microphone. If any specific questions come up, she can step up and let the public know there's no basis to her ex's claims." He turned to Hadley. "You can say the suit originates with your ex, but don't say anything else about him. We don't want to give his lawyer any ammunition."

Hadley tried to think of something—anything—that might persuade MacAuley to leave her behind. "I'm not wearing my dress uniform!"

"The regular kit makes you look more approachable."

"Why couldn't *I* look approachable?" The chief tugged at his jacket, scowling.

"What are you, a girl? Stop complaining."

A girl? Really? You use "girl" as an insult? Hadley seethed while they walked the four blocks to the town hall. Anger was great at pushing back

fear—she figured that was why men spent so much time being angry—
but even the dep's casual sexism wasn't enough to keep her stomach
from flopping over when she saw the news vans parked outside.

"Just two?" The chief looked over his shoulder as they entered the
building.

"Unless it's a big story, Channel Eight and Capital News are the
only ones who send their own crews up here." MacAuley held the door
open for Hadley. "There'll be a camera guy who shoots footage for the
Albany stations, the AP stringer, and a reporter from the *Post-Star*.
Maybe someone from the *Times-Union*; they've had a guy up here
doing stories from the fair."

It didn't sound like a lot, but when they entered the aldermen's
session room, it felt as if the entire East Coast press corps had arrived.
Several heads turned as they came in and Hadley told herself they
probably weren't staring at her alone.

"Ah, hell. Ben Beagle." The chief pasted on an insincere smile and
nodded at a sandy-haired man in a Snoopy tie. "I hate that guy."

MacAuley managed to both smile at the *Post-Star* investigative reporter and frown at the chief as they passed Beagle and moved toward
the front of the session room.

The space where the aldermen met wasn't large; in the usual run
of things, it only had to hold a handful of people with business before
the board, a few lawyers and witnesses, and the usual scattering of
town-politics junkies who never missed an open session. The reporters and three cameramen wouldn't have filled the left front row if
they had all been sitting side by side. The chief and MacAuley had
a brief, low-voiced discussion about holding a mic that ended when
MacAuley dragged the podium from the end of the aldermen's bench
and centered it in front of the town shield.

Hadley thought there would be more ceremony—maybe an
introduction?—but the chief simply stepped up to the podium and
said, "Thank you all for coming."

Hadley took a parade rest position, which required a certain amount
of concentration, since she hadn't done it since she'd graduated from
the academy. She focused on looking ticked off, which might not have

been what the dep had in mind by "good optics," but was an expression no one would associate with the word "porn."

When the chief got to the part about the previous deaths, there was a shift in the room, a sharpening of attention and interest that was almost audible. The TV reporters and Beagle went heads-down over their phones, typing like mad. When one of the men glanced up and caught Hadley's eye, she rearranged her features from ticked off to foul tempered.

She had done what she could to separate herself from the woman in those films: no makeup, hair as short as her twelve-year-old son's, mom clothes when she wasn't in her unflattering uniform. But short of going around like the Phantom of the Opera, she couldn't disguise her face.

"Any questions?" the chief asked, and she snapped back to attention. Hands shot up. A woman with a microphone asked, "Chief Van Alstyne, if this suspicious death was preceded by two other identical killings, why was it first released as a possible hit-and-run?"

"We wanted to make sure the circumstances were the same as the previous two, uh, incidents. We couldn't rule out hit-and-run until the autopsy." He pointed to another TV reporter. "Ms. Bevins."

"Chief, you have no idea of the identity of the dead woman?"

"None. We've released her photo to you; we're hoping the public will be able to help us with that. Yes, you."

"Greg Donovan, *Albany Times-Union*. The Millers Kill Police Department is facing a vote this fall to shut it down and replace its services with the state police. What would you say to residents who might point to three unsolved deaths as a reason why the state police ought to be doing the investigating rather than a small-town police force?"

"Not to denigrate the work of the state police, but they were in charge of investigating the first killing and dismissed it as death by misadventure. My department knows the three-town area better than any state investigator, and, not to knock their professionalism, I would say we care a lot more than they do about what happens here."

Donovan leaped into the chief's pause before he could point to another reporter. "Caring is great, but do you have the resources the state police could bring to bear on this case? Have you considered calling them in for help?"

The chief opened his mouth, but MacAuley bumped him aside, smiling. "We're calling you all in for help. Here's your chance to show up the troopers."

The reporters laughed. MacAuley continued. "As Chief Van Alstyne said, we don't know how or why these deaths are connected. While we'd love to finally close the case from 1972, we need to focus first on what happened this August nineteenth. Whoever is responsible for that death may well be incapacitated or in jail or dead. We know whoever is behind this recent tragedy is alive and out there somewhere."

Bevins spoke up. "Deputy Chief MacAuley, are you cautioning area residents?"

"We're urging them to use common sense. If you're a young woman, don't go off with strangers. Make sure people know where you are and when you're expected back. Keep control over your drinks in bars."

Ben Beagle's hand shot up. "Deputy Chief MacAuley. You say the person who killed the young woman in 1972—"

"We're not using the word 'killed,'" the chief interrupted. "We have no evidence, then or now, of foul play."

"Okay, the person who left her dead in the road may be in jail or dead." He held up his phone. "According to the *Post-Star* archives, one of the suspects in the mysterious death in 1972 was twenty-year-old Russell Van Alstyne."

27.   "Wow." Clare muted the volume on her mother-in-law's television. Margy, sitting on the sofa next to her, kept shaking her head. "It wasn't *that* bad," Clare said.

Margy looked at her.

"All right, it was that bad. The deer-caught-in-the-headlights look is never good. He should have stopped talking after he said he hadn't been charged."

"He should have let Lyle MacAuley handle the whole thing, that's what he should have done." Margy bent over the bouncy chair where Ethan had been batting at black-and-white figures strung from a frame. "Sometimes your daddy's an idiot, Ethan, and that's a fact."

"I wish he had just *talked* to me about what happened back then. I could have at least pointed out a few pitfalls."

Margy looked up at her. "Is he doing the strong, silent man routine?"

Clare clicked off the remote and rose from the sofa. She grabbed the backpack she used to carry her son's bits and pieces and began tossing things in. "Yes, and I don't get it. He's always been, well, not forthcoming about certain events in his past, but at least willing to share them with me."

"Mmm. I bet he hasn't said much about Desert Storm, either."

"Other than the fact he was there, and drinking? No." Clare paused, an Elmo doll in her hand. "Which is odd, because I was there, too. It was my first deployment."

"He probably didn't go into the end of his service, before he came here."

"No." Clare frowned. "Okay, this is really bothering me, now."

Margy stood up and stretched. "When he came back from 'Nam, he wouldn't hardly say a word. I wasn't any fool, I knew it was because he was hurting inside. Sometimes, when you're carrying around too much pain, you don't want to open your mouth because you're afraid you'll start yelling and you won't stop."

"It sounds like you're speaking from experience."

"You don't get to be my age without having a few pains, sweetie." Margy squeezed Clare's arm. "Then there are the other things you don't want to think about. The things you messed up bad. The time you cheated on a test at school, or the night you lied to your parents to sneak out with your friends." She looked at Clare. "The days when you drank when you were pregnant."

"I didn't know—"

"I'm not blaming you, sweetheart. I'm just pointing out there are some things we don't want to think about because we're ashamed of ourselves. Now, if it's an ongoing problem"—thankfully, Margy didn't say *Like you wanting a drink*—"you're going to need to confront it. But if it's not going to happen again, it's all right to let it lie. You don't have to 'deal with' or 'process,'" she made air quotes, "fibbing to your mom and dad when you were a teen, because you're a grown-up. If you want to stay out with your friends until four in the morning, you just do it."

Clare bent over Ethan. "Not with a baby in the house."

"Ha! No, well, don't worry. Being a parent gives you a whole other set of moments you're going to mess up and not want to think about ever again."

"Yeah, I've already gotten a head start on those." She wiggled Ethan out of the bouncy chair and hoisted him up, pressing kisses into his fat cheek. On the sofa, her phone rang.

Margy picked it up. "New York City area code."

"Oh! I bet it's my new intern." She exchanged the baby for the phone and walked into the kitchen. "Clare Fergusson here."

"Clare? It's Joni Langevoort. Is this a bad time?"

"Absolutely not. I'm just picking up the baby from my mother-in-law's place."

"Is she the one you mentioned when we were talking? The political one?"

Clare glanced at Margy's refrigerator, covered with stickers urging the viewer to stop war, disinvest from fossil fuel companies, and vote Green. "Oh, yes," Clare said.

"Good. You can ask her for me. My folks are having a dinner party to honor my dad's replacement at Barkley and Eaton—Dad's retiring soon—and my mother said it would be a perfect time to discuss the Save the Police campaign."

"That's a lot better than the Committee for Public Safety."

Joni laughed. "Isn't it? Anyway, I already spoke with Mrs. Marshall, and she's bringing her gentleman friend with her, so this is your invitation. Please come with your husband and your mother-in-law.

123

Is she Mrs. Van Alstyne? Oh, hang on." The sound of Joni's voice was muffled for a moment. "My mother says to invite your father-in-law as well. Sorry."

"Margy is a widow, but thank you."

The widow in question had drifted into the kitchen, Ethan on her hip. She raised her eyebrows at Clare. Clare switched the phone to speaker so Margy could hear.

"Well, if she has a gentleman friend like Mrs. Marshall has, he's welcome, too. Friday at seven— Oh, hang on." More muffled talking. "My mother wants to know if that was your husband on the news just now."

Clare and Margy exchanged pained glances. "Yep, that was Russ."

"Huh. Well. That should make for interesting dinner conversation." Joni dropped her voice. "It'll be nice to have someone else in the spotlight instead of me."

"You were saying Friday at seven?"

"That's right. Casual cocktail dress. I'll text you the address."

"Thanks, Joni. And thank your mother for me."

"A few of my parents' friends who are also summer people will be here, so be ready to hit them up for a contribution."

"I may leave that part to Mrs. Marshall. Thanks again. See you tomorrow." Clare put her phone in her pocket. "How would you like to be a founding member of the Save the Police Committee?"

"Finally! An organized campaign! If Lacey Marshall is involved, we'll raise enough money to get mailers to every voter in the three towns. I admire that woman."

"Me, too." There was a small pile of folded baby clothes on the kitchen table—Margy had taken to doing Ethan's laundry when she was babysitting. Clare carried them into the living room and packed them in Ethan's diaper bag. "My one worry is that Joni is doing this because I'm supervising her internship at St. Alban's. I don't want her to think the price of admission is helping Russ keep his job."

The kitchen door creaked open. "Mom, you left the door unlocked," Russ said. "Clare's bad habits are rubbing off on you." He walked into the living room like a man wearing a lead overcoat. When he hugged Clare, it felt more like he was using her to keep from falling over. "I thought I was picking up Ethan?"

"I came over to watch the news with your mom."

"Oh, God." He flopped into the recliner Margy kept for him and shut his eyes.

"Did you see it?" Clare asked.

"I didn't have to. I lived it." He opened his eyes and pointed a finger at his mother. "You're thinking I should have had Lyle do the press conference. And you would be right."

Mercifully, Margy didn't unload any more hard truths on him. Instead, she laid Ethan on Russ's chest. One big hand came around and clasped the baby. Russ sighed.

"Don't you worry, son. You'll figure this one out. And Clare and her new intern and Lacey Marshall and I are going to put together a nice fundraiser for the Save Our Police campaign."

Russ opened one eye. "What in the heck is the Save Our Police campaign?"

"It's a citizens' advocacy group formed to raise awareness of the ballot initiative." Clare perched on his chair's roll arm. "Or at least, it will be as soon as Mrs. Marshall registers it. It'll raise money for informational mailings and ads, and otherwise support the continued existence of the Millers Kill Police Department."

Russ groaned. "Clare. I thought you weren't going to take on any more projects for a while." He said "projects" the way someone might say "nuclear waste." "Any spare time you have should be spent sleeping."

She didn't bother to engage with that statement. "We've been invited to a dinner party at the Langevoorts' summer home this Friday night, to confer about fundraising and tactics."

"Tactics."

Margy patted her limp and overgrown perm. "I guess that means I'll need to get Cousin Nane over to do my hair. Cocktail casual. Do you suppose that old blue shirtdress of mine's good enough?"

"Between the nursing and the baby hips, I don't know if I can fit into any of my old dresses." Clare shouldered the diaper bag. "Lucky for you, you can get away with your khakis and blue blazer."

"Great." Russ got up from the chair, still holding Ethan. "They'll go with the bag I'll need to wear over my head until people forget that press conference."

AUGUST 1952

28. "So the girl was from New York City." Jack eyeballed himself in La Belle Dame's window as he set his hat on just so.

"The *dress* was from New York." Harry couldn't tease the kid about his vanity—he himself had mastered the art of casually dropping his hat over his bald spot. "Lots of people come and go from the city. I visit there once a month."

"Really?" Jack looked impressed. "I've never been. I mean, when I was in the air force, I transited through New York. But I didn't see anything except Port Authority." He frowned. "I've never really been anywhere other than Texas for basic training and upstate."

Harry patted his shoulder. "You've been here, and you've been paying attention. That's good enough." He left his jacket slung over his arm as they began walking toward the car. "Okay, she was wearing a pricey dress from a New York City department store. What do you think might explain that?"

"You mean, other than she comes from the city and has money?"

"That's one possibility. Can you think of any others?"

Jack stepped around a sticky mess on the sidewalk where somebody had dropped an ice-cream cone. "Sure, she's local and her family's rich enough for her to shop for her clothes in New York."

"But there's been no missing persons report in our area."

Jack frowned. "She's visiting? Like one of the summer residents at Lake George or up in the mountains?"

"Again, no missing persons report. And what's-his-name, Detective Carruthers's partner, was right when he said she looked Italian or Franco. I don't know of any of that type with summer homes in these parts."

Jack nodded toward a young couple walking on the other side of the street, the girl in a fresh dress and the boy looking like a hood in jeans and a rolled-sleeve shirt. "What if she was from the city and sneaking around with a guy her parents didn't know about? I can imagine her telling her folks she's going up to Lake George with her friends Patty and Mary Lou, but really she's there with the boyfriend."

"Which means Mom and Pop might not be expecting to hear from her for a while. Good thought. What other possibilities?"

"Someone who could afford a hundred-dollar dress brought her here, or met her here."

Harry nodded. "I wouldn't dismiss the first idea, but I think the second is more likely."

"But if she wasn't a local with someone who'd notice she was missing, we're back to prostitutes and—" Jack broke off and snatched the hat from his head. "Margy!"

In front of them, a woman had just exited a shop door and was trying to tug on her gloves while juggling two large carrier bags. The bags weren't the only thing that was large—she was well along with child. She smiled at Jack, and Harry could see why the kid seemed dumbstruck. She was as cute as a Kewpie doll; tiny chin, rosy round cheeks, dimples, and a cloud of dark curls.

"Jack! I haven't seen you in I can't remember when!" From the way Jack was staring at her stomach, Harry guessed it had been at least four or five months. She finally got the gloves on and extended her hand. "Chief McNeil. I know you, but you don't know me. I'm Margy Van Alstyne."

He shook her hand. "Young Edward Van Alstyne's wife?"

"No, I'm married to his cousin, Walter."

Ah. Walt Van Alstyne. One of those golden boys who went off to fight and never seemed to get over it come peacetime. His officers had had Walt sleeping it off in the drunk tank a few times. Had trouble keeping a job, too, although if his wife was filling up shopping bags at a pricey Glens Falls store, he must be doing better.

"May I?" Harry asked, reaching toward the bags. Jack's paralysis broke and he darted forward, snatching them out of Mrs. Van Alstyne's hands.

She blinked. "Thank you, Jack. How have you been? What are you doing here?"

"We're working on a—"

Harry cut the boy off. "I'm helping Jack with some shopping. Giving him a mature point of view."

Mrs. Van Alstyne dimpled again. "I don't know if he needs that. Jack was *born* mature. He was voted 'Most Studious' for our class yearbook."

Harry smiled. "Can we walk you to your car, Mrs. Van Alstyne?"

"Thank you, yes. I'm just a couple blocks down the street." She nodded toward the bags that Jack held against his chest, like a doorman who needed one hand free. "My mother suggested finishing the layette shopping earlier rather than later, but she probably didn't mean to do it on a ninety-degree afternoon."

Harry gestured her forward. Jack crowded in on the other side of her, causing a shopper walking in the opposite direction to swerve aside and give him a filthy look.

"Sooner rather than later?" Jack waved at her very obvious belly. "You look like you're ready right now!"

Mrs. Van Alstyne blushed, and Harry glared at the kid. There were some things polite people didn't discuss right out on the street.

"Really, Jack." She set one hand atop her stomach. "If you must know, I'm due in mid-November."

"I'm sorry. I was just so . . ."

"Surprised?" She smiled. "I don't blame you." She turned toward Harry. "Walt and I have been married four years now, and this will be our first."

"Congratulations." Harry held out a hand to help her off the curb. "You must be excited."

"Oh, I am, I really am! And Walt is over the moon."

"I bet," Jack said. Harry glared at him again while handing Mrs. Van Alstyne up onto the next sidewalk.

"Oh, it's much better in the shade, isn't it?" She pointed to a worse-for-the-wear Chrysler parked beneath one of the Norway maples that lined the street. "That's mine." She opened the latch on her purse and handed Harry the keys.

He unlocked the car, leaving the driver's side door open to air it out. Jack put the bags on the passenger seat before turning to Mrs. Van Alstyne. "Margy, I apologize. In my, umm, surprise, I forgot my manners."

"Oh, Jack." She took both his hands. "It's my fault, too, for falling out of touch. Tell you what, why don't you ask Dorothy Ketchem out for Saturday next and the two of you come to our place for dinner and bridge?" She looked at him seriously. "You know she's sweet on you."

"I know." He nodded his head. "Okay. Let's do that."

She smiled. "Friends?"

"Friends."

She kissed his cheek. Harry helped her into the driver's seat—no graceful way to do that when a lady was as far gone as she was—and she rolled down the window, waving at them as she drove away.

"Friend of yours," Harry observed.

"Yeah." Jack shook himself like a wet dog. "Chief, there's a possibility we haven't considered. The dead girl wasn't wearing a ring, but that doesn't mean she wasn't married. If she was, and her husband was the one responsible for dumping her, that would explain why there's no missing persons report."

Harry nodded as he watched Mrs. Van Alstyne's car disappear down the street. "That's a thought, Jack. That's a thought."

AUGUST 1972

29. At the car, Russell had folded himself into the front seat. He had taken off his T-shirt and was pressing it against his face. Jack got in, slammed the door, and reversed down the drive. He went up the road a good half mile until they were well out of range of the farmhouse, then pulled over. "Let's see it, then."

Russell lifted his head. Jack winced. The boy's nose was bleeding, as was a cut over one eye and his split lip. "God almighty, boy, your mother's going to think I worked you over with a lead-lined hose." He shifted into drive and got back onto the road. "C'mon, we've got to get you home. If you don't get some ice on that, your face is going to puff up like a parade balloon."

Russ grunted, which Jack took for agreement. "You surprise me. He certainly got the better of you in that tangle."

Russell shook his head. "Nuh-uh." He moved his injured lip carefully around the words. "Didn't know how to fight. This"—he spread his fingers above his face—"dun't stop you."

"It doesn't stop you, huh? What does, then?"

Russell pointed. His gut, his balls. His knee, his elbow. Jack thought back to the hold the boy had on Isaac before he'd been hauled away. Russell, he realized, had been an inch away from dislocating Isaac's shoulder and shattering his elbow. He dwelt on that as he navigated through the rolling fields bright with Indian paintbrush and loosestrife, over Veterans' Bridge and into town, traffic picking up on this Monday morning, then hooking onto Old Route 100 by the river, rising north and west toward the mountains and the rough, rocky beginnings of the Hudson.

Finally, he said, "It wasn't a fair fight. I'm glad you didn't hurt him badly."

Russell flashed him a look before letting his gaze drop to his hands. "I was afraid," he mumbled.

Jack nodded. "You thought you might not be able to stop."

Russell nodded. "If you . . . hand t' hand, you're not supposed to hold back."

"But you did. You were angry, and surprised, and you still held yourself back." He glanced over at the boy. "That's the mark of a man, Russell. Self-control. Control yourself, and you control the situation. Without self-control, a man's nothing but a bully and a brute."

Russell nodded, slowly, then closed his eyes and sank into the seat. Even at that, there was still a wire strung tight through him, ready to lash him from rest at a moment's notice. *Are you that afraid they've turned you into a killer, boy?*

Jack felt about as bad as a man could feel when he knocked on Margy's door, her battered son leaning against him. He saw her face splinter with fear, and in the next moment, smooth into matter-of-fact concern, seating her boy at the kitchen table, wrapping ice cubes in a dish towel, fetching him aspirin. It was a reenactment of all those times Jack had steered her husband home, sodden with drink, and had stood by helplessly as Margy tended to the man—aspirin and water and first aid if Walter had fallen down or walked into a door.

It had created a bond and a bar between them, all those intimate scenes of bitter duty and stoic humiliation. Walter had been dead these four years, and Jack had begun to hope . . . but the sight of a lanky Van Alstyne tipped back in the kitchen chair brought it all back, Margy's tight lips and worried eyes, Jack's frustration and silence.

Just like always, he waited until after she had settled her walking wounded in bed. Like always, she returned to the kitchen and offered him coffee. This time, he took her up on it. She didn't ask him anything until they were both seated at the table, white crockery mugs in hand.

"It was my fault," he said.

Margy raised an eyebrow. "If you're the one who beat him up, you're in better shape than I thought."

He snorted. "No. The actual walloping was done by another youngster. What I meant was, it was my fault Russell was there." She gestured for him to go on. "He came to talk to me this morning. Did you know that?"

Margy shook her head wearily. "I don't seem to know much about what he's doing these days."

"I thought that might be the case. He'd remembered the name of the girl he tried to pick up at the college bar in Saratoga."

Margy folded her hands around her mug. "I told him not to go speaking to you without a lawyer present." Jack nodded. "And you did anyway."

He spread his hands. "Margy, I'm a cop. That's my job."

She ran a hand through her glossy dark curls. He noticed a few threads of silver glinting in the morning sunlight. "I'm not blaming you, Jack. I just . . ." Abruptly, she stood up. Opened a cupboard and removed an ashtray and a pack of cigarettes. "I'm trying to cut back." She sat down, leaning away from him as she lit the cigarette and inhaled. She sighed with relief and glanced to where the clock over the sink announced it was eleven. "I was hoping to get to noon today."

"I'm sorry to bring trouble to your door."

"The trouble is living with me. Go on, tell me what happened."

"I had a . . . hunch about where the dead girl may have come from. There's this hippie commune over to the old Stevenson place, and—well, never mind the details. I brought Russell along."

She stared at him. "What? Why?"

He looked down at the milky surface of his coffee. "I wanted to see what stirred up. If being there made Russell uneasy. If anyone recognized him."

Margy stood, her chair screeching back across the linoleum floor. "Get out of my house."

"Margy—"

"I mean it, Jack! That was *low*. Sneaky, scheming, *and* illegal. You were violating his Fifth Amendment rights. *And* you got him beaten up!"

"One of the kids started needling him about being in the army—"

"I don't care what caused it!" She strode to the kitchen door and flung it open.

Jack rose and set his coffee mug in the sink. "I'd like to believe he isn't responsible for that girl's death. I'm starting to develop other leads." He crossed to the doorway, stopping in front of her. "I want—I very much want—to prove him innocent."

"But if you can't, you'll go ahead and arrest him."

"Is that what you want from me? To ignore anything I find or sweep it under a rug? To throw over everything I've held true for the past twenty years?" He lowered his voice. "What if he is guilty, Margy? Do you want him to walk away whistling? Do you want him to learn there are no checks and no consequences to his temper?" They were close now, so close he could see the wetness caught in her eyelashes. "Tell me what you want me to do and I'll do it. You want

132

me to queer the investigation? Tell the girl's parents we had no leads? Pin it on somebody else? Tell me what to do. I'll do it for you."

She burst into tears. "God *damn* you, Jack Liddle!"

He folded his arms around her and held her tight against his heart while she cried. "Shh," he said. "Shh. Oh, sweetheart, don't. I'm sorry."

She pushed a little away from him and wiped her eyes with the heels of her hands. He fumbled for his handkerchief and held it out for her. She took it, wiping away the salty streaks on her cheeks, then blowing her nose. She looked at the handkerchief, then at him, dismayed.

"I have another one. A good cop always carries backup." Her bow-shaped lips quivered in an almost-smile. He put his arm around her waist again and brought his face close, their foreheads almost touching. "Margy. Sweetheart. You know I—"

She set her fingers against his mouth. "Don't. Don't say it."

He ducked a little, so he could look into her eyes. "Am I wrong? Is this all just . . . me being a fool, and you being kind?"

She shook her head. Whispered, "No."

He felt all those old routines and roadblocks tremble, on the brink of falling down, and because he wanted so badly to knock them over he stayed silent. Margy was right, trouble lived at her house, and he wasn't going to add to it. He held her for a moment more—that much he'd allow himself—then stepped back.

"Next time, if I need to talk with him, I'll come here."

She nodded.

"I think it'd be good for him to spend time around men who don't . . . make war for a living. I know your dad and Mr. Van Alstyne are both passed, but somebody." The boy had spent the last two years being shown one way to be a man. He needed to see another, and, although Jack would never say it aloud, he was certain Walter hadn't stepped up to the plate while Russell was growing up.

Margy nodded. Smiled a little. "You'd better come here for that, too, then."

30. Russ took the morning Cossayuharie patrol so Hadley could meet with the town lawyer. He was pretty sure she'd have rather walked the route barefoot than spend the time with an attorney, but they were all making sacrifices these days. Midweek after what passed for the morning rush hour in the country, his was practically the only vehicle on the road, and he was preparing to turn back toward town when his radio cracked on. "Fifteen-fifty-seven? Dispatch."

He keyed the mic. "Dispatch, this is fifteen-fifty-seven, go ahead."

"Shirley Bain's called a couple times. Thinks a drug gang's moved into the old Cunningham place."

Russ rolled his eyes. "That's at least two miles from her house. Usually she goes for something closer to home." Mrs. Bain was a sweet old lady who called the police several times a year, convinced she was being menaced by vagrants, thieves, and criminals. The calls inevitably happened when her son, who lived in Manhattan, had failed to check in with her for a few months. They had a standard form saved for her; just change the date and the particular bump or rattle that had set her off and she was ready to forward it to her negligent offspring, who would up stakes and visit for a weekend to make sure she was okay. Lather, rinse, and repeat.

"I'm still in Cossayuharie, Harlene. I'll take it." He decided to check out the long-abandoned Cunningham house first, so when he stopped by Mrs. Bain's, he could assure her that no, the farmhouse up the road wasn't being used as a drug depot, or biker gang headquarters, or brothel. Actually, that last was a possibility, in that some teenagers might have discovered the shuttered house was the perfect sheltered spot to play a little slap-and-tickle.

His first glimpse of the place made him wonder if Shirley Bain had seen something that wasn't just in her imagination. The heavily overgrown drive had been cut back, and a double row of squashed and dirty grasses showed where a vehicle or vehicles had passed through to the house. Russ bumped slowly up the ruts, emerging through the

134

hedgelike tangle of bramble and saplings into the sunny meadow surrounding the house. There were no other cars at the end of the long drive, but the house had clearly seen visitors recently. Several windows were propped open with squared-off sticks, and old sun-faded drapes were puffing and flapping in the warm summer wind. One of the front steps had been pried clean off, the punky boards tossed in the grass next to a hammer and a can of nails. Russ tested the step above before putting his weight on it. The porch planking had also been decimated, empty spaces gaping, a handsaw left near the edge. Russ could see fresh cuts where someone had been sawing off the ragged, pulpy ends of the still-intact boards.

Balanced between the gaps, he knocked on the door. No answer. He tried the handle. It turned. He swung the door open onto a wide center hallway containing a sixty-pound bag of plaster, mixing buckets and drop cloths, and a box filled with measuring tapes, a level, and assorted paddles and draggers for plastering. The place was clean of dust and cobwebs, the floor swept and the windows clean. He turned back toward the door and spotted a cooler with a travel mug resting on top.

Either the house was the hangout for super-neat Girl Scouts getting their wall repair badges, or it had been sold. He'd tell Mrs. Bain and she could come over with a bag of her chocolate-chip cookies and meet the new folks. When he got back to town, he'd double-check with Roxanne Lunt—if the Realtor hadn't sold the property herself, she'd know who had.

He was on the porch, watching his steps to keep from falling through, when he heard the voice.

"Hey, there. Find what you were looking for?"

Russ almost stumbled. He glanced up just long enough to see an old man in jeans and a plaid shirt. Keeping his eyes on his feet, he crossed the remains of the porch. "Sorry to trespass. Your neighbor up the road saw some activity and asked us to check it out." He jumped off the steps and headed toward the man. "I'm Russ Van Alstyne, chief of—" The old man was grinning at him. Washed-out blue eyes, heavy grooves, thick-set shoulders—"Chief Liddle!" Russ felt himself straightening like a rookie at parade drill.

"Nice to see you again, Russell." Liddle held out his hand. "Nice to see you in the uniform. Suits you."

Russ's right arm twitched with the effort of not saluting. He took Liddle's hand and shook. "It's a pleasure to see you again, Chief. What are you doing here?"

Liddle looked up at him. "Is that question personal? Or professional?"

"Oh." Russ gestured toward the house. "Shirley Bain lives down the road. Winton Bain's widow, you know?"

"I know Shirley, ayup."

"She gets a little, uh, gun-shy when she sees or hears something amiss. So I came out to check everything over, let her know she didn't have anything to worry about."

"Good." Liddle slapped his arm. "That's good, old-fashioned community policing."

Russ felt his face warm from the praise.

"As to why I'm here, my mother was a Cunningham before she was wed. This was my grandparents' house. It went to my aunt, and when she passed, to her grandkids. My cousins once removed? Second cousins? Anyway, the four of them never could agree on what to do with the place. None of 'em even live on the East Coast by now. My wife died last year and I was looking to leave Florida—never liked the place, only moved there 'cause Dorothy wanted—and they offered to let me have it for a fair market price less the back taxes owed."

Russ tilted his head to look at the roof. Both chimneys were marred by cracked bricks and the asphalt shingles were curled and mossy. "So . . . about fifty bucks, then?"

Liddle laughed. "Not much more! I like working with my hands, though."

"I remember."

"I never did settle to the sort of hobbies everyone else does in retirement. I figure this place'll keep me busy from now until the day they carry me out feet-first."

"You should pay a visit to my mother. Talk about not settling for hobbies. I had to arrest her once for an unpermitted demonstration."

Liddle laughed. "That sounds like M—your mom."

"Have you been to see her? How long have you been in town?"

"'Bout a week. I've got my RV over at Lockland's Whispering Pines, been busy trekking back and forth between here, there, and that new Home Depot they've got over to Fort Henry." A gust of wind swept over the meadow, shivering the grass and the Queen Anne's lace. The leaves on the maples and ash trees reversed, showing their paler undersides to the sky. "I didn't know if I ought to look her up. I don't want to make her uncomfortable."

Russ shook his head. "No, no, no. She was never anything but grateful for the way you treated my dad. And for what you did for me."

Liddle smiled sideways. "I saw you on the news last night. Speaking of doing for you."

Russ winced. "I'm not a great public speaker."

The older man grew serious. "Is it true, then? There's been another death? Like before?"

"Identical. To both times. I'm treating them as connected."

Liddle frowned. "Bit of a stretch, considering the first girl was found—what, fifty-five years ago?"

"Thereabouts. *You* treated the cases as related."

"Except there wasn't much to go on from the '52 death. Chief McNeil did the best he could, but he was hog-tied by that piss-poor state investigation." He looked up at Russ. "Have you questioned anyone working at the county fair?"

"You mean the carnies? No. I didn't think it was a likely avenue. First, it's hard to imagine anyone still working those rides who had been here in 1972. And second, you never got anything definitive from them."

"I never got anything definitive on anyone, Russell, which is why you're still listed as a person of interest in that old file."

Russ pinched the bridge of his nose beneath his glasses.

"Chief McNeil had a theory that the girl might have come from the traveling show," Liddle went on. "Now, Natalie wasn't with the carnies, but she was as in the wind as it was possible to get back then; no last name, no fixed residence, no past, no future plans." He sighed. "Not that she had a future."

"You remember her."

Liddle pierced him with a look, and Russ realized the old man's eyes weren't faded as he had first thought. Not faded at all. "I remember every detail of the ones I couldn't save. Don't you?"

Russ thought of the dumpster in Stuttgart, and the bag, slick with rancid lettuce and potato peelings, and the baby inside the bag. "Yeah," he said. "I do."

"Have you got an identity on your victim?"

"Not yet. That's why I made an ass of myself on TV. I was hoping getting the girl's picture out might open up a lead."

"Try the midway and the county fair. It's damn hard for anyone to slip between the cracks these days, but those folks can come pretty close."

Another swirl of wind stirred the leaves. The ancient curtains fluttered out the open windows. "I will." Russ turned to go, the words "see you around" in his mouth, when he realized that wasn't enough. "Come to dinner Friday night." He could count on one hand the number of times he'd spontaneously invited someone to his home. "I'd like you to meet my wife and my son. Well. He's not like a grown son. He's a baby."

Liddle's eyebrows went up, but he didn't say anything.

"We'll have Mom over. Trust me, with Clare there, you won't feel awkward for more than a minute." He could feel himself smiling without meaning to. "She has a way of lighting everything up."

Liddle rubbed the back of his neck. "Well . . . it does sound better than another can of Dinty Moore in my RV. And you can give me the lowdown on this resolution the town's putting up for vote." He looked Russ up and down. "I'd hate for you to be the last man to put on that uniform."

31.   Russ suspected it wouldn't be as easy to get information from the midway workers as it had been back in Chief McNeil's day, when cops could show up, play the heavy, and get what they wanted. He was right. Pointed toward the management office—a large RV at the edge of the fairgrounds that also seemed to be

the manager's home—he was met by a guy who looked like a pugilist out of an old boxing movie, short and powerful, with a huge strapband chest and arms like a stack of boulders. He was maybe five or ten years older than Russ, but he still looked like a man you wouldn't want to meet in a dark alley. Or a deserted country road.

"Trouble?" He stood in the doorway, blocking Russ's view of the room within.

"I hope not. I'm Chief Van Alstyne of the Millers Kill Police Department—"

"I know who you are. I saw you on the TV last night."

Russ kept his face still, but he could feel the tips of his ears heat up. "You've got the advantage of me, then. You are . . . ?"

"Brent Hill. I'm the manager." He stepped back and the door shut in Russ's face. Russ blinked, frowned, and put his hand on his gun. He had just keyed on his radio to alert Harlene when the door swung open and Hill reemerged, a thin stack of papers in his hand.

"Chief?" the radio said.

"Ten-two, dispatch. Over." He slapped the mic onto its Velcro patch. "Mr. Hill—"

"I'm required to show law enforcement officers the following documents. State license." He handed a paper to Russ. "State Department of Employment compliance records." Two pages. "Department of Health and Safety and Department of Environmental Protection certifications." Two more pages. "State tax registration and vendor's license. County registration and permit. Town permit." He handed the rest of the papers to Russ.

"Mr. Hill." Russ didn't try to keep the annoyance out of his voice. "I'm not here about paying your taxes or dumping your fry oil. I'm trying to identify a young woman who was found dead in Cossayuharie on Saturday. Your midway was already on site and setting up that Friday."

"Anything other than my permits, you're going to need a warrant for." The door closed in Russ's face. Again. This time, he banged hard against the fiberglass. The door swung open. "Was I not clear? No warrant, no questions, no searches, no looking around. And don't try to talk to my people behind my back. They'll just send you here."

"Mr. Hill—" Desperate for leverage, Russ shook the papers in his hand. "What about your certifications?"

"Keep 'em. They're copies." With that, the door slammed shut, and no amount of knocking could get Hill to come out again.

Swearing under his breath, Russ retreated to his cruiser, where he called Lyle. "I need you to get a warrant for Rusty's Amusements. I want to be able to see their employment records and talk to the personnel. I've been blocked by the manager."

"Which unit?"

"Which unit of what?"

Lyle's voice was patient. "There are three individual units. East, West, and South. Rusty's is their corporate owner."

Russ looked through the sheaf of papers. "Uh . . . East."

"Great. Now, do you have any suspicions or reasons that might induce Ryswick to give it up?"

"Check the '72 report. Chief Liddle questioned the carnies back then. See if there's any mention of Brent Hill."

"That's it?"

"Be creative. And fast." Russ hung up. He decided to stroll around and chat with the hired help a bit. Despite Hill's assurances, some of them might be willing to open up. At the very least, he could get Italian sausage with onions and peppers for lunch.

32. Joni Langevoort had already proved her worth to Clare by agreeing to take Elizabeth de Groot's Wednesday sick visits, allowing Elizabeth to hold down the office, enabling Clare to help out at the county fair fish fry. She had already had childcare arranged for Ethan in the form of Russ's niece, Emma. The cascading responsibilities gave Clare a headache, but not nearly as bad as the pain she'd have if she had to scare up a babysitter later in the week. For a moment she let herself remember the kick of the go-pills she had brought back from her deployment—amphetamines—and how they would sweep through her brain like a broom taking down cob-webs in a cellar. *God,* she craved a little help sometimes.

Elizabeth had pointed out there was volunteer coverage for all the hours the booth was in operation, but Clare tried to make a personal appearance at every outreach program, musical event, or fundraiser the church had. She doubted any customers would be suddenly struck with the urge to convert, but a welcoming smile and some friendly small talk could go a long way in leaving a good impression of the local Episcopal community. Clare genuinely enjoyed serving food and meeting people face-to-face.

Unfortunately, she wasn't face-to-face with anything except a cooler full of ice and halibut. "I can't feel my fingers," she said, scooping fish out and dropping them into a galvanized tub of cold water barely warmer than the ice cubes. "I think I'm getting frostbite."

Anne Vining-Ellis, who had emptied her cooler twice as fast as Clare, dumped her remaining ice on the dusty grass beside their tent. "Let me see." She examined Clare's hands. "You're fine. Get back to work, you whiner."

"You're a hard woman, Dr. Anne."

"Rhode Island breeds 'em hard."

It was, in fact, Dr. Anne's hometown connections that enabled the St. Alban's annual fish-fry lunch at the county fair. Two of her cousins were commercial fishermen out of North Kingston, and they sold the church haddock and redfish at cost. Their little refrigerator truck made the trip from Rhode Island to Washington County early every morning; thus the hand-lacquered wooden sign above their tent: NEW ENGLAND FISH FRY—FRESH CAUGHT TODAY.

They would begin serving lunch in forty-five minutes, so preparations were in full swing. Clare and Anne were decanting the second wave of fish; the tubful that had defrosted earlier was beneath a long Formica ta-ble. Anne's son Will and her husband, Chris, passionate fishermen both, were beheading, skinning, and boning the haddock. At another table, Delia Hall was grating cabbage and carrots for the coleslaw while Celia Wakefield whipped pickle and lemon juice into mayonnaise.

Doug Young was carefully pouring thirty pounds of frozen French fries into individual wire baskets next to the still-lidded fryer. The two other fry cooks, both of whom had been doing the annual job long before Clare had become their rector, were outside setting up tables and folding chairs beneath the large pop-up tent that was their dining area.

Clare dumped her ice and tried to rub some feeling back into her hands with a soggy towel. "Now what? More fish?"

"Not until these have a chance to defrost." Anne headed to the commercial-size boxes of picnic goods: five thousand paper plates, ten thousand plastic utensils. "Let's set the tables and put the rest of the dinnerware where the guys can reach what they need."

Clipping checkerboard tablecloths in place and squaring napkins into baskets, Clare couldn't see when the guys turned the old fry-o-lator on, but she sure could smell it. First the slick of hot grease, then the mouthwatering odor of meal-covered fillets, just the way Mother used to make them. Grandmother, in her case.

She got the knives and forks into their canisters on the prep table and switched out her plastic apron for a clean cotton one just in time for the first wave of customers. The next hour passed in a blur of serving food, busing tables, restocking the fry cooks, and another turn at defrosting fish. After that last, Dr. Anne tossed her a tube of hand lotion and said, "Why don't you take a break? You haven't seen any of the fair yet."

"I'm not going to argue with you on that one." Clare rubbed the cream into her reddened knuckles and put the container on the table. "I'll be back in twenty." She ducked out of the tent, rounded the refrigerator truck, and was free.

The day was brilliantly sunny and blessedly dry, with a breeze off the western mountains, which made the heat bearable. Clare gave Emma a quick call to check in, and was informed Ethan had played most of the morning, taken his bottle, and was now sleeping like a marathoner after a training run. He always seemed to sleep better with Emma or Margy. Clare tried not to think of Dr. Underkirk saying her own anxiety was probably manifesting itself in her child's behavior. She needed to work on keeping a calm, clear head. Well, wasn't that what she was doing right now? Twenty minutes of no responsibilities, just enjoying the beautiful day and the faces of happy people all around her.

She wasn't interested in the midway, so she skirted the edge of the exhibitors' lot—cars and horse trailers and trucks parked in haphazard rows atop flattened grass—and struck out for the craft displays. Unlike the food tents and the midway, the exhibit halls were year-round structures, high-roofed enough so that with the help of strategically placed fans, they remained comfortable in the August heat. Strolling past pies and breads and pastries on display and lingering over the jams and preserves was almost as relaxing as a glass of wine. Cooking was the only domestic art she could claim, although you wouldn't know it by her recent efforts. Since Ethan had been born, her repertoire consisted of whichever grain or pasta she could boil in under ten minutes, some chopped veggies, and canned tuna. Deep breath. *Calm mind. Quiet mind.*

She picked up an informational brochure on home canning in the almost-certainly vain hope she might do something creative with the tomatoes coming out of her mother-in-law's garden. In the same vein, she took recipe cards she probably wouldn't use and entered her name for a set of cookware she didn't need.

With one more longing glance at the homemade pies, she headed back to the St. Alban's fish fry, this time by the direct route through the midway. She had never cared for the carnival side of fairs; the music was too loud, the rides couldn't compare to actually flying, and if she wanted a cheap stuffed animal, she'd get it in a store. She could feel a headache coming on as she pressed through the milling crowds of people to the accompaniment of lights and bells and shouts from the game booths.

She bought a coffee from the First Lutheran Church stand—in her heart, she felt the Lutherans always had the best coffee—and was shamelessly spooning too much sugar in when she heard her husband's voice from behind her.

"Hey, lady. Buy a poor guy a cup of joe?"

She spun around. "What are you doing here?"

He grinned at her. "Nice to see you, too, darlin'."

She laid a couple dollars on the counter for Russ's coffee. "You know what I mean. How come you're not tracking down leads?"

"You mean doing legwork?" He held up his heavily shod foot and wiggled it back and forth.

"You're never going to let me live that down, are you?"

"Nope." He accepted his cup, adding as much sugar as Clare had. One of the many reasons she loved him. "And I am *developing* leads."

"At the Washington County Fair." She didn't try to keep the skepticism out of her voice. "You think one of the 4-H'ers did her in?"

"The traveling show came up in the prior investigations in '52 and '72. I thought it would be a good idea to check it out." He headed toward the midway's main drag and Clare fell in step beside him.

"Did the previous investigations find anything to link the girls' deaths to the carnival?"

"Well . . ."

"So essentially, you're just repeating fifty-year-old prejudices against carnival workers, right? Because they have tattoos and travel around, they must be suspect?" They swung wide to avoid three summer camp counselors attempting to corral their charges.

"No," he protested. "Hell, the kids at the high school have more tattoos than carnies nowadays. But this is the same show that's been setting up here in Washington County for the past sixty years. And the killings, if that's what they are, all happened while the fair was going on."

As they passed between the Tilt-A-Whirl and a sno-cone truck, Clare had to raise her voice to be heard over the pop songs keeping the beat with the rattle of the ride machinery. "*If* they were killings?"

"Dr. Scheeler hasn't ruled out some sort of overdose."

Clare raised an eyebrow. "Three young women who happen to OD under identical circumstances, decades apart?"

"Yeah, that's my thought, too." Russ took a drink of his coffee. "Anyway, the manager wasn't willing to let me take a look at the personnel files, so while I'm waiting for Lyle to show up with a warrant, I thought I'd stroll around and take in the sights."

"And question people without permission?"

"I need a warrant to get into the *files*. I don't need any permission to walk around a public place and talk with folks." He gave a grin that showed his eyeteeth. "After all, it's not like they can't tell I'm a cop." He tapped his badge.

Clare tried not to smile. "I appreciate you taking time from your interrogations to walk me back to the St. Alban's booth."

He ducked to avoid a faceful of helium balloons. "Actually, I'm walking this way because I want to talk to the guy running the shooting booth. There was a girl working the taffy apples who said he'd been sneaking away and acting shifty. She thought he might be dealing. Granted, she clearly didn't like the guy, but she may be onto something."

"Or she may be an ex-girlfriend."

He grinned. "Watch out, darlin'. My cynicism is rubbing off on you."

"Believe me, nobody knows more about the vagaries of the human condition than priests."

He nodded toward a *Wild West Shoot-Out!* sign. "This is my stop."

She kissed him. "If you can, come by the St. Alban's booth. We're down that way, close to the vendor parking. Fried fish lunch. For you, no cost."

"That's the best offer I'll have all day. Do I need to check in with Emma?"

"No, I called her. Ethan went down for his nap with no trouble."

Russ didn't say anything, but she could read his expression. *Still sure day care's not the right choice?* She waved as she walked away. No, she wasn't sure day care wasn't the right choice. Parents were supposed to go by their gut feelings, right? But how was she to know if her gut was acting in Ethan's best interests, or only out of guilt? Maybe they could compromise, and get a caretaker to stay with Ethan at home. But what if they went to the trouble of vetting and hiring a woman and then, God forbid, the towns voted to close the police department? No way her salary and Russ's army pension would stretch to cover a nanny, not to mention the possibility they'd have to move for a new job for Russ—she pressed her hands against her forehead. *Quiet mind. Calm mind.*

The noises behind her broke through her self-absorption. Over the shrieks of riders and the cries of barkers, she could hear shouts. She spun around to see a young carny racing down the midway road, headed straight for her. Or—she glanced to where she could see the St. Alban's tent behind her—the parking area.

Fairgoers were leaping out of his way, leaving a mingled roar of "Hey!" and "Watch it!" and "What the hell?" in his wake. And behind that, Russ, pounding down the lane.

One glimpse told her he wouldn't be able to overtake the sprinting man. She didn't have time to think; she acted. She stepped back as if to get out of the carny's path, then launched herself at him in a full-body tackle.

He barreled into her, toppling them both, thudding, rolling, and then he was squirming out of her grip, up on his hands, knee in the dust, boot on the road, and then he lurched sideways, breaking her hold.

But it was enough. Russ raced past her and slammed into the young man with eighty pounds more than she could muster. This time, the carny stayed down. Russ, straddling his back, pulled his arms behind him and hitched him with handcuffs. "Clare, are you okay?"

She got up, swiping at her blouse in a vain attempt to get the dust off. "I'm fine."

He stood up, hauling the carny with him. "Kid, you're under arrest for resisting—" He broke off as he turned the young man around. Skinhead shave, short beard, tattoos around his neck.

Clare sucked in her breath. *"Kevin?"*

33. The crowd was coalescing around them. Reverend Clare was staring at him, eyes wide, mouth open, and Kevin knew her next words would be, "What on earth are you doing here?" The chief's grip was already loosening on his collar.

So he head-butted the chief. Kevin didn't have enough leverage to make much of a dent, but Van Alstyne stumbled back, his hand automatically tightening, yanking Kevin along with him. Kevin let himself fall against the chief's chest. "Arrest me. Make it look good." He pitched his voice just loud enough for the chief to hear.

Van Alstyne spun him around and put him in a hold. "That was a bad mistake, kid. Assaulting an officer." The chief searched him for weapons, brutally and efficiently. "Say good-bye to your job, 'cause you're going to be sitting tight in jail when the show moves on." He shoved, and Kevin staggered forward.

Reverend Clare was right in front of them, hands on her hips. "Russ?"

The chief walked Kevin past her, aiming for the parking area. "Stay out of it, Clare." Kevin shook his head slightly. "No, wait. Come with me so I can take your statement." He raised his voice to be heard over the throng. "Anyone else want to come down to the station and fill out a complaint?"

That was more effective at crowd dispersal than a gas canister. Kevin kept going, Van Alstyne's hand hard against his back, head hanging down in defeat—which also made it harder for anyone to get a clear look at his face.

He could hear a ripping sound as the chief unhooked his shoulder mic. "Dispatch, this is fifteen-fifty-seven, come in."

"Go, fifteen-fifty-seven." Kevin had to bite his lip to stop his smile at the sound of Harlene's voice.

"Dispatch, requesting available unit to transport an arrestee at the fair, over."

"Why can't you do it yourself? Over."

The chief muttered beneath his breath. "Because I'm waiting on Lyle for that warrant, *over*."

"Don't get your britches in a knot." There was a long pause. "Okay, fifteen-thirty is on his way with the paperwork. He can do the pickup when he gets there. O-ver."

"Thanks for your cooperation. Fifteen-fifty-seven out." The sound of the chief's satisfaction as he got the last word was enough to tip Kevin over. He bent double, coughing like he had end-stage TB to keep from laughing.

"Ke— Kid, are you okay?" And just like that, the concern in Van Alstyne's voice swung him from hilarity to grief. He felt as if a great hole was opening beneath his feet. He gasped, and to his horror, burst into tears.

"Russ, he needs help."

"Mmm. I think I know what it is. Will you go distract the folks at your lunch counter while I get him to the parking area? I don't want anyone to see him. Come meet me out past the horse vans when you can."

"All right."

Kevin heaved for breath, trying to control himself. The chief steered him forward, sideways, forward, sideways, and Kevin realized there was grass beneath his feet and dozing trucks and caravans around him. "Hang on," the chief said, and there was a click and his arms were free. "Go ahead and sit down. No one can see us here."

Kevin collapsed, wiping his eyes. "God, I'm sorry."

Van Alstyne sat down more carefully. "How long have you been undercover?"

"All summer."

"Twenty-four/seven?"

Kevin nodded.

"Jesus. That's hard." The chief squeezed his shoulder. "Sometimes, when you get out from under, it hits you that way. It's just a reaction to having to be so in control the rest of the time."

"Thanks." He blew his nose on the bottom of his T-shirt. *Sorry, Mom.*

The chief smiled a little. "So you're obviously not patrolling the streets of Syracuse. Can you tell me what's up?"

"Yeah." Kevin recrossed his legs and tipped his head back against the warm edge of a tire. "I'm working for the State Task Force on Domestic Extremism. Detailed from the SPD."

"That's a pretty short time from being the new transfer to serious undercover work."

"I volunteered."

The chief snorted. "*That,* I figured."

"They really needed guys who looked like they could be in their late teens or early twenties. I've always had a young face."

"True. So what are you doing *here*? Trying to disguise yourself a few miles away from your hometown—that takes brass balls."

Kevin laughed. "Believe me, I didn't mean to wind up here. There's a National Socialist group in Syracuse, so the city is a center point for organized neo-Nazis. But those are the old guys, the ones who go to meetings and make crappy handouts." He held out a hand as if offering Van Alstyne a booklet. "The real growth, and the scary stuff, are the guys who are on the Internet."

"Like Stormfront?"

Kevin nodded. "There are cesspits online that make Stormfront look like ladies swapping knitting patterns. That's how I got started last winter, in the computer crimes unit." He automatically patted his pocket for his cigarettes. "Most of the losers posting are just jerking each other off—they'll never do anything in real life."

"But there are others . . ." the chief offered.

Kevin nodded. "Who need a way to hook up. To transport arms and drugs. They make their bank by drug sales."

"Rusty's Amusements?"

"They've got guys on the inside. It's pretty anonymous—we're in one place for a week and then move on. So I got hired by Rusty's— that's a story in and of itself—and I was supposed to be working for a unit that's traveling through the western part of the state. Chittenango and Wyoming counties."

"But . . ."

"But at the last minute, they needed a bunker man here. So they got me."

"And you got an ulcer worrying about someone recognizing you."

Kevin stroked his beard. "I practically guzzled Miracle-Gro to get this to come in faster."

The chief laughed.

"Russ?"

Van Alstyne stood up, groaning a little. "Over here, Clare." He waved a hand. Reverend Clare rounded the rear of the van and immediately dropped to her knees beside Kevin. "It *is* you." She hugged him fiercely. "Are you all right? *Please* tell me those horrible tattoos aren't real."

"They're not." Kevin laughed. "At least, not all of them."

"Thank goodness." She sat back on her heels. "What can we do to help you?"

He glanced up at the chief. "Can you book me and keep me overnight?"

Van Alstyne frowned. "If you go into the county jail, you're almost guaranteed to be recognized by somebody you had a run-in with over the past five years."

"I mean, not really. But if you just release me after resist and battery, it's going to look weird."

"Why did you run?" Reverend Clare asked.

"Word was there was a cop walking around asking questions. When I saw the chief headed toward my game—" He ran his hand over the stubble on his head. "I just didn't trust him not to out me." He looked up at Van Alstyne. "Sorry."

"No need to apologize. I might have without meaning to." The chief reached a hand down and hoisted Reverend Clare to her feet. "Keeping you for a while would be useful. There's a possible connection between the show and a case in progress. I'd like to go over it with you, get your input. The question is, why should I let you go after a twenty-four-hour hold?"

Kevin grinned as he stood up. "I thought Reverend Clare could talk you into it. You know, sort of a Christian ministry?" He turned to the chief. "My backstory is that I have a juvie record, but no arrests as an adult."

"So I plead for a poor boy who made some unfortunate choices so he doesn't lose his job?"

Van Alstyne looked at his wife. "You have to admit, it sounds just like you."

"I can give him a ride back to the fair tomorrow," Reverend Clare said. "That ought to seal the deal."

"Sounds like a plan." The chief kissed her briefly. "Back to the fish for you, darlin'." The Reverend Clare waved as she disappeared

around the corner of the van. The chief pulled out his handcuffs. "Okay, Kevin. I never thought I'd be saying this, but get ready for your perp-march." He grinned. "I can't wait to hear what everybody back at the station has to say about your new look."

34. Swapping Kevin for a records warrant went smoothly, mostly due to Lyle's years of experience. Russ doubted there was anything that could surprise him; certainly not their former junior officer decked out like a hipster skinhead. The deputy raised his bushy eyebrows and said, "Guess I'll hear your story in the car, kid. Get in."

The interview with Brent Hill was less of a seamless experience. Judge Ryswick, as usual, had issued a very focused warrant, compelling Hill to allow Russ to compare the current employment records with the copy Chief Liddle had made in '72 and examine those that matched. Hill read through it standing in the door to his trailer, and only after he finished did he step aside to let Russ in. It was a tiny office, almost overwhelmed by a large desk and—Russ did a double take—a safe in the corner. A series of shelves held a printer, stacks of manuals, and what looked like a CB radio rig. Two chairs; one well-worn and comfortable, one plastic.

Russ took the plastic seat across from Hill, who unlocked a drawer and tossed a manila folder onto the desk. Russ opened it and spread the papers out. "Old-fashioned."

"Oh, I got a laptop." Hill thumbed toward the shelves. "But when you're on the road every week from Memorial Day to mid-October, you don't want to trust important stuff to a computer. Generator fails, or we got no Wi-Fi, and then what? Besides, I got most of it in my head." He tapped his skull. "F'rinstance, I can tell you right now the only matches you're going to find are me and Joe LaVoie, who sells tickets." He twisted and his spine cracked audibly. "Rigging and striking a carnival's a young man's game. Once you've sprained your shoulder or strained your back a few too many times, you're gone."

Russ adjusted his glasses and began comparing names. "So why is it you're still here?"

Hill laughed. "I'm the owner. Whadja think? Rusty was my dad. He had me work every job there is in a show, starting when I was fifteen. Used to say if you were going to run a carnival, you had to be able to fix a class-C ride at night in the rain with nothing but a wrench and a spool of electrical wire."

"Sounds like a smart man."

"Oh, he was. Built this up from five rides and a Skee-Ball alley into the biggest show in New York."

"And what about Joe LaVoie? Why's he still here?"

"Joe's always been the inside money guy. He did accounting for my dad. Now he's retired, he drives his RV up from Florida in the spring and works the circuit with me till fall. He's reliable and honest, which is a premium in a cash-only business."

Russ jotted down Hill's and LaVoie's information. "You lose much from the other ticket takers?"

Hill propped his elbows on the desk. "I assume every gal sitting in a booth is skimming at least three to five percent and handing it over to her boyfriend."

"That's a lot of shrinkage." Russ slid his finger down and down the list of names, birth dates, social security numbers.

"What can I do? I fire 'em if I can catch 'em."

"What about this guy?" Russ tapped the paper. "Aaron Kaspertzy? I've got a Jim Kaspertzy listed in 1972."

"Aaron's dad. The carnival business gets into the family blood sometimes, you know?"

Russ handed Chief Liddle's list to Hill. "Anyone else here who has a kid or a relation working in the show now?"

Hill looked over the old police report, shaking his head. "Nope. Not here. I got a couple guys in the western unit whose parents both worked for my dad, but nobody in this show."

"Okay." Russ squared the papers and handed them back to Hill. "Thank you for your cooperation."

"You're welcome. Now I got a question for you. You picked up one

of my guys today. Do I need to find somebody to take his job for the rest of the season? Because thet's gonna be a pain in my ass."

Russ paused, as if weighing his decision. "He ran from questioning. And resisted arrest."

"So he's stupid. And by the way, I told you not to be talking with my people. Is he wanted? Didja find anything on him?"

"No. And no." He looked at Hill. "You know he's got a juvenile record?"

"In a carnival, it'd be surprising to find a kid who *didn't*. C'mon. He's a hard worker. I need him."

Russ frowned. "I'll consider it." He opened the door and paused. "Oh, one other thing."

"Yeah?"

"Can you tell me where you were last Friday night?"

35. It sounded like a party was in progress in the squad room. Coming down the hallway, Hadley checked her watch: five o'clock. Yeah, it was time for the evening debrief. For a moment she was seized by a sickening fear—her ex had sent more tapes, or pictures, or something awful, and right now her past was on display to her fellow officers, and they were laughing, and she didn't have enough strength to go through this *again*—and then she heard the chief say something in a teasing voice, and she knew it was all right.

She punched in her number and hung her squad car keys in the cabinet before entering the room. It was more full than usual—all of second shift and half of third—and everyone was clustered around someone in the middle. Harlene turned and saw her and said, "Oh, my gosh! Hadley, you better get over here and see what the cat dragged in."

"I'm the cat in this story," the chief added. He waved her forward and Eric and the dep stepped out of the way and she was face-to-face with Flynn for the first time in seven months.

At least, she thought it was Flynn. She stared at the beard, the barely there hair, and the *tattoos, my God,* twining down his arms and around his neck. Only his eyes, wary and waiting, were the same.

"Well, hell," she finally got out. "It's the evil Flynn from the *Star Trek* Mirror Universe."

The room exploded with laughter. "She's got it," Eric crowed. "Kevin's evil twin!"

The chief held up his hands. "Okay, everybody, let's settle down and get this briefing over with." Several of the guys slapped Flynn on the back as he headed to what had been his seat when he was in the department. The chief hitched himself up on the table. "First, for those of you who didn't hear it earlier, Kevin is working undercover for the State Task Force on Domestic Extremism, courtesy of the Syracuse PD, and it's extremely important you tell no one about seeing him here. At least, about seeing *Officer* Flynn here. Kevin, what's your cover name?"

"Kevin Flynn."

The chief looked at him.

"Do you know how many Kevin Flynns are out there? It's the Irish-American version of John Smith."

"I'll take your word on it. At any rate, *evil* Kevin is supposedly on twenty-four-hour hold. He'll be released back to Rusty's Amusements tomorrow. In the meantime, I've brought him up to date on our Jane Doe investigation, and he's agreed to help out with any information he can provide." The chief pointed toward Noble. "Noble, how are we doing on identifying the victim?"

"No luck at the motels and the amusement parks," Noble said. "We got a *lot* of calls after the TV interview, and I'm running those down."

"Anything that stands out as likely?"

"Nope."

"Probably the usual fruits and nuts," MacAuley said.

"Knox."

She took a breath to make sure her voice was completely normal. "After spending the last two days in the company of rapists, Peeping Toms, and up-skirt fetish boys, I'm sorry to say I haven't found any we can bring in for questioning. As much as I'd like to." In the back of the room, Urquhart said something beneath his breath.

"Paul?" Van Alstyne said. "You have something to share with the team?"

"No, Chief."

"Good. Knox, every possibility we can cross off brings us that much closer to the answer."

"Except when it doesn't," the dep said.

The chief gave him a look. "Thank you, Lyle. Eric, how are we doing on the technology front?"

"All the cell numbers within the tower triangulation check out as local. Mostly kids texting."

"Which suggests, but doesn't confirm, that she was killed elsewhere and dumped." He pinched the bridge of his nose beneath his glasses. "If we had security cameras on our roads, this case would be closed by now."

"Dream on," MacAuley said. "It took four years and a fatal accident to get a new light out on Sacandaga."

Noble frowned. "With the number of road miles we've got, I don't think the town could afford security cameras for 'em all, Chief."

"Or for any." Van Alstyne sighed. "I was just blowing off steam, Noble. How about the dress?"

The dep looked at his notes. "It's a brand called Tory Burch, which I guess is a thing. The main store's in New York, but of course you can buy it online, so it could have been purchased anywhere. It cost four hundred bucks, which the lady I spoke with said was midline. Seems pretty damn expensive to me."

Everyone looked at Hadley. "Really?" she said. "Because I'm a girl? I do all my shopping at Goodwill, don't ask me."

"Okay. So it was either a big splurge for someone like us, or a moderate expense for the summer people." The chief nodded toward the whiteboard, where MacAuley had written names and info in bright blue. "We have two men who were persons of interest back in '72 who are still living here—three if you count me. Neither Terry McKellan nor Isaac Nevinson have particularly sound alibis; a waitress at Harborside Burgers recognized McKellan's picture but couldn't place him on the date"—he looked at Noble, who nodded—"and Nevinson's daughter vouches for him but . . ."

"They seemed very tight when I interviewed her," MacAuley said. "He's the one who raised her after the parents split up."

Paul piped up from the back. "What about your alibi, Chief?"

Van Alstyne smiled a little. "I have a priest who can testify as to my whereabouts."

"Doesn't get much better than that," the dep said. "What about the other POI from '72? The carnival?"

"Two guys who were here that summer and are back again; a seventy-four-year-old retiree named Joe LaVoie and the owner, Brent Hill, who's about my age." The chief turned toward Flynn. "Kevin, what can you tell us about Rusty's Amusements?"

"The show's headquartered in Syracuse, with three units. The oldest one has been touring eastern New York since right after World War Two. The newer two cover the western half of the state and the southern tier." Flynn sounded—older? More assured? Different, at any rate. Hadley bent to her notes. Taking down every word would help her ignore his voice and focus on the information.

"The show is also a vehicle for connecting white supremacists. At this point, I don't have any evidence that Brent Hill is involved or that he's even aware of the issue."

Hadley put down her notebook. "How can he *not* be aware of guys with six-six-six and SS lightning-bolt tattoos?"

Flynn rubbed his arm. "Oh, he's fine with casual racism. You notice there aren't any people of color employed there. But as long as you're a hard worker and polite to the marks, he doesn't care about anybody's political beliefs. And I'm dead sure he'd fire anyone he thought was transporting drugs."

"So, I can see why the state is interested in these guys, but how does any of it relate to our case?" MacAuley tapped the picture of Jane Doe where it was pinned to the board. "Our victim was white. As was the girl in '72. And the one in '52, come to speak of it."

"A white girl dating a black guy?" Eric suggested.

"That's a pretty narrow window of time in the '72 case, but I suppose it's possible," the chief said.

"Were there white supremacy groups back then?" Hadley asked.

"Ah, youth." MacAuley crossed his arms. "That was the era of the Black Panthers. You *bet* there were white supremacy groups around."

"And the Klan was still active in this area in the early fifties," the chief added.

"The Klan? Get out!" Hadley couldn't picture it. "Were there even any black people *up* here back then?"

"They mostly went after Catholics," Noble said. "They set my granddad's hay on fire one year in the Great Depression."

The chief held up his hands. "This is all interesting, but we're getting way off point. Kevin. Was there anyone missing from the show Friday night into early Saturday morning?"

"Friday night we were rigging, so no. Later on? Nobody from my RV, but I wasn't paying attention to anyone else. It's possible someone left and came back before morning call, but they'd have to be really motivated. Rigging is exhausting. Most of us stagger to our bunks and sack out as soon as we're done."

"What about Hill? Does he work hands-on during the rigging?"

"No, he supervises. I mean, not everyone is hoisting steel and setting lines, but everyone is scrambling to get set up. We arrive at a site and open the next morning, whether it means working through the night or not."

MacAuley pointed to the board, where the ME's estimated time of death was written in numbers five inches high. "That doesn't leave much time for our unsub to pick up a girl, kill her in a way that leaves no trace, and dump her."

"He knew her previously?" Eric said. "She traveled with the carnival?"

Kevin shook his head. "I didn't recognize her, and I've been with the show since Memorial Day."

"Could our unsub be someone associated with the fair?" the chief asked. "Outside vendors? Um, maybe . . ." He glanced around the room for a suggestion.

"There are a lot of people and organizations who're part of the county fair, Chief." Hadley set her notebook on her lap again. Clearly her plan to write everything down and say nothing was not working out. "All of the ag and arts and crafts buildings are permanent. So are a bunch of local groups' booths. The Rotary, Kiwanis, stuff like that. They must have people at the fairgrounds every year around the same time as the carnival."

"And now we're back to half of Washington County as suspects." The dep capped his dry erase marker with a noise suggesting he'd like to do the same thing to the case. "We've got nothing to go on, and now every voter in the three-town area knows we've got an unexplained death we can't close." He turned to the chief. "If we don't break something, Russ, we're going to look like we can't find our asses with both hands and a flashlight."

Kevin snorted. The chief gave him a look before addressing them all. "Believe me, I know it's frustrating. You have to realize every dead end gets us closer to the right path. This is obviously a case that's not going to be broken without a lot of—" He paused, and his mouth twitched for a moment. "—legwork. Keep at it. We'll get there. Dismissed." He slid off the table. "Kevin, you can stay with us tonight."

Flynn shot her a glance. "I was hoping to catch up with Hadley, Chief."

I need to talk to you. Not over the phone.

"Yes! That would be great. We could . . ." Her voice trailed off.

"Go out for dinner? That'd be a great way to keep undercover. I'm sure no more than half the folks who'd see you would recognize Kevin. The rest of 'em would just see the ordinary, everyday sight of a cop and a skinhead eating together. Nothing memorable about that."

Hadley winced.

The chief went on. "I'm going to smuggle him into our house and he's not leaving until Clare takes him back to the fair tomorrow morning. Why don't you drop by later this evening?"

She and Flynn exchanged equally desperate looks. She could just *imagine* talking over all her dirt where the chief and Reverend Clare could hear. Flynn opened his mouth.

"Why don't you stay with me and Granddad," Hadley blurted. The chief looked at her. "The kids would love to see you again. And, and, I could drive you to the station in the morning and Reverend Clare could pick you up here."

Flynn shut his mouth. Blinked.

"Do you have a guest room?" Van Alstyne said.

"We have a very comfortable fold-out couch in the family room. *And* no baby crying in the middle of the night."

"Oh, that's nice." The chief looked like he might angle for an invitation. "Okay, Kevin. Whichever you prefer."

Flynn looked at her closely. She tipped her head. "Sure, then. I'll go with Hadley, Chief."

"Fine. Just don't let anyone spot you coming and going. I'll see you two bright and early tomorrow." With that, he left the room. Hadley almost called him back. By his face, Flynn was thinking the same thing. Silence descended. "My car's out back," she finally said. "You go out the old prisoner entrance. I'll meet you there."

He nodded. Gestured her out into the hall first. As she strode past the dispatch center, she thought, *Thank God I live close by*. Because this was going to be the most awkward car ride in history.

36.   The car ride wasn't as bad as Kevin had anticipated, mostly because they both stayed silent from the time they got into Hadley's purple POS car—he couldn't believe the thing was still running—till they reached her place. He had taken a large hoodie from the lost-and-found and drawn it low over his face. The car's AC was on the fritz, but they drove with the windows rolled tight, so he was sweating like a Saturday-morning jogger by the time they arrived at her granddad's bungalow on Burgoyne Street. God, he hoped he didn't stink. They went in through the screened porch out

back, and the relative coolness of the kitchen felt like plunging into the river. He stripped off the hoodie and laid it over the back of a chair.

Hadley still wasn't looking at him. "Granddad, I'm home!"

"He's not feeling good, Mom." Hudson, Hadley's twelve-year-old, didn't look up from his spot in front of the game console in the family room. "He went upstairs to lie down."

She glanced back at Kevin. "I better go look in on him. Genny, Hudson, put the Nintendo down and come say hi to our guest."

"It's Kevin! Yay!" Geneva, Hudson's ten-year-old sister, ran across the kitchen to give him a hug. "We haven't seen you in *forever,* Kevin. Look, I finally have all my grown-up teeth in the front."

"Hey, Kevin." Hudson, past the hugging age, shook hands. "We've missed you at track."

"I miss it, too, buddy." Kevin had been the volunteer assistant coach for the middle school's cross-country and track teams. "How'd you do this spring?"

"Not as good as the cross-country last fall, but we did place higher than Greenwich for a change."

"Good job." Kevin let the kids pull him into the family room, and by the time Hadley returned, looking cool and collected in shorts and a sleeveless top, he was sitting on the floor, learning the finer points of Kar Krash 3000.

"Mom," Genny said, "Kevin has fake tattoos! Can we get fake tattoos?"

"No."

"I told him beards were so over."

Hadley bit her lower lip. "Well. I trust your knowledge of the trends." She gestured toward the kitchen. "I'm going to let you kiddos play Nintendo a little longer tonight because Kevin is going to help me in the kitchen."

"Sweet," Hudson said.

"No offense, Kevin, but you're too old to be a hipster." Genny took the joystick from Flynn. "You should go for the retro grunge look."

"The retro grunge look?" he said when they were in the kitchen. "I don't even know what that is."

"And she's just starting fifth grade. Imagine what she'll be like in middle school." She took a bowl of London broil in marinade out of the fridge.

"Um. How's your grandfather?"

She shook her head. "He insists on taking the kids for ice cream or fast food and then stuffing himself. Then he has to take another insulin shot, and his gut acts up, and God knows what it's doing to his arteries."

"Sorry."

"Yeah. Well." She reached for a baking pan on the bottom shelf.

He couldn't help watching her shorts tightening, feeling himself respond, and feeling sick about doing so. "What can I do to help?"

"There's some salad stuff in the crisper. Would you grab it?"

He found a head of leaf lettuce, a cucumber, and some green onions. She had a bowl on the kitchen table with a few ripe and misshapen tomatoes, clearly a gift from some gardening neighbor. "You know how to make a salad, right?"

"Yes."

"Hey, I don't know. You didn't know how to make a baked potato, and that's about as basic as it gets."

"Oh, believe me, I know I was way too ignorant for you."

She spun around, cutting board in one hand and knife in the other. "What's that supposed to mean?"

"Nothing. Never mind. Let's just stick to what we need to talk about." He crossed to the sink and washed his hands. "Knife? Peeler?"

She gestured. "In that drawer. The salad bowl's in the cupboard beneath."

He retrieved the tools and bowl and took a seat at the table. She had her head down, watching carefully as she sliced the meat into thin strips. "Okay. What we need to talk about. You first."

Now he had come to it, he didn't have the faintest idea what to say. Somehow, he had imagined Hadley as reticent and shamed when they finally saw each other again. Maybe a little desperate, needing him to rescue her from her ex again. Obviously a fantasy, because she was never reticent, refused to be shamed, and didn't need anyone except her kids.

"I guess I just wanted you to know that if it comes down to it, if Dylan's suit goes to court, I'll make sure you're cleared."

She put the knife down. "What does that *mean,* Flynn?"

"It means I'll tell them I put a bag of meth in his suitcase."

"Did you? Because I know I didn't. And Dylan may be an asshole," she dropped her voice, "but he's not stupid enough to carry on a flight. Besides, there wasn't enough for sale, just for use, and I know Dylan. If he had enough to get high, he would have done it, not packed it for later."

"I will say I put the meth in the bag." He enunciated every word. "That's all you need to know."

"Oh for God's sake." She took a chair, facing him across the table. "What the hell were you *thinking,* Flynn?"

He picked up the cucumber and began peeling it. "If I had been the person who—"

"You did it, Flynn! Just . . . admit it. It's not like I'm going to rat you out."

"You're going to be a witness under oath, Hadley." Saying her name out loud was strange. "The attorney's going to ask you if you saw me slipping the meth into your ex's bag. You'll say no. Then he's going to ask you if I ever confessed to you or spoke to you about it. And you're going to be able to say no to that, too."

"Oh, God, Flynn." She pressed her palms against her forehead. "You could lose your badge over this."

"Then I go to law school like my mom continually bugs me about. Dylan was always going to be able to hold the kids' custody over your head because of the . . . what you did. Now he's got a conviction for possession and intent to transport. That evens the playing field."

She stood up abruptly and walked back to the counter. She lined the pan with tinfoil and covered it with a broiler rack. "You didn't know about my porn career that night."

He felt his throat close up. "No. Obviously not."

"Then why?"

"Because I know you. I've seen you under fire, and chasing down bad guys, and driving through zero visibility, and the only time I've seen you scared was when he threatened to get custody from you. So I knew . . . it was something bad."

"Oh, yeah." She laid the meat strips onto the rack. "Something bad. Bad enough so when you found out, you dumped me without a word and disappeared. To goddamned *Syracuse*."

His jaw tightened. "Look, you got whatever you wanted out of me. Don't pretend your feelings were hurt."

She tossed the pan into the oven and slammed the door. "Pretend? Pretend? You—" She glanced toward the family room, where the kids were still battling it out for world dominance. "You think I let anybody in like that? My God."

She threw her oven mitt on the counter and stalked out the back door. He could see her through the windows, pacing around the screened porch, her lips moving in what he assumed were curses she didn't want the kids to hear.

He was *not* the one in the wrong here. And he sure as hell didn't want to rehash what had happened that night. Coming in at the end of his shift, the guys clustered around the screen, and those images . . . he screwed his eyes shut to chase them out of his head. They had made love that afternoon. At least, he thought of it as making love. Obviously, that wasn't her take on it. And he had been too *stupid,* too *naïve* to know. God, he was hopeless.

The timer dinged. He stared at the oven. Was he supposed to take the meat out? Put something on it? Turn the temperature down? Growling beneath his breath, he walked to the kitchen door and opened it. "The timer went off."

She stalked past him as if he wasn't there. She slid the pan out and swiftly turned the slices over with a spatula before returning it to the oven. She turned to him. "You. Are a jerk. Which shouldn't have surprised me, since every guy I ever get close to turns out to have been a jerk."

"Me?" Kevin stood up. "I *never* treated you with anything less than respect and complete honesty."

"Oh, really?" She made a motion like a swinging baggie.

"Forget that. You know what I mean. I told you honestly how I

163

felt. I told you about my inexperience. God, when I think about how I must have seemed to you! Sweet virginal Kevin, too dumb to realize he's being played."

"Shh! Keep it down!" She yanked the door open and shoved him onto the screened porch. "Is that what this is about? Because I wasn't some untouched vestal, too?" She shut the door behind her.

"Oh, for chrissake, Hadley, I knew you weren't a virgin. I just didn't expect you to be a *pro*."

"I was a performer," she hissed.

"Performing with dicks in you. It's not exactly Shakespeare, is it?"

"I'm not going to apologize for what I did, Flynn. I was young, I made some bad decisions, and I regret—I *deeply* regret—the way it's affected my kids. But I'm not ashamed of having sex. I notice you were fine dipping your wick until you found out some other guys had been there first."

"Some other guys?" He was so frustrated he couldn't stand still. "Hadley, I thought what we had was special."

"It *was* special, you idiot."

"Then how come in two years you never found time to mention to me, *Oh, by the way, Flynn, I used to act in porn.* Jesus, yes, it horrifies me to realize everybody I've worked with for the last five years has seen you orgasming."

"I was faking."

"Oh, that makes it much better. And I'm sick to my stomach when I realize what I must have seemed like in comparison."

"For God's sake, Flynn, I wasn't comparing—"

"But the part that really gets me? That really rams home how little you thought of me? The fact you didn't trust me. Forget the relationship part. I thought we were *friends*. But even when you were scared your ex was going to get the kids, you still didn't come clean. You couldn't be honest with me, and I had to find out by walking in on the rest of the department watching you banging two guys in full color. Christ, of course I transferred to Syracuse. How could I stay?"

The evening air was still heavy and damp. Outside, he could hear grasshoppers buzzing, and the distant shouts of kids playing.

"I'm sorry," she finally said. "I should have told you. I didn't because I knew it would cause everything to fall apart."

"Yeah? Well, you got that right."

"You could have at least stayed around to talk about it. You never gave me a chance to explain, or apologize, or anything. I got to work the next day and the chief told us you'd taken your accumulated sick days and you were gone."

"You could have called me, Hadley. I didn't change my number."

"Oh, I'm sorry I didn't call you while I was dealing with the worst crisis of my working life! I didn't know if I was going to be fired, if I was going to have to resign, let *alone* if some jackass like Paul Urquhart would start blabbing and I'd have to move the kids *again*—"

"You don't get it, do you? Your worst crisis is when you're *supposed* to call the people who love you. But no, of course you wouldn't do that. You wouldn't have told me about your ex if we hadn't been stuck working together. You won't ask anyone for help, because you don't trust anyone." He thumped down onto the picnic bench, shaking his head. "You know, it's true. I don't know anything about sex. But at least I know how to be a human being in a relationship."

Hadley took the bench across from him. "I did trust you. I trusted you to have my back when we worked together. I trusted you to spend time with my kids, and to help me get them back from Dylan, and I trusted you when we . . ." She trailed off. "I told you I was ready to try. You and me. And then you left without a word."

"You know what I kept hearing in my head that night? You telling me, *It's just sex, Flynn.*" He leaned across the picnic table. "We were together three times, and at least two of them, you jumped me like you were scratching an itch. So when I found out you had been a porn star? It made sense. I finally believed what you had been telling me all that time." He hated that he sounded so bitter, but he couldn't help it.

"You know what I finally believed? That you loved me. You told me you did time and time again, and I ignored it, because you were young, and I was the first woman you'd slept with, and how *could* you love me, some boy whose life had barely started, and me with two kids and a mountain of debt and so much baggage I need a U-Haul to make it through the day." She stood up. "But you convinced me, Flynn. You made me believe it. For the first time in fifteen years, I thought maybe I *am* loveable." She laid her hands on the picnic table and leaned over him. "And I got smacked in the face for it."

She crossed to the kitchen. "So I guess I was right the first time. It *was* just sex." She slammed the door, leaving him alone.

Kevin crossed his arms on the picnic table and laid his head down, too exhausted for the moment to sit upright. Jesus, Mary, and Joseph. So much for feeling better if he let it all out. He still felt like he had a gut full of poison inside, but now his outside was lacerated, too, as if he'd been scoured with acid. His head seemed to be stuffed with greasy rags. He let his breath empty out and focused on the knot of hunger in his stomach, the smell of grass clippings from beyond the screens, the feel of the wood beneath his arms. Just being for a moment. Breathing in. Breathing out.

He didn't notice Hadley was back until she sat down at the end of the bench. He jerked upright. She held her hands up. *Pax.* "Dinner's ready."

"Oh. Okay. Thanks."

"Just one more thing. Not about us. I mean, not about our . . . relationship."

"All right. I guess."

"The lawsuit. They're going to depose you at some point. What are you going to say?"

That I thought I was being your knight in shining armor. That I wanted to hurt someone who was hurting you. That I was an idiot.

"I don't know," he finally said. "I just don't know."

AUGUST 1972

37. Jack gave Gifford the photo and the kids' descriptions of Natalie No-Last-Name and sent him down to Poughkeepsie to find out what he could with the new information.

"Finally," George said. "My mom always hoped I'd go to college."

"I'm afraid you've got the wrong equipment for Vassar." Jack signed the petty cash receipt and handed the money to the sergeant. "Don't try to get back tonight. Just phone in if you turn over anything. And bring back your receipts." He handed the cash box to the secretary.

George winked. "I might need someone to take notes. You interested in a trip downstate, Harlene?"

She turned as red as a prize tomato, but after a moment, she managed to get out, "Not with you, George Gifford!"

Jack grinned. "Thatta girl!" Harlene spun around and headed to her office, keeping her speed down just enough to qualify as a walk instead of a retreat.

George spoke quietly. "If I get the names of her parents, do you want me to notify them?"

Jack shook his head. "Thanks, but that's my job. Speaking of which"—he glanced at his watch—"I need to get over to the bus station."

◆ ◆ ◆

He was in luck. One of the two ticket agents at the Glens Falls bus station had been working last Friday. Jack slid the Polaroid Fran had given him across the white laminate counter and through an arch in the Plexiglas window.

The agent studied it. "Maybe?"

"She got dropped off here around three thirty. She might have gone next door to get something to eat."

"I may have seen her in the waiting room. I can tell you I didn't sell a ticket to anyone who looked like that."

"How busy was it?"

"Friday afternoon in August? Busy. The four thirty-six from New York City is always full of husbands joining their families for the weekend. You can't walk through the parking lot for the station wagons picking folks up."

"That's the one that continues north to Plattsburgh, right?"

"That's right. In at four thirty-six, leaves at four forty-four."

Jack took that to be bus speak for sixteen before five. "What if she was headed south? Say, to the city?"

The agent jerked a thumb toward two large black-and-white posters hanging next to a soda machine. Jack could see long lists of stops and times in ordered columns. "Southbound arrives six A.M., two thirty in the afternoon, and eight at night. If your girl was here at four, she was either planning on going north, or she was waiting for the bus from New York." He slid the Polaroid through the opening as if he were returning change.

"Was there another agent here? One who might have sold her a ticket?"

"Sure. Scottie Kilmer. He's off today and tomorrow."

"Can you get me his address and phone number?"

"Give me a sec, and it's yours."

While the agent was in the back office, Jack thought about the timing. Arriving at three thirty sounded just right for someone traveling north—enough time to grab a burger at the lunch counter next door and make the bus with plenty to spare. But why north? Most of the stops between Albany and Montreal were small towns that flourished during ski or swim season. Maybe her people were summer visitors? But if that were so, why didn't she get on that bus?

"Here you go." The agent slid Jack a piece of paper with an address and number jotted on it. "If you can't reach him at home, he'll be in Wednesday at one P.M."

"Thanks." Jack walked out of the station and went to the lunch counter next door.

"Sorry, Officer, but Friday afternoon's not my shift," the waitress said. He collected another name and address, along with the information that, just like at the station next door, it was always busy on Friday for them. "Since D and H cut off the train service last year, everybody comes up from New York by bus. Tough for Fort Henry, but it's great for us."

Maybe Natalie was meeting someone from New York? Of course, there were a lot of stops between there and Glens Falls, but Vassar College, going to Florida on spring break—it all indicated a girl whose family had money, and in this day and age, that meant downstate.

The heat was shimmering off the sidewalk as he made his way

back to his vehicle. Her family may have money, but Natalie didn't. Her share of the communal funds might have stretched to a burger and a bus ticket, but not much further. So she needed cash. Or someone to bail her out. Which might be the reason she was waiting at the bus station for the Friday coach from New York.

He unlocked his car door, and the heat from inside felt like a solid wall. He went around and opened the partner door to let some air flow through, and suddenly had an image of Margy Van Alstyne doing the same thing. Here in Glens Falls. When had that been?

He shook his head. He needed to go back to the commune, find out if Natalie had made a call or used a pay phone in the days before she left. He could also check the Western Union office in town, though he didn't expect that to pan out. It was a long walk from the bus station; if she had been waiting for a wire, she would have had Isaac drop her off there.

The temperature inside the car dropped from blast furnace to uncomfortable. He got behind the wheel and pulled out of the parking lot. At the red light, a trio of girls crossed the street in front of him, all long tan legs and long silky hair. The sense of how little he knew, and how fast time was passing, dug into his chest with hot fingers. He'd gotten this far on guesses and gut feelings, but sooner or later, his luck would run out. Before that, he needed something solid to build the investigation on.

THURSDAY, AUGUST 24, PRESENT DAY

38. Clare collected Kevin from the police station at 7 A.M. Since yesterday, he had picked up a baseball cap and a hoodie; combined with his tats and his none-too-clean clothes, he gave even Clare a start until he stuck his head in the window and smiled his sweet everyday smile. He slid into the passenger side, then twisted around to look at Ethan, strapped into his baby seat. "Oh, wow," Kevin said. "So this is the little guy."

"That's him." She signaled and pulled onto Main Street.

Kevin adjusted his hood around his face. "He doesn't look much like the chief." There was a pause as they both digested that, and then he blurted, "I don't mean I think—you know. He doesn't look like you, either!"

Clare laughed. "As near as I can tell, most babies just look like other babies." She turned onto Route 117 by the Stewart's and immediately slowed down for Millers Kill's version of rush-hour traffic. "He does sort of bellow like Russ does."

Kevin laughed.

"That coffee is for you." She pointed toward the go-cup in the console. "I didn't know if you had time to get any at Hadley's. How did it go over there?"

Kevin's mouth flattened for a moment. "It was fine. We talked a bit. I got to hang out with the kids. I turned in pretty early."

"Hmm." She had a few theories in that direction, but if he didn't want to bring it up, she certainly wasn't going to. "I also have a backpack of necessaries for you next to Ethan. We give them out to homeless people or folks down on their luck who come to the church for help. It's got some clothing basics, a prepaid phone card, lightweight food you can fix with hot water—stuff like that."

His expression loosened up as she spoke. "I don't need any of that, you know."

"You can send us a donation to cover the cost later, if you want." They passed the exit for Glens Falls and traffic opened up again. "But if you really were who you're pretending to be, I'd give it to you." She flashed him a grin. "I thought it would bolster your cover."

Kevin shook his head. "I'm not sure if it was a loss or a gain when you decided to go into the ministry instead of law enforcement, Reverend Clare."

She laughed. "Be sure to tell that to Russ."

A billboard up ahead advertised the Washington County Fair in old-fashioned circus lettering. Cars and trucks were already turning onto the road that led to the vendor parking area. "Where should I let you out?" she asked.

"Main gate, if you can. I'm going to have to report in to Mr. Hill and let him rake me up one side and down another anyway."

She frowned. "Are you going to be in trouble?"

He grinned. "For evil Kevin Flynn, trouble is good. Bolsters my cover."

She rolled her eyes. The front gate was still closed, but she could see a few people beyond the entryway, moving with a speed and purpose that marked them as staff instead of visitors. She put the car into park and turned to Kevin. "Be careful. I know you have a whole organization behind you, but please know if you need to, you can call me anytime, night or day."

He smiled a little. "You know, that's exactly what the chief said, too."

He got out and opened the back door to retrieve the backpack. Ethan stared at him with the utter solemnity possessed by infants and funeral-goers. Kevin leaned in and booped the baby's tiny nose. "Hang in there, little dude. Your parents are some of the good guys."

She was about halfway to Margy's house when her phone started ringing to the tune of "I fought the law and the law won."

"Hey, sweetheart," she said.

"Hi, darlin'. Kevin get off okay?"

"He did. I can't say I'm not worried about him. He seems so . . ."

"Young? Yeah, to me, too. But he's got six years of experience under his belt. And he's a smart kid. Mostly. Are you headed to Mom's?"

"Uh-huh."

"Good. Two things: one, Ben Beagle was here sniffing around for information."

"It's not 'sniffing around,' love, it's his job."

"Whatever. You know how Beagle gets up my nose. I had Lyle talk to him. The point is, if he approaches you, don't tell him anything."

"Why on earth would he ask me anything? I'm not a member of the department and I don't know anything more about the case in '72 than the general public does." *Because you won't talk to me about it.*

"Oh, he already covered the cases in today's *Post-Star*. Now he's doing a story on the chief of police having been a suspect. What a load of bull hockey."

Clare pressed her lips together to avoid screaming. Russ *had* been a suspect, and as far as she knew he *hadn't* been cleared, and how was she supposed to help or defend him if he wouldn't open his big fat stubborn mouth about it? She took a deep breath. "Okay." She took another. "Say nothing. Got it. What was thing two?"

"I invited Jack Liddle to dinner Friday night."

"What? *Please* tell me you're joking. We're already committed to the fundraiser at the Langevoorts' house on Friday. To raise money to get the word out about the referendum and maybe save your police department and everyone's jobs!"

"Okay, okay, I'm sorry. I forgot." There was a pause. "Can't we just bring him along?"

"Russ, you don't just add people to an invitation—" Her intern's words popped into her head. "Wait. Maybe he can come as Margy's date. Joni said she was welcome to bring an escort."

Russ laughed. "*That* will be a new one! Mom's last date was during the Truman administration."

"I'm sure she'll be fine with it. You need to call Mr. Liddle right away though, and see if he's up for a dressy sit-down dinner."

"Good point. I'll handle it. Have a good day, darlin', and kiss Ethan for me. Love you."

"Love you, too." And she did, even though there were times she would cheerfully run him over with her car. She dropped the phone into her tote as she pulled into Margy's drive. "Here we are, baby boy. Grammy's house."

Margy was descending the granite steps before Clare had even crossed the dooryard. She reached out toward the diaper bag. "Let me help you with that."

"Thanks. I swear, I went on month-long deployments with less stuff than Ethan needs for one morning."

"Be grateful you don't have real diapers and rubber pants like we did when Russ was a baby. Now *that* was a pain to travel with." She bumped the door open and they both went into the kitchen. Margy set the diaper bag on the table and took Ethan. "Hello, my smart and clever and accomplished boy." Ethan made a noise that might have been *gla!* and smacked Margy's mouth with his hand. She kissed his fingers. "Violence is never the answer, sweetie."

"I have to dash," Clare said. "About the fundraiser Friday—would you mind a tagalong? The former police chief is back in town and Russ accidentally invited him to dine with us tomorrow. I thought we could salvage the situation by having him be your escort."

"Tom Sheffield? I guess that would be okay."

"No, the one who was chief when Russ was back from Vietnam."

"Jack Liddle?" Margy shifted the baby to her other hip. "Jack Liddle's in Millers Kill?"

"He's renovating an old family house in Cossayuharie? I think? If it's a problem, I'll tell Russ he has to reschedule."

"No, no." Margy patted her hair. "No, I'd be . . . happy to catch up with Jack. I just . . ." She looked down at her stubby frame. "Last time I saw him, I still had a waistline."

Clare hugged her. "You look beautiful just the way you are. There are people twenty years your junior who can't keep up with you." She kissed Ethan's cheek. "Bye-bye, my little sweet potato. Mama loves you." Predictably, he started to cry. She dashed out Margy's door, her child's angry shrieks following her all the way to her car. Margy claimed he always cheered up within minutes, but it didn't make parting from him any easier. She tried more deep breathing as she peeled out of the driveway. *Quiet mind. Calm mind.*

Back at St. Alban's, Elizabeth had already taken Joni on what she liked to call her "rounds"—visiting shut-ins, the hospital, and the infirmary. Clare was desperately grateful to have her morning cleared, giving her the chance to catch up on overdue phone calls and paperwork. Lois had scheduled two late-afternoon marriage counseling sessions with couples who had left the required three meetings until the last minute, but other than that, she was free to work on Sunday's sermon. Maybe—please God—she could finish the first draft without having to take it home to work on it.

She had just hung up from a call to one of the soup pantry's food providers when she heard Lois talking to someone from the other room. A moment later, a sandy-haired man in glasses and a Snoopy tie stepped through her door. "Hi, there, Reverend Fergusson."

Lois appeared over his shoulder. "I'm sorry, Clare, he wouldn't take no for an answer."

"That's okay, Lois. Hi, Ben. Why don't you come in and have a seat."

She didn't think Ben Beagle had visited her office before, but he somehow knew to avoid the lumpy love seat. He took one of the admiral's chairs. Clare rose from her desk and joined him. "If you're here about the recent death, I don't have anything to say. I'm strictly a civilian. I don't know any more than anyone else in town."

"Reverend"—Ben grinned at her—"that wasn't true even before you married the chief of police."

She tried to repress a smile. The trouble was, she *liked* Beagle, despite having had his investigative spotlight turn on her in the past. "All right then, let's just say I'm under strict orders not to talk about it with the press."

Ben leaned back in his chair as if he were at home in his family room. "You know, I'm pretty sure you're not the sort to listen to strict orders from your husband."

"I might mention my vestry is never happy when I get into the paper, unless it's an—"

"Easter message of hope, yeah, I remember." He gave her what she assumed was a sly look that didn't quite work on his boyish face. "How about this: if you'll talk to me about Chief Van Alstyne being involved in two identical murder cases, I'll make sure the inaugural fundraiser of the Save the Police Department organization gets covered. Pictures and everything. The more publicity the better."

"How do you know about that? Never mind. One"—Clare held up a finger—"it's still not confirmed that any of those deaths were intentional. And two"—she added a finger—"I don't think any amount of gauzy coverage of rich people writing checks would outweigh a headline implying my husband is a suspect. Heck, *I'd* vote to close up the department if I thought that was true."

"I'm not implying your husband is a suspect."

"Unless you're titling your story 'Ten Weird Coincidences You Won't Believe!' there's no other way to parse it."

Ben spread his hands. "Have you thought the killer might be targeting your husband?"

Clare snorted. "He's missing by a mile, in that case. Besides, Russ wasn't even *born* when the first woman was found."

"His mother, maybe? The Van Alstyne family?"

"Do you actually *believe* any of that?"

"Nah." Ben grinned. "But you have to admit, it's a hell of a story. Three identical murders—"

"Not proven."

"—in the same place, at the same time of year, but separated by decades." He winked at her. "Do you know how many people are going to subscribe to the web-only edition of the *Post-Star* just to read about it?"

She made a noise of frustration. "Do you know how many people are going to start thinking we don't need a police presence in the three towns if they can't instantly solve this case?"

Ben's face sobered. "Reverend, it's not my job to advocate. The editorial page can root for the MKPD all they want, but I'm here to dig into the facts and report them clearly and honestly."

"I know." She sighed. "I was just blowing off steam. You want a quote from me? Here it is: I have every reason to believe the Millers Kill Police Department will quickly find the person or persons responsible for the young woman's death and bring them to justice."

Ben folded his notebook and rose from his chair. "Thanks very much, Reverend." He paused in her doorway. "I'm just going to point out we have quotes almost identical to yours. From 1972."

39. Clare was finishing a tomato and mayo sandwich when she heard Elizabeth de Groot's voice calling from down the hall. "Clare? We're back, and we have a visitor!"

Clare stuffed the rest of her sandwich in her mouth, felt something wet give way, and managed to get her hand up in time to keep a blob of mayonnaise from staining her blouse. Unfortunately, she wasn't deft enough to prevent the stream of tomato juice and seeds from hitting her right on her bosom, which was larger, since she was nursing, than it had been at any other time in her life.

She was rubbing her chest with a paper towel when Elizabeth stepped in. "Really, Clare."

"Sowwy," Clare mumbled around the remains of her sandwich.

"Get yourself presentable and come out to the sanctuary. Joni's mother is here, and we want her to be impressed."

Clare wiped her hands and tossed the paper towel into the wastebasket. She showed her teeth to the deacon. "Okay?"

Elizabeth sighed. "Good enough. Don't grin too much."

As they approached the sanctuary, Clare could hear Joni repeating the same history-of-St.-Alban's tour she had been given two days ago. When Clare and Elizabeth entered, her intern was at the back of the church, pointing out the "unique herringbone pattern laid with reclaimed Civil War—era bricks."

"Hello," Clare said. She didn't have to raise her voice: the church had been designed to carry sound in an era before microphones and speakers. "I'm Clare Fergusson."

Joni's mother bore a striking resemblance to her daughter; tall and athletic with an angular face and a thick swoop of hair that was probably kept red at great expense. "Audrey Langevoort." She held out a hand that still had dirt beneath clipped fingernails. "I'm so pleased to meet you."

"The pleasure's mine." Clare shook hands, feeling more relaxed about her tomato-scented blouse. Mrs. Langevoort's outfit was very much like Margy's summer uniform: cropped jeans, a T-shirt, and a light shirt thrown over all. Several sizes smaller than Clare's mother-in-law's, and it didn't come from Kmart, but Clare recognized the look of a passionate gardener.

"I had to pick up some things at the Agway," Mrs. Langevoort said, "and I thought I could stop by so we could meet before Friday night."

"Thank you so much for being willing to open your home on such short notice."

"I'm glad Joni thought of it. We had already planned a get-together honoring Kent's successor; this gave me an excuse to open the party up to our delightful neighbors instead of just having stuffy financiers." She gestured toward the rose window above the brass-and-marble high altar. "What a lovely church."

"Thank you," Clare said. "We have a wonderful congregation to match."

Mrs. Langevoort smiled. "We'll have to join you some Sunday before we go back to New York."

Clare gestured to the center aisle, and they walked toward the front of the church. "Are you headed home soon?"

"Usually the county fair marks the end of our summer—we head south to the city the weekend it closes. This year, I'll be staying on. We've almost completed construction of a house on Lake George, and I need to be here for the final punch list. And of course, Joni will be here to work on the internship."

"You're building a new house? Year-round?" The older Adirondack camps were almost never winterized; they became uninhabitable by late October or early November.

"The camp belongs to the company," Mrs. Langevoort said.

"Dad's retiring soon," Joni added. "He and Mother wanted to stay on in the area."

"Have you lived here through a winter?" Elizabeth sounded skeptical.

Mrs. Langevoort laughed. "No, but we've been here for skiing quite a bit. And believe me, the city in January is no picnic."

"So Joni will be living in the new house in Lake George?" Elizabeth asked.

"Don't worry, I've got four-wheel drive and good winter tires."

"It'll be a great help to us." Mrs. Langevoort squeezed Joni's arm. "We'd like to have the place ready by next summer, which means we need someone there for the painters, carpet-layers, paper hangers—"

"Furniture delivery, finish carpentry, landscapers . . ." Joni grinned at her mother.

"Oh, we're not even *thinking* about landscaping until next year!"

The pieces of the Langevoort family dynamic began to fall into place. Joni spends the summer in the city while her father is in the North Country, the two of them overlapping at their camp for a scant few weeks. Mrs. Langevoort, meanwhile, creates the perfect opportunity for Joni to stay out of her father's way until her December operation, and be useful to the family to boot. An internship in the area must have been the missing part of the plan; something that enabled Joni to continue to work toward her MDiv degree.

Clare smiled. No wonder Audrey Langevoort was amenable to their fundraising dinner.

Joni tugged her mother's hand. "Mom, come and see the undercroft. It's amazing. The basement has a basement."

"Oh, darling, I'd love to stay and get the insiders' tour, but Bors has the car, and he's picking me up"—Audrey looked at her watch—"well, just about now."

"Oh, Bors." Joni drew out the name until all Clare could picture was a herd of wild swine. She looked inquiringly at her intern. "Bors Saunderson is the new crown prince. No, wait, I mean *princeps imperialis.*"

"Be nice," her mother said. "And technically speaking, *princeps* would be the equivalent of *imperator.*" She pressed her fingers to her lips, trapping a laugh as she looked at Clare's and Elizabeth's expressions. "Bors is going to take over the company from Kent. Who insisted Joni study Latin all through her school years. After drilling her on those innumerable tenses, I got better at it than she was."

"Has it helped you any with Hebrew or Greek?" Clare asked.

"Not one little bit."

Audrey gave her daughter a sideways hug. "Anyway, your dad's been taking him around and introducing him to the area, and today it's my turn." She held out her hand to Clare. "Reverend Fergusson, I look forward to seeing you again Friday."

"Clare, please." Clare shook her hand. "Thank you again for the invitation."

"You're doing us a favor. Hearing your husband speak in person will give us something besides business to talk about. We saw him on the evening news!"

Clare and Elizabeth waved goodbye, identical stiff smiles on their faces.

"That went well," Elizabeth said.

"Right up to the part where she said she saw Russ putting his foot in it on Channel Eight. We're going to spend the entire dinner explaining the 1972 case, aren't we?"

"Cheer up." Elizabeth's voice was dry. "The days when being associated with a crime made you persona non grata are long gone. Nowadays, just being on television is enough to make you a celebrity, never mind what for. Who knows, maybe you can raise more money with a little whiff of scandal."

"What he's hoping is that he can raise a few informants with that little whiff of scandal." Clare sent up a brief prayer. "As much as he hated it, I think he'd go on TV every night if he could just get some clue as to who that poor girl was."

Elizabeth raised an eyebrow. "Well. Let's hope it doesn't come to that."

AUGUST 1952

40. Faced with the possibility his Jane Doe could be a missing wife, a runaway girlfriend, or a working girl, Harry took the simplest possibility to start with. Prostitutes frequented bars, hotels, motels and, in the busy season with men coming and going from vacations in the mountains and Lake George, train and bus stations. In Harry's experience, wherever they were, there was at least one barkeep, concierge, front-desk man, or security officer getting a kickback for steering clients her way and making sure she

didn't get tossed out. Photos in hand, he started making the rounds as soon as his shift was over at five.

Cossayuharie he skipped, despite the fact Jane Doe's body had been found there. The only commercial establishments in the farm town were a couple feed and seed stores and a livestock auction barn. Glens Falls and its environs were also out—they had their own force. He didn't mind treading on the state police's toes, especially since they were putting in the minimum effort to find the dead girl's identity, but he wasn't about to cheese off his closest colleagues. He might call the Glens Falls chief tomorrow, though, and ask if the staties had passed any information on to him.

So, Millers Kill and Fort Henry. The girl had been young, fresh-faced even beneath the layer of makeup she had worn, so he started at the top: the Rensselaer Arms Hotel in Fort Henry. Close to the train station and the landing for the canal that joined the Kill with the Hudson, it had been the hotel for well-heeled businessmen since the 1860s. He had taken his mother to the Rensselaer's impeccable dining room for her sixtieth birthday. He was almost as old now as she had been then. He caught a glimpse of himself in the glass doorway and straightened his tie.

Inside, he realized he wasn't the only one who had gotten older. The rich Turkey carpet in the lobby was shiny with wear in places, and there was a crack in the plaster wall along the staircase sweeping to the second floor. The brass fittings around the registration desk gleamed, but part of the elaborate mahogany carving had broken away.

"Can I help you, Officer?" The man behind the desk might have been the same one there on Harry's mother's birthday. Hell, he might have been there on his grandmother's birthday; the fellow looked older than God.

"Hi. Harry McNeil, Millers Kill Police." Harry slid the photo across the mahogany surface. "I'm trying to discover the identity of this young woman. I don't think she was a local. Might you have seen her?"

The receptionist lifted the eight-by-eleven with a liver-spotted hand. "Goodness. This appears to be a dead woman."

His expression made Harry shift with embarrassment, as if he had committed a faux pas by not mentioning it first. "Yes, sir. We're trying to find out who she is, and notify her kin."

The elderly man tched. "I can't say I recall her as a guest."

"Um. She might not have been here as a guest. Exactly. Are you—is there another man on the night shift?"

"I am, as it were, my own night manager." He slid the photo back toward Harry. "You get to be my age, it's hard to sleep at night. Might as well take advantage of it."

"Yes, sir."

"She might have been a guest at our restaurant, of course. Please feel free to speak to our maître d'hôtel. He might recognize her. Pretty girl."

"Yes, she was. Thank you, sir." Harry crossed the lobby to where a narrow hallway led left to the dining room and right to the bar. He went right. The bar showed the same signs of long-postponed maintenance; unmatched chairs at the small tables, splits in the leather bumper edging the bar counter. Two standing fans tried to move the overwarm air around. A pair of men sat in the corner with drinks and documents in front of them. Two salesmen after a good day? There was more booze than paper—maybe a bad day.

The barkeep, who had been washing glasses, perked up as Harry entered. "Help you, Officer?"

The man was a good twenty years younger than Harry. He figured he could be less diplomatic than he had at the desk. He laid the photo on the bar and introduced himself. "We found her dead and we're trying to ID her. She may have been a working girl. I'm wondering if she was ever in here?"

The barkeep held up his hands. "I don't aid and abet illegal behavior."

Harry sighed. "Look, I'm not setting up a sting. I'm not interested in whether girls are working here or not." Honesty pricked him. "Well, so long as it's not leading to fights." He touched the edge of the photo. "Whoever she was, she had family, and they'll never know what happened to her if we can't figure out who she is. Can you help me?"

The barkeep glanced toward the hallway. "I really don't have girls in here. Mr. Beekman"—he jerked a thumb toward the lobby—"would have a stroke. If any of our guests ask me, I send 'em to the Canalmen's Rest. And I suggest if they come back here, they make sure the dame's walking on the side away from Mr. Beekman."

"Do you get many men looking for company?"

The barkeep waved a hand at the near-empty space. "This place is dying. People want slick-looking motels with air-conditioning and swimming pools. I'm here because Mr. Beekman pays me enough to make up for the tips, but when he goes toes-up . . ." He shrugged. "Probably be the wrecking ball for the old girl."

The Canalmen's Rest was a bust. It was lively, but the crowd was 90 percent men stopping by for a quick one on their way home. The other 10 percent were two middle-aged couples having predinner drinks. Neither bartender admitted to knowing any prostitutes, and Harry was obviously several hours too early to see if there were any likely women. The second-best hotel was a repeat of the Rensselaer Arms, except without the attention to keeping everything as clean and polished as possible. Maybe everyone really was staying at the new Howard Johnson's out by the Northway, but Harry found it hard to imagine girls turning tricks under the orange roof.

The next bar he tried was too nice—it looked like a jet-set airport lounge and had an even mix of young men in narrow suits and young women in wide, flirty skirts. Prostitutes didn't go to date bars—why compete against straight girls? He was looking for a place that attracted men, in groups or alone, but not someplace they took their wives and girlfriends. Which is when he thought of Sal's.

Sal's was on the road toward Minot, just outside the town lines of both Millers Kill and Fort Henry. It had a small menu of Italian food, a huge bar, and had long been the place to listen to fights or ball games while hoisting a beer. Sal's son Steve had added a television when he took over from his old man. Harry was pretty sure the Perazones were running book on the side, but there wasn't any mob involvement that made itself known, and no law enforcement agency had ever had to come out to settle trouble. Anyway, it wasn't in his jurisdiction, which is why he had been there many times himself. He'd never noticed any girls working the bar, but then, he'd been well off-duty and focused on following whatever fight was on the radio.

"Chief McNeil!" Steve Perazone was manning the front himself. "Here for some dinner? My ma's made ravioli tonight. Like little angel pillows. You'll swear you've died and gone to heaven."

"Thanks, Steve. Not tonight."

The host spread his hands. "I'm afraid you missed the Dodgers game. They folded in the seventh. Philly took it ten to four."

"Ouch." He looked toward the bar. Maybe five or six people, mostly men. He pulled the photo out of its envelope. "We have a Jane Doe we're trying to identify." He passed the picture to Steve. "She may have been—"

"I've seen her." Steve crossed himself. "Poor thing."

The surge of *Yes, yes!* was like a burning shot of whiskey hitting his bloodstream. "What's her name?"

The host handed the picture back. "I don't know. I remember her because she's Italian. Was Italian. Not many of us around here."

"Italian like you? Or right off the boat?"

"I'd guess second generation, like me. She didn't have an accent but . . ." He shrugged. "You can tell."

"I think—we're working off the possibility that she was a prostitute." Harry took a breath. "I'm not trying to pry into how you run your place—"

"It's okay." Steve smiled. "Look, if girls come in here and meet a guy, it's none of my concern what happens after they leave my place. I don't take any money and I don't make any introductions." He paused. "I did ban a guy once, when a girl came in with a black eye he'd given her. A man who hits a woman, his business I don't need."

"Was my Jane Doe a regular?"

Steve laughed. "There are no regulars. You've been in here yourself. Most of the guys who come to Sal's are a lot more interested in a fight or a game than they are in playing slap-and-tickle." He sobered. "Your *Tizia*—your Jane Doe—was here maybe four or five times this summer. Maybe she was working. Maybe she was homesick for *pasta con fagiole*."

"Did you ever see her leave with anyone?"

"Maybe?" The host shrugged. "But I couldn't tell you who if he was standing here in front of me. I noticed her, like I said, because she was Italian. It didn't occur to me she was a working girl until now."

"She was discreet."

"Or she was just here for the food. I hope we're not speaking ill of the dead." Steve touched his chest.

"You said this summer. Can you remember when you first might have seen her?"

"I'm not sure. After Memorial Day, though, and not before."

"Okay. Thanks for your help."

"Anytime, my friend." Steve shook his hand. "Come back for the Lamott fight next Saturday. Ma's making meatball bombers. You'll think you've—"

"Died and gone to heaven?"

Steve cocked a finger, grinning. "You've got it."

Harry sat for a long time in Sal's parking lot. The new information made him less certain, not more so. Jane Doe—what had Steve called it? *Tizia*—could have been a prostitute, in the area for the summer season. If she was cautious and discreet, she might move around a lot, one night in Lake George, another in Glens Falls. Which would mean she had her own car, which would eventually turn up as abandoned. He sighed. Unless she was renting, and the landlord seized and sold it.

On the other hand, she might be a seasonal worker, cleaning rooms at one of a hundred hotels or resorts between Lake George and Saratoga. Maybe she did show up at Sal's because she missed the taste of home. Maybe she had the bad luck to meet a man who seemed nice. Harry ground his head against the steering wheel before straightening and starting the car. Still a lot more hours in the evening. Still a lot more bars and hotels to check out. He shifted into gear and headed off into the sunset.

THURSDAY, AUGUST 24, PRESENT DAY

41. As it turned out, Russ didn't need to call Jack Liddle to clue him in on Friday's fundraiser; Liddle called on him. Russ was trying to shape his notes from yesterday into some sort of report for the Syracuse PD and State Task Force on Domestic Extremism when he was stopped by a noise he'd never heard before coming from Harlene's station. *Good God, she's dying.* He was through the door, hand already pulling out his phone to call the ambulance, only to see Harlene wrapped around Jack Liddle, the two of them rocking back and forth like long-lost relations.

"You old reprobate! Why didn't you tell me you were back? How long are you here for? How are you?"

"I don't think he's going to be able to answer until you let him breathe," Russ said. He held out his hand. "Good to see you in the station, Chief."

"Well, you said I could drop in anytime." Liddle kept one arm around Harlene while he shook Russ's hand. "I can't believe you still have this sweet young thing working here." He gave Harlene a squeeze. "You figure out how to make a decent cup of coffee yet?"

"Actually, *I* make the coffee."

"Probably for the best."

Liddle yelped as Harlene smacked him. "I've outlasted four police chiefs so far, and I'm taking my vitamins so I can outlast this one, too." She nodded toward Russ. "You should see him after I take my vacation. Begging me not to retire."

"She won't tell us where the keys to the restroom are."

Liddle laughed.

"I'm glad you came by. I was going to call you"—Russ made a quick calculation of the awkwardness of the two of them in the office that had once been Liddle's—"but we can head into the squad room and have a chat."

Harlene gave Liddle a kiss on the cheek and let him go. In the squad room, Liddle walked the perimeter, looking at the maps of the

185

three-town area and the view from the tall windows. "It doesn't look as different as I would have thought."

"The town isn't any more generous with its funding than it was in your day."

"Less, it sounds like." Liddle shot him a glance. "How popular is this idea about shutting down the department?"

"Hard to tell. The economy's not great, and state taxes aren't going down any time soon. If the town can hold the line on increases for a few years, all the better for some folks."

Liddle shook his head. "Not enough people left who remember when Cossayuharie and Fort Henry had to rely on the state police."

"That was when you started, right?" Russ hitched himself onto the pine table and watched with some bemusement as Liddle did the same.

"Right. I've got nothing against the staties—I started out as a trooper myself. But their mission isn't to serve individual communities. It's not their strength." Liddle nodded toward the whiteboard, currently covered in Jane Doe information and theories. "It was the first of these killings that got Harry McNeil up in arms to join up the three towns. It was just the police force at first, you know, with Cossayuharie and Fort Henry tossing in for a couple new officers. Merging the administrations and the town boards came later, when folks realized they could save money by . . ." He pushed his hands toward each other.

"Centralizing?"

"Yep. And now they want to hand it over to the state again. Chief McNeil must be rolling in his grave."

"I've been rereading your file on the 1972 Jane Doe case."

"I imagine you would be."

"You weren't trying to find connections to the earlier case."

"Not many," Liddle agreed. "My prime suspects were all young men—those two hippies out at the farm."

"And me."

"And you." Liddle cocked his head. "You didn't do it, did you?"

Russ laughed. "No."

42. The chief came back into the squad room after saying goodbye to the one-hundred-year-old cop. Which wasn't really fair, Hadley acknowledged; the man had been in good shape, kind of stocky and square, but holy God, if he'd been the chief when Van Alstyne was young he must be older than dirt.

"You said you had something?"

"Yeah." She set her laptop on the table and flipped it up. "I've been following up on the call-in reports, and like you said, most of them are junk." Wading through the voice messages and e-mails this morning had made organizing autopsy photos seem like a fun job. Psychics, heavy breathers, confession junkies—no wonder Noble had wanted a break. "However, there's one that looked promising." She enlarged the e-mail so the chief didn't have to put on his reading glasses. "This guy's the general manager of the Water View, a restaurant on Lake George near Bolton Landing. He said the missing girl resembled a waitress who'd been working for him. She had last Thursday and Friday off, and didn't show up for work Saturday. He hasn't seen her since. He attached a picture they took of the staff on the Fourth of July—see?" She switched to the photo and blew it up. "This is the girl." She pointed to a smiling blonde. "What do you think?"

The chief frowned. "Did you talk to the manager personally?"

"He's not in until three. The woman I spoke with over the phone did confirm one of their waitstaff had skipped out and hasn't shown up yet."

"Follow up. Take the good photos with you, and see if you can find out anything about a roommate, her background, whatever. See if anyone has more pictures of her. It's hard to tell from one group shot."

"Okay." She folded up the laptop.

"And Knox?"

"Chief?"

"I didn't say anything this morning, because we want to keep it on the QT, but thanks for putting Kevin up last night."

She wondered if Kevin had said anything to Reverend Clare. "Happy to help, Chief."

189

◆ ◆ ◆

It was a beautiful day to drive north to Bolton Landing—the hills in falling waves of smoke and slate blue and green-black to her left and brilliant flashes of the lake to her right. Hadley tried to appreciate it—she had read an article on improving your life by improving your outlook—but mostly she watched her problems scuttle back and forth across her mental windshield. What to do about Flynn. Would the porn story get out? Where could she get a decent job if the department closed? How to get Granddad to pay attention to his health. Nasty little things with no solutions, breeding more and more worries in the dark.

It was noticeably cooler next to the lake than it had been in Millers Kill. The Water View was a rambling white clapboard building, with green shutters and wide porches facing Lake George. Hadley could see why she had never heard of it—even from the pea gravel parking lot, she could tell she couldn't afford to eat here. Through a screen of balsam trees, she could glimpse another building, definitely *without* a water view—probably the staff dorm. Rental property was out of reach for most college students working in Lake George for the summer; many of the large hotels and restaurants solved the problem by providing housing. Which, Hadley supposed, had the added benefit of keeping them close at hand and accountable.

She headed for the restaurant first, walking past a few Beemers and Mercedes as well as several beat-up station wagons. In Lake George's older-is-better culture, the wagon owners might have more in the bank than the folks with German imports. The sun-dazzled green and blue outside made the interior cave-dark for a moment, nothing but the clink of cutlery and the rising and falling of many conversations. She blinked her eyes, and was just adjusting to gleaming wood and brass when a voice hailed her.

"Good afternoon." A professionally friendly young woman was looking at Hadley from behind a podium. "Do you have reservations"—her face changed as she registered Hadley's uniform—"Officer?"

"I'm looking for the food manager." It seemed like a silly title. Weren't they all food managers in a restaurant?

"What can you tell me about her?"

"Oh, goodness." The older woman took a deep breath and sat up straighter. "Let's see. Her name is—was Gabrielle Yates. I'll get her personnel file to you before you leave."

"Family?"

"Not to speak of. She came out of some foster-home situation in Kentucky—I think her parents, if they're alive, are drug addicts. She had been working in the hospitality industry since she was sixteen. We hired her last summer, she did a good job, we rehired her this year. She was twenty-two. So young."

"Did she know anyone here in New York? Did she have a boyfriend or people she was close to?"

"She might have met some people last year. Generally speaking, the summer employees tend to flock together, though, so I'd be surprised if she had made any friends among the locals. A boyfriend? I never heard of one."

"Could she have been"—Hadley searched for a term that wouldn't sound offensive—"entertaining men?"

"Prostitution? No, don't apologize. Believe me, thirty years working in restaurants and you see everything at least once. I don't think so. Not necessarily for moral reasons, but Gabrielle was starting to think of her future."

"Wanting to continue working for the same company in Florida?"

"Most people don't realize it, but the hospitality industry offers a great deal to disadvantaged workers. Someone like Gabrielle, without a high school diploma, can wind up earning more than a typical high school teacher. Or for immigrants, like me. I started out as a cleaner with barely a dozen words of English."

"I see your point." Hadley took a sip of tea, letting the picture of Gabrielle Yates coalesce in her mind. "She was starting to think about getting ahead in life, rather than just living in the moment."

"A very good summation, yes."

"May I see her room?"

"Of course." Mrs. Beshir picked up the phone, asked for Tori. The same girl who had escorted Hadley down the hallway appeared, carrying a cardboard container for leftovers. Hadley deduced no one left the food manager's office empty-handed. When she handed Hadley the box, it weighed at least ten pounds. "Please keep us informed. If her relatives don't . . . claim her, we'd like to take care of her."

"I will."

Walking over to the staff dorm, Hadley questioned her escort, but Tori, at eighteen, was not part of the older, legal-drinking group Gabrielle had hung out with. "I know she liked to party. And I heard she was DTF." She saw Hadley's puzzled expression. "Down to—"

"Got it. Guys, or girls?"

"Guys, I think."

"Did she ever bring somebody back to the dorm?"

Tori shook her head. "We're not allowed to have guests in the dorm. They say it's a liability thing." She rolled her eyes.

The staff dorm itself was whitewashed and airy, plank walls and creaking wooden floors, with high ceilings to draw the summer heat up and away. Hadley imagined it was what cabins in sleepaway camps were like. Gabrielle's room was simple: an iron bed, unmade, a narrow desk and chair beneath the screened window, a painted bureau and pegs head-height along the wall instead of a closet.

Hadley searched the drawers. A lot of tops and shorts from Walmart, which Hadley recognized because it, along with Goodwill, was where she did most of her own clothes shopping. Floaty short dresses and skirts hung from some of the pegs. The footwear in the corner was all flip-flops and sneakers.

There were condoms in the desk drawer, as well as a full array of makeup and nail polish. No phone. No bills, no paperwork—like most of her generation, her life was probably online, accessed through the missing phone.

Hadley turned around, trying to wring something more from the small room. Not much to show for twenty-two years. "Where did she like to go? When she went out?"

Tori blew out a breath. "I don't know. There are a lot of bars in Lake George. Some of the girls like to go to brunch at the yacht club place. You know, maybe they could meet a rich guy?" She rolled her eyes again. "She was supposed to go to the fair with us this past Monday."

"Yeah?"

"She had gone last year. She told me it was a lot of fun." Tori paused. "I guess we know why she missed it now."

43. Russ caught Knox as she was walking in. "Good. I was about to call you. I just got the royal summons from the mayor's office. The town lawyer's shown up and he wants to talk to you about your ex-husband's lawsuit."

She screwed her eyes shut. "Oh, Christ."

"I told them as your supervising officer, any professional misconduct was my responsibility. So I'm going to sit in on the interview."

"Really?"

"Really. I'm not going to let anyone hang you out to dry, Knox."

"Thanks. That's . . . thank you."

The town hall was just a couple blocks up Main Street, so they walked. "I'm sorry this is taking time away from the case," Knox said, as they passed storefronts devoted to yarn and bad landscape paintings.

"I'm not so worried about the case as about the referendum. I mean, yeah, we need to close the case, the sooner the better. But I'd like to see this business put to rest and forgotten before Election Day rolls around."

"You think something like this can be forgotten?"

A group of tourists crossed the street toward them. He tried to smile in a way that said *Welcome! Please spend your money here.* "Are we talking about the lawsuit? Or what's been happening with you?"

She looked away.

"I'm not going to lie and say people won't remember if they're pressed. But I can tell you that as soon as a juicy new story comes along, the old one gets put away. Look at Clare and me. These days, I bet only twenty percent of conversations in the greater Millers Kill area involve our scandalous relationship."

Knox was laughing as they walked through the door. He hoped he had helped; at times his most recent hire reminded him of a galvanized line that wired two halves of an ancient maple together in the front yard of his boyhood home. He had watched it from his bedroom window as it held through thunderstorms and blizzards, assuming it would last forever. Then one mild summer morning it snapped with a sound like a thousand cicadas, and the two halves, each as large as a full-grown tree, smashed to the ground. During the cleanup, his grandpa Campbell had found one end of the line. It was loose, deformed, with dozens of tiny wires splayed out at the end, as if they had been trying to escape. "Remember this when you're building something, Russell." Grandpa looked across the yard at Russ's mother. "Everything has a breaking point."

"Chief?" Knox had paused halfway down the hall.

"Sorry." He strode after her. The clerk waved them through to the mayor's office.

Jim Cameron was in his usual uniform, rolled-up shirtsleeves, bright tie, pressed khakis. He looked like a *GQ* cover next to the other man in the room. "Russ." The mayor nodded. "I don't know if you've met Julius Arlam from Arlam and Bales."

Arlam was in his sixties, shorter than Knox and with the kind of belt-busting belly that only comes with lovingly tending it over the decades. His few hairs, white and gray, were mounting a stand-up protest against his encroaching pink scalp. His suit, despite being some indestructible drip-dry polyester, managed to be both rumpled and stained. All in all, he looked like he ought to be at Belmont, betting on the sixth, rather than practicing law.

"No," Russ said. "I met Mr. Bales."

Arlam shook his hand. "For your employment contract, I bet. Bill Bales is the guy you meet when you're talking about defined benefits. I'm the guy you get when someone needs a beat-down." He looked Knox up and down before taking her hand. "You must be the young lady with the creepy ex-husband."

Knox didn't seem charmed.

"Let's all sit down, shall we? My firm is going to charge you a ridiculous amount for this. We might as well get the most out of it."

Russ was impressed by Arlam's ability to make the mayor's office seem like his own. He took a seat as the lawyer flipped open a yellow pad and clicked his pen. "Okay, Miss Knox—"

"Officer Knox." Hadley's voice was firm. "In this context, anyway."

"Officer Knox, right. What's your version of events?"

She gave Arlam the same rundown as Russ had heard. A little more precision about the times and action, a little less information about her emotions. Arlam muttered *hmmm* and *uh-huh* as he wrote on his legal pad. "Okay, Officer Knox. Now tell me if you asked Officer Flynn to mess up your ex for you."

"No! I told you—"

"Were you and he lovers?"

Knox turned a shade of pink Russ had never seen before. "What?"

"Lovers. An item. Dancing the horizontal hokey pokey."

"We did not have a romantic relationship." Knox spoke like each word was costing her a hundred bucks. "He's eight years younger than me."

Arlam's eyebrows went up. "That's a kind of chastity belt, now? Chief Van Alstyne, what's the age difference between you and your wife?"

"Thirteen years," Russ growled. "And our department has a no-fraternization policy."

"It's nice you think that makes a difference." Arlam turned back to Knox. "So you're saying that out of the blue, this guy you've only ever worked with decides to plant a schedule II(d) drug in your former husband's suitcase all on his own? For funsies?"

"I'm not saying that at all! I left the room with my kids while Flynn—Officer Flynn—held Dylan to prevent him from attacking them! Or me! I don't *know* what happened after that!"

"Good." Arlam set his pen down. "That's the essence of your story, and that's what I need you to get across when the opposing counsel deposes you."

"I thought you were representing me!"

Arlam screwed up his face. "I represent the *town,* young lady. My interest in you is making sure you're not going to crack under pressure and confess to conspiracy to endanger. That would put us all in a very uncomfortable—not to mention costly—position."

Russ leaned toward Knox. "If you want an attorney of your own, the union can help you out."

"I don't know." She jammed her fingers into her boy-short hair, reminding Russ of the way Clare would unpin and pin the knot at the nape of her neck. "Part of me feels I shouldn't need a lawyer because I didn't *do* anything." She glared at Arlam. "As for Flynn, I can honestly say he's quite possibly the most straitlaced guy I've ever met."

"He does have that reputation," Russ agreed.

"If I can ever locate Officer Flynn and get a deposition out of him, I'll be sure to keep that in mind."

Russ focused on keeping his face still. In his peripheral vision, he saw Knox glance at him, then away.

"You two wouldn't have any knowledge of his whereabouts, would you?"

"Officer Flynn is working for the Syracuse Police Department. He doesn't report to me anymore."

"A little birdie told me opposing counsel is having a hell of a time finding him. They sent somebody to his parents' house." Arlam grinned, foxlike. Russ could swear he saw a feather drooping from the corner of his mouth. "He royally cheesed off Assemblywoman Flynn, which, since she might be our new representative, is all to the good for us."

"What happens if they can't find him?" Knox asked.

Arlam waved the question away. "Sooner or later, he'll surface, and the sheriff's department will serve him. In the meantime, you two will be getting deposed." He shot a look at Knox. "Try not to get so shrill next time."

Knox narrowed her eyes and opened her mouth. Russ set his hand on her sleeve. "You'll need my deposition as well?"

"They're going to want to know about Officer Flynn's training, your departmental standards, how you secure evidence, where the meth came from—that's assuming he didn't just buy it somewhere—"

Russ shook his head. "No way. I'd sooner believe my mother was buying meth than Kevin Flynn."

"I'd sooner believe it, too," the mayor murmured.

Russ glared at him. "As for evidence, we were working a case that involved meth, but the MKPD didn't take possession of any product. It all went to the Essex County Sheriff's office." From the corner of his eye, he saw Knox tense.

Evidently, the lawyer noticed it as well. "Officer Knox? Does that square with your recollection?"

"Um. Most of it went up in a fire, but yes, anything that remained was secured by the sheriff's department."

She spoke the absolute truth, but there was still something there. Russ didn't know what, but he knew he wanted to hear about it before Cameron and Arlam did.

"I'd really like to get Officer Knox back on patrol. If you're done with her, I can give you the rundown on our training and procedures."

Arlam frowned. "I guess."

Knox bolted from her seat. "Okay. I'll see you at the briefing, Chief."

"Or even before then," Russ said mildly. He caught her eye.

She blinked rapidly, but didn't respond. Once the door had swung shut behind her, he turned like a man facing a firing squad. "All right, Mr. Arlam. What do you want to know?"

44.

The chief returned an hour after she had fled the town hall. Hadley desperately wanted to get in her cruiser and disappear—even roadwork detail sounded good right now—but she made herself stay and write up her notes on this morning's interview with Mrs. Beshir and Tori the waitress. Van Alstyne poked his head into the squad room just as she was finishing up. "Knox? In my office."

She stood up, squaring her shoulders and tucking her uniform blouse into her waistband. In his office, the chief closed the door. Hadley's stomach lurched. He always kept the door ajar when she was in here with him.

He sat at his desk and gestured for her to take the chair opposite. "I want you to tell me what you didn't tell the attorney," he said.

"Um . . . I . . ."

"Knox." He leaned forward. "When we were talking about the meth in evidence. There was something you kept back." He tapped his desk. "Tell me."

"Oh, God." She covered her eyes. "I don't know."

"Did you plant the drugs on your ex-husband?"

"No." She was absolutely sure of that.

"Then what?"

She filled her lungs with air. Breathed out slowly. "You know the dep sent us to Albany to dig up leads on the location of the meth house or to find someone who was inside the organization."

"Yes."

"We ran down a guy. He was carrying, maybe five or six envelopes." She held an imaginary glassine square between her fingers. The chief nodded. "Flynn tossed them into his glove compartment after we frisked the guy. We were in his SUV because of the weather."

"I remember."

"There was . . . it was confusing. We were talking with the feds, and the DEA, and the Albany PD, and then I got a call from Harlene saying Dylan had taken the kids, and I was so scared . . ." She took another deep breath. "We never turned the envelopes in. We got the kids, and there was that terrible ice storm to get through, and we were all run off our feet, and . . ." She looked at her lap, tight-lipped. Then she raised her eyes to meet his. "Chief, I swear to you, I had completely forgotten about them until I heard from the Albany Airport Police. A courtesy call. Blue to blue."

"And they told you what?"

"Dylan's carry-on had been searched, and they found meth on him."

"Why didn't I hear any of this back in January?"

"Because literally, when I got back to the station, I walked right into . . . the guys had all seen . . ."

"The videos."

Her lips twisted. "A parting shot from Dylan. If he couldn't control my life, he could at least ruin it." She sounded as bitter as salt water, and she didn't care.

"And you never saw the drugs again."

"Flynn—" She steadied her voice. "Flynn resigned the same day."

Van Alstyne sat back. "Do you think he went to Syracuse because of the missing meth?"

She paused for a moment. She had confessed to the chief because this lawsuit was going to involve him and the whole department. But her brief relationship with Flynn? That wasn't anybody's business but her own. "Maybe? I don't know. I didn't think he was the kind of guy to run away from problems."

"Neither did I," the chief said dryly. "On the other hand, I never thought he might frame up someone, either."

"We don't *know* that for sure."

"You suspect it, though." She nodded. "Did you think so at the time? When you heard from Albany?"

She nodded again. "What do you want to do, Chief?" She swallowed. "Do you want me to resign?"

"I told you a couple days ago that wasn't necessary. I haven't changed my mind." He pinched the bridge of his nose beneath his glasses. "I don't know what I want to do." His eyes sharpened. "No, I do know something. I know I need to talk to Kevin Flynn."

AUGUST 1972

45. "I've got a name for you."

Jack tightened his grip on the receiver in his hand. "George, I could kiss you."

Gifford laughed. "I'm holding out for someone prettier than you, Chief." There was a rustling sound of paper near the phone. "Okay, the registrar ID'd her. Natalie Epstein, born October eighteen, '52. Father is Harold Epstein, 41 West Seventy-second Street, New York."

"The city. I knew it."

"I got his home and work numbers. Ready?"

Jack scribbled it down. "Did you get the contact info of any friends? Roommates?"

"She dropped out last year, after the first semester. Her roomie from the year before is studying abroad." Jack could hear Gifford rolling his eyes at that.

"That's fine. The father's the real lead."

"You want me to keep heading south and see if I can interview him?"

"Let me try him on the phone first. If anything sounds hinky, I'll contact the NYPD before we see him in person. Don't want to poke a stick at New York's Finest."

"I hear you. Okay, I'll see you back at the shop."

"Good work, George." Jack hung up. He carried the notepad he'd been writing on to his secretary's desk. "Harlene, I want you to connect me to this long-distance number. Send it straight to my phone."

"Sure." She settled her headset gingerly over her bouffant hair, then paused. Jack guessed she'd get the job done a lot faster if he wasn't hanging over her shoulder and retreated back to his office. It took her a few minutes to sort out, but eventually the phone rang. He picked it up. The other line rang twice, then a professionally polite voice answered, "Kriggs, Epstein, and Springer."

Law firm? Accountants? "I'd like to speak to Mr. Epstein, please."

"Mr. Harold Epstein? Or Mr. Leonard Epstein?"

"The former."

"I'm afraid he's going into a conference. May I take a message for him?"

"This is Chief John Liddle of the Millers Kill Police Department. I'm calling about his daughter Natalie. I need to speak with him in person, as soon as possible."

"Oh!" There was a pause. "Um. Please hold, while I try to get him for you."

The line went to the blank non-tone of hold. Jack doodled on his notepad, circles and swirls that became big looping curls. He crosshatched over them and was about to open a drawer for his scheduling folder when he heard a click and a sigh. "This is Harold Epstein." The man sounded resigned to hearing bad news.

"Mr. Epstein, this is Jack Liddle of the Millers Kill Police—"

"If it's bail money, I'm not paying it."

Jack blinked. "No." Better to get it over with quick. "I'm sorry to tell you this, but your daughter is dead."

There was a long pause. "Is this some kind of sick joke?"

"Mr. Epstein, I'm sure this is a shock, and if I could have told you face-to-face—"

"Where is Millers Kill? Near Poughkeepsie?"

"We're in the southern Adirondack region. About an hour and a half north of Albany."

"North of Albany. Jesus Christ."

Jack thought there were worse places to die, but perhaps that wasn't Epstein's point. "I have a few questions about Natalie—"

"Are you sure it's her?"

"Her roommates have confirmed her identity, but we'd like a family member to come up if possible." He paused, but there was no reply. "Did you know your daughter had left Vassar?"

"I knew she dropped out, if that's what you mean. I told her if she couldn't carry through with something as simple as studying goddamn English, she wasn't going to get another cent from me. Goddammit. I can't believe it. Wait, I gotta get something to write with. What did you say your name is?"

Jack repeated his name and position, and gave Epstein the address and phone number of the station. "Like I said, we'd like you or another family member to ID her, but in the meantime, I'd like to find out what you knew about Natalie's activities."

"I knew squat. She came home after the fall term, told me she wanted to get a *real* education from life, and proceeded to hang around the house for a month, sleeping all day and going out all night. I told her get a job, or leave, and she left. Goddammit. Goddamn—" There was a wet slap of sound. The man was crying. Then the phone went dead.

"Crap." Jack hung up. He went into Harlene's office. "I lost the call."

"Oh, no." She looked at her switchboard.

"No, no, it's nothing you did. I got the father, and he was understandably upset. I'm going to give it ten minutes and call him back." Time enough to get started on the schedule for next month, at least.

He had gotten as far as penciling in extra cars in the school zones for the first week of September when his phone rang. "It's Mr. Epstein, calling you back," Harlene said when he picked up. "Hang on."

There was a click. "Mr. Epstein? It's Jack Liddle."

"This is Leonard Epstein, Chief Liddle. I'm Natalie's brother. I understand you have some questions."

The brother sounded shaky, but in control.

"I do, thanks. Your father said Natalie left home about a month after dropping out of college. Do you know what she did? Where she went?"

"She read about some commune in Virginia, and went there for a couple weeks. Then she worked her way down to Florida. I know her plan was to meet up with some of her Vassar friends for spring break. That was the last we heard from her."

"That was when? February?"

"March. Dad says she was upstate?"

"At a sort of mini-commune with a few other kids. It sounds like she and your dad didn't part on the best of terms. Is there anyone else she might have been in contact with? Maybe her mother?" It wasn't unheard of for a kid to keep a line open to Mom without the dad knowing about it.

"Our mother died when Nat was little. If she had been in touch with me or any of my brothers, we would have told Dad. Nat's the— was the youngest. We all looked out for her."

"I see. How about a few days ago? According to the people she lived with, Natalie decided to leave the commune. One of them drove her to the bus station in time to meet the northbound coach from New York. She didn't have much money, and we don't know of any reason why she'd head further north. Could she have called someone to come up and rescue her?"

"I guess? I can't think of anyone off the top of my head. Sorry."

"Okay. I know it's a lot to absorb. When one of you comes up to identify her body—"

"That'll be me."

"Good. Before you head north, could you look through Natalie's belongings? We're particularly interested in any address books or diaries she might have had. Anything that might connect her to someone at that bus station." Jack didn't mention the possibility that she had wandered away and been picked up by some random guy, because if that was the case, he had absolutely nothing to go on. *Except Russell Van Alstyne,* a cool voice in his head reminded him. He focused on Leonard Epstein, detailing his plan for busing up tomorrow morning. "Great. Thank you. We'll see you then."

"Chief Liddle? Just—one thing I didn't get from my father. How did Natalie die?"

THURSDAY, AUGUST 24, PRESENT DAY

46. Clare figured hitting up the library with a baby carrier in one hand and a tote bag of board books in the other must be the most pitiful version of playing hooky possible. Lois had already left for the day, and Clare had told Elizabeth she and Ethan needed an air-conditioning break. And that her books were due. The neat brass chime of the bell over the door sounded like a guilty toll in her ears. The books were an excuse. She was here to do some research.

Michael Penrod was at the massive oak desk that served as check-out station, reference desk, and director's office. "Reverend Clare!" His cheerful face immediately drew in. "I'm afraid you've got the wrong day. Tot Time was Wednesday."

She hoisted the tote onto the desk. "I do come to the library for things other than Tot Time." Penrod made a noncommittal noise as he transferred the small square books into the return basket. "At least, I used to."

He held up the only adult item in the bag: Louise Penny's latest mystery. "Did you like it?"

"I didn't finish it. The only free time I have is in the bathroom, and I didn't have to go frequently enough to make it to the end before it was due back."

"Mmm. Tough to get in reading time with a baby." Penrod slid it to the side, undoubtedly planning to check it later for unpleasant odors or toilet-paper bookmarks. "There are only a couple patrons here, if you want to spread a blanket out for Ethan in the children's room."

"Actually, I was hoping you could help me. I'd like to look at some old newspapers."

"Old as in last week?"

"Old as in 1972."

"Okay . . . which ones? We have a pretty limited supply on hand, although we do have a digital subscription to the *New York Times* that lets us use their archives."

"No, strictly local. I think. The *Post-Star* and whatever else was publishing in the Millers Kill area."

"That would be in the microfilm stacks in the basement. Um—" He looked at Ethan, sucking his fist in his carrier. "It's not a terribly kid-friendly environment."

"I'll keep him strapped in. If he starts to get fussy, we'll leave." She had milk-bombed Ethan and put on a fresh diaper before leaving the church, so she was hopeful he'd stay content for the next little while.

Penrod gestured toward the reading room, where the afternoon sun poured in through tall Palladian windows to light a single elderly man who appeared to be napping in one of the worn leather chairs. "Like I said, we're not too busy at the moment."

"With the heat, I'd think everybody would be here." Clare plucked at her clerical blouse, letting the cool air in.

"They're at the fair. At the end of the school year all the local kids get an admission pass and tickets good for one free ride for Thursday. If you have a couple of youngsters, this is the day to go."

"How many kids stop after the one ride?"

"Well, that's why it's smart marketing, isn't it?" The entrance to the basement was squeezed in between the children's room—once the library office—and the restroom—formerly a closet. Penrod removed the childproof gate blocking the stairway and set it aside. "Watch your step," he warned.

Clare hugged Ethan's carrier to her chest as she maneuvered down the narrow circular stair, installed long before modern building codes. She could feel the temperature dropping as she descended. "This is where we keep the microfiche and microfilm readers." Penrod led her into a windowless room. "This one's for microfilm." He pointed to a rectangular machine the size of a dorm refrigerator weighing down a long, narrow table. "Do you know how to use it?"

"Unless they've changed since my college days, yes."

"You're all set. This one dates from the early sixties." The librarian thumped the battleship-gray metal. "They made 'em to withstand a nuclear explosion back then."

"Looks like the room can, too." The interior cinderblock walls had been painted white in an attempt to maximize the overhead fluorescents, but the exterior walls were the original nineteenth-century granite.

"It can." Penrod beamed with pride of ownership. "In the fifties, the basement was an official fallout shelter." Clare had no good response for that. "All our materials are in the stacks, arranged by publication and date." He pointed to a small wooden card catalog. "No computer down here, so you have to look things up the old-fashioned way, I'm afraid."

"I remember how to do that, too."

"You'd be surprised," the librarian said. "I'll be upstairs if you need me."

Clare set Ethan's carrier on the table next to the microfilm machine and attached his latest dangling toys to the handle. The baby strained for the black-and-white shapes, and once he had his fingertips on one, began batting it furiously. Clare shook her head. "I'm not sure you appreciate the educational nature of your toys, baby boy."

Ethan banged away at a zebra-striped triangle while she located the boxes containing the 1972 runs of the *Post-Star* and the now-defunct *Greenwich Journal*. She started with the Glens Falls paper. Threading the tightly wound celluloid strip through the machine's bars and rollers was trickier than she remembered, as was forwarding to the right month. She had to go back and forth and finally adjust the image by hand until she was looking at August 19, 1972.

She scanned past headlines about taxes and protests and county commissioners. The paper covered a lot more national news in 1972 than it did today. She paused at a story about Nixon's reelection campaign. If she recalled correctly, the Watergate burglary was happening right around the time this paper was rolling off the presses. Who was it who said *Newspapers are the first draft of history?*

Some things stayed the same. There was a full-page ad for the Washington County Fair, and a story about a 4-H kid hoping to take home a blue ribbon for his calf. Two car accidents involving tourists from downstate. In the Women's section—Clare rolled her eyes hard—one of the weddings announced had taken place at St. Alban's, and the society photos of summer people at fundraisers and parties could have been taken this past weekend, if you allowed for bigger hair and wider ties.

She moved on to the next day. Nothing. In the August twenty-first paper, she spotted the first story about the death, a small column headed BODY FOUND IN MILLERS KILL, POLICE INVESTIGATE. It was short on details and speculation.

The next day's paper had more. The story was twice as large, and had moved to the front of the Local section. The MKPD had ruled the death suspicious, but were withholding details about how the victim had died. She was still unidentified, but there was an artist's rendering of what she would have looked like in life. In the August twenty-second edition, her picture was replaced by a photo of Russ in uniform: skinny, shorn, and looking too young to be out of school yet. Clare touched the screen over the image. It was his official ID, taken when he was fresh out of boot. She looked at Ethan, nestled in flannel, gumming his hand. Tried to imagine him going off to war in eighteen years. How had Margy done it?

The recently returned soldier was a person of interest in the girl's death, the story read, and gave the basic facts about Russ's military service. He had been the star forward for the Millers Kill basketball team in '68 and '69, which she hadn't known, and his mother was active in the local antiwar movement, which she had. The implications that Russ had been a good kid twisted by the war seemed pretty clear.

The next day the story was front-page. The girl was identified as a member of a commune in Millers Kill. The members of the group had refused to talk to the reporter, but their neighbors had apparently been happy to share the unconfirmed details—drugs, orgies, and organic farming. All of them seemed to be equally suspicious to the neighbors.

The next day the front-page slot had been replaced with a look at the county fair. There was a letter to the editor about the mysterious death, though, pointing out that returning vets weren't all unregenerate killers. It read as a pretty low bar to Clare.

There was an update story on the twenty-fifth, but nothing new. Two days later it had gone back to a small column inside the local section: POLICE STILL SEEKING ANSWERS TO DEATH. "Aren't we all," Clare said.

Ethan was still wearing himself out on the padded triangle, so she rewound the spool to a few days before the crime and began skimming. She wasn't looking for something particular—just seeing if anything caught her eye. If she was being honest with herself, she had to admit she wasn't sure if she was trying to help Russ out, or to see if there were parts of the story he hadn't shared with her. She was confident he'd never lie to her, but the fact he'd never mentioned being a suspect in the death of a young girl made her . . . suspicious? No, that wasn't the right word. Concerned.

Caught up in her own head, she was already a page past when she realized she had seen the name Langevoort. That *had* to be related to her new intern. She dialed back to the Business section, where a small article announced the president of Barkley and Eaton, Lloyd Harrington, was handing the reins over to his chief financial officer, Kent Langevoort. Joni's dad. Barkley and Eaton, blah, blah, blah, headquartered in New York but with deep roots in the Adirondacks, thanks to founder Samuel A. Barkley. Not much else useful. Langevoort was only thirty-one, which seemed awfully young to be taking over a company. Of course, people seemed to mature earlier back then. Her own parents had married right out of college and had four kids by the time they were twenty-seven.

She kept dialing the pages forward, but her train of thought had jumped the track to tomorrow night, and the fundraiser, and meeting Joni's parents' friends. She ought to do some homework on Barkley and Eaton but she didn't need to crank microfilm in a basement for that information.

Her phone began playing "I fought the law and the law won." Russ's ringtone. She snatched it out of Ethan's diaper bag and answered. "Hey."

"Hey, darlin'. Are you busy right now?"

She pressed the rewind button. The spool whirred into action. "Nope. What can I do for you?"

"I need to talk with Kevin, but I can't waltz up to him in the midway and ask for a chat. I don't want to leave messages on his phone, just in case."

She pulled the spool out and maneuvered it back into its case one-handed. "So you figure the friendly local priest who helped him out might check up on him?"

"Would you?"

She grinned. "Help with an investigation? I thought you'd never ask."

47.

The downside of undercover work—well, one of the downsides—was that you actually had to do the job you'd been hired for. For some cops, that meant hanging around street corners and going to raves. Kevin had met one guy who'd been investigating an ice-cream parlor suspected of laundering drug money. Two months scooping cones and mopping up after kids who'd dropped their treats. At the time, Kevin had felt sorry for him, but right now, after a full day of shouting pitches at passersby, wheedling guys into laying down for one more chance at winning a teddy bear for the girlfriend, and constantly restocking, resetting, sweeping up BBs, stomping boxes, wiping off the counter—he'd spend the rest of his life in a nice, air-conditioned sweet shoppe and count himself grateful. Or, more to the point, in a nice, air-conditioned squad car with a radar gun.

But now, finally, it was five o'clock, which meant the end of his shift. As a new jointy, he got morning and midday, the least profitable time. The older, more experienced agent got evening to close, when the lot was packed with young adults with money to burn and enough alcohol in their systems to make them indifferent as to how much they lost. Kevin could see the man headed his way to take over. Except when he stepped out of the sun's glare, it wasn't the agent. It was the boss.

"Hey, Mr. Hill." Was he blown? He'd seen at least four people on the midway today who could have ID'd him, although no one showed any signs of recognizing straight-arrow Kevin Flynn behind the beard and tattoos. "You subbing in for Don?"

"Yeah. Lemme in."

Kevin unlatched the side door and swung it open. Two bodies behind the counter made him realize how small the joint was.

"How's it been today?"

"Crazy." Kevin pulled the plastic tub where he tossed tickets off the shelf. It was more than half-full.

"Good. Good." Hill looked over the plush display; stuffed animals hung in thick garlands, the big bears looming over the target board. "How's your stock holding up?"

"I went through three boxes today, but they didn't all move. I like to keep the display really flashed."

"You got good instincts, kid." Hill turned toward him. "You're not going to have any more trouble with the cops, are you?"

"No, sir."

"'Cause you know, if I catch you selling drugs on my show, I'm kicking you out and you walk home. It don't matter how good a worker you are."

"I know, Mr. Hill. I'm not dealing."

"I don't expect my people to be choirboys, but I got rules. No drugs and no turning tricks."

211

"I'm definitely not doing that."

Hill cuffed him on the back of the head, laughing. "Okay. Get those tickets to Joe, he'll mark your tally. Make sure you—Uh-oh, look at this. Is that the minister who brought you back?"

Kevin followed Hill's gaze and sure enough, there was Reverend Clare, black dress, white collar, looking like she was out to save souls.

"Never known a preacher to do a favor for free," Hill said. "There's always a pitch on the backside."

The reverend reached his booth. "Hi, Kevin." She smiled brightly at the boss. "Hi, I'm Clare Fergusson." She stuck out her hand.

"Brent Hill."

"Kevin, I was wondering if I could take you out to dinner. If you get a break, that is."

"Um . . ." He didn't want to seem eager.

"You're in luck, Pastor. I'm relieving him right now." Hill's eyes gleamed with amusement. "Go on, Kevin. Say a prayer for me."

"No, no, no, nothing like that. Just a burger. And maybe I could set you up with a bag of groceries."

"That would be great!" Kevin didn't hide the enthusiasm in his voice. Carny work didn't pay much; Hill wouldn't think it strange for him to jump at a meal *and* thirty or forty bucks' worth of groceries. He unlatched the door and let himself out. "Um. I have to drop my tickets off at the office."

"I'll bag and tag 'em for you, kid." Hill lowered his voice. "Remember, there ain't no such thing as a free lunch."

"I'm parked by the main entrance." Reverend Clare pointed and strode off. She kept up a steady flow of loudly pitched questions as they made their way through the lot—Was the job hard? How did he get health care if he needed it? What were his living conditions like? Kevin got so lulled by the give-and-take of her do-gooderism he was startled when they passed through the gates and her voice dropped. "Russ needs to speak with you."

"Why? I mean—"

She unlocked her car. "We're going to the rectory. Don't worry." She grinned. "You really are getting dinner and a bag of pantry staples." She slid into her seat. Kevin got in. Inside, her car smelled like antiseptic wipes and old milk. "I hope this is okay. I don't want to raise any suspicions on the part of your coworkers."

"Don't worry. If I'd thought it would look bad, I would have blown you off. As it is, the old guy in the booth is my boss, and he thinks it's hysterical that you're going to swap a meal for the chance to proselytize me."

She shifted and pulled out of the parking area. "Oh, you're in luck, then. I've got some day-by-day booklets and prayer guides I can send home with you."

Kevin had been to the chief's old house before. Every summer, he and his wife—his first wife—held a cookout for the department. He guessed the chief would eventually figure out something similar at the new home, but until now, no one from the department had been there, as far as he knew. The MKPD, he corrected himself. Forget staying in character, being back in Washington County was making it hard for Kevin to remember he wasn't part of the Millers Kill family anymore.

The rectory driveway was made private by a tall hedge between it and the church grounds. The reverend parked nose-in, tight to the small carriage house that maybe served as the garage, so the passenger door was facing the steps up to the side entrance. Someone would have to be standing on the sidewalk right in front of the house to see him exiting the car, and even then, he'd be hard to identify.

Nevertheless, Kevin took the steps two at a time. The door opened before he reached it and the chief hustled him inside. A complaining "Hey!" kept him from shutting out his wife.

"Sorry," the chief said. "Kevin, thanks for coming. I know anything out of the norm can be dangerous to an undercover investigation, so I appreciate it."

With a heavy *woof*, a russet Lab mix bounded across the kitchen floor, butting into the reverend. "Easy, Oscar." She pushed against the dog's head. "Let me get the door closed."

"Um. It's no problem, Chief. It's just, I don't know if I have any more information that might help you. I haven't heard any talk about anybody seeing a girl, or getting into trouble." He hadn't heard much talk about anything. He was going to look like he spent the summer playing hooky on the state task force's dime unless he managed to make contact with someone directly involved with the drugs-for-firearms deal.

"Yeah." The chief rubbed the back of his neck. "It's not about that."

The picture snapped into focus. The legal papers he had read at Hadley's dining room table. He had been so swept up with his own involvement, and what it might mean for her, he'd barely registered the other party to the complaint. The Millers Kill Police Department.

"The lawsuit. From Hadley's ex." The dog, done with greeting Reverend Clare, shoved his muzzle into Kevin's hand. He scratched the broad, hard dome of the mutt's head, his mind racing.

"Why don't you two sit down?" Reverend Clare tied a *Have you hugged an Episcopalian today?* apron around her waist. "Russ, where's Ethan?"

"In his bouncy chair in the living room." As if on cue, the baby squawked from beyond the kitchen. Kevin knew a little bit about babies—he had been nine when his youngest brother was born—and he translated the demanding noise into *Why isn't anyone paying attention to me?*

"Want me to get him?" Kevin asked.

The chief looked as if Kevin had offered to perform a card trick. "Please," Reverend Clare said. "Right through there." She pointed to the swinging louvered doors.

Their living room was what he would have expected: some nice antiques, overstuffed furniture, overflowing bookcases. The baby was in a Jolly Jumper in front of the gated-off fireplace. As Kevin approached, he kicked his feet against the floor and sent himself up a good five inches into the air. "Nice one," Kevin said. "The Millers Kill basketball team is going to be glad to see you fifteen years from now."

He slid the baby out of the seat. Ethan stared at his face for a moment before reaching for his beard. "You like that, huh? Your dad doesn't have one of these." He hoisted the jumper—more like a piece of playground equipment than baby furniture—and toted both into the kitchen.

"Thank you, Kevin."

"Let me help you with that." The chief took the jumper out of his hand and placed it on a rubber mat near the pantry door. He didn't sound any different, but then, he wouldn't. Cops dealt with liars all the time, and the side effect was you became a better liar yourself. It was a tool in the kit, like a Maglite and a Taser. Use it to help others, you keep civilians calm and bluff witnesses in investigations. Use it for yourself . . . you wind up dropping nine grams of methamphetamines into your lover's ex-husband's suitcase.

"Kevin?" The chief was looking at him. "Can I have the baby?"

"Oh! Sorry. I was . . ." He decided to not try to explain what he was. He transferred Ethan into the chief's hands and took a seat at the table. Oscar laid his head in Kevin's lap and whined. *Even a dog knows how pitiful I am.* Kevin sighed and scratched between Oscar's ears.

The chief sat down, Ethan straddling one of his legs. The two of them looked across the plain pine table at Kevin with identical blue eyes. "So. Kevin." The chief huffed what might have been a sigh. "Knox tells me she showed you the summons from her ex. The lawsuit."

"Yeah." Kevin glanced toward Reverend Clare. Her back was turned toward them, her hands peeling and chopping. "I read them."

"You realize you're a party to the suit. They'd have served you already if they knew where to find you."

"Yeah, I know how it works, Chief."

"Dylan Knox was stopped and arrested at the Albany airport when a drug-sniffing dog turned up suspicious packages in his suitcase. He claims they weren't his, and that you, Hadley, and the MKPD conspired to frame him for possession." The chief sounded exactly like he did when laying out facts at a briefing. Kevin half-expected to turn around and see Deputy Chief MacAuley writing on a whiteboard.

The chief looked at him expectantly. Kevin shrugged. "He would say that, wouldn't he? I mean, I once picked up a guy who claimed he just happened to catch three bottles of OxyContin someone threw out a window."

"Chad DuKuys." The chief snorted a little. "I was amazed he actually had brains enough to get Oxys. I'd have figured him for the kid whose friends would sell him baby aspirin." Ethan burbled, as if in agreement. "However." The chief's face sobered. "I don't think Dylan Knox is dumb. Mean and vindictive, yes. But not dumb."

Kevin kept his face calm and his voice even. "I don't know what you want me to say, Chief."

"I'd like you to say you had nothing to do with nine grams of meth getting into the man's luggage."

"Okay. I had nothing to do with—"

"Kevin." The chief caught Ethan one-handed as the baby tried to fling himself onto the floor. "Let me rephrase myself. I'd like you to tell me the truth."

Kevin had taken a hike with the Boy Scouts one summer, with an overambitious, inexperienced dad leading the troop. They had gone over a hill and down a gentle slope, following one of the thousand small streams that cross and recross the Adirondack valleys. They had noticed the stream swelling and rising, thanks to a distant line of thunderstorms over the western mountains, but no one had thought to turn back until they reached a spot where the narrowing hills on either side ended and the now-boiling water spilled into a vast and boggy arboreal swamp. Behind them, the stream-side trail was flooded. Ahead of them, the prospect of picking their way from hummock to hummock. Either way, return or go on, someone was going to get a soaking.

Kevin could feel the water splashing at his feet. He knew Chief Van Alstyne. It wouldn't matter his motivation, it wouldn't matter that Hadley's ex had been blackmailing her and threatening to take her kids away. If Chief knew Kevin had planted those baggies of meth, he'd say so. He'd do his best to shield them, of course, because that was also who he was, but the damage would be done. Dylan Knox would be exonerated and Hadley and her kids would come out the losers.

"I don't know where he got those baggies, Chief. Hadley told me he liked to live fast. I know he did drugs when they were together."

The chief leaned forward, causing the baby to crane his neck upward and examine his father's chin. "What about the meth you copped in Albany?"

216

"The DEA guy's bait? I left it at Albany South Station."

"Knox says she never saw you take it from your car."

"Not to throw doubt on Hadley's recollection, Chief, but we were at the station when she found out her ex had taken the kids from her granddad and was planning to leave the state with them. She was a little preoccupied." He was amazed at how easy it was to lie to the chief, so long as he ignored the ache in his stomach and the tight feeling in his chest.

"And that's your story?"

"Do you want me to change it? I mean, if you're looking for a fall guy to definitively get the MKPD off the hook, I'll do it, but it's not my first choice."

"No, no, no. For Christ's sake." At the stove, the reverend coughed. "Pardon my French," the chief said to her back. He turned toward Kevin. "Are you willing to testify to that?"

"Sure." His mouth felt like cotton.

The chief's eyes narrowed. "Kevin . . ."

"Kevin, would you like a drink? I have water, lemonade, and I think there's some flavored seltzer in the fridge." Reverend Clare set three glasses on the table.

"Thanks. Water's fine." He couldn't tell exactly what the dynamic was between husband and wife, but the chief sat back, frowning slightly.

Kevin had never seen anyone bustle before, but there was no doubt that was what Reverend Clare was doing. She poured water, laid bowls and silverware, handed out napkins, and settled a bowl of pasta salad on the table with such purposeful activity it quashed all conversation. She took her seat and said, "Grace," in a tone that was more order than invitation. Kevin and the chief obediently bowed their heads. "Bless, oh Lord, this food to our use and ourselves to your service. Amen." She nudged the salad toward him. "So, Kevin. How is the investigation going?"

◆ ◆ ◆

It was full dark when Reverend Clare dropped him by the back entrance to the fair, where the carny campers were squared off between

217

power poles and electrical lines. As he stepped out of her car, she handed him a bunch of pamphlets. "As promised. Try to look as if you've been preached at all evening long."

He nodded. His nerves were still stretched to a thin line from the chief's questioning. It wasn't going to be difficult to seem uncomfortable.

"Be safe. I'll be praying for you."

"Thanks." He watched her reverse, and then her red lights trailing away into the night. He swiveled his shoulders to loosen the kink in his upper back. Past the trailers, the midway was still going full bore, lighting the sky in brilliant colors, like fireworks fallen to earth. The music from the various rides were a blur of noise from this distance. He had learned to sleep through it.

God, he felt so alone.

Most of the campers were dark as he walked past them, the only noise the dull roar of air conditioners and fans in windows. The night shift was at work, manning the games and rides that would be active until midnight. The day shift was bedded down, sleeping while they could. Tomorrow and Saturday would bring the biggest crowds of the week, followed by Sunday and the break-down that afternoon.

"Hey, Kevin." Aaron Kaspertzy was sitting on a lawn chair outside his trailer. The end of his cigarette was a bright ember in the gloom. "Heard you went off to get converted."

Sitting in the neighboring chair felt like dropping back into his life, as if the Kevin who had lied to the chief while accepting his hospitality was the fake, and the real Kevin had always been the high school dropout and drifter. He waved Reverend Clare's pamphlets. "I dunno about being converted, but I got a good meal for free."

"Any cigarettes?"

Kevin laughed. "No." Kaspertzy held out his pack. Kevin took one and lit it. The first drag felt dangerously good.

"You're not planning on jumping ship, are you?"

"Hell, no," Kevin said. "What would I do, flip burgers? I make better money here, and I like the job. It's, you know, man's work. Not something meant for teenagers after school."

"I just thought, after that run-in with the law, maybe . . ."

"Yeah, that wasn't my best moment." Kevin took another drag on his stick. "I got into a little trouble a couple years ago. There's still some stuff nobody's ever connected me with. Guess I got a little paranoid when that cop came toward me." He mimed smoking weed.

"I hear you, bro." Kaspertzy stretched his legs out. "We all do some dumb shit when we're young. I once got into a fight, sent the other guy to the hospital."

"You get picked up?"

"Naw. I had friends who worked the circuit south. I hit the road and joined up with their show until things cooled off up here."

"What happened to the guy?"

Kaspertzy shrugged. "He healed up. Came out with a funny-looking face, I heard."

Kevin snorted.

"The trick is, to get past the age when you're doing shit for dumb reasons. That guy, we got into a fight because he hit on the girl I was with. I can't even remember her name now. It's not like I still couldn't put somebody in the hospital." He flexed his large bicep. Kevin held up his hands. Kaspertzy laughed. "Not you. I mean, you got to have a purpose in life. Something you're fighting for."

"That would be nice." Kevin took a long drag on his cigarette. "That would be good."

Kaspertzy slapped him on the back, a blow that tilted him halfway out of the lawn chair. "You're all right, Kev. I like you. Hey, you better hit the rack. We'll talk more later."

Kevin could hear the snores of his roommate through the thin wall between their tiny bedrooms. He stretched out on his bed, indulging in one last drag on his cigarette before snuffing it out.

Contact.

AUGUST 1972

48. Leonard Epstein arrived on the noon bus, the first to get into Glens Falls from the city. Even on a weekday, there were a good number of folks spilling through the gate into the station. Hippies in patched vests, farm wives clutching boxy purses beneath their arms, and a mix of vacationers and businesspeople.

Epstein was middling height, in pale pants and a plaid jacket that made him look exactly like a lawyer taking the day off. He was older than Jack had expected—in his early thirties.

Jack introduced himself. "I'm sorry to bring you up for such a miserable reason." He gestured to the door. "I'll take you over to the morgue to get the worst of it over first, and then we can talk in my office."

Outside, Jack had parked his Fairlane in the POLICE ONLY space. "How's your father doing?"

"It was a hell of a shock." Epstein climbed into the passenger seat. "He and Natalie always had a tough relationship. Now—" He shook his head. "Well, there's no chance to mend it now, is there?" He pulled a pack of cigarettes out of his jacket. "Mind?"

"Go ahead." Jack pulled out and began threading his way through the lunchtime traffic. "Why a difficult relationship?"

"Natalie came along quite awhile after the rest of us. Change-of-life baby, I guess. We were all teens and she was a toddler, we were all boys and she was a girl . . . and then Ma died when Nat was seven." Epstein rolled the window down and exhaled a stream of smoke. "I can understand it now, from my vantage point as a father myself. I don't know what I'd do if I lost my wife. Probably what Dad did, which was hire a series of sitters."

"Not the easiest way for a little girl to grow up," Jack observed.

"No. And she let everybody know it by acting up constantly. If there was trouble anywhere, Nat would find it." He pulled out Jack's ashtray and tapped his cigarette. "She worked at our firm a couple summers after graduating high school. Front desk. I had hoped it would . . . show her

220

the possibilities. We would have loved to have her manage the office after she graduated."

"Not so much?"

"Oh, she was great with the *clients*. It was just family she fought with constantly."

"You said you didn't know she was up here."

Epstein shook his head. "If she had just called. Hell, sent a letter. It doesn't matter how busy we were. Somebody would have come up here to get her." He looked outside the window, as if the leafy residential street they were driving through was the most interesting thing he had seen all day. When he finally spoke again, his voice was smaller. "Sometimes I think she felt like she wasn't really part of the family. But she was. She was to us."

The visit to the morgue was cold, formal, and excruciating. Natalie's brother identified her with a jerk of his head. Dr. Roberts gently replaced the sheet over the girl's waxen face. "I'm sorry for your loss, Mr. Epstein. Chief, may I have a moment of your time?"

Jack gestured Epstein toward the tiny waiting room at the end of the hall. "I'll be right with you." When they were alone—or at least, the only living people in the room—he turned back to Dr. Roberts.

"There was semen," she said without preamble. "Obviously, I didn't want to mention it in front of her brother."

"Huh. According to them, neither of the boys at the commune had had sex with her. Well, not for several days before she left." Jack rubbed his lips. Time to haul Isaac Nevinson and Terry McKellan into the station for questioning. Separately. They might lie to save themselves; he didn't think they'd lie to save each other. "You said she hadn't been raped."

"There wasn't any sign of force. That's not to say she wasn't scared into cooperating." Dr. Roberts slid the girl's body back into the mortuary refrigeration unit that served as their cold box. "However, she had alcohol and the remains of a light dinner in her stomach. That says 'date' to me."

"Pretty fast work if it was a stranger."

Dr. Roberts shut the narrow door to the unit. "Times have changed since we were young. You don't even need to buy girls dinner first now."

Jack glanced toward the door. "When will you be ready to release the body?"

Dr. Roberts spread her gloved hands. "You tell me. There's nothing more I can learn from her except how, exactly, she died. And that's utterly stumping me. I've consulted with two other pathologists, and neither of them has been able to help."

Jack wanted to bang his head against the tiled wall. How the hell was he going to prove a homicide when he couldn't prove the cause of death?

"Sorry." Evidently, Dr. Roberts was also a mind reader. "I know that's not what you wanted to hear."

Jack waved her apology away. "It's not your fault." He gestured toward the hall. "You have everything you need? Photos, slides, blood samples?" He held the door open.

"Everything and then some. If I were Dr. Frankenstein, I could re-create her."

The warmth of the hallway was delicious after the chill of the pathology room. He rolled his shoulders to unkink them. "Okay. I'll authorize the release. I'll suggest a few local funeral homes to Mr. Epstein, and they can handle the transfer down to New York."

The midday sun hit like a blast furnace when he and Epstein walked outside. They made the drive to the police station in silence, Jack considering his lack of leads, Epstein smoking. Jack asked Harlene to bring them coffee before ushering Natalie's brother into his office. They sat facing one another across the bare expanse of Jack's desk. "Mr. Epstein, I'm going to ask you some questions. I don't mean to upset you, and I certainly don't intend any insult to your sister's memory. But the more information we have, the more likely it is we can find the man responsible for her death."

"I understand."

Jack folded his hands. "First off, did Natalie have a serious boyfriend in her past? Or a boy who wanted to make it serious?"

"She went steady with a kid from her high school. Jerry Blume. But they broke it off when they went to college."

Jack jotted the name down. "Where is Mr. Blume now, do you know?"

Epstein smiled sideways. "Studying cinema at UCLA."

Jack crossed the name out. "Anyone else who might have carried a grudge against her?"

"My dad?" Epstein's attempt at a laugh turned into a sigh. "I can't imagine anyone. She's always had—she always had a whole gang of friends. Girls, boys . . . kids liked her. She was more of a trial to adults and teachers, but no one's going to come upstate and, and kill a girl because she sassed him in class." He frowned. "What about the people at this commune she was at?"

"I've questioned them, and they're still on the table as potential suspects. The two boys there have alibis my men are running down."

Epstein leaned forward. "What about the other girls? Maybe one of them was jealous of Nat? I mean, they're saying women can do anything a man can nowadays."

Jack nodded. "True. But we know from her, um, examination that Natalie had had a few drinks and a meal shortly before she died." He paused. "She also had sex. Our theory—my theory—is the man she was with is the one who killed her."

Epstein sat back in his chair. He blew out a breath. "I guess I'm not surprised."

There was a rap at the door and it swung open, revealing Harlene with her tray. This time, she hadn't included any pastries. He would have to work on her sense of *interview* versus *interrogation*. She set the coffee cups and fixings between them. "Anything else, Chief?"

"Yes. Harlene, can you ask one of the men to bring up the dress from the evidence locker? And write out a list of local funeral homes and their phone numbers for Mr. Epstein. We're going to be releasing his sister's body." Her eyes went wide, but she nodded and disappeared behind the door again.

"If she didn't have any likely boyfriends, was there anyone up here she might have known? Family friends summering at the lake?"

Epstein smiled wryly as he reached for his cup. "Don't take this the wrong way, Chief Liddle, but our friends don't summer up here."

"Oh." Jack sat back. "Too far from the city?"

"Too Gentile. When I was a kid, there were still hotels and resorts upstate that wouldn't take Jews. We founded our own places decades ago, and even though times have changed *a little*"—he dropped a sugar cube into his cup—"we tend to vacation where we're sure we'll be welcome."

"Huh." Jack drummed his fingers along the edge of his desk, eyes unfocused. "Do you think—is it possible she could have been picked out *because* she was Jewish?"

Epstein set his cup down abruptly. The two men looked at each other. Finally Epstein said, "Have you had any anti-Semitic instances around town? Vandalism? Swastikas painted on buildings?"

Jack shook his head. "No, I'm glad to say."

"Well. The sort of people who attack Jews have to work themselves up to it. And they're never subtle. They want the world to know. There isn't anything you haven't told me about how she was found, is there?"

"Nothing to make me think of this. I do have a question about how she was dressed—" Another rap on the door interrupted him. George Gifford stuck his head in. "Good timing. Come on in, Sergeant."

The dress Natalie had been wearing when they found her was on a hanger and draped in plastic. It looked like George was delivering it from the dry cleaner's. Jack introduced the two men and had George hold the dress up. "Her roommate at the commune said she'd never seen your sister with this dress. Do you recognize it?"

Epstein shook his head. "No. And it's not the kind of dress Nat would have picked out."

Jack's eyebrows went up. "You're certain."

"About that I am. Nat's clothing got more and more outlandish—" He paused. Let out a breath. "Sorry, that's my father speaking. Nat wore hippie clothes and nature-girl dresses and things she picked up at army-navy surplus stores. That dress," he pointed at it, "is what a Brearley girl would wear to a country club dance."

Jack didn't know what a Brearley girl was, but he got the gist of it. "All right. Thank you." He nodded to George, who left to return the dress to the evidence room. "Is there anything else you can tell me, Mr.

Epstein? You were going to check at home for any writing or pictures that might shed some light onto what happened to her."

"There wasn't anything. I mean, notebooks from college and high school. Some letters from friends she'd saved. She didn't keep scrapbooks or a diary. Nat was the sort to go out and do things, not to write about them." Epstein's voice cracked at the last, and he turned his head away.

Jack murmured something about getting the list and left his office. Leonard Epstein had been in company all day; he deserved a moment alone.

Harlene had not only gotten the names and numbers of the local funeral homes, she'd typed them up. "Good work," he said.

She pinked up. "I just wish there was more that I could do. That poor man." She tore a message slip off her pad and handed it to him. "Margy Van Alstyne called while you were in your meeting. She'd like you to call her when you can."

He refrained from asking *Did she sound like she's still ticked at me?* He had some dignity, after all. In his office, Epstein had gotten himself under control. He thanked Jack for the list. "I'll set something up with our funeral home."

"I appreciate you coming up for this," Jack said. "It's the hardest thing in the world, I know. Can I give you a ride back to the bus station?"

Epstein checked his watch. "It's . . . I've only been here two hours?" He looked up. "It feels like two days." Jack recognized his face. He had seen it before on people who had come to the end of themselves. You can soldier on and do everything you have to, but sooner or later a part of you just sat down, in a corner, in the dark.

"I bet you haven't eaten anything today." Jack's voice was gentle. "There's a burger place next to the station. Let's get over there and grab you a late lunch. They'll bag it up for you and everything."

They both went into the luncheonette; the giant electric hamburger on the sign hit Jack hard enough to set his stomach growling. Epstein wasn't the only man who'd neglected to eat yet today. There was the usual crowd—the only time it was empty was between buses. He let Epstein order first and then asked the counterman for five burgers

225

and an equal number of fries. May as well take some back for the guys on duty.

He heard someone say, "Len Epstein!" and then several voices chiming in. He turned to see a group of men closing in on his guest. He didn't have to ask to know they were from the city. Their clothes were a shade brighter and a touch more casual than Epstein's, but they were all cut from a similar cloth.

He left Epstein alone to talk with the three—no, four—men. There was hand waving and a few shoulder slugs and laughter. Apparently, Natalie's brother wasn't going to fill them in on why he was here. Well, who could blame him? Their orders came up as the men picked up their suitcases, promising to save Epstein a seat.

Jack tucked his large sack beneath his arm and handed Epstein his bag. The younger man reached for his wallet. "My treat. It's the least I can do." Jack gestured with his chin. "I thought you didn't have any friends here?"

"Business acquaintances. Our law firm does work for their invest-ment bank, and they handle several of our clients' accounts." Epstein shouldered his way through to the door, Jack on his tail. They both squinted in the sunshine. "Their boss has a cabin up here. Hunting and fishing and that sort of thing." Epstein's tone showed what he thought of the typical Adirondack pursuits.

"Do you think any of them might have known your sister?"

Epstein opened his mouth. Closed it. Pursed his lips. "I'll ask. But it's got to be a really, really long shot."

Jack didn't tell him long shots were about all they had left now. "Call me if you find out anything. Or if you come across anything of Natalie's that might . . ."

"Shed some light? I will." He shifted his lunch bag and shook Jack's hand. "Thank you, Chief Liddle."

"Thank me when we've found your sister's killer."

"I look forward to that." Epstein bared his teeth in a sort of smile. "I look forward to sitting behind you in the courtroom when the son of a bitch gets sentenced to the chair."

FRIDAY, AUGUST 25, PRESENT DAY

49. "Maybe I shouldn't go."

"Russ!" Clare glared at him from the passenger seat of her car. He preferred his truck, but he wasn't going to try to squeeze a couple of octogenarians in the crew seat. "First, this evening is about helping *your* people stay off the unemployment line. Second, the time to back out was at home, not pulling into your mother's driveway."

Since he was, in fact, slipping the car in next to his mom's station wagon and his niece's little Honda, he didn't have a good argument for that. "I could stay here with the baby and Emma."

"I'm sure Emma loves you, but she didn't sign up to spend her last Friday night before heading off to college hanging out with her uncle. She's here to earn money babysitting." Clare unbuckled and opened her door. "I'll grab the stuff. You get Ethan."

Ethan smiled toothlessly at him while Russ unhitched the baby seat. "Here's a tip, kid. Never take a job where you have to go to parties in a suit."

He wasn't actually in a suit, but it felt like one. Khakis, a white button-down, and a navy blazer. Not his style. The crowning glory were the pair of deck shoes Clare "happened" to buy for him because they were "on sale," which he didn't believe for a minute. She had coerced him into *just trying them on,* and now he was wearing the damn things.

Clare paused on the doorstep. "You look great. Very sophisticated and handsome."

"I don't look like me," he said. "I look like some guy named Brett who sails on Lake George and who has apps on his phone." Russ didn't trust apps on his phone.

"Oh, good Lord." Clare opened the door. "Margy! Emma! We're here!"

Russ set Ethan's carrier on the kitchen table and unbuckled the baby. From the living room, he could hear the women carrying on about how good they all looked. Clare did look good, and he had

227

already said so. She was wearing this sleeveless black dress with a high neck and about a hundred tiny buttons all down the front. He was hoping to have a chance to unbutton them at the end of the evening. He hoisted his son and brought him into the living room. "Heeeere's John—Holy crap, Mom, what did you do to yourself?"

Clare glared at him. Emma glared at him. His mom glared at him. "I mean . . . jeez." Her hair, instead of its usual poodle perm, was fluffy and swirling around her face. She had *earrings* on. And a long necklace, over a drapey top and pants he knew he'd never seen before. "Are you wearing *makeup*?"

"Let me be the first to apologize on behalf of my husband, the grunting caveman," Clare said.

Mom shook her head, making her hair move in ways no eighty-year-old lady's hair ought to move. "No, I raised him. I have to take the blame."

Emma smacked his arm. "Uncle Russ. Don't be weird."

"*I'm* weird? Suddenly my mom looks like—" It was the look in his mother's eye that made him finally hear himself. "A beautiful glamorous actress," he finished. He kissed her cheek. "Mom, I'm sorry."

She squeezed his hand. "It's okay, son. I know you don't take well to change."

"Uncle Russ is afraid you're going to catch the eye of some rich New Yorker tonight and he'll whisk you away to the city and we'll never see you again." Emma plucked Ethan from Russ's arms.

"The only thing I'm going to be doing with a rich New Yorker is squeezing him for a donation to the Save Our Police campaign."

"SOP? That's what we're going with?" Russ rolled his eyes.

"How much do you know about organizing, son?"

"Not much."

"That's right. So stand back and let the professionals do their job. You're here to look good and sound like a caring civil servant."

"I *am* a caring civil servant."

His mother patted him on the cheek. "Then you shouldn't have too hard a time of it tonight, should you?"

The doorbell rang. "I'll get it," he said, grateful to escape from the snickering women.

Chief Liddle—*Jack*—had on the Southern version of Russ's getup; green pants and a pale plaid jacket. He had a potted plant under one arm. "You look like you're ready to start your own golf club," Russ said, shaking his free hand.

"Too bright?" Liddle plucked at his lapel. "Too many years in Florida, I guess."

"No, no. Come on in. I can't wait for you to meet my wife." Saying that, about Clare, still gave him a deeply satisfied feeling. "Should I . . . ?" He held out his hands for the plant.

"It's for your mother."

"Oh. Right." He led Liddle into the living room. "Mom, I'm sure you remember Chief Liddle." He turned to Clare. "And this is my wife, Clare Fergusson." Clare looked at him and tilted her head. He turned back. The two older folks were still standing there, his mom looking flushed.

Damn. He had worried that seeing Chief Liddle might bring back painful memories. All those nights he had knocked on their front door, Walter Van Alstyne drunkenly in tow. Russ had come to grips with his father, both his sunlit highs and his dark lows. He wasn't sure his mother ever had.

"Jack." Mom touched her chin. "It's so good to see you."

"Margy. You haven't aged a day." Liddle held out the plant. "I would have brought cut flowers, but I remember you used to like gardening."

She took the plant. "A dieffenbachia! I know just the place for this." She smiled over the leaves.

"And *this* is my wife, Clare," Russ repeated. Liddle turned, a peculiar expression on his face.

"Chief Liddle, what a pleasure to meet you." Clare did that thing where she kind of glowed at someone. "Russ has spoken of you so many times with such affection."

Liddle laughed. "Really? Did he tell you about the time I caught him lighting tires on fire at the dump?"

Clare's eyebrows rose. "No. But I'm dying to hear about it."

"And over here—Emma, bring Ethan over—this is our son." Russ scooped the baby into his arms, and Ethan responded with a heart-melting smile.

"What a little cutie." Liddle looked past the baby toward Mom. "I see you in him, Margy."

With his blond hair, blue eyes, and blocky head, Russ thought he looked a lot more like his father than anyone else, but he guessed that might not be the politic thing for Liddle to say at the moment.

"And this is my oldest grandchild, Emma McGeoch." Her grandmother gave the teen a nudge and Emma dutifully shook hands with the elderly man.

"My goodness, that's some age range. Are you in college, young lady?"

"I'm headed up to SUNY Plattsburgh next week." Emma had the same smile Russ got when he thought of Clare. No doubt, she was more than ready to fly the nest. He glanced back down at Ethan, watching all the interactions from the crook of his arm. He would be seventy-one when his boy started college. If he made it that far.

Clare nudged him. "Why don't you hand his royal highness over to Emma, and we can get on the road."

He refrained from asking again about staying behind. It might not be so bad, with Jack Liddle to talk to. He was actually going to have the men up front and the ladies in the back on the way over, but somehow his mom and Liddle wound up sitting in the back with Clare riding shotgun as usual. Mom spent most of the ride catching Liddle up on the Save Our Police campaign—what there was of it to this point. What a name. "Too bad we're not a sheriff's department," he said quietly to Clare. "Then it could have been SOS."

"How about Save Our Badges?" she suggested. He laughed.

The road to the Langevoorts was typical of summer homes in the mountains. First a winding paved road, then a gravel-covered turnoff leading to several private drives, then another long stretch of rutted, beaten dirt. There were a few places that had modernized with asphalt and culverts over the years, but most people who came to the Adirondacks liked to keep it rustic and traditional.

The parking area was half full of cars, which meant Clare had been right to jog him about leaving. They weren't the first, or the last.

Liddle got out of the vehicle, crossed behind the rear, and held the door open for Russ's mother. Clare, who had exited under her own power, gave Russ a pointed look. "I'll do it for you, darlin', but you have to have the patience to stay put until I collect you." He tucked her hand in the crook of his arm.

"Yeah, that's not really my style," she said. "What a lovely camp."

It was a picture-perfect example of High Peak style, all creamy varnished logs and deep eaves. His mother nodded approvingly at the full-to-bursting garden beds between the house's facade and the rock walls encircling it. "Nice. Mostly native plants. I wonder if Mrs. Langevoort does her own gardening?"

"I think so," Clare answered. "When I met her, she was on her way to a nursery." There was a broad slate walk to the doorway, with only an overhang to keep off the rain. "That's odd. Don't these sort of places usually have a porch?"

"It's on the other side of the house," Liddle said. "Wraps around on two sides." Russ looked at him. "I've been here before. A long time ago, but it hasn't changed much. It belonged to Lloyd Harrington, then."

"He was the last president of Barkley and Eaton," Clare said. "Evidently, Kent Langevoort took over from him. And now, of course, he's handing the reins over to someone else."

"And so the wheel of time turns," Liddle said. "Makes me miss the old days, once in a while."

"Trust me," Margy said. "If you were a woman, you wouldn't be nostalgic at all."

"Humph. Maybe not."

The door opened to a slim woman who could have been Russ's age or a decade older—she had definitely done something to iron her face out. Audrey Langevoort, he assumed. "Clare! Wonderful. I'm so glad you could make it." Clare did the introductions all around, and they followed Mrs. Langevoort into a wide expanse of a room, anchored by a jazz trio beside a set of French doors open onto the velvet night.

231

Beyond a log archway, Russ could see a second set of French doors swung wide. The wraparound deck.

"What a lovely home," Clare said.

The interior had the same varnished logs, with a river stone fireplace dominating the wall that, Russ guessed, usually marked out the dining area. It had been cleared of any furniture, leaving space for guests to mingle and dance. In the open kitchen to their left, caterers in white and black worked with quick, precise movements.

"Thank you! I did some updating when it came into our hands, but mostly I've left well enough alone. The bathrooms—well, you can imagine, Mr. Harrington never married so it was all men all the time up here. And I tore down the kitchen wall so I didn't feel like the maidservant when I was making dinner. Let me introduce you to my husband, and he can take your drink orders."

Mr. Langevoort was in the second room, which was filled with a comfortable mix of leather and chintz furniture, arranged for conversation or watching the TV over the second fireplace. The bar was in the corner, complete with a small refrigerator and a wet sink.

Langevoort had the kind of firm handshake that was just shy of aggressive, and was the sort of hail-fellow-well-met rich guy that set Russ's teeth on edge. It was probably reverse snobbery, he admitted, but he almost preferred the summer residents who clearly viewed him and the rest of the force as lackeys—an armed version of the waiters circulating throughout the house.

"What's your poison, Russ?" Langevoort asked.

"Just seltzer, thanks." Russ snagged a little crab cake from a passing server.

"Designated driver, eh? I bet you never get pulled over!"

Russ propped a smile on his face. His mom took a glass of wine, and Clare, after a longing look at the bottles, accepted a ginger ale. Liddle asked for a whiskey on the rocks, and whistled when Langevoort showed him the label. "You don't skimp on your guests, do you, Mr. Langevoort?"

"Please, call me Kent. And no, we certainly don't. Might as well use money for what it's good for, right?" He handed over Liddle's glass. "It can't help you with the important things in life." Langevoort glanced past Russ, who turned to see a tall, striking redhead enter through the French doors.

"Oh, that's Joni," Clare said brightly. "Let me introduce you." She got a grip on his jacket sleeve and started pulling him toward the woman. "I think there's an unstated quid pro quo for tonight." Her voice was pitched to reach his ears only. "We get to rally support to save the department, and in exchange, we run interference between Joni and her dad." Her voice rose as they intercepted the Langevoorts' daughter. "Hey! You look great. This is my husband, Russ Van Alstyne."

"I am so glad you're here." Joni hugged Clare. "It gives us something to talk about other than the market. Or me." She looked at Russ. "I found Wall Street boring even when I was working there. I was trapped on the deck between a couple of guys droning on about derivatives, and I thought, if I don't get away I'm flinging myself into the lake."

"I hear you," he said.

"Why don't you let me introduce you around and you can start chatting people up about the vote. I don't know if Mom is actually going to ask people to pull out their checkbooks later on, but you might as well soften them up beforehand, just in case."

Russ looked around. The men—and he had to give Clare credit— were all dressed like he was. The women had a gloss that came from expensive haircuts and face creams. There were definitely Millers Kill citizens who would have blended into the group seamlessly, but Russ knew all of them, at least by sight. "I don't think there are any actual voters here tonight."

"They're better than voters," Joni said. "They have money."

50. R uss was nothing if not determined to do his duty. Clare knew he'd rather be manning the speed gun next to the old barn on Route 9 (which, he had informed her, smelled like rotted hay and mice) than having the same conversation over and over and over again with summer people. He was good at it, though.

Clare had long thought he was the best representative the movement to save the department could have, probably because he genuinely believed the things he said about community policing and making the three-town district better and safer for everyone.

The rooms grew more crowded. Seeing so many partygoers with drinks in their hands was not good for her; her craving for alcohol was like a mosquito whining in her ear. She could feel her heart rate rising. Standing next to Russ as he tried to explain to a concerned forty-something couple that the "person" who kept opening their gate was probably a bear, she tried to distract herself by surreptitiously people-watching. Joni was back out on the deck again, as far away from her father as she could be while still on the same floor. Margy and Jack Liddle seemed to be performing the same sort of song and dance she and Russ were doing—two police chiefs for the price of one! What a bargain. Margy didn't touch Liddle and he didn't touch her, but even from across the room Clare could see they were connected by something. Tension? A past? Russ was oblivious to whatever it was, which might be just as well.

An arm slipped into hers and she turned her head to see Audrey Langevoort. "How are you doing?" she asked.

"Fine. Great. Russ has been able to answer lots of people's questions."

"Summer residents have just as much at stake as year-round ones do when it comes to policing. Maybe more. Full-timers don't have houses that stand empty half the year."

Clare looked up at the soaring ceiling, braced by gleaming logs easily a foot and a half in diameter. "This place looks year round."

"It is. We came up in the winter more frequently when Joni was a—" She caught a word before it could escape. "—a teen. We skied most weekends. Drove up as soon as he got home from school and spent all day Saturday on the slopes. Church on Sunday morning, then I got to relax with a book in front of the fire while the guys, while Joni and Kent, got in some more time on the mountain. I'd make a meal we could eat in the car and we'd be back in New York by ten or eleven." She was looking into the middle distance with a complicated smile. "Those were good times."

"You're going to miss this house."

"Oh, am I ever." Audrey sighed. "But it goes with the business. Like an entailment in England in the olden days. Everything goes to the firstborn son." She glanced toward the deck.

"Which should have been Joni?"

"That was Kent's dream." Audrey shook her head. "Joni—she wasn't Joni then, of course, but—she struggled through an economics degree to please her father. Then she got an MBA to please her father. He blames her quitting the firm on her gender issues, but the truth is, she never enjoyed the work. She felt called to the priesthood since she was in college. It's just that when she finally came out as a woman, it seems to have freed her up to come out as someone who hates finance as well."

"I can't imagine the kind of bravery that must have taken. You must be very proud of her."

"You know? I am." Audrey gave Clare's arm a little shake. "Let's rescue your husband from the Neilsons, and I'll introduce you to the fellow Kent picked to take over all this."

Russ was more than happy to be pulled away. "How hard is it for people to keep their trash cans locked up?" he asked rhetorically.

"They're new," Audrey said. "They'll learn. And here's someone else new to the area. Bors, this is Chief of Police Russ Van Alstyne and his wife, the Reverend Clare Fergusson. Russ and Clare, Bors Saunderson." They shook hands. Saunderson was pale and damp, more like a nineteenth-century invalid who came to the mountains for the air than someone who might hike and ski and swim in the river. Clare supposed climbing to the top of Barkley and Eaton didn't allow a lot of free time for outdoor sports.

"A police chief and a minister." Saunderson gave an unconvincing laugh. "I feel like I ought to start confessing."

Russ looked him straight in the eye. "Do you have something you need to confess?"

Clare slapped his arm. "Excuse my husband."

"Actually, Bors, the Van Alstynes are here tonight in part to take the heat off of you." She turned to Russ and Clare. "Bors is a genius in the C Suite, but he hates being the center of attention." She shifted. "The town this house falls in—your house, soon—is proposing to abolish the police force. It's coming up for a vote this fall, and Russ is going to tell us all why that's a bad idea." She raised her voice slightly as she spoke, bringing in several nearby onlookers. "And you're all going to write a big check to the Save Our Police fund, so we can sleep safe at night in the city, knowing someone is keeping an eye on our houses!" Several people laughed in an appreciative way. A caterer caught Audrey's eye, and she nodded. "Let's move outside for dinner, shall we?"

"Outside" proved to be down a set of wide stairs that followed the wraparound decks to a lawn that fell away in a wide bowl to the tree line. Clare could see the house had been built into the side of a steeply raked hill, with a full walk-out story beneath the first floor. "See?" Russ said. "This is what I'm thinking about for our place."

"Your place?" Mr. Liddle asked.

"We've bought a small house—" Clare began.

"A small wreck," Russ added.

"On Lake Inverary. It's in a protected area, so the only way we can expand is up." She glanced up to where the deck railing was silhouetted against the bright lights inside. "Except that's got to be twenty feet high."

"Obviously, ours won't be that tall." Russ turned to Jack. "We can't actually move the footprint to cut into the hill, so I'm thinking of a suspended walkway from the road to the top floor—"

Fortunately, Audrey Langevoort corralled him before he could launch into his really detailed description of his future construction plans. "Russ, you're sitting at my table. Clare, if you follow Bors, you two will be at Kent's table."

A rectangular white tent lit from within by hundreds of twinkling lights was settled, like a barge in a fairy tale, at the flattest spot in the curving landscape. Servers were going in and out of a smaller tent, pitched discreetly to one side.

"A second kitchen?" she asked her escort.

"Must be," Bors said. "Otherwise, they'd need hiking boots to get back to the house." He led her through the crowd of people performing the dance of the name tags—picking one up, putting it down, moving to a new spot. She saw someone nab a cherry tomato off the salads waiting for them. She prayed it wasn't hers, and her prayers were answered when, ahead of them, Kent Langevoort stood up and waved.

"Here you are. Welcome." He pulled out the chair next to him, in front of what seemed to be an untouched salad. "Reverend Fergusson."

"Please, call me Clare." She took her place. Saunderson, after a glance at his name tag, sat down next to her. The grandmotherly lady on Kent Langevoort's right hand was the wife of the COO, while Saunderson's other partner was a summer resident Clare knew slightly from her efforts to promote recycling programs throughout the three towns. The rest of their dinner companions were a similar mix of high-level Barkley and Eaton people and well-connected seasonal locals. Audrey knew how to plan a table. Clare wondered if Bors realized everyone was here for his benefit.

Langevoort was deep in discussion with the grandmother, so Clare turned to Saunderson. "Have you spent much time in the Adirondacks?"

He shook his head. "Just on trips here, with Kent. He likes to throw a boys' weekend a few times during the year."

Clare suspected the glass ceiling was more like a glass wall at Barkley and Eaton. Surrounded by a glass moat. "Well, you'll have a lot to discover once this place is yours. I'm originally from southern Virginia, so it took me awhile to get used to it, but now I snowshoe and cross-country ski right alongside the natives." She couldn't help looking toward Russ, who was two tables away, paying close attention to an elderly woman she thought might be part of Margy's native plants project.

Saunderson glanced toward Langevoort. "I don't anticipate spending that much time up here. I prefer the city."

"Oh." She speared a forkful of delicate greens. "Does your spouse work there as well?"

"I'm not married." He looked at Langevoort again. "It's hard to combine a social life with climbing the corporate ladder."

"Really? I knew a Barkley and Eaton guy who was quite sociable. Hugh Parteger."

"Oh, Hugh." Saunderson made a dismissive gesture. "That's his job. Schmoozing the prospective clients, keeping little old ladies and golf-playing geezers happy."

Clare smothered her laugh in her napkin.

"Hugh could probably make a deposit into the bank if one of the secretaries helped him. The actual business is *complicated*." Saunderson's face took on some color. "We're not just a hedge fund. We're a private bank, *and* an investment firm, and there has to be a wall between those two sides. We serve clients all over the world, with every sort of investment vehicle, and we're also starting to get into direct corporate capitalization."

"Like, um, venture capitalists? The guys in Silicon Valley?"

"Right." Saunderson stabbed his fork toward her. "That's my baby. It's the future, right? B and E's motto has been 'Preserving capital, growing wealth' since it was founded. But we can't keep on doing things the way they did in the roaring twenties."

"I can see why Kent chose you to be the next CEO."

"Owner. I'm going to be the next owner of B and E."

"Really?" Clare tried not to sound too startled. "I thought . . . I mean, I assumed . . ."

The grandmother next to Langevoort leaned toward Clare. "I know, it's odd. Barkley and Eaton has always been a privately held company. But instead of diluting the shares through family members, the owner picks a new head and everything goes to him. Or it could be a her, I suppose."

Langevoort grunted. Clare turned toward him. "So . . . after you retire, you won't have any continuing interest in the company?"

"We have a pension plan. And of course, I have my private investments and savings. But no, once the business transfers to Bors, I'm out."

"I've never heard of that sort of arrangement."

"Mr. Barkley came up with it. He said if it worked for the Romans, it would work for us."

"The Romans?"

"In ancient Rome, for the most part, they didn't pass imperial rule from father to son. Instead, the emperor would choose the most talented man of the next generation and adopt him. That way, they kept continuity but didn't risk idiot or incompetent heirs."

Clare raised an eyebrow. "What about Caligula? Or Nero?"

"They prove the point," Langevoort said. "They were blood family members. Have you heard of the Five Good Emperors?"

"Maybe?"

"The greatest century of the empire. All adopted as adults by the previous emperor."

"It sounds odd, but it works," the grandmother said. "Barkley and Eaton has thrived as a private company for eighty-four years. There are very few other businesses that can say the same."

"Actually, the period of the Five Good Emperors also lasted eighty-four years." The activist summer resident smiled sheepishly. "Sorry. Classics major at Barnard. I can't stop myself."

"What happened after eighty-four years?" Clare asked.

"Civil war. Power grabs. Assassinations."

"In other words, a typical week on Wall Street." The finance guy next to the grandmother laughed.

Langevoort gave him a quelling look. "Eventually, the Romans ran out of men who were willing, able, and competent. We, fortunately, have escaped that fate." He raised a glass to Bors, and the rest of the table followed suit. Clare stared at her sparkling water, as if she could change it into wine with wishing. "To Bors Saunderson," Langevoort said. "Who's willing to do the hard, relentless work to get the job done."

51. As Harry's Buick chugged up the switchback mountain road, he wondered when he was going to get his free time back. A few phone calls from his office were okay, but he didn't feel right working the state police case on his own taxpayers' dime, so he had been squeezing in the investigation before work, in the evening, and on his day off. Or, as today, on his lunch hour.

He downshifted and pressed on the accelerator. He had spoken to his counterparts at the Lake George Police Department and the Warren County Sheriff's office. They both kept pretty close track of their summer residents, the ones in expensive water-view houses and the ones in honky-tonk motor courts alike. Neither was aware of any domestic disturbances around the time of the girl's death, or of any oddities like a young woman alone at a family camp.

Which left his neck of the woods. Which, at the moment, was practically vertical. Millers Kill hadn't seen a boom in the tourist trade like Lake George, and they had never appealed to the rich society types who flocked to Saratoga Springs for the racing season and then flew away again. What summer camps they had were old, built by the generation who went up to the mountains on now-defunct railroads to hunt bear and deer and moose and to take the air. Nowadays the air was in Arizona, apparently, but there were still descendants of those Victorian camp builders who came faithfully or grudgingly every summer. Those that still had money tore out the heavy wooden beams and curlicue carvings in favor of glass walls; those whose fortunes had dwindled had to make do with dark interiors and grandma's bric-a-brac.

He had visited the van der Hoevens and the Griswolds; two families who had held on to the inherited cash and had long, low, modern summer camps to show for it. Both places had been stuffed with enough wives, children, and grandparents to make Harry confident that no man could possibly have been sneaking around long enough to *find* a girl, let alone deck her out and dump her body.

Next on his list was the Barkleys' camp, an old-fashioned log building distinguished by a long porch lined with rocking chairs. When Mrs. Barkley had been alive, the window boxes had been full of geraniums and ivy; as Harry drove closer, the bare wooden troughs made the front of the house look like a blank face.

There were several cars parked along the grassy verge of the curved drive, all of them late-model Lincolns and Buicks and such, the dust from the mountain road scarcely showing on their glossy wax finishes. He was surprised to see anything other than Mr. Barkley's well-preserved Ford; the days of young guests and house parties had gone along with their only son, dead on an Italian hillside trying to take a redoubt from the Germans.

The door opened as Harry exited his car. It took him a moment to recognize Samuel Barkley; it had been three years since he had seen the man last, in a condolence call upon Mrs. Barkley's passing. Her widower had had the physique you'd expect of a man who'd spent a half century having three-martini lunches and taking meetings behind a desk.

The man on the porch, on the other hand, looked like he could have just been released from the army. His waist was small, his chest was large, and he glowed with vitality, despite his white hair. It wasn't until he reached the bottom of the steps that Harry could see the lines and wrinkles proclaiming Barkley's age.

"Chief McNeil!" The banker shook his hand. "It's been too long."

"That it has." Harry gestured to his own expanding stomach. "I'm getting old, and you look like you've found the fountain of youth."

Barkley grinned. "After Edie passed, I started spending less time at the office and more time at the swimming pool. Started riding again when I was up here. Dropped sixty pounds, and my doctor says I've got the heart of a twenty-year-old. And I'm not giving it back to him!"

Harry dutifully laughed at the old chestnut.

"So what are you doing up here? Come to see if I was still alive?"

Harry shook his head. "Wish it was just that. There was a girl left dead in a road in Cossayuharie a few days ago. She's not local, so I'm looking to see if any of our summer folks might recognize her."

"Left dead? Was it a hit-and-run accident?" He turned toward the assemblage of automobiles. "I can't imagine any of my guests having anything to do with such a thing, but please. Go ahead and take a look."

"No, the medical examiner didn't think it was a car accident." Harry tried not to sound like a kid explaining how his ball went through a window. "To tell the truth, he isn't sure what killed her."

"He isn't sure?" Barkley didn't quite look at him as if he was a crackpot, but it was close. "So . . . she wasn't *killed,* she's just . . . dead?"

"It could be natural. Or accidental. Or malicious. But either way, she's a Jane Doe I'd like to identify. Would you mind if I had your guests take a look at her photo?"

Barkley gestured toward the steps. "Most of them came up from the city in the past two days, so I don't know if they'll be any help, but you're more than welcome to come in and ask your questions."

Inside, the camp had the distinct feel of a womanless house—none of those pieces of lace and little doodads a wife or daughter-in-law might have put around. Instead, it had reverted to its origins as a hunting camp, with antlers, hide rugs, and a bar that would make any fancy hotel proud. "We were just having some drinks before dinner. Can I get you something?"

Harry held up a hand. "Thanks, but no." The banker steered him past a leather davenport toward double doors opened wide. The view from the parlor, endless green and blue mountains fading to the distance, was enough to distract Harry from the men gathered in what looked like an old-fashioned smoking room.

"Gentlemen, this is Chief Harry McNeil, our local constable. Chief McNeil, these fellows all work very hard for me, and are here for a little R and R in the fresh Adirondack air."

Most of the men didn't look as if they'd traveled past Twentieth and Broadway. Four were wearing lightweight pants and coats that would snag and tear within ten minutes of walking through the woods. Another had on what Harry assumed was a golf shirt and sweater. The bridge game dealt out on a card table didn't speak much of the great outdoors.

"Sorry to disturb you with some unpleasant business, but I need you all to take a look at some pictures for me. We have an unknown dead girl we're trying to identify, and we're asking our local summer visitors for help." He didn't want the men passing the photos around hand to hand; he'd never get an unfiltered reaction from them. "If you could come into the front room one at a time, we can keep this separate from what looks like an enjoyable afternoon."

It felt like something out of a silly detective novel, each one of the men walking through the double doors and pondering the face and full-body photos of the dead girl. Unlike the suspects in a mystery story, however, none of Barkley's guests were considerate enough to gasp or turn pale when seeing the pictures. To a man, they all shook their heads and murmured some variation of "What a shame." The last of them, one of the blue-blazered fellows, added, "None of us have laid eyes on any girls since we left the city. It's a stag weekend." He made a face. "Unfortunately."

Barkley came up beside him to examine the picture. "Pretty girl," he said. "I hope you find out who she was and what happened to her."

"I don't suppose any of your young men in there have had a chance to get away on their own, have they?"

"Well, yes, on the horses. Lloyd and Charlie are out on a ride right now."

"The rest of us aren't allowed to ride." The blue-blazered fellow sounded as if his parents hadn't smacked him enough as a kid.

"That's because the rest of you aren't competent to ride in the mountains without laming my stock." Barkley turned to Harry. "I've had to have the vet up here five times so far this summer." Harry gave him a look of genuine sympathy. Barkley was summer folk, but he respected the mountains like the locals did.

"Maybe I can come back when your other two guests are in. Just to cross them off my list." Harry looked around the room. Everything neat and clean and polished. There was probably a maid or cook. "You have quite a place here." He drifted over to the long lawyers bookcase beneath the stairway. A lot of histories. A shelf of thick textbooks, probably the dead son's. And a whole lot of titles in, if his schoolboy studies hadn't deserted him, Latin. You could tell a lot about a man from the books on his shelves, and Barkley's said he was a man far happier in the past than in this present.

"Thank you." Both of them heard the noise from outside; a heavy clop-clop and the whicker of a horse that knew its stable was near. Barkley smiled. "Looks like you won't have to make a second trip. Come on outside."

Two men were dismounting in the dooryard, both of them dressed sensibly in denim jeans and sturdy shirts. The horses—ponies, really—were a pair of dark bays, with muscular legs and sweet eyes. Barkley introduced the aforementioned Lloyd and Charlie, and Harry did his routine and showed them the pictures. Neither of them could help. At this rate, he might as well ask the horses.

After they led their mounts around the side of the cabin, Harry indulged his curiosity. "What's really going on up here? Those boys playing cards inside don't seem like the types to indulge in wood sports."

The banker man smiled. "You have a keen eye, Chief McNeil. I'm planning to retire. I thought I'd be passing the business on to my son but . . ." He shrugged. "So instead, I'm turning the whole kit and caboodle over to one of these sharp young minds. You've seen them all. Can you guess which one it is?"

"One of the riders."

Barkley laughed. "Got it in one."

"Like you say, I've got a keen eye." Harry opened his car door. "Let me know if anything comes up, please. If anyone happens to remember anything."

"I will. Say, you didn't tell me—where did your men find the girl?"

Harry forced himself not to scratch the back of his neck. "Cossayuharie."

Barkley's eyebrows went up. "I thought that was patrolled by the state police?"

"I'm . . . helping out. The state police don't always have the time to . . ."

"Actually do what they're paid for?"

"Not how I'd phrase it." Not that he disagreed.

The banker nodded. "Just keep in mind what Horace said, Chief. *Non omnia possumus omnes.* We can't all of us do it all."

FRIDAY, AUGUST 25, PRESENT DAY

52. Clare wondered if anyone at the table knew Langevoort had wanted Joni to take over the company in his place. Was his anger because she had come out as a woman? Or because she had decisively dumped the future he had planned out for her? When Clare had told her parents she was giving up her military career to become a priest, they had been deeply concerned. Well, deeply concerned on her father's side. Her mother had been appalled, in part because she envisioned Clare in a life of poverty, and in part because she thought it spelled doom for her daughter's chances of ever getting married and producing grandchildren.

"Clare?"

She had zoned out of the conversation. The recycling advocate was looking at her. "I'm sorry, what?"

"I was wondering how the investigation was going?"

Investigation into what? She could feel her cheeks start to redden. "It's going very well. Lots of development." That ought to cover almost anything.

"Good. It's terrifying to think there might be a predator out there stalking young women. I won't let my daughter go out without a friend—and they have to check in several times during the evening."

A man farther down the table who was with the international affairs department laughed. "I bet she loves that!"

"I don't care. Until the police have someone in custody, I'm making sure she's keeping safe. At that age, it's not like they think of it themselves."

"Are they close to finding out who did it?" The man across the table from Clare addressed her. In fact, the entire company was looking at her.

"Obviously, I can't reveal any information the police department hasn't already made public. But I think it's common knowledge they're waiting on DNA and toxicology tests from the state crime lab, and it's been my experience as someone, um, adjacent to investigations that once that information is in, the case will be closed very quickly." She pasted what she hoped was a deeply confident expression on her face.

"And, of course, it wouldn't look good for the local cops to have an unsolved murder leading into a referendum on their very existence," International Affairs said.

Clare leaned back to let the waiter take her salad plate. "It wouldn't, no. But I can honestly assure you Chief Van Alstyne would be putting the same effort into closing the case even if the towns had just voted to preserve the department and give everybody raises. He's a pretty driven guy." She tried to control the dopey smile she got when she talked about Russ.

"How long have you two been married?" the recycling woman asked.

"Ten months." There was a chorus of *Aww, newlyweds,* and the conversation thankfully switched to marriage and weddings.

The caterers were coming out with the main course. Clare pulled her phone from her clutch and held it in her lap. "Just want to check in with the sitter," she said to Langevoort.

Instead, she texted Russ. Better open w how well the u/x death investigation is going. Everyone at my table is v concerned.

A few seconds later, she felt her phone buzz in response. Will close dept myself if we can get out of here sooner.

Breastfeeding makes a great excuse, she texted. Just thinking about Ethan gave her a little pre-nursing tingle. She had her portable hand pump in its bag in the truck, just in case.

Good. Keep it up next 4 years.

She smiled and leaned into the table, focusing on being a good listener while sending supportive thoughts Russ's way. It was a lively group, in part because it was well lubricated. The waiters came around like clockwork, filling Bors's glass to her left and Kent's glass to her right. After the second time she had waved the wine away, they didn't offer, but she was aware of every pour and every drink. She tried to console herself with the thought that at least she wasn't getting red-faced and sweaty or pale and glassy-eyed, like her dinner companions.

Dessert and coffee were rolling out when Audrey Langevoort stood and tapped her knife against her glass. As the various conversations settled down, she said, "Thank you all so much for coming out to honor Barkley and Eaton's new leader. It's an exhausting, challenging, life-changing job, as I know almost better than anyone—" She paused, and her audience obliged by laughing. "—but Kent and I know he'll be brilliant. Bors, stand up and take a bow."

Saunderson scraped his chair back and stood, raising his hand to the assembly. He looked less like a man taking a victory lap than a boy being called on to perform at a recital. He sat down quickly.

"Now. We're going to get our other guest of honor to speak for us about the change—the drastic change—the town is proposing. Police Chief Russ Van Alstyne."

Russ stood up and nodded toward his hostess. "Thanks, Audrey." He raised his voice to be heard throughout the tent. "Folks, first let me assure you the Millers Kill Police Department is working round the clock to find the person responsible for the recent death of the young woman found on McEachron Hill Road. We know her identity, although we're waiting on finding her next of kin to release it. We've had a steady stream of information coming in on our hotline, and a great deal of physical evidence that's being examined by the state crime lab. I know some of you may remember a similar unexplained death back in '72. I know I do." He rubbed the back of his neck and—there was no other word for it—chuckled. Clare was impressed. Apparently, his speaking improved in inverse proportion to the presence of reporters.

"That was a long time ago, and we have forensic tools today that would have sounded like science fiction back then. We *will* find whoever is responsible." He looked around the room in a way that reminded Clare of the time she'd seen him interrogating a suspect.

"Now, is this why you should stand behind keeping an independent police department? Maybe. To be honest, the state police can do just as good a job with major investigations as we can. We use their crime scene technicians and their labs. But I can guarantee you, they don't *care* about the three towns the way my officers and I do. This is where we live, and shop and go to church and raise our kids. We know these communities and we're committed to maintaining the peace and safety of every resident, whether they're here year-round or seasonally. I could stand here for half an hour listing all the ways we make you and your families and your homes more secure. And yes, that includes writing you a ticket so you don't get into an accident with someone else who's up here enjoying our beautiful mountains and lakes." The audience laughed. "But you're smart folks. I don't need to lay out every particular for you. So I'll finish by thanking you for your support, and saying I hope my officers and I have the privilege of serving you for many years to come."

He sat down to enthusiastic applause, only some of which was due to his brevity.

"Nicely done," the grandmother said.

"I'm glad to hear him sound so certain about finding the killer." The recycling activist looked around the table. "Am I the only one with a daughter here for the summer?"

"There's Kent," the man at the far end of the table said. Langevoort gave him a look that should have peeled his skin.

"I think Joni's a little out of the age range," Clare said. "The girl who was killed—all the previous girls—were in their very early twenties."

"Previous girls?" someone said.

"In 1972," Clare amended.

"That remains unsolved, correct?" Langevoort gestured toward Clare. "The *Post-Star* said there weren't any arrests, even though the police had several suspects."

"Persons of interest. No, they never got any further in the investigation. I know Russ is hoping finding this girl's killer will shake something loose."

Langevoort looked skeptical.

"I don't think anyone expects them to solve a thirty-something-year-old murder," the recycling woman said. "Just get the nut who's running around right now."

Clare smiled. "I have no doubt that will happen." She pushed her chair back. "Now, if you all will pardon me . . ."

She touched Russ's shoulder as she passed. "A word?" He excused himself and followed her to the edge of the tent. "Do you think we need to stay much longer? 'Cause if we do, I'm going to have to—" She lowered her voice as several people brushed past her, evidently also heading for the toilets now the speeches were over. "—get the pump from the car."

"Oh, babe. You're turning me on."

"I could kill you right now and no jury with a woman on it would convict me."

He laughed quietly. "Apparently, there are going to be fireworks, but we don't have to stay for those. Just let me check with Mom and Chief—and with Jack and make sure they're okay with slipping out early."

"All right. I have got to get to the bathroom right now before I burst. Can you come up to the house and tell me if I need to hook myself up?"

"I'll grab the pump out of the truck if you do."

She stretched up and kissed him. "Your execution is stayed."

"Ma'am, thank you, ma'am."

There was only one caterer in the kitchen, cleaning and packaging the leftovers. "Bathroom?" Clare said.

"Um. The master bedroom one and the powder room are occupied. You have to go upstairs or down."

Clare chose up. After she emptied her bladder, her breasts felt even more full. Ten o'clock feeding time was definitely coming up. She checked herself in the mirror. No embarrassing leaks on the front of her dress. Yet.

As she descended the stairs, she heard the caterer say, "Sir, what are you doing? Sir? Oh, my God!"

Clare jumped the last two steps and swiveled toward the kitchen. The caterer was staring, horrified, toward the deck. She spotted Clare and pointed. "He . . . I . . ."

Clare ran through the den. There was no one on the deck, but she could hear screams coming from the tent—and then she saw it.

A strip of white—part of a sheet, perhaps?—double-knotted around the railing. The taut line led straight down. *Holy mother of God.*

"Clare!" Russ was a dark blur pounding up the lawn. "Cut him down! Cut him down!"

She whirled, bolted for the kitchen. "Knife! Knife!"

The caterer's eyes darted over the enormous island. She grabbed a large chopping blade and thrust it toward Clare, handle reversed.

Clare raced back to the deck. She dropped to her knees, wrapped one hand around the sheet—*pulled so tight, oh God*—and sliced. The steel was wickedly, blessedly sharp. The fabric parted with a curl of threads. Another slice. Then another.

"We've got him!" Russ shouted. "Let him drop!" She severed the rest of the sheet with a final cut, dropped the knife, and bent over the railing. Twenty feet below her, like the mourners at the cross, Russ and Jack Liddle tenderly cradled the sprawled, still body of Bors Saunderson.

53. It took twenty agonizing minutes for the ambulance to arrive. Russ, Mr. Liddle, and a friend of the Langevoorts who announced he was Red Cross certified took turns performing artificial respiration. Aside from a thready pulse, Saunderson remained unresponsive.

Langevoort, a man of action reduced to ineffectiveness, handed out flashlights and directed several guests to the turning points along the private road, to prevent the ambulance from getting lost in the mountain dark. Joni rose to the occasion magnificently, corralling the remainder of the company and leading them back to the tent, where they could vent their shock and their suppositions without crowding the spot where the three men were working to save Saunderson's life.

Audrey Langevoort fell apart. "I don't," she sobbed. "I don't . . ." She clutched Clare's hand. They were sitting on the sofa in the den together, Clare's arm tight around the older woman.

"I know," Clare said. "I know. It's terrible."

"Why?" Audrey wailed.

"I don't know. We may never know." Clare took a breath. "Did he seem depressed?"

"He always seemed depressed!" Audrey bent over, her body shaking. She started to gasp for breath.

"Audrey? Are you all right?"

Audrey waved her hand in front of her face. "Panic . . ."

"You're having a panic attack." Clare glanced around, but the only other people in the house were a few of the catering staff, huddled together in the kitchen and speaking in low tones. "Do you take any medicine for anxiety? Audrey?"

The woman nodded, then pointed a shaking finger toward the other room. "Bedroom," she gasped.

"In the master bedroom." Clare stood, still holding Audrey's other hand. "In your nightstand? Or the bathroom?"

"Bath," Audrey wheezed.

"Okay, I'm going to leave you for just long enough to get your pills. I'll be right back."

The bedroom light was just inside the door. Flicking it on, Clare saw the large bed had been torn apart, pillows tossed on the floor, duvet half-fallen to the floor. The top sheet was missing. Clare turned her face away and crossed to the bathroom. Its marble-swathed luxury seemed almost obscene under the circumstances. She opened the top drawer nearest to the door and was rewarded by a clattering of pill bottles and makeup. She recognized prescriptions for high blood pressure, for acid reflux, for insomnia. There were three—three!— bottles of pain pills. Audrey's doctor was generous with her scrip. There were two medications she had never heard of. She took those and stepped back.

She stared at herself in the mirror for a heartbeat. She wasn't thinking, exactly, but some decision had been made, because her hand went out of its own volition and closed around one of the bottles of pain pills. She watched looking-glass-Clare as she slipped it into her pocket, and she remembered getting the dress, and her delight at discovering it had pockets, so useful, so easy, and then she was walking out of the bathroom with two bottles of pills in her hand and one hidden away in the mirror-skirt. Which was also her skirt.

She asked the caterers for water and three of them tried to serve her at once. She took the first proffered glass and crossed the wide room to Audrey's side. "Audrey?" She held out the pills. "I wasn't sure which one it was."

The woman took one. "Seconal." She tried to open it, but the childproof cap defeated her.

"Let me," Clare said. The label read *One as needed* so Clare shook out one and handed it to Audrey, holding out the glass of water at the same time. Audrey downed the pill, closed her trembling hand around the glass, and took a deep swallow.

A distant siren wailed. "Listen," Clare said. "The ambulance is here." The siren grew closer and closer and then cut off, leaving a silence that was like sound in its wake. Then the slamming doors, and the shouts of "Down here!" and the crunch of footsteps running across the gravel drive.

Audrey lurched upright. "I should . . . I should go with them." She teetered, half up and half down.

Clare wrapped her hands around the older woman's arms and gently guided her back to the couch. "I'm sure someone is going with him. I don't think you're quite in a state to be at the hospital."

Audrey looked up at her. "Will you go? I mean, find out. Make sure he won't be," her breath hiccupped, "alone."

"I will." Clare handed Audrey the glass of water. "Why don't you see if you can drink the rest of this? I'll be right back."

Audrey nodded. Clare let herself out the side door to the deck, avoiding the yawning opening with the sheet still knotted around the railing. She ran down the wraparound stairs. It was impossible to believe she had come up them—she glanced at her watch—only half an hour ago. She found Russ and Mr. Liddle standing in the same spot, looking up the hill toward the flaring ambulance lights.

"Did they already take him?"

Russ reached for her and pulled her close. "Yeah. Kent Langevoort's going with them." He tucked her beneath his chin and shuddered slightly. "Jesus." He drew back and studied her face. "Are you okay?"

"I guess?" Behind her, she could hear the ambulance fire up and roar out of the parking area in a spatter of gravel. "Did we get to him in time? Will he recover?"

Beside them, Mr. Liddle made a noise. "No coming back from a hanging, they say." He looked up at Russ. "You ever seen one before?"

"No. Most of my career was military. People use guns." He hugged Clare hard. "I hate suicides. I hate 'em."

"If it was suicide," Mr. Liddle said mildly.

Russ released Clare. "Let's see if we can nail that question down."

"What do you mean?" Clare glanced up at the deck. The handsbreadth of sheet and the broad knot looked like a wide-jawed skull. "There wasn't anyone else up there. I would have seen anyone leaving the deck."

"Would you have?" Russ followed her gaze. "It's pretty wide, and mostly in the dark. And I'm betting you were very focused on what was going on right in front of you."

"Are we waiting for your people to get here?" Mr. Liddle asked.

"No. I notified Dispatch, but I didn't see the need to take anybody off duty. Not stretched as thin as we are."

Mr. Liddle jerked his chin toward the stairs. "Good enough. You go talk to the folks that were inside. I'll start getting statements from the ones in the tent. We're going to want a guest list to compare."

Even under the grim circumstances, Clare was a little amused to see Russ follow the old chief's orders and head for the stairs. *You can take the man out of the police force,* she thought. She went up behind him. "There was a caterer cleaning the kitchen," she said when they reached the side door. "The young woman with the ends of her hair dyed pink."

"Well, that makes her easy to pick out from a crowd." Russ held the door open for her. "Who else was inside when you got here?"

"She said the powder room and the master bathroom were occupied. I'm pretty sure Bors was in the master bedroom. The sheet—" She made a tugging gesture with both hands.

"I see. Was he alone?"

"I have no idea. And no, I don't know who was in the powder room. I was focused on reaching the upstairs bathroom as quickly as possible at that point."

"Okay, darlin'." He glanced around the open space of the dining room and kitchen.

Before he could position her someplace innocuous, she pointed toward the living room. "I'm going to check on Audrey Langevoort and see how she's settling down." Russ raised an eyebrow. "She was upset and had a panic attack. I had to get her anxiety medication." At once, she became aware of the pill bottle in her pocket. "I'll see if she has the guest list."

The corner of Russ's mouth turned up. "Good girl."

No, I'm not, really.

Audrey's Seconal was evidently the real deal. She was relaxed on the sofa, looking as if she had just had a stiff drink and a back rub. "Oh, Clare. Thank you so much. I'm sorry I got so emotional."

"Your husband went with the ambulance, so there'll be someone at the hospital with Bors." Clare sat down. "Russ wants to know if you have a guest list available."

"Of course. Whatever I can do to help."

"Audrey, can you think of any reason why he would want to kill himself? You said he always seemed depressed, but I spoke with him at dinner and he was definitely excited about the promotion. Well, excited about some aspects of it, at least."

"'Depressed' was probably the wrong word. Serious, maybe. Somber. Bors was a perfectionist. He couldn't be happy if something was ninety-nine percent good. It had to be a hundred. You know the type?"

"I've met a few. Do you think the responsibilities of taking over Barkley and Eaton were weighing on him?"

"I do, yes." Audrey pushed back her hair. "He certainly didn't act like a man who had just been given the opportunity of a lifetime when I arrived."

"He was here before you?" She glanced toward the ceiling as if she could see through to the second floor. "Has he been staying here?"

"Yes. He and Kent spent last weekend here while Joni and I were in the city. Kent likes to bring groups of his executives up here—"

"I heard."

"Right. So he brought Bors up to make the offer. Then they had a working weekend to map out the future of the company. Joni and I got here Monday evening."

Clare blinked. "You pulled this whole evening together in four days?"

Audrey laughed a little. "Thanks, but I'm not that good. No, Kent asked me to set things up a few weeks ago. He had a press release ready to go and everything. He just hadn't formally asked Bors."

Clare wondered if, stuck up in the Adirondack woods, Bors had felt he couldn't refuse his boss's offer. She had a friend who had accepted a marriage proposal because it was in the middle of a restaurant with everyone else looking on with heart-shaped eyes. She had given the ring back less than a week later. But how do you break up when the engagement's already been announced on Bloomberg News and the *Wall Street Journal*?

"Did Bors have any particular friends at the company? Anyone he might have confided in?"

"Not that I know. He was a workaholic. Not unlike Kent, which is one of the reasons he got the job."

"How about the opposite? Was there anyone at the company who was jealous of him? Disliked him?"

Audrey looked at her as if she had grown a second head. "You mean, enough to somehow drive him to suicide? In a week's time? I find that really hard to imagine."

54. Calvin Ogilvie found Jack at the coffeepot. "Helping yourself? I thought rank hath its privilege."

"Harlene's half day. What do you have for me?"

Cal handed him a file folder. "Statements from David Reyniers and Cyndi Bradford, the two at the Flying Dutchman."

Jack flipped open the folder. "This the fellow Russell Van Alstyne fought with?"

"Yep. According to Reyniers, Van Alstyne was bothering the girl. He stepped in, words were exchanged, and Van Alstyne laid him out flat."

Jack raised his eyebrows. "He said that?"

"No, he talked around it for five minutes. He *boxes* for *Cornell*." Cal drew the words out. "Embarrassed to have his ass handed to him in the first five seconds."

"Is that why he didn't report it to the Saratoga police?"

"That, and the girl evidently fell on him, crying."

"Hmm. What did she have to say?"

Cal gave him a sly look. "Once I assured her I wasn't going to share any of what she told me with Reyniers, she admitted she picked out Van Alstyne because she thought he'd provoke the other boy."

Jack snorted. "Tactical flirting?"

"I've always said women are smarter than we are."

"You've got the right of it, there." He handed the papers back to Cal. "Anything else?"

"Nope. Everything about Van Alstyne's timeline checks out. Except for that six-hour period unaccounted for." He thumbed toward the hallway. "George brought your two hippies in."

Jack picked up his coffee. "He put 'em in separate rooms?"

"Yeah." Cal shook his head. "The hair on boys nowadays. I'm so glad I've got daughters."

"They do it *because* it drives us crazy. Didn't you ever do anything to put the wind up your old man?"

"Yeah. Joined the Tenth Mountain Division and went to Italy."

Jack smiled a little. "Think how much easier it would have been to simply stop visiting the barber."

He decided to start with Isaac Nevinson, figuring time spent waiting in an interrogation room would do half the work for him on young Terry McKellan. "Mr. Nevinson. Thank you for coming in."

"Did I have a choice?"

Jack kept his voice mild. "You're not under arrest."

The young man sprawled in his chair, boots planted firmly on the floor, arms crossed. Jack sat across from him. "We've got the autopsy report on Natalie back."

Nevinson straightened. "Do you know what happened to her?"

"Some." *Not enough.* "When was the last time you saw her?"

"I told you, that afternoon. When I dropped her at the bus station."

"Mm-hmm. And before that?"

"What do you mean? We were at the farm before that."

"I'm thinking she may have told you a little more than you're letting on. In an intimate moment, maybe. You were sleeping with her, right?"

"Three or four times! Jesus, we weren't, like, a thing."

"How about the day she left? One more for old times' sake?"

"Oh, my God. Old people should *not* talk about sex. No, we didn't have one for the road. I don't need to try to make it with some chick who's pissed off at me. There's plenty of other cool girls around."

"Did Natalie make any phone calls before she left?"

Nevinson blinked at the sudden change. "We don't have a phone at the farm."

"How about at the bus station?"

"How would I know? I let her out at the curb and drove off."

"You didn't even wait to see her inside? Make sure she had enough cash for the bus?"

"It was broad daylight out! She's a big girl, she can take care of herself."

Jack watched Nevinson's face as he realized what he had said. "Demonstrably, not."

Nevinson hung his head. "Sorry."

"How about at the carnival? Did she use a pay phone there?"

"I didn't see her. Nobody else mentioned it. Nobody else made any calls, either."

"Okay." Jack pushed away from the table.

"Can I go now?"

"I want you to stay right there while I talk to your buddy. See what he has to say about everything."

Nevinson groaned.

Terry McKellan, in the other room, was sitting bolt upright, knees together, hands flat on the table. "I saw Nat talking with some guy at the fair," he began.

Jack sat down slowly, beckoning him to continue.

"I didn't want to say anything because I went to get Italian sausage, too." The boy looked down at his lap. "And fries and soft-serve ice cream." He wanted to make a full confession, evidently.

"Tell me what you saw."

"She was leaving the sausage stand when I got there. We kind of looked at each other, and she did this"—he held his finger to his lips—"and I nodded. So we were both cool."

Illicit sausages. This generation had a lot to learn, Jack thought.

"I was waiting in line, not, you know, paying attention to her, but as I was looking around, I saw her talking to a guy."

"What did he look like?"

"He was straight, you know?"

"Straight as in . . . square? Short hair?" He thought of Russell's barely-grown-out army cut, and his heart sank.

"Yeah. And he was dressed very, you know, establishment. Chinos and a short-sleeved shirt. Like something my dad would wear."

"Was he an older man?"

"I don't think so. He was, you know, regular sized?" He gestured to his lean midsection. "He didn't have any middle-age potbelly or anything."

"Height? Eyes? Hair?"

McKellan screwed up his face. "Definitely taller than Nat. Light hair, I guess. I couldn't see his eyes. They were over by where the games start, by the one where you throw a dart into a balloon. It was, I don't know, too far to see any details."

"What about her body language?"

"Her what?"

"How was she standing? Stiff, like she was talking to a stranger? Leaning in, like it was someone she knew?"

"I guess . . . sort of in-between? Like maybe she didn't know him, but she wouldn't mind getting to know him, right?"

Jack leaned back in his chair, thinking.

"Am I in trouble, sir?" McKellan had the hippie look down—long hair, tie-dyed shirt, ratty jeans—but it was all surface. His anxious tilt forward and bright, open eyes said, *I used to be a Boy Scout, and I'm going back to the troop as soon as I can.* Jack had no doubt McKellan would be in chinos and a sports shirt himself within a year. Maybe less.

"This is very important, son, and I need you to tell me the truth." The boy nodded. "When was the last time you, um, had relations with Natalie?"

McKellan blushed. "The end of July? Right around the beginning of August."

"And then she and Isaac were together."

He looked down at his lap again. "Yes, sir." Jack thought of what Fran had said. *We're breaking beyond traditional bourgeois morality.* It looked like that was considerably more difficult for some of the commune's members.

"Do you know the last time Isaac was with her? Slept with her?"

McKellan twisted in his seat. "About a week after that. Maybe ten days."

Two weeks ago. Fran had been right, Nevinson certainly hadn't seemed to be moving on Natalie due to some great passion. Jack wondered if the young man was enough of a dog in the manger to want Natalie back if he saw her with another man. Someone like the stranger from the carnival.

Jack stood up and leaned over the table, bracing himself on his hands. McKellan shrank back. "Did Isaac talk about your testimony today? Did he tell you what to say to me?"

McKellan shook his head, eyes wide. "No, sir!"

"Okay. Stay here." Jack shut the door and crossed into Nevinson's room. He didn't bother to sit. "Isaac. Did you see Natalie talking to a man at the fair?"

The kid frowned. "No. The girls split right after we got to the fair, and Terry peeled off after a while. I didn't see anyone until we all met up at the end of the evening." He brightened. "Hey, I've got witnesses! I was talking to a bunch of the farmers showing there. I collected their business cards."

Nevinson was more committed to the hippie lifestyle than McKellan, maybe, but no young man who collected business cards from ag supply salesmen was destined to overthrow capitalism. "Okay. Wait here."

Jack found his sergeant in the bullpen. "Go ahead and let the boys out, George. Thank 'em for their cooperation and all that."

"You get anything?"

A mysterious man who couldn't be identified at the fair. No hint of who she might have had sex with on her last, fatal night. Jack sighed. "I got more questions. No answers."

FRIDAY, AUGUST 25, PRESENT DAY

55. Russ met up with Jack Liddle outside the dining tent. He had the guest list in hand, passed to him by a tense-faced Clare, who had briefed him on what Audrey Langevoort had told her and then said, "I'm getting the pump," before heading out the door.

Liddle held up a pocket-size notebook. "I took down the locals' names and numbers and let them go. No one had even heard of Saunderson before the party tonight."

"You still tote a notebook around?"

Liddle made a face. "Force of habit. I don't feel dressed without one."

"Are you still carrying?"

"Not to a party, Russell."

Russ noticed Jack didn't actually answer the question, but he let it go. The caterers had set up an impromptu bar on one of the dining tables and were passing coffee around, which would mean a lot of overcaffeinated drunks on the road later. *One thing at a time.* "Did you find out anything useful from the Barkley and Eaton people?"

Liddle shook his head. "Saunderson was the fair-haired boy. Literally, I guess. No one was surprised he got the top spot. Kept his nose clean, worked six days out of seven, didn't have any unsavory habits as far as anyone here knew."

"Personal life? Financial problems?"

"I'm afraid you're going to have to turn to the NYPD for that. No one up here seems to have known him that well." Liddle gestured toward the house. "Did you get anything up there?"

"As far as I can tell, the only people in the house at the time were Saunderson himself, Clare, one of the caterers, and a Mrs. Fike in the powder room." He pointed to her name on the guest list.

"Yeah, I cleared her husband to go. He's waiting for her."

"The only one to see anything was the caterer, who spotted him when he reached the deck. She said he was alone and had something white around his neck."

Liddle blew a breath out. "The musicians?"

"Gone as soon as we went down for dinner. I took a look at the guest room he's been staying in."

"Anything?"

"Well, he had some condoms in his shaving kit, so he wasn't a monk. Otherwise . . ." Russ shrugged. "No prescription or other drugs. Clothing for a week in the mountains. One of those books on improving your efficiency. His laptop."

"We should get a look at that. And his phone."

"I'll see if Kent Langevoort knows the passwords. Otherwise, I'll have to get a warrant, and I can guarantee Judge Ryswick won't issue one based on what we have right now." Russ rubbed his lips.

"You're thinking this is a straight-up suicide attempt."

"Right now I am. What about you?"

Liddle nodded. "He wouldn't be the first person to hide his personal troubles away. Maybe the strain of the new responsibilities was the final straw. Or maybe—a business thing like this is bound to get some press coverage. A story in the *New York Times*. Definitely in the *Post-Star*. Maybe there's something he doesn't want exposed."

Liddle frowned. His sentence hung in the air like a weapon someone had tossed into the middle of an argument.

Russ stared at the older man. "Are you thinking what I'm thinking?"

"No." Liddle shook his head. "That's complete supposition."

"We have a girl who was killed a week ago. Now we have a guy, who was here a week ago, trying to off himself despite just being handed a top-of-the-line Wall Street job on a silver platter."

"Uh-huh. And do you have a single other thing to link them together? A piece of evidence? Any way that they overlap other than being within the same fifty square miles of each other?"

"No, but—"

"How many suicides does the county average in a year?"

"Ten or twelve."

"So maybe two or three in your jurisdiction."

"Yeah, but—"

"How many have you had so far this year?"

Russ paused. "None." He looked back at the house. At the twenty-foot-high deck he had admired. "Okay. I get your point. I want to close the murder and that's making me grasp at straws."

Liddle snorted. "You know where that saying comes from?" Russ shook his head. "It's a proverb about a drowning man clutching at reeds in desperation."

"Reeds are straws?"

"Everything was straw in merry old England. Here's the thing, Russell. Usually, when you pull on a reed, it comes up out of the mud. But some of them, once in a while, are rooted deeply enough to let a man haul himself to safety." Liddle tapped the side of his head. "As soon as the words were out of my mouth, I thought of your murder. Intuition is an important tool in a cop's arsenal. But it's worthless without meticulous casework to back it up."

"We're going to have to cross our t's and dot our i's. I get it."

"First you have to *find* some t's and i's, Russell. Right now all you have is a soggy straw."

Russ exhaled. "Better let the rest of the guests go, as long as we have their contact information." He glanced into the tent again. "How's Mom holding up?"

"She's talking with people who own three houses like they're her next-door neighbors. Your mother's a remarkable woman."

"I know. Let's get her home before she drops." Not to mention Clare. And himself. He was exhausted by the events of the evening, aching from performing CPR for so long, and had an increasing itch of unease about Ethan. This was the longest they had both been away from him.

Russ called Kent Langevoort's phone and left a message about the laptop while Chief Liddle—*Jack,* Jesus, he was going to have to stop thinking as if he were still a teen—told the remaining guests and catering staff they were free to go.

Up at the house, he left Clare's new intern in charge of her mother. "We'll be fine. A good night's sleep, hopefully, and then we're having everybody from B and E back for a breakfast meeting." Joni turned to Clare. "I may not make it to assist on Sunday. I'm sorry."

Clare hugged her. "Take all the time you need."

"It's not that. It's going to be a delicate time for the business. Transitions are always tricky, and something like this happening? There are going to be a lot of clients and market partners needing reassurance. And to know we have a plan going forward."

"We?" Russ said. "I thought you were out of the company."

She sighed. "Yeah, well. It's not always that cut-and-dried, is it?"

They drove back to Mom's place in silence. Ethan, doing his usual trick of being good for everyone except his parents, had taken a bottle at ten and fallen asleep. Emma left with a wad of cash in her pocket and a cheerful, "See you for October break, Grandma!"

"Are you going to be okay to drive home?" Russ asked Liddle.

"How about a cup of tea?" His mother went to the sink and began filling the kettle. "Not as bad as coffee at this hour, but it'll help perk you up."

Liddle smiled. "I'll take that offer."

"None for us, Mom. Clare and I need to get Ethan home."

She crossed the kitchen and kissed him. "Need to get yourself home, more like. Drive safe."

"I always do."

Liddle barked a laugh.

"I always do *now*," Russ amended.

Ethan stirred when they fastened him into the backseat, but he passed out again as soon as the car was in motion. "I've been thinking," Clare said. "When Joni was talking about how the business could be affected. Do you think that might have something to do with it? Could there be some sort of, I don't know, terrible loss Saunderson was covering up? Or embezzlement? Or fraud?"

He hadn't. And all of those sounded more probable than the theory that Saunderson had something to do with Gabrielle Yates's death.

"I think . . ." He paused. Clare laid her hand on his arm. "I think I really, really need a fresh perspective on all this."

56. "I think you're out of your ever-lovin' mind," the deputy chief said.

The chief crossed his arms and leaned against the briefing room table. "Don't hold back, Lyle. Tell me how you really feel."

"Some poor bastard from out of town tries to off himself last night, and you decide, based on zero evidence, that he's our killer. What I *really* think is too many sleepless nights with a new baby have got you delusional. I had three of my own, I know how it works."

"I'm not delusional." The chief looked at Hadley, who had been trying to sneak a peek at the headline story in the Saturday *Post-Star*. "Knox, what do you think?"

I think this is a no-winner. "About your mental health, Chief? Or about not getting enough sleep with a baby in the house?"

He gave her a look that said, *Nice try.* "About Bors Saunderson as a possible suspect."

She chose her words carefully. "I understand you wanting to tie two out-of-the-ordinary events together. You always say you don't believe in coincidences. And it *is* really strange that someone with no prior signs of depression should hang himself at his own congratulations party. But"—she nodded toward MacAuley—"I have to agree with the dep. Saunderson was a rich workaholic Wall Street guy. Gabrielle Yates was a poor girl from Florida. Where is there even a point of contact for them?"

"The fair."

Hadley shrugged helplessly. "Okay, she went to the fair. And maybe he did, too. But Chief, everybody goes to the fair. They get over one hundred thousand visitors during the course of the week."

The dep nodded approvingly.

"And there's one other thing, Chief. We've been working this as if it's connected to the 1972 killing."

"For good reason." MacAuley thumbed toward the whiteboard, where the known facts of all three similar deaths were scrawled in black erasable marker.

"Bors Saunderson was, like, four years old back then. Which means we've got no follow-through from the earlier killing."

"Copycat?" The chief's voice indicated he thought it was a weak argument.

"A copycat from our area I could buy," MacAuley said. "If some smart townie accidentally killed Yates, I could just . . . *just* . . . see him remembering the old case and staging her body drop to look like it. But that requires one"—the dep held up a finger—"the perp be a local guy and two"—he held up a second finger—"the perp be at least somewhere around your age. Saunderson is from downstate and he's not even forty. Not likely to get any older, either."

The chief sighed. "Knox, what's the report from the hospital?"

"He's alive and in intensive care. I guess the big danger is from pneumonia or something like that, because of the compromised breathing tube."

Van Alstyne pressed a finger against his mouth, thinking. "Okay. You two both make good points. However, I still want to canvass the folks at the fair."

"Russ—" MacAuley began.

"I know we're short on manpower. I know." The chief pointed toward Hadley. "Knox, you handle it. Get a photo from . . . I don't know, see if you can print one from the internet. If not, ask up at the Langevoorts'. Change into civvies. I went there in uniform and I suspect I left a less-than-ideal impression on the management."

"Civvies?" She tried to make the word squeak less.

"You've done it before."

MacAuley tipped his head toward her. "Consider it the uniform of the day, kid."

"Meanwhile, I'm headed over to the Water View. Maybe Saunderson went to dinner there. If we can put him and Gabrielle Yates in at least one spot together, we should be able to get a warrant for his DNA." The chief tossed the folder to the dep. "Lyle, get the paperwork ready. And call Dr. Scheeler, see if anything's come in yet."

MacAuley shook his head. "This is completely ass-backwards."

"I know. But we've tried it front-forwards and we've got nothing. If this doesn't pan out—" He spread his hands. "Well, at least we can't have less than nothing."

◆ ◆ ◆

She felt like an idiot showing her badge at the gate. "I'm with the MKPD," she began.

"Yeah, yeah. Hold your hand out." The bearded man stamped a strip of purple on the back of her hand.

"Um . . ."

He sighed. "Go to the main ticket booth at the entrance of the midway. They'll set you up."

She wished she had her uniform on. Her poly-blend armor made her feel aloof, tough, above the crowd. In shorts and a sleeveless top, walking all alone through the throngs of fairgoers, she looked like a loser. Who even comes to a fair by themselves? They had been so slammed at the shop, she hadn't been able to bring her kids—instead, they went with Granddad. Plus, men didn't leer at her when she was in uniform. At least, the sober ones didn't.

She spotted the main ticket booth by the queue stretching out in front. She strode to the rear and got in line behind a man with two preteens. All three of them, dad and kids, had their noses buried in their phones, the kids playing games, the adult tap-tap-tapping away with his thumbs. Divorced dad, she decided. She had dated her share of them back in California, something she never wanted to do again. Date, that was. Of course, that meant she might never have sex again, and wasn't that a cheerful thought? She was pretty sure there were apps for no-strings hook-ups that encompassed even Millers Kill, but as a mom with two kids in school, she wasn't going to risk it. Imagine if the guy on the other end was a teacher? Or worse, one of her kid's friends' parents? She had already experienced being the bad girl of the PTA, and she'd left California because of it.

"Miss? Miss?"

Hadley blinked. She was first in line. Crap. She fished her badge out of her pocket. "I'm with the MKPD—"

She didn't get to finish the introduction. The girl behind the glass unspooled a long string of tickets and tore them off. "Here you go."

Suddenly, the behavior of the man at the entry gate made sense. She pushed the tickets back through the booth's crescent opening. "I'm not here for freebies, and you shouldn't be offering them to cops anyway. It's illegal." The girl looked at her like she was crazy. Hadley unfolded the picture she had downloaded from the B and E company site. "I'm trying to find out if anyone remembers seeing this man." She pointed to Saunderson.

"You're kidding, right?" The girl shook her head. "I can't remember people five minutes after I've taken their money." She looked over Hadley's head toward the line now stretching out behind her.

Hadley stayed put, blocking off the window. "Okay, then. Who *is* good at remembering faces?"

"Joe. Old Joe. He manages the tickets and the money."

"Where can I find him?"

"He doesn't work mornings. He'll be back in the trailers, behind the midway. All right?"

"All right." Hadley released her spot at the window and started walking. She skirted the edge of the midway until the rides and booths gave way to an agricultural display field. Spectators in a rise of bleachers cheered as a border collie raced through its paces, rounding a herd of fat sheep and moving them out.

Hadley kept going, the midway on her right and the show field on her left becoming a grassy parking area filled with livestock trailers. Beyond them, however, pitched a little farther back from the noise and smell, was a cluster of RVs, pickups, and trailers, many with lawn chairs and folding tables set up outside.

A man and a woman sat at one of the tables, with the remains of a late breakfast or early lunch scattered between them. The woman smiled when she spotted Hadley, revealing the loss of several teeth. "Hey, hon. You've gotten lost. What are you looking for?"

"Actually, I think I'm in the right place. I'm looking for Joe? The girl who gave me the name called him Old Joe?"

The man and woman laughed. "One of the kids," the man said. "Yeah, I'm sure Joe seems about a hundred years old to them." Since the couple looked a hard sixty, Hadley began to wonder if Joe might not in fact be close to the century mark.

The woman rose. "He's in his trailer. C'mon, hon, I'll knock you in." She led Hadley to a small, round Airstream trailer with a wide mat of artificial turf beneath a striped awning. "Nice, hah?" The woman rapped on the door. "These things come back in style. Joe keeps getting offers to buy it." She shook her head. "Sixty years old, and kids want it to take pictures. Crazy." She knocked again. "Joe? There's a cute young lady out here wants to see you." She winked at Hadley. "That'll bring him."

The door opened. Joe did indeed look a couple decades older than her helpful guide. He was wiping his hands on a small towel. "I was in the can, for chrissakes. Can't a man have some peace around here?" He looked down at Hadley. "Who're you?"

She held up her badge. "My name's Hadley Knox, and I'm with the MKPD."

The woman looked at her sorrowfully. "Hon, you should'a led with that."

Hadley spread her hands. "No one's in trouble. I'm trying to see

Liddle sighed. "Didn't think so."

"My problem is, I don't have any viable suspects, so I'm forced to look at what this death has in common with the other two."

"Summer people. The carnies. Chief McNeil had them both on his list."

Russ nodded. "We're looking into those."

"Chief McNeil was certain the unsub was from away, because the dead girl wasn't from around here. My investigation veered in the opposite direction, because it seemed most likely to me that Natalie was killed by one of her lovers, or by someone she picked up at the bus station."

"Which you couldn't prove."

"To my regret. My point is, you're already ahead of us, because you're focusing on the bigger picture."

"It feels more like I'm flailing around in a sea of possibilities."

"You need to consider a man who was here in '52 and '72 and who's still around today. Like me."

"You?"

"Sure." Liddle slid off the desk and walked to the whiteboard. "I was here for all three deaths."

"Please don't take this the wrong way, but I'm having a hard time picturing this last killing done by a seventy-eight-year-old. Especially when they all had such an obvious sexual component."

Liddle snorted a laugh. "It doesn't fall off when you start collecting social security, Russell."

"I can't tell you how happy I am to hear it. Nevertheless—"

Liddle held up a finger, an abstracted look on his face. Russ shut up.

"Obvious sexual component," the former chief finally said.

"Mm-hmm."

"We all approached these cases as sex-related crimes. You, me, Chief McNeil."

"Yeah . . ."

"What if they're not? What if the makeup, the dress, all that was a distraction? Camouflage, if you like."

"Camouflaging what?"

"A different motive for murder."

"Such as . . . ?"

Liddle shrugged. "Control. Money. Secrets. If I knew, I could clear the case for you, Russell."

"Chief, I may have something—" They both looked to where Hadley stood in the doorway. "Am I interrupting?"

"Chief Liddle, this is our newest officer, Hadley Knox. Knox, Jack Liddle, who was chief here when I was a kid."

"Pleased to meet you, Officer." Liddle shook Hadley's hand. "And it's time for me to go."

"I'll walk you out." In the hallway, Russ remembered Clare's dire warnings about Friday night. "Look, I invited you to dinner without checking with my wife. Turns out we have a Save-the-MKPD fund-raiser that evening."

"I understand." Liddle opened the front door, letting shimmering, tar-scented heat into the foyer.

"No, no, we've scored an invitation for you, if you're willing to climb into a jacket and shine your shoes, which is what Clare says I have to do."

Liddle laughed. "I can manage that, if you really think I won't be a fifth wheel."

"You'd be evening our numbers out. Mom was going to have to go stag, but you can be her escort. If that wouldn't be too awkward."

"Huh." Liddle scratched the back of his neck. "Well. I guess not, if it's all right with Margy. Thanks."

"Having another chief of police there can only help our cause. After all, you've already helped me by giving me something new to think about."

One foot on the granite steps, Liddle turned back. "The chief doesn't go it alone, Russell. We can all use a little help now and again."

"Of course." The young woman gestured to an even younger girl, clearly still in her teens. "Tori, will you show this officer to Mrs. Beshir?"

The girl led Hadley past the kitchen entrance and opened an unmarked door onto a long, windowless hallway. Unlike the public areas, the floor was bare wood. No need to hush dozens of footsteps back here, Hadley guessed.

The girl knocked and opened another featureless door. "Mrs. Beshir? There's a police officer to see you."

The small room looked like a food product convention in miniature—a wall of shelves held cans, boxes, tins, binders, books, and measuring scales. The woman who rose from the tidy desk to greet Hadley looked a bit like something warm and comforting to eat—a raisin muffin, maybe, or a coffee bun, if those pastries were dressed in bright colors and a hijab.

"Hello." She stretched out her hand. "You must be the officer I spoke with earlier."

"Hadley Knox, yes, ma'am."

"Sit, sit." Mrs. Beshir gestured toward one of the chairs facing her desk. "What can I get you?" She picked up an old-fashioned phone receiver. "Have you had lunch?"

Hadley waved the offer away. "Nothing for me, thanks."

"Okay. Just some tea, then." She pressed a button on the phone. "Stefan? A tea tray and meze, please."

"Really, I don't—"

Mrs. Beshir sat. "As I said earlier, the general manager is technically in charge of the staff. He does all the hiring and firing—not that I'm saying that's necessary! We usually get a good group of kids."

"But you'd be able to identify one from a picture?"

"That's why I said 'technically.' When their boyfriends break up with them or when they don't know if they want to return to college in the fall, they tend to come talk with me. Probably because I'm *not* their supervisor."

There was a knock and the door opened. A man in a stained chef's tunic entered, balancing a huge tray laden with a complete tea set and at least a half-dozen dishes of finger food. The cook flipped open a tray stand, set the tray down, and with a flourish, left, shutting the door behind him. Mrs. Bashir took a small plate and began filling it with items. "Gabrielle—she's the girl who is missing—I would describe as 'work hard, play hard.' This is her second summer with us. She very much enjoys the nightlife around the lake, but she always shows up in time for her shift and does her best. I think this year she's hoping to be part of the winter crew in Florida. The owner of the Water View has a large restaurant in Sanibel." She handed the plate and a white napkin to Hadley.

"Oh, I can't really—"

"How do you like your tea?" Mrs. Bashir was already pouring.

Hadley knew when she was beaten. "Milk, no sugar."

The cup and saucer were placed on the desk in front of her. "Eat," Mrs. Bashir commanded. "Try the koumus, the little puff pastry. And the stuffed grape leaves. They're delicious."

Hadley dutifully popped the pastry into her mouth. It *was* delicious. She wiped her fingers on her napkin and opened the folder she had brought. "Would you mind taking a look?"

Mrs. Beshir held out a hand. She examined one photo, then another. She laid them on the desk, all the animation drained from her face. "Oh, dear."

"Is it Gabrielle?"

The food manager sighed. "You know, I persuaded my manager to contact your office after I saw the news on TV. We had called the Lake George Police when she didn't show up for her weekend shift, but they said a young adult at a seasonal job . . ." She shook her head. "They don't consider her a missing person for at least three days."

Which explained why the girl wasn't flagged in their initial lists of MPRs. "When did you last see her?"

"She was scheduled Wednesday, and I saw her in the restaurant that night. She had Thursday and Friday off, due back for Saturday lunch. It's not unusual for a staff member to be away during their days off. I didn't think she would *actually* be . . . hurt." Mrs. Beshir looked at the pictures again. "She was a lovely girl."

if anyone remembers a certain man visiting the fair." She pulled the picture out of her pocket. "I was told you're good with faces, Mr., uh, Joe."

He stepped down from the doorway. "This about that girl who died? Your boss was here a couple days ago, acting like he thought one of us done it."

"I can promise you, it's nothing personal. We're running down any and all leads." She spread the photo open. "Do you by any chance remember seeing this man?" She pointed to Saunderson.

"Yeah," Joe said.

"Yeah?" the woman asked.

"Yeah . . ." The instant agreement made Hadley suspicious. If the old man thought he was taking the heat off someone at the fair . . . "What makes him so easy to remember?"

"First off, he was really pale. Like he'd been living under a rock pale. Second, he and his friend were rich. Don't see a lot of rich folks going for the rides. They go to, I dunno, Disney World instead."

"How did you know he was rich?"

Joe shrugged. "Clothes. Hair. Can't you tell when you see 'em?"

She thought for a moment. "I guess I can. You said he was with a friend?"

Joe tapped the picture. "Yeah. This guy."

"They were together?" She couldn't remember if the chief had included Langevoort in the report. "Okay. Anything else you can recall?"

"They asked where the shooting gallery was. I thought maybe they were queer for each other, because, you know, most regular guys go to the shooting gallery to show off for girls."

She decided to ignore the offensive comment. "Do you think who-ever runs the shooting gallery might remember them?"

Joe looked at her. "How the hell would I know?"

"I'll take you there, hon." The woman seemed ready to forgive Hadley's failure to identify herself as a cop for a chance at getting more interesting gossip. She led Hadley through the encampment, across a width of half-dead grass crossed and crossed again with thick black power lines, and into the noise and fried-grease smells of the midway itself. "It's right over here, hon. He's a nice boy. New this year, but very polite."

Hadley saw the gleam of red hair before they reached the booth. *Of course. Of course it's goddamn Kevin Flynn.* He hadn't told her where he worked at the carnival, but the universe hated her, so here they were, her in what felt like way-too-revealing shorts, and him in his bearded, tattooed, where-did-all-those-muscles-come-from glory.

He spotted her when she was still a couple yards away. She saw the momentary flare in his eyes, swallowed immediately by a keen-edged smile. He leaned on the counter. "Hello, there, pretty lady. Want to try your luck?"

The woman beside her cackled. "Don't let her make you run away, Kevin, but she's a cop!"

He rolled his eyes. "I'm never going to hear the end of that, am I?"

She patted him on his bearded cheek. "Nope."

"Um." Hadley fumbled for her badge. "I'm Hadley Knox, from the MKPD."

"What can I do for you, Officer?"

"I'm, uh, trying to find out if anyone remembers this man." She smoothed the picture on his counter. "Well, both of them. Joe, Old Joe, said they asked him for directions to the shooting booth."

"It's about the girl who died near here," the woman helpfully supplied.

"I already told the cops I don't remember seeing the girl."

Hadley pointed to the picture. It was easier when she looked away from Flynn. "How about one of these men?"

Flynn picked the paper up, frowning. "Do you mind?" He stepped back into the shade of his booth to inspect it more closely. "Yeah. I think I do remember the pale guy. And I definitely remember this one." He tapped at the picture of Langevoort. "He won flash." He pointed up at the enormous and expensive-looking plush toys hanging front and center in his booth. "I don't hand out many of those, and I try to remember who takes them if they come around again."

Hadley couldn't help asking. "Why?"

Flynn handed her the picture. "Because the point of the game is for the marks to lose their money, not for me to throw stock." He smiled slowly. "Ma'am."

The older woman elbowed Hadley. "I told you he was polite!"

"Hey! Debbie!" The woman turned around. A skinny man with more tattoos than Flynn was trotting toward them. "Boss wants to know if you can swing in for Weezie."

"Can do." She turned back to Hadley. "I gotta go, hon. Don't let this one sell you any after-hour tours!" She walked away, laughing.

"You really recognize the guy?"

Flynn pulled a water bottle from beneath the counter and took a swig. "Yeah. What's the deal?"

"He's a VIP with Barkley and Eaton. New York finance firm. He tried to kill himself out of the blue last night, and the chief's got a hair up his butt, thinking he might be connected to the vic."

"Because they both came to the fair? That's a reach."

"Yeah, but . . ." Hadley tried to put the pieces together. "If they *did* intersect, where else could it have been?" She paused. "The chief is checking out the restaurant where Yates worked. If Saunderson ate there, we'll have two points where he and Gabrielle intersected, which will get a warrant for his DNA."

Flynn lifted a cloth off a hook and began wiping down the toy rifles racked at the front of the booth. "You're still working from a conclusion backwards. That's not like the chief. That's *really* not like the chief."

"He's pretty desperate to close this case. I think he's worried about the ballot measure. If they vote to close the department, we're all screwed."

"Syracuse is hiring."

"Yeah, I don't think so. You're not making it look like the best career move."

He pulled back. "I'm doing something important here. I've connected with one of the guys who seems to be involved. I'm getting close to having some real evidence."

"I'm not attacking your—" At the last minute, she remembered to

271

drop her voice. "Your *work*. I never said you weren't good at what you *do*." If that implied he was lousy at what he *was*, well, that was fine.

He nodded. "Don't knock yourself out with the compliments." She opened her mouth and he raised a hand. "You better go. I don't want anyone wondering why I'm chatting with a cop." His lips thinned. "I've had enough encounters with the law already this week. Next time, just slap down some tickets and play the game."

"Don't worry, Flynn. I'm done here." She turned, and turned again to fire one last shot. "I think we're both done here."

57. "You're back," Lyle said. "That was quick."

Russ stepped fully into the squad room. "Have you heard from Knox yet?"

"I have. She got two separate IDs from people who remembered Saunderson and Langevoort at the fair. They bought tickets and won a prize at the shooting game."

"Both of 'em, huh? I guess that wouldn't preclude Saunderson from picking up a girl later." He laid his find on Lyle's desk. His deputy picked up the evidence baggie, read the slip of paper inside, and whistled. "Well, I'll be damned."

It was a charge slip from the Water View. Bors Saunderson's name, with his signature over it, was imprinted from his card. On the top, the ticket was printed with the date, the station, and the waitress. Lyle looked up.

"There isn't another Gabrielle waiting tables, is there?"

Russ shook his head. "No. It was her. Serving Saunderson dinner."

Lyle squinted at the total. "Not just him. Unless that place is even more expensive than I thought."

"It's pretty pricey, but no. The manager who pulled this for me confirmed that was an average price for dinner and drinks for two people."

"How did you get this?"

Russ grinned. "The manager's old-fashioned. He keeps all the paper copies until the bookkeeper comes in at the end of the month. Once she reconciles everything, they get shredded."

Lyle glanced at the calendar. "You are the luckiest sonofabitch to walk this planet."

"Don't I know it. Get on it; I want that warrant request to Judge Ryswick ASAP."

◆ ◆ ◆

Russ had the paper in hand an hour and a half later. He met up with Dr. Scheeler in the lobby of the Washington County Hospital. "What's the news?" Russ asked, shaking Scheeler's hand.

"Nothing from the state labs yet." They walked toward the elevators. "Your man is in the ICU. They want to send him to Albany, but he's not stable enough to make the trip."

"What are his chances of recovery?"

Scheeler pinched his thumb and forefinger together. "Slim. The trauma to the larynx creates major pulmonary and respiratory problems."

Russ stabbed the UP button. "But we got to him almost immediately."

"The bulk of the damage is done in the first impact to the throat. That's why it was the preferred method of execution for so many centuries. It was quick enough to be considered humane." They stepped into the elevator.

"Anyone here with him?"

"Your wife was coming in when I arrived." Scheeler selected the floor.

"Anybody not professionally charged with visiting the sick?"

"His boss has been here the whole time, the nurses said. I guess there's family coming from the Midwest somewhere, but they haven't made it yet."

"Good. The last thing I need is to explain to a bunch of grieving relations why we're swabbing their son or brother's DNA."

The charge nurse at the ICU station took a look at the warrant. "I need to get a doctor here to okay this."

"We just need a cheek swab," Russ said, as Scheeler said, "I *am* a doctor." The nurse shook his head and paged the ICU internist. A

273

white coat showed up within ten seconds and signed off on the orders record.

Russ waited by the central station as Scheeler and the nurse went into Saunderson's room. Clare came out, followed by Langevoort; they both spotted Russ at the same time.

"Chief Van Alstyne." Kent Langevoort looked twenty years older than he had the night before. "What are you doing here?"

"Checking in." Clare narrowed her eyes, but didn't say anything. "How is he?"

"Not great. Although they're very hopeful."

"Mmm." Russ glanced around the antiseptic hallway. "Have you had a chance to get out?"

Langevoort shook his head. "I feel like I ought to stay with him until his parents get here."

"I understand. It sounds like you two are pretty close."

"I guess so. We weren't drinking buddies, but Bors has been working for me for almost a decade. And of course, we've spent a lot of time together in the run-up to naming him as my replacement."

"We're trying to get a sense of why Mr. Saunderson tried to kill himself. Do you have any ideas?"

Langevoort shook his head. "None. It seems . . . ridiculous, in a word. I was handing him the world on a silver platter."

"There are a lot of stresses to the position, though." Clare's voice was thoughtful.

"He could have just turned it down. I didn't hold a gun to his head." Langevoort scrubbed his face with his hand. "Sorry. That's not very appropriate, under the circumstances."

Scheeler and the nurse reemerged from the room. Scheeler crossed the hall, sample bag in hand. "I'm going to see if I can get a look at his tox screen for you."

"Thanks," Russ said. "Call me when you know anything." The medical examiner vanished around the corner, headed toward the elevator bank. "Mr. Langevoort, did you know anything about Bors's personal life?"

"He was straight. He dated some. He hasn't had a long-term rela-

tionship that I know of since he joined the firm. He's not very close to his family, but I think that's because they're blue-collar people back in Minnesota, not because of any falling-out." Langevoort rubbed his face again. "I was actually telling him he ought to find a wife not long ago." He looked at Russ, then at Clare. "You need to have somebody in your corner. Somebody to remind you your life is more than the job."

Clare smiled a little. "Somebody to get you to take your kid hunting and skiing?"

"Yes."

Hunting. Well, that would explain the shooting range at the fair. "You and Bors came up from the city last weekend?"

"Friday afternoon, yes. Audrey and, and, Joni were gone that weekend, so it gave us some quiet time to work."

"And the two of you came up on some earlier weekends this summer?"

"Sure. I had all the candidates for the job up around the Fourth of July. I narrowed it down to Bors and two others, and had each of them up for a one-on-one weekend."

Russ stepped aside for a phlebotomist pushing a cart full of rubber-stoppered vials. "Did they know about each other? The candidates, I mean."

"Obviously, everyone at the Fourth of July house party knew what they were there for. I tried to keep the later trips very hush-hush. I came up here almost every weekend, and I asked my individual guests to simply let people know they were going to be away. I wanted to keep an information blackout until I'd made my choice."

"And he'd accepted," Clare said.

"Well, yes, of course." Langevoort frowned. "Maybe I'm not following you because I'm so damn tired, but what possible connection does any of this have with Bors trying to kill himself?"

Russ spread his hands. "I don't know. I'm trying to get a picture of the man to see if any of this makes sense. Did the two of you go to the fair this past weekend?"

"What?"

"The Washington County Fair. Did you go there?"

"Yes. Sure. I go every year. Last weekend was the only time I was going to have, so I took Bors."

"Did he meet anybody while he was there?"

Langevoort stepped back. "All right, now you've *really* lost me."

"Let me put it this way. You went to the fair together. One car or two?"

"One car, of course."

"Did you leave the fair together?"

"Yes." Langevoort sounded impatient.

"While at the fair, did Mr. Saunderson meet anyone, chat with anyone, or go off with anyone?"

"No. Not to my knowledge. We weren't joined at the hip, but we stuck fairly close together." Langevoort raised a hand. "That's all for me right now. I'm going to go back in and sit with Bors. Reverend Fergusson?"

"I'll be in in just a moment." She watched him disappear into the ICU room. The she turned on Russ. "What's this all about? And why was the medical examiner taking a DNA sample?"

"How did you—"

"I can recognize a cheek swab, Russ. What's going on? Poor Kent feels badly enough already."

Russ dropped his voice. "Gabrielle Yates was Saunderson's waitress a couple weekends ago. And they were both at the fair the same day." She gave him a look. "I *know* it's a stretch."

"I've got one word for you. Why?"

"Think of what you said last night in the car. Maybe he *was* involved in financial hanky-panky at Barkley and Eaton. He knows he's in the running for president, he knows there are other guys being considered—unless you believe no one talked about their weekends in the Adirondacks with the boss?"

Clare shook her head. "I think Kent was underestimating the power of gossip."

"Me, too. So he gets up here and Kent offers him the job."

"And he feels trapped into saying yes."

"You thought about that, too?"

She nodded. "But that's an argument for his feeling overwhelmed and trying to find a way out. Not for killing a girl he's met maybe once."

"Maybe she said something and he snapped." He moved his hands through the air, trying to shove pieces into place. "I've got a man who tried to kill himself on what should have been one of the best nights of his life. I've got a woman dead for no discernable reason, from no identifiable cause. I know they met at least once, and they could have met twice."

Clare took his hands in hers. "I understand what you're trying to do. Now I want to ask you a question. What happens if there is no connection? What happens if you can't close this case, just like Jack Liddle couldn't close *his* case?"

"Or how Harry McNeil failed to close his case?" The manic energy that had been driving Russ all morning dropped away. He let his shoulders sag. "I don't know. Any time murder goes unpunished, it's a loss. For the victim, if for no one else. Right now . . ." He squeezed her hands. "There's just so goddamn much at stake."

"You're afraid this could make or break the vote to dissolve the department."

He nodded.

Clare released his hands and reached up to cup his jaw. "You need to keep that in your mind, love. Don't let that fear drive you to put an innocent person behind bars."

He snorted. "I doubt Saunderson is going to make it long enough to do any time."

She stepped back. "I wonder if your subconscious realized that, just before it decided he would make the perfect suspect?"

She left him in the ICU hall, wondering as she had so many times over the years, if he really knew himself at all.

58. "Margy? We're here." Clare entered her mother-in-law's kitchen with a bowl of potato salad balanced in her arms. Margy always said not to bring anything to Sunday dinner, but the one time Clare had arrived empty-handed, she felt the ghost of her grandmother Fergusson shaming her all afternoon long. "Margy?" She stepped forward to get out of Russ's way as he came up the steps, baby carrier in hand.

He looked over her head to the empty kitchen. "Must be we're eating out back."

They had begun having Sunday dinner at Margy's shortly after they were married. Not every Sunday—particularly in the winter, Clare was needed for Evensong or small concerts at St. Alban's as often as not, but they managed the get-together at least twice a month. It was the old-fashioned concept of Sunday Dinner, a full meal at three in the afternoon, although with Margy, you were as likely to get vegan chickpea stew as you were to see roast pork and dumplings.

She followed Russ around the corner of the house to Margy's backyard, and sure enough, there was a blue-and-white cloth on the picnic table beneath a spreading maple tree. Smoke rose from the small grill—which was manned by Jack Liddle. Margy was lighting citronella coils that had been studded into the ground like wards against evil spirits.

"There's my boy!" Margy went straight for Ethan, making it clear who her boy was now.

Russ let his mother take the carrier. "Chief—Jack." He shook the older man's hand. "Didn't expect to see you again so soon."

"Margy kindly extended the invitation to me. I told her I'd come if I could bring the burgers."

"Did she lecture you about how cows are destroying the climate?"

"Only beef cattle!" Margy hoisted Ethan from his carrier.

"Dairy cows fart methane, too, Mom." Russ leaned closer to Jack. "My sister and brother-in-law run a herd with two hundred head of milkers. It puts Mom on the horns of a dilemma."

Jack grinned. "I'm moooooved by her predicament."

Clare set the salad bowl on the table. "Next person to pun gets stuck with diaper duty for the rest of the day."

Both men prudently shut up.

Margy surrendered Ethan back to his father and headed to the house. Clare followed her. "Jack seems like a very nice man."

Margy made a noncommittal noise.

"Did you know him well? Back when he was police chief?"

They entered the kitchen. "You know what it's like around here. Everybody knows everybody else." Margy went to her refrigerator, covered in flyers and bumper stickers urging the reader to give peace a chance, buy local, and reuse, reduce, and recycle. She pulled out her ice bin and set it on the counter. "Can you get the sodas out of the pantry for me?"

Clare hoisted a pair of six-packs and set them beside the ice. "It's just . . . you seemed pretty friendly the other night. He brought you a plant."

Margy shot her a look. "He's well brought up." She opened the cellar door and retrieved a battered Coleman cooler that must have been at least as old as Clare. "But, yes, I knew him before he was chief of police. We went to school together." She slid the cooler across the floor. "Go on and put the sodas in there."

"Really?" Clare tried to keep the speculation out of her voice. Perhaps they had a schoolyard romance. Margy had been a girl in the run-up to World War II. Maybe they . . . her imagination failed her. History wasn't her strong suit. Maybe they collected scrap metal together? From what she had heard about Russ's Campbell grandparents, that didn't seem like the kind of thing they'd condone.

"Really." Margy sounded amused.

Clare settled the last soda can into the cooler and straightened. "What about after you graduated?"

"After graduation, he went into the air force. There was a draft on, remember. I started working at the town hall, and then I met Walter—of course, I had known who he was, but he was several years older than me—and he was handsome and dashing and practically a war hero . . ." She sighed. "By the time Jack was out of the service, Walter and I were engaged." She gave herself a small shake. "Not that it would have made a difference if we weren't. Jack and I were friends, not boyfriend and girlfriend." She grasped the ice basin and upended it into the cooler. "Can you carry this outside? I'll bring the ketchup and mustard and what-all."

Jack's burgers were meltingly good. Even Margy had one, "Just to be polite," and polished it off with enthusiasm. Russ ate three, which made Clare realize they probably ought to switch up their cold pasta or tabbouleh salad habit a bit. Afterward, they spread the play quilt in the shade and laid Ethan down to stretch and kick. Margy had just gone into the house to bring out dessert when Russ's phone rang.

He checked the number. "Got to take this." He moved a few steps away, out of the shade into the bright sunshine. "Van Alstyne here."

Clare would have happily listened in, but Jack leaned across the table and said, "That was some potato salad."

She smiled. "It's not a tricky dish."

"Sometimes it's the simple ones that are most satisfying. I had to teach myself to cook when I—"

"Wait. Wait." Russ stalked back toward them, waving one hand. "The chief investigator for the 1972 case is here." He swung a leg over the picnic bench and sat down. "Yes, he's still alive." He shot an apologetic look at Jack. "Hang on, I'm putting you on speaker. Okay, go ahead."

"Can you hear me?"

"Loud and clear. I have Jack Liddle with me, you'll have seen his name on the old files." He turned to Jack. "This is Daniel Scheeler, our ME. Dan, can you repeat what you just told me?"

"I know how your victim died. I know how *both* the victims died."

59. "What?" Clare said.

"How?" Jack asked at the same time.

"Who's that?" Scheeler asked.

"It's my wife. Just go on with it."

"They died from an overdose of secobarbital sodium. It's a short-acting barbiturate, the same stuff they use for veterinary euthanasia and in lethal injections. It kills very fast—within thirty minutes to an hour if it's in pill form. It knocks you out and depresses the respiratory system. You die without a mark on you."

"I thought you weren't getting the tests back—"

"For another week, I know. This was driving me crazy. I took all my samples down to the lab in Albany. I've been here since yesterday afternoon." That explained the slightly manic edge to the doctor's voice. "Once I knew what I was looking for, I checked the blood and stomach contents from 1972."

Jack frowned. "Why didn't Dr. Roberts find this when she did her tests?"

Russ looked over Clare's shoulder. She twisted around to see Margy heading toward them, chocolate cake in hand.

"Because there *was* no blood test for barbiturates back then. They didn't develop a reliable marker until the late seventies. Back then, most overdoses were diagnosed because the remains of the actual pills were found in people's stomachs. In this case, my theory is someone put the secobarbital sodium in the alcohol served to both women."

Margy settled her cake on the table. She nodded as Russ held up a finger. "So, we're looking for someone with access to veterinary medicine?"

"Or for someone with Seconal, although it's rarely prescribed anymore."

Clare felt a flush of cold through her body, surging with each heartbeat. Her hand closed, as if around a pill bottle. "Russ." She looked at her husband. "Audrey Langevoort has Seconal. It's what I gave her for her panic attack."

Russ swore.

"Russell!" his mother said.

"Who's *that*?"

"My mother. Are you sure about this?"

"Yes."

Russ jammed his hand into his hair. "Okay. I need you to fax everything you've got to the department as soon as possible."

"Will do."

"Dr. Scheeler?" Jack's voice shook. "Thank you."

"You're welcome, uh, Chief Liddle."

There was a moment of silence after Scheeler hung up. Jack Liddle rubbed his lips. "There wasn't a blood test for it. Jesus Christ. All these years . . ."

"What does this mean?" Margy remained standing.

"It means Kent Langevoort killed Gabrielle Yates and Natalie Epstein." Russ's voice was grim.

Jack shook his head. "We can't place him here when the Epstein girl was killed."

"I think you can," Clare said. Both men looked at her. "I was going through the local papers from that summer. At the library. They have them on microfilm." Russ spread his hands wide, his gesture saying *Really, Clare?* "I was curious! You didn't want to talk about what happened."

"What did you find?" Jack asked.

"There was an article about the new president of Barkley and Eaton being chosen at a weekend retreat. Right around the time the murder was in the news."

"Kent Langevoort."

Clare nodded.

Jack looked at Russ. "What about now? You're going to need more than the fact his wife has a prescription for Seconal."

Russ stood up. "We know Langevoort was at the county fair the same day as Gabrielle. He went with Saunderson." He paced toward the tree trunk. "We've got Saunderson at Gabrielle's restaurant a few days before. She was his waitress. Maybe Langevoort was with him."

"Any evidence of that?"

Russ shook his head. "No. The tab was enough for two meals, but we don't know the other diner. No one at the Water View could remember."

Clare swallowed an acid piece of guilt. "Maybe Bors stole the pills. They were right there in the master bathroom. Anyone in the house could have accessed them." Her voice faded away.

Jack squared his hands on the blue-and-white tablecloth. "Objectively, Saunderson looks better than Langevoort."

Russ pivoted and paced toward the grill. "What about your case, then? Saunderson sure as hell didn't put Seconal into Natalie Epstein's drink in 1972."

"Langevoort was around back then . . ." Jack looked at Clare, who nodded. "But we can't connect him with Natalie—" His face went blank for a moment in a way that reminded her of Russ, looking inward, following his own thoughts through the dark and back out into the light again. "Sonuvabitch." He jerked to his feet. "Leonard Epstein. The brother. There were a bunch of men he knew at the bus station. His law firm did work for their investment company." He slapped his pockets as if looking for a car key. "We have to get to the station."

"Why?" Margy looked doubtful.

"Because Russ can use the state license database to get his current address and number. If he can confirm those men were from Barkley and Eaton, we have a connection between the Epstein family and Langevoort's business."

"Do you think he'll still remember? After all these years?"

Jack looked at her. "Do you still remember the day Walter died?"

Margy's face stilled. "Every detail."

Jack spread his hands. *I rest my case.*

"Langevoort could have picked Natalie up the afternoon she left the commune." Russ paced back toward the tree. "A face she knew, an offer of dinner and drinks . . . maybe the Seconal was an attempt to roofie her that went wrong." He stopped in his tracks. "What about the new dress?"

Jack shrugged. "The Jane Doe in '52 had a new dress as well."

Russ froze in place for a long moment. "You said this might not be a sex-related crime."

Jack tilted his head.

"What if it's something . . . weirder? Something more like a ritual?"

"That would explain the fancy dresses. And the missing accessories. The shoes and such. Trophies."

"Wait a minute." Margy put her hands on her hips. "I think you two are going down the White Rabbit's hole here. Are you suggesting the folks in charge of an investment bank are making some sort of pagan human sacrifice?" She snorted. "I don't much approve of greedy capitalism, but even I wouldn't go that far."

Clare thought of the discussion at her table, the night of the party. "It's not pagan sacrifice," she said tentatively. "It's pagan adoption."

Russ sat down across from her. "Go on."

"At my table the other night, we were talking about the transfer of the business to Bors. Kent and one of the older women were comparing it to Roman adoption. A son is taken on, often as an adult, and has all the rights and responsibilities a son by birth would have."

Jack sat down as well. "What's that got to do with murder?"

"This is something I actually know about. We studied it in seminary, because Paul uses a lot of language about Christians being the adopted children of God—"

"Clare."

"Right, sorry. So in the ritual of adoption, the birth parents symbolically sold their son to his new family. Money was exchanged. After that, the adoptive father was the *pater familias* to the new son. He had absolute power of life and death over him." It made a fascinating analogy when you started to dig into Paul's epistles, but she was pretty sure Russ and Jack weren't interested in that part.

"So . . . killing a girl is like a payment?" Jack looked at Margy, who spread her hands.

"No," Russ said slowly. "Killing a girl puts you under the absolute power of your new 'father.'" He made quote marks around the word.

"Kent told me he was retiring on his investments. All financial ties to the company he had owned and run for however many years would be cut."

Russ was nodding along to her words. "But what if you wanted an insurance policy? Something to guarantee the new owner would treat you right. Maybe keep doing things the way you thought they ought to be done."

"Aaah." Jack's eyes lit. "Not trophies. Evidence. Held back just in case you needed leverage against your replacement."

"Which means somewhere, some place, Gabrielle Yates's shoes and phone and whatever else she had on her is tucked away. Secure." Russ rapped his knuckles against the tabletop. "Where?"

"The murders took place here. You wouldn't want to risk being caught transporting any items, so . . . close. Millers Kill or nearabouts."

Russ nodded. "The camp?"

Jack shook his head. "With family and guests and a cleaning service in and out? No. Maybe a hole dug in the woods?"

"The camp goes to Bors, though." Clare's mouth flattened. "Or it would have. If it wasn't your property, it'd be a lot harder to go tramping through the forest looking for a cache. Assuming you'd want to be able to get at it quickly just in case." She looked toward Russ. "The Langevoorts are building a new retirement home, by Lake George."

"Same issues Jack just listed for the camp. Except maybe even less secure, with builders and plumbers and electricians on site."

"Maybe he has a safe-deposit box." Margy sounded exasperated. Everyone looked at her. "I may not be trained in law enforcement, but I've got my common sense. Why on earth would anyone dig a hole in the ground when they could stash it away in a bank?"

Jack smiled. "Common sense indeed."

"We need to lock this down as quickly as possible." Russ set his hands on the picnic table and pushed into a standing position. "I'm afraid I may have put the wind up Kent yesterday. The ME and I went to the hospital to get a DNA sample for Saunderson and I had a few questions for Langevoort."

"He started grilling the man," Clare translated.

"If he's smart—and there's no reason to think he's not—he'll already be weighing getting rid of the evidence. It's of no use if Saunderson dies, which seems likely." He looked to Clare for confirmation. She nodded. "Clare. Can you find him and stick with him? Either at the hospital or the camp, you can be there for, you know, pastoral support. I don't want him alone with Bors Saunderson and I especially don't want him alone with his family. Guys backed into a corner sometimes decide to take everyone else with 'em."

Jack frowned. "You want your wife involved in that?"

Russ grinned his most wolflike grin. "If you knew Clare, you wouldn't ask that."

She felt like a lamp lit from the inside. "If Margy will keep Ethan."

"Good girl. If you can find out if he has a local bank . . ."

"I will."

"Don't take any risks. You're just there to make sure he's not out destroying evidence. If he leaves, call me. No legwork."

Her mouth curved in a helpless smile. "No legwork."

Russ turned to Jack. "Okay. Let's get over to the shop and see if we can track down your Mr. Epstein. It's hard enough getting a warrant from Judge Ryswick on a working day. I hate to think how pissed off he's going to be when I show up at his house on a Sunday."

60. Clare had mastered the trick of talking on the phone while breastfeeding—she switched on the speaker and balanced the phone on her shoulder. She could carry on a conversation, and any distinctive smacking or gulping noises were muted by the distance. Ethan was a dedicated nurser, latching on with a single-minded focus and not releasing until he was full. After almost five months, they were both pros at it.

"I thought I would stop by and lend my support, if it wouldn't be too much. I've been worried about your parents." That was certainly true.

"I am, too," Joni said. "Dad's just been wrecked over this. We finally got him to leave the hospital this morning. Mom forced him into bed and he was out like a light. I think it's the first real sleep he's had since the night before the party."

"What's the latest on Bors?"

"Not good news. He's got some sort of pneumal infection now. They're hitting him with wide-spectrum antibiotics, but it's looking increasingly grim."

Which may explain why Kent was willing to come home. If Bors's death was assured, he didn't have anything to worry about on that front.

"Would this be an okay time?"

"Please. I would love to talk with someone who's not falling apart at the seams. I may throw you at my mother so I can get outside and take a walk. She doesn't want to leave Dad alone, and I don't want to leave her alone, so the two of us are stuck here overeating."

Clare smiled a little. "At least you're not overdrinking."

"That's next."

Clare promised to get there as soon as possible, and finished the call just as Ethan finally fell asleep, his mouth sagging open to spill the last of the milk onto her stomach. He stayed asleep through burping and handing him over to Margy. Clare kissed his fat cheek. "I'll be back as soon as I can."

"Take care of yourself." Margy cupped the back of Ethan's head. "You've got a lot more to lose nowadays."

"Don't I know it."

There were only two cars in the Langevoorts' parking area when Clare arrived. Joni greeted her at the door. "We had everyone from B and E here yesterday. Most of them have gone back to the city by now."

"How did the meeting go?"

Joni smiled wanly. "I was able to give my counseling training a real workout. We spent the first two hours just processing everybody's feelings."

The temperature inside was pleasantly cool. One of the upgrades Audrey Langevoort had mentioned Friday night, no doubt. The kitchen and dining area seemed even larger without the party crowd.

"How much of a problem is the company going to have with Bors's . . ." Clare didn't want to say "death."

"Incapacitation?" Joni walked to the gleaming stainless steel refrigerator. "He's the CFO. That's a key position that has to be filled, preferably from within the company, which creates another vacancy in upper management, and so on."

She retrieved a jug of lemonade and waggled it toward Clare.

"Yes, please. What about your father?"

Joni pulled out two glasses. "Obviously, it slams the brakes on his retirement plans. Which isn't a disaster—he's only sixty-seven. When he took over the company back in the day, the previous owner had cancer, which, of course, no one knew because in the early seventies, no one mentioned that sort of thing." She poured and slid Clare's glass across the smooth soapstone island. "He died within a year."

"Are you talking about Mr. Harrington?"

Clare and Jodi both turned toward where Audrey Langevoort was closing the master bedroom door behind her. "Your father was very good to him." She crossed to Clare and embraced her. "It's so nice to see you again, Clare. Thank you for coming."

Clare winced inside. If Russ was right, her presence here might keep Kent Langevoort from destroying whatever evidence there was of his crimes. That was the important thing, the most important thing, but it didn't stop the unpleasant poking of her conscience, accusing her of manipulating her position as a priest and as a friend.

"Darling, can you pour me some?"

"With or without vodka?" Joni reached for another glass.

"Without. I'm afraid if I touch any booze I'll just keel over like your father."

"Is he still asleep?" Clare gestured toward the bedroom door.

"Yes, thank heavens." She accepted her lemonade and climbed onto one of the woven leather stools nestled beneath the island's lip.

Clare took another one. "You said Kent was very good to his predecessor."

Audrey nodded. "Took care of all his medical expenses. Private nurses at his home, experimental treatment at Sloane-Kettering—everything insurance didn't cover."

"At any rate, Dad's perfectly healthy." Joni leaned across the island from the other side. "So it's not a huge problem if he has to take another year to find a new CEO."

Audrey shot her a look. "Easy for you to say, kiddo. You're thirty-two. I've been looking forward to your father's retirement since before you were born."

Clare would rather smash her glass and slice her wrists with the shards than listen to Audrey talk about her hopes for a future with her husband. *How do you feel about disgrace and despair and once-a-week visits to Clinton, Mrs. Langevoort?* That was the truly evil part of crime. No one escaped. Victims stretched out in all directions. "I have a question." Anything to derail the conversation. "Do you know what Bors's personal bank was?"

Audrey frowned. "No. Why?"

"On Friday, Russ mentioned checking his accounts. In case there were financial reasons behind his suicide attempt." True. Russ's theory had changed, but he did say that on Friday.

Joni groaned. "Oh, God. Embezzlement. We didn't even think of that." She rubbed her forehead with the butt of her hand. "Now that really *could* be a disaster."

Clare held up her hands. "Just a thought. What's Mr. Langevoort's personal bank?"

"HSBC." Audrey frowned at her daughter. "But there's no reason to think Bors would have the same one. We're at HSBC because they're right on the corner by our condo."

HSBC was no good. There wasn't a branch within three counties of Millers Kill. She folded her hands around her glass. Okay. Russ was going to get a warrant, based on information from the medical examiner and the brother of the previous victim. Hopefully. He and his officers would then be able to search this camp. It wasn't her responsibility to figure out where Kent Langevoort might be hiding away evidence of his and Bors's crime.

Unless . . . if Russ's questions really had made Kent suspicious, the first thing he'd do would be to start hiding his tracks. If he had a receipt from a bank or a key to a safe-deposit box here, those things could disappear as soon as he woke up.

"Clare?"

Her head jerked up. "Sorry. I was woolgathering. What?"

Joni smiled at her. "I was wondering if you'd do us a big favor and stay here while Mom and I took a walk."

"I don't want Kent to wake up to an empty house," Audrey said.

Clare didn't believe in divine intervention in human affairs, but if she did, this would be a giant billboard sign from the Almighty. "Sure. Yes. I'm sure you could both stand some fresh air and exercise."

She waved them farewell from the front porch and stood there a long moment as the two women turned left out of the parking area and took the long narrow road through the woods. She thought about Gabrielle Yates and Natalie, who apparently still had family waiting to find out what had happened to her. She thought of the third woman, nameless and forgotten. *The last thing we can give the dead is justice,* Russ had said once. There was nothing she could do to stop the pain heading for the Langevoort women. But there was something she could do for the dead. She turned and went into the house.

She went upstairs first, to the guest bedrooms. Russ had searched Saunderson's room the night of the party, with Audrey's permission, and hadn't found anything. But if Kent had already started covering his tracks, stashing anything incriminating with Bors's things was a quick and easy way to begin.

There was nothing obvious to her eye. The small writing desk was empty, Bors's laptop already in police custody. She quickly and methodically riffled through the pockets of his clothing hanging in the closet and slid her hands along the dresser drawers. She heaved the mattress up—nothing—and then spent too much time smoothing the bedding to make it look untouched.

The other three rooms upstairs were guest bedrooms, empty and unused. She twisted her hair against the back of her head while she considered. Langevoort was a workaholic. They came up here frequently. He must have a workspace. She had already seen the main floor, so that left the walk-out basement.

She went down one flight of stairs and paused in front of the master bedroom door. She didn't hear any sounds. She continued down the next flight of stairs, which opened up onto a long family room. A pool table sat near the stairs, bracketed by a narrow bar, and beyond it, a massive sectional sofa would give loungers the chance to watch either a wall-hung wide-screen TV or the mountains, framed by the wall of French doors facing the outdoors.

There was a narrow hall, barely six feet long, across from the bar. It had an open door on each side, one to a bathroom, the other leading to what was obviously Joni's room. Clare hissed in frustration. Maybe there was an outbuilding she had missed? She turned back to the stairs, which was when she saw the small room behind the pool table. Its door was invisible to anyone descending the stairs.

She tried it. Unlocked. The room inside was utterly dark. She swept her hand along the wall and was rewarded with the lights snapping on. It was a windowless office almost filled by a desk and chair and a set of bookcases. Someone had made an attempt to brighten the space up with a pair of skiing posters and a fake fiddle-leaf fig tree, but they couldn't change the vibe of Getting Things Done.

She ignored the closed laptop squared on a wide leather blotter. She had neither the time nor the expertise to tackle it. Instead, she slid into the chair and began going through the drawers.

The wide center drawer was filled with loose papers, pens, pencils, the detritus every office collected. The right top drawer was more of the same, with a small graveyard of old calculators and decrepit phones thrown in. Beneath that was a slide-out file drawer. Clare bent over, her fingers flicking through the file tabs, the physical manifestation of time tick-tick-ticking past. Spreadsheets, market reports, sales brochure designs, research. She stopped at one labeled BANKING and pulled it out, but it was filled with complicated forms from commercial banks she didn't even pretend to understand. She slid it back into place and continued.

FUNDING, PROSPECTS, UNLABELED, PRESS AND PUBLICITY—she stopped. Reached for UNLABELED. Inside were eight full-page receipts. The logos changed, and the name went from McKenzie Full Service to McKenzie Self-Store, but they all seemed to be from the same storage unit company. The oldest was dated 1970, the newest just last year.

The listed renter on the newest receipt was the same as that on the oldest—Lloyd Harrington. Who had been dead for thirty years.

There was a key at the bottom of the folder.

She took a breath. Pulled her phone from her back pocket and laid the key on the desktop. Took a photo of it. Put it back in the file. She smoothed the most recent receipt over the laptop's cover and photographed it. Put it back in the file. She was about to pull out the oldest receipt when she heard thumping overhead.

Heart racing, she slid the file back into place. Shut the drawer. Stood up and shoved the chair back into place.

"Clare?"

She opened the door and turned out the lights simultaneously. "Clare?"

On tiptoe, she bounded toward the center of the room, as awkward as a gazelle in toe shoes. "Down here!" She shoved her phone back into her pocket and pressed her hands against her flaming cheeks. She headed up the stairs.

Audrey and Joni were bracing themselves against the front door, taking their sneakers off. "We got into some mud," Joni explained.

"Were you checking out the downstairs?" Audrey walked past Clare toward the kitchen sink.

Clare nodded. "I missed the tour Friday night," she managed.

"I'm not going to miss that pool table, I'll tell you." Audrey ran herself a glass of water. "We've scrubbed, we've sprayed, we've cleaned the carpet, but the smell of cigars will not come out."

Joni joined her mother. "God, I remember the first time Dad included me with the 'big guys.' One scotch and a cigar and I spent the rest of the evening barfing out back." She shook her head. "The crap I put myself through trying to pretend to be someone I wasn't."

Her mother put an arm around her. "Hey. No more of that." She rose up on tiptoe and kissed Joni's cheek. "You are who you are and we love you."

Joni smiled down at the older woman. "Thanks, Mom."

Clare thought they must be able to hear the sound of her heart breaking for them. She took a breath. "I need to make a phone call. Can you excuse me?"

Outside, she walked away from the house, decided that wasn't enough, and got into her car. She was tempted to turn on the ignition and start driving and not stop until she reached Virginia. She sat for a moment, her hands on the wheel. They were shaking, she noticed. She thought about the bottle of pain pills. She had tucked them in the glove compartment, behind the papers and small flashlight and bag of almonds and extra hairbrush. Her plan had been to sneak them back into Audrey's bathroom. She realized that wasn't going to happen. She reached for the small door, then curled her hand into a fist.

No. No. *Quiet mind. Calm mind.* She focused on breathing, in, out, in. She needed to call Russ. She picked up her phone and pressed his number.

"Hey, darlin'. Are you okay?"

"I'm fine." She closed her eyes. "I mean, I feel like I'm abusing their trust the whole time I'm chatting with Audrey and Joni like there's nothing wrong, but . . . yeah, other than that, I'm fine."

"If you want to pull out, just let me know. I'll get Eric McCrea up there. It'll tip my hand, but I'm not so concerned about that anymore. Jack and I are making real progress here. We're figuring out which bank officers to notify as soon as we've gotten the warrant."

"It's not a safe-deposit box. It's a storage unit."

"What?"

"I found receipts dating back to 1970, all in the name of Lloyd Harrington. There was a key in the file, too."

Russ paused. She could picture him, staring into the middle distance. "Could it be something personal? Old stuff that belonged to Harrington?"

"He died in the early seventies. The latest receipt is from last year. I took a picture of it, and of the key. I'm going to send them to you."

"Send it to my e-mail. It'll be easier to print off as part of our warrant request."

"I will."

"Are you sure you're okay? You sound . . . Seriously, darlin', you don't have to do this. I can have Eric out there in twenty minutes."

"No. Thank you, but no. I feel like I ought to be there for them. Even though they don't know what's coming."

"All right. If anything gets hairy, leave."

"I will." She sighed.

"Promise me."

"I promise."

"Hey," he said. "I'm holding on over here."

She smiled. "Good. Because I'm not letting go."

61. Judge Ryswick frowned as he leafed through the papers Russ had assembled. Being in chambers with the man always made Russ feel like a juvenile delinquent about to be dressed down. Standing in the judge's dining room wasn't an improvement. He had thought changing into his spare uniform at the station would seem more professional, but he was afraid it just made him look more like an asshole.

"Can I get you something to drink, Chief?" Mrs. Ryswick was as sunny and serene as her husband was dour and dismal.

"Thank you, no, ma'am." The Ryswicks were in golfing gear. The deputy chief clerk, whom Russ had called, had caught them at the nineteenth hole of the Glens Falls Country Club. "I'm sorry to interrupt your Sunday."

She patted his arm. "You already apologized, Chief. It's fine."

Ryswick said something beneath his breath.

"Your Honor?"

Ryswick looked up at him. "I see reasonable cause for searches pertaining to Bors Saunderson. Kent Langevoort, less so."

Russ pointed to the faxed statement from Leonard Epstein, who, thank God, still lived in New York and practiced at his family firm. "Mr. Epstein confirmed corporate officers from Barkley and Eaton did business with his firm, where his sister worked for two summers, at the end of high school and after her first year in college. Barkley and Eaton officers, including Kent Langevoort, were at a corporate retreat outside Millers Kill during the time Natalie Epstein was killed."

Ryswick grunted. "What about this storage unit business? Where did you come up with that?"

"A confidential informant."

"That's not going to fly in court."

"My men are ready to execute the warrant simultaneously at the storage unit and at Mr. Langevoort's vacation home. We expect to be able to find independent verification. As well as evidence that Mr. Langevoort was directly involved in the death of both women."

"Hmm. Good luck with that." Ryswick reached for his phone. "Stacy? It's Ronald. Can you meet me at the courthouse? I need you to draw up a warrant for the Millers Kill police." He flipped the folder shut and handed it back to Russ. "Make this count, Chief Van Alstyne. I hate to disturb my clerks on their days off."

• • •

Russ had guessed there wasn't going to be anyone at McKenzie Self-Store at five o'clock on a Sunday evening, and he was right. He had brought the lock-pop with him, a thirty-pound drill that could pith out an entire locking mechanism. It was going to be overkill for Langevoort's unit, which had been knocked up out of cheap corrugated metal a long, long time ago.

Jack Liddle stared around at the mostly deserted industrial park stretching around them. FOR RENT signs hung on several long, low buildings, and the parking lots and roads connecting them were cratered with unfilled frost heaves and potholes. "I remember when this was a busy place."

Lyle MacAuley handed Russ a pair of work gloves and protective glasses. "It's definitely gone down since I've been here."

"That building there, with the rusty roof? That was my cousin Ed's business. He put together little electronic things. Smart guy, went to RPI."

"Probably made in China now." Lyle gestured for Jack to step back. Russ hefted the lock-pop and switched it on. It bucked and shook in his hands. He pressed the bit end against the metal lock plate and grimaced at the resulting shrieking whine.

"I hate these things," Lyle shouted at Jack. "Last one we had to go into had kiddy porn. They oughtta be outlawed."

Russ lurched forward as the drill broke through. He reversed the power, pulled it out, and switched it off. "Okay, we're in." He handed the machine to Lyle while he stripped off the gloves and goggles. He had asked his deputy chief to ride along to assure there would be no questions about planting evidence later. In fact . . .

"Lyle, drop that in the car and bring back the camera, will you?" The MKPD didn't have shoulder cameras for its officers yet, but Russ had popped for several small video recorders out of his own pocket.

Lyle returned, latex gloves on, camera in hand. "This is going to look like that show where the pickers go into the storage units." He tossed a pair of gloves to Jack.

"Let's hope this isn't as stuffed with crap as those ones are." Russ grasped the handle at the bottom of the door. "Okay, start recording." He yanked the door up.

The storage unit was empty, except for two cardboard boxes at the very back. Russ snapped on his evidence gloves and walked forward. He picked up one box and brought it to where the late-afternoon sunlight spilled across the storage unit's opening. He bent over and gently pried the flaps apart.

A pair of sneakers sitting on brightly colored cotton. He lifted them out, the fabric unfolding into a fluttery summer dress. Beneath it was a small square purse with a long strap. "Jack, can you hold these?" He handed the clothing to the older man.

Russ opened the purse. Lipstick, mints, a phone and a wallet. He flipped the wallet open.

"Is it hers?" Lyle stepped forward, still recording. Russ held up the fabric rectangle so the camera could capture Gabrielle Yates's face in the Florida driver's license. He closed the wallet and exchanged it for the phone. It wouldn't turn on. Russ slid the back off. "SIM card's gone."

Jack peered over his arm. "Is that the part that tracks location?"

"Yeah." There was a yellow bandanna left in the box. Russ stooped to pick it up, and revealed a cheap digital camera beneath it, similar to the one his deputy chief was using. Unlike the phone, the camera powered on. The thumbnail pictures displaying in its two-by-two screen were too small for Russ to make out. He scrolled down to the first photo and selected it. It opened, filling the screen with a smiling Gabrielle Yates, bright-eyed and alive. She had the yellow bandanna in her hair. He scrolled forward through the photos. Gabrielle and Bors Saunderson, drinks in their hands. Gabrielle modeling the Tory Burch dress, pretty and pleased. Why not? It might have been the most expensive piece of clothing she ever had, foster kid that she was.

Lyle peered over his shoulder. "What do you think the deal was with the dresses?"

"Part of the ritual, whatever it was? Maybe a soft payment in exchange for sex?"

Jack shook his head. "It's to put them off guard. These were wealthy men. They'd say, 'Hey, let me take you out to a fancy restaurant for dinner. Here, I've got something you can wear that'll fit right in. Gosh, you look pretty. Go ahead, honey, it's yours.'"

Russ thought of Gabrielle's wallet and handed the camera to Jack. Inside the back compartment, neatly folded, was the receipt for the dress. It was difficult to make out the scrawled signature, but Russ had no doubt the credit card imprint would be Saunderson's.

Jack made a noise. Lyle and Russ leaned in to see. No longer bright eyed, Gabrielle half-leaned in Saunderson's arms, her face glazed. He was peeling the pretty dress away. Jack handed the camera back to Russ. "It's the Langevoorts' place."

"Yeah."

"You think there'll be any forensic evidence left?"

"I doubt it. They have a cleaning service. Odds on he had them there the day after." Russ tilted the camera.

Jack held up his hand. "I don't need to see it." He set the dress and sneakers back in the box.

Lyle, looking over Russ's shoulder, switched off his own camera. "Oh, Christ." He shook his head. "Jesus, he filmed everything."

The pictures of Bors folding her limp body into a large garbage bag were close to unbearable, but Russ made himself press on until the final image, her body as he had seen it, stretched out on McEachron Hill Road, the bare glimmer of dawn along the horizon.

"There's not a sign of Langevoort in those pictures, is there?" Jack nodded toward the camera, as if he didn't want to get too close.

"Yeah, but how else could they have been taken? It places him there as much as if he'd put himself in the frame."

"He could argue Saunderson had a tripod." Russ turned the camera off and set it back inside the box. "Set the camera to go off regularly every couple of minutes or so."

Lyle made a noise.

"What's in the other box?" Jack pointed toward the rear of the storage unit.

Russ walked back and hoisted it against his chest. It was larger, older, and heavier than the first box had been. He set it on the floor and glanced at Jack. "This might be the evidence for your case."

Jack shook his head. "Langevoort's not dumb enough to leave that behind. My guess is, this place stays secret until the current owner dies. Then the next guy inherits it. First thing he would do is destroy anything implicating himself."

Russ bent over and unfolded the flaps. "Huh." Slim leather shoes with short, curved heels, their color stained with a thin layer of mildew. White wrist-length gloves, the kind women wore in old movies.

"Oh, dear lord." It sounded like Jack was praying. "It's Jane Doe. This is what Harry McNeil was looking for."

Russ handed the shoes and gloves to Jack. Beneath them, neatly folded, was a stiff, wide-skirted dress, still shiny despite the patches of mildew. Beneath the dress, a flouncy skirt with layers of netting riddled with holes. A garter belt and flimsy stocking were likewise moth-eaten.

"A purse." Jack pointed. "Is there a purse?" Russ thrust his hand beneath the froth of feminine apparel and came up with an embroidered clutch. He opened it. Not much different from Gabrielle's despite the intervening years—a lipstick, a small handkerchief, a box of Chiclets. He handed the wallet to Jack, who opened it.

"Carmella Marino." He shut his eyes for a moment. "We got her, Harry. Carmella Marino."

Lyle leaned over the box. "He wasn't involved in this one, was he? Langevoort?"

"Not if my theory is correct. I think old Mr. Barkley and Lloyd Harrington, his successor, did this."

"In 1952."

"When Barkley decided to make him his heir."

Lyle scrubbed at the top of his head as if he was trying to knock his thoughts into order. "And when old Mr. Barkley died, Lloyd Harrington inherited this."

"Not this." Jack waved at the cheap metal walls. "This place didn't go up until '69 or '70."

Lyle pointed to the box. "But this evidence, this was somewhere Harrington had access to. But instead of destroying it, he moved it here. Why?"

"Jack said it this afternoon, when we were trying theories out. This is a trophy." Russ straightened and twisted his back. "Maybe Langevoort and Saunderson committed rape and murder as some sort of cold-blooded pact to gain power. But Harrington"—Russ tapped the box with the toe of his boot—"Harrington liked it. Hmm."

He bent over again. His tap had dislodged a small cylinder from beneath the clothes. He pinched it between his fingers and held it up. It was a metal film canister, its top screwed on tight. "What do you want to bet is on this film?"

"Not old home movies." Lyle's voice was dry. "You think Langevoort hung on to all this because he's a freak, too?"

"I don't know. So far he's managed to keep himself well away from all this. Except for the fact he's presumably been paying for this place for the past thirty-odd years, there's nothing directly tying him to the murders. Lots of circumstantial evidence, no smoking gun."

"I won more cases with the former than the latter, back in my day." Jack carefully replaced Carmella's purse in the box and then straightened. "I think Langevoort kept it as a smoke screen. This is evidence Lloyd Harrington committed murder. He was also around and involved in Natalie Epstein's death. But he died a year later. The murder was still an active case." He made a face. "Not very active, to my great regret, but still out there. If I had just managed to break something, and connected it to Barkley and Eaton—well, Langevoort could have pulled this box out and said, 'Hey, I found this in my boss's effects after he died.'" He sighed. "If I had had evidence Harrington was the killer in '52, I would have accepted him as Natalie's killer. Yeah."

Lyle slid the MKPD camera into his breast pocket. "I'd dearly love something that ties Langevoort in a little more tightly."

"We go with what we've got." Russ bent over to fit the items more securely back in the box. "We wrap and seal these in evidence tape and—" his fingers brushed against something that was neither cloth, nor leather, nor metal. He pulled it from where it was, flush against the side of the box. An 8-by-11 mailing envelope, brown, unsealed. He stood. It had no writing on the outside.

"Developed pictures?" Lyle raised the camera again, to catch the image.

Russ flexed the mailer. "I don't think so. Not stiff enough." He opened the flap carefully and pulled out a sheet of paper, covered in florid writing that could have been done by a calligrapher. His eyes dropped to the bottom, It had been signed by Lloyd Harrington. He looked back up at the opening. It was a paragraph in Latin.

"Can either of you read what this says?"

Jack pulled his glasses down and squinted at it. "That's the word for father, and there's son. Uh, hand, heart . . . sorry, that's all I know." He reset his glasses. "My last Latin class was about sixty-five years ago."

The next paragraph was, thankfully, in English. "'I, the undersigned, having had a life put into my hands, likewise put my life into the hands of my father, Samuel Barkley—'"

"Hot damn," Lyle murmered.

"That confirms the link," Jack agreed.

"—'to be sealed by a worthy sacrifice of youth and beauty'—That would be the girls—'and to be so bonded by seed and blood as a natural father and son, owing all due support, loyalty, and obedience to my father while inheriting all his worldly goods.'"

"What. The. Hell." Lyle shook his head. "What does that even mean?"

"Clare said the folks from Barkley and Eaton were talking about this Roman adoption thing that passed ownership of the company from one man to the next. I'm pretty sure most of them thought it was a metaphor. Apparently, not for these guys."

Lyle looked horrified. "Was this how Romans adopted?"

"Absolutely not. I remember that much from my history classes." Jack crossed his arms. "I'm sure there was a legal document, and maybe they sacrificed a bird or something, but this? This is two guys who wanted to rape and murder, coming up with a fancy reason to justify it. 'Blood and seed.' God."

Russ tilted the page to better catch the light. "The rest of it's a list of what the new son owes to the father. Financial support, listen to his advice about the company, keep him 'as befits the father of a great man,' provide him with company—do you think that means visiting him on Sundays? Or did Harrington have to supply more girls? Jack, Harry McNeil didn't have any other cases like this, did he?"

"No. But Harrington would have been living and working down in New York City. God knows how many bodies he could have slipped into the East River."

Russ eased the paper back into the envelope and replaced it in the box. "Let's see if there's one of these in the other box."

There wasn't. "Not surprising." Lyle pocketed the camera. "Langevoort has everything he needs to blackmail Saunderson into doing whatever he wants. No need to slap his name on some freak-show document."

"Keep him as befits the father of a great man," Jack murmured.

"Russ, should we be looking for possible sexual assaults by Langevoort as well?"

"I don't think so. My hunch is, this isn't a sex thing, like it was for Barkley and Harrington. I think he's doing this in a very clear, calculated way, to have control over Saunderson."

"Then he's insane," Lyle said flatly. "All that stuff about financial support and a say in the company? He could just put it in a goddamn contract."

"Yeah, but . . . there's a difference between legal obligations and the way a father influences his son." Russ tried not to think of Ethan. He didn't want his baby boy in this place, even if it was only in his head.

"They weren't father and son."

"You don't have to be kin to one another," Jack said. "Sometimes, you don't find a father until you're all grown up."

Russ's phone rang. He pulled it out of his pocket and checked the caller. Clare. "Hey, darlin'. Everything okay?"

"Kent just left the house." Her voice was low and tense. "I tried to talk him into staying, Audrey and I both did, but he wouldn't listen. Should I follow him?"

"No. Eric is manning a speed gun on the county highway a mile down from the Langevoorts' private road. If we need to, he can keep eyes on Kent. Did he say where he was going?"

"The hospital. But Russ—he went down to his office first. He could have taken the key to the storage unit. Or he might have more of the Seconal to finish off Bors. I don't know."

"That's fine. We've got him either way. You sit tight. I'll talk to you soon." He hung up. Swung around to the pair behind him. His teeth felt sharp when he grinned. "Lyle, let's get these boxes secured. I think Langevoort's coming to us."

He called Hadley and sent her to the hospital with orders to not allow anyone except listed medical personnel into Bors Saunderson's room. Then he had Lyle park the car at the end of the storage units. They pulled down the door of the storage unit with themselves inside. Closed up, it was very dark and very hot. The hole where the lock had been shone like a flashlight near the cement floor. "He's going to notice that," Jack said.

"Yeah, but he'll still want to check and see if the boxes are here."

"Is he in good shape?" Lyle asked. "Works out?"

"I don't know. Why?"

"Because our average age is sixty-four. We're going to have a hell of a time catching him if he bolts."

"Speak for yourself," Jack said.

There was the sound of tires on asphalt. They all stilled. Russ unsnapped the top of his holster. The car stopped. A door slammed. Walking footsteps that switched into a run. "What the hell?" The voice was low to the ground, as if the speaker had squatted down to take a better look at Russ's locksmithing skills. The door jerked up, and there, outlined in the beautiful August sunshine, was Kent Langevoort.

"Aaah!" He quivered for a second, open-mouthed, as if he had been rung inside a bell. His eyes darted left, right, and then he settled. His face smoothed into a mask.

"Jack?" Russ handed him his cuffs. "It was your case."

The old police chief stepped forward. "Kent Langevoort. You're under arrest for the rape and murder of Natalie Epstein, and criminal conspiracy in the rape and murder of Gabrielle Yates, and accessory after the fact in the rape and murder of Carmella Marino. You have the right to remain silent . . ."

62. Russ himself came to the Langevoorts' house with Eric McCrea, Hadley Knox, and a technician from the state crime lab. He sat Joni and Audrey on the sofa in the living room and dragged a chair over to face them. Clare perched on a hassock halfway between her husband and the Langevoorts, which felt just about right.

As the officers and the technician spread through the rest of the house, collecting evidence, Russ told the women what had happened. His voice was gentle, but his unwavering recitation of the details—telling them exactly what he had found in Kent Langevoort's storage locker—made the experience like watching two people having nails hammered into their flesh. She wanted to cry mercy for them, until she realized this was a hard kind of mercy, giving them the truth without false hope or euphemism.

Neither of them, she noticed, said *I can't believe it* or *He'd never do that,* although Audrey had started to weep halfway through Russ's description. Joni went to fetch her mother's medication, only to find it in an evidence baggie. With Russ's nod, the gloved technician took a single pill out and handed it to Joni, who gave it to her mother with a glass of water. Clare watched the technician reseal and relabel the bag. The bottle of hydrocodone sitting in her glove compartment filled her head until she was certain anyone looking at her would know what she had done.

Russ got to the end of it. He asked, "Do you have any questions?"

The Langevoorts sat in silence for a moment, hip to hip on the sofa, Joni's arm around her mother. Finally, Joni said, "Can we see him?"

Russ shook his head. "Not yet. He's being processed into the county jail. You'll be able to be there for his arraignment and bail hearing."

"What about an attorney?"

"He called someone. I don't know who."

"Probably Brenda Kenty. She handles our family stuff." Joni's mouth twisted. "She helped me with my name change; this is going to be something different."

"I'm sure she'll recommend an experienced criminal lawyer," Clare said.

Russ's phone buzzed in his pocket. "Excuse me, please." He got up and crossed into the kitchen. Clare listened to the low tone of his voice, his words inaudible.

"What about the business?" Audrey spoke for the first time. "My God, what about the business? Bors is on his deathbed and God knows how long it will take for your father to fight this. What happens to the firm?"

Joni glanced at Clare, then at her mother. "You're still co-owner with Dad, right? The lawyer can make out power of attorney papers for you. You can sign them and then you'll have legal authority to do anything necessary."

"Me? I don't know anything about the firm!" She put her hands over her face. "Oh, my God, what is this going to do to the client base when the news gets out? We'll be lucky if they don't all jump ship.

And the ones who don't are going to want complete accounts of their portfolios."

Joni hugged her. "See? You do know something about the firm."

Her mother clutched her hand. "You're going to have to go back. You have to head it up until your father gets out of jail."

"Mom—"

"Joni, you have to. We're going to need someone strong and smart at the top and you're the strongest, smartest person I know."

Joni closed her eyes for a moment. "How can I resist that? Okay, Mom. I'll do it."

Audrey sighed and collapsed back against the sofa cushions. Joni turned to Clare. "It looks like I won't be able to do my internship with you—" She broke off. Frowned. Clare could see on her face the precise moment she realized. "You knew about this."

Clare hesitated. "I knew Russ suspected your father, yes."

"How long?"

"Just this afternoon. If he had any inkling about it beforehand, he didn't tell me."

"Why did you come over here?"

Clare forced herself not to twist on the hassock like a prisoner in the dock. "I came over to see if I could help."

"And?"

"And to make sure Kent didn't go anywhere without alerting the police. And to be here if he offered violence to you or your mother." *And to poke around and see if I could find anything incriminating.* She couldn't bring herself to admit that out loud, not the least of which because she didn't want to taint the MKPD's case against Langevoort.

"Wow." Joni stared into the middle distance for a moment. "I think when I'm not so completely numb, I'm going to be really pissed off at you."

"You have every right. I'm not very happy with myself at the moment, either."

Joni made a noise. She stood, pulling her drooping mother upright. "Why don't you do something *actually* useful and see if the bedroom's clear so Mom can lie down."

Russ was still on the phone. Clare caught Hadley Knox ascending from the lowest level with several folders wrapped and stickered as evidence. "Sure," she said. "We've cleared it."

Joni vanished into the bedroom with Audrey and emerged a couple of minutes later. "The drink and the Seconal will keep her out for a while. Thank God." She walked back to the living room. Clare followed. "Mom thinks Dad is going to come home at some point. But that's not going to happen, right?"

Clare spread her hands. "That's going to be up to a judge and jury."

"What do I do? What the hell am I supposed to do?"

"What do you want to do?"

Joni looked at her. "Burn this whole house down and salt the earth beneath it." She passed the sofa and slid open the screened portion of the French doors. "I always loved this place. I loved coming here. We had our best times together as a family in this house." She leaned over the railing. Clare joined her, carefully avoiding the place where the unhappy Bors—she was going to have to stop thinking of him as a victim, she supposed. The guilty Bors. The repentant Bors? It would be too pat to imagine he had been trying to pay back a life for a life. No, he had been drunk and terrified of everything coming out and had chosen to skip all that now faced Kent Langevoort: public disgrace and prison and the shame of his family.

"I caused this."

Clare jolted back to the here and now. "What? No, Joni, don't be ridiculous."

"I precipitated it, then. Dad was so furious with me when I came out to him. He fought me transitioning every inch of the way. I was his *son,* he needed a *son,* why couldn't I just *see* that. I blamed transphobia; I thought he was stuck in the last century. And then I quit the firm. And he had to find someone else to take over."

Clare put her hand on Joni's arm. "It's not your fault your father was so hidebound he couldn't envision a woman running Barkley and Eaton."

"He didn't think of me as a woman. He's never thought of me as a woman. He thinks I'm a boy in a dress, and that no one would respect me or follow my lead."

"Listen. I don't know much, but I do know you can't save someone else by destroying who you are. You can't start with a lie and expect to build anything good and lasting on top of it. Your father had choices, Joni. He could have taken the company public. He could have issued shares, so he wouldn't be dependent on the whims of the next owner. He could have recognized you for who you are and trusted you. He could have done a hundred other things instead of going through with that sick, perverted 'adoption' ceremony. You are not responsible for his blindness and his lack of common humanity."

Joni nodded. She turned back to the railing, and they stood side by side, looking at the hills shading from green to blue to gray as they rose into the High Peaks. Eventually, Joni said, "That's a good speech. Could you e-mail it to me once a week while I'm down in the city?"

Clare surprised herself with a laugh. "Sure. If you hurry up with what you have to do and get back to your studies."

"I don't know. I may try to combine the two. I have no idea what it feels like to work in finance when I get to set the rules. Maybe we can switch to ethical investing. I can't pay back what the company owes to the women who died. I can try to pay it forward, though."

"Sounds like it might be a good start."

They turned around at the sound of the screen door opening. Russ's face was grim. "That was Lyle. The hospital called. Bors Saunderson died about an hour ago. Pneumonia."

Joni let out a breath. She tucked her hair behind one ear. "I'll tell you one thing I know from my studies. The First Letter of Paul to Timothy. 'For the love of money is the root of all evil: which while some coveted after, they have erred from the faith, and pierced themselves through with many sorrows.'"

63. Jim Cameron was waiting for them at the door of the town hall. "This isn't good," Lyle muttered.

"Congratulations, Russ. Lyle." The mayor pumped their hands as if he thought water might gush out. "That was some top-notch work. Closing three murder cases at once." In fact, it had been on the front page of the Glens Falls *Post-Star* for two of the last three days running. Ben Beagle had pestered Jack Liddle for his three-generational view; Russ had been grateful to have the spotlight on someone else for a change.

Jim ushered them down the hall, past the clerk's office. "I think the good publicity is behind the Algonquin Waters asking for this meeting."

Russ stopped Jim in the conference room antechamber. "When you say 'Algonquin Waters,' who, exactly, are we dealing with? Because the owner is in federal prison." Russ had helped to put him there, in fact, an arrest he still considered one of the highlights of his career.

"The court-appointed board of trustees is the ultimate authority for BWI, but right now we're talking with Danielle Howe. She's the lady picked by the board to manage the day-to-day operations—the temporary CEO, if you will—until John Opperman, um, returns."

"She was one of Opperman's VPs," Lyle added.

Russ's mouth twisted. "You'll excuse me if I'm not wild about the idea. Captains of industry aren't high on my list right now."

Jim turned to face him dead-on. "If the biggest employer in town throws its weight behind the Save Our Police campaign, it could make all the difference come November."

Lyle's bushy eyebrows went up. "I didn't know you cared, Jim."

The mayor gave him an exasperated look. "I keep telling you two *I want to keep our independent police force*. It's the best thing for the town. Even if it is busting our budget."

"Okay." Russ gestured toward the door. "Let's see what Ms. Howe has to say."

Every one of the aldermen was at the table. Jim introduced them to Ms. Howe, a tall, trim woman about Russ's age, with swinging hair right on the halfway mark between blond and silver. Lyle gave her one of his most charming smiles and murmured something Russ couldn't hear; when Lyle released her hand, Russ noticed she wasn't wearing a wedding ring. He gave his deputy chief a sidelong look.

"Thank you all for agreeing to meet me on such short notice." Howe opened her briefcase and removed a stack of folders, which she handed to Bob Miles on her left. He took one and passed the rest along. "The BWI board of trustees has been concerned about the proposal to replace the Millers Kill Police Department with the state police for some time. As I'm sure you're all aware, tourism is on the rise throughout this area. The Algonquin Waters has seen an eight to ten percent increase in visitors each year since it opened. We know from our internal polling that one of the things that attracts our guests to the area is its feeling of safety and security." The handout reached Russ. It was several pages inside a tinted plastic presentation folder. The top page was titled A PROPOSAL TO MAINTAIN MILLERS KILL'S EXISTING POLICE FORCE.

"If you look on page two, you'll see some quotes from our guests. One mentions enjoying the small-town atmosphere where they can let their children 'off leash.'" Howe smiled. "Another comments on how a visible police presence has encouraged her to keep returning to our area as a woman traveling alone."

Next to Russ, Lyle's shoulders tensed. *Yeah, I know. It didn't help Gabrielle Yates.*

Harold Collins leaned back in his seat. "Ms. Howe, I'm sure I speak for us all when I say we want to keep the Algonquin Waters resort happy. The problem is the cost to our taxpayers."

"Which is what our proposal addresses. As you all know, part of the agreement with the town of Millers Kill during BWI's siting of the Algonquin Waters Spa and Resort was a ten-year tax abatement. In laymen's terms, the resort gets a pass on property taxes. The board of trustees has directed me to offer to amend BWI's agreement with the town and to begin paying the resort's property taxes in full, starting retroactively with the beginning of this financial year."

Jim Cameron blinked several times. "We'd get a property tax payment. This year."

"And next year, and so on and so forth. If you look on page four, we have an estimate of our taxes due based on your current mill rate. Obviously, you would want to do an independent assessment."

"Obviously," the mayor echoed.

Garry Greuling gave Russ a surreptitious thumbs-up from across the table. "Ms. Howe, thank you. This is exactly the miracle we need to save our police department."

"Wait." Bob Miles held up a hand. "Can we get the measure off the ballot at this point?"

"No." Jim frowned. "But we can certainly get the word out to everyone that the circumstances have changed."

"Let's ask the county election board if we can include a handout at the polls," Greuling said.

"A voting guide? Maybe not at the polls, but we could do a mailing—"

"Gentlemen." Danielle Howe's voice cut across the rising debate. "BWI does have one stipulation to this offer."

Russ leaned forward. *This is it*. Unlike Mr. Greuling and Clare, he didn't believe in miracles. He had been waiting for the other shoe to drop.

"Road widening," Lyle said under his breath. Russ nodded. That was the next logical step after the new light. Widen the Sacandaga Road and put in an interchange.

"The board of trustees would like you to replace the current chief of police."

The room went silent. Everyone stared at Russ. He moved his mouth. "What?" he finally said.

Howe nodded toward him. "Chief Van Alstyne, I mean no disrespect to you as an individual. But over the past several years you've been involved in personal scandal and have been the subject of a state internal affairs investigation."

"Russ was cleared," Jim snapped.

"In addition, the department had an officer accused of excessive force last year and two more named a week ago in a suit for false imprisonment and tampering with evidence."

"How do you know—"

"I'm sorry, but the BWI board of trustees has lost faith in Chief Van Alstyne. Obviously, our organization cannot and should not pick the next person to head your police department. But we can say our funding is contingent on your finding that person."

"This is bullshit!" Lyle stood up, his chair rocking away from him. "Russ led the investigation that put your sleazy boss away, and this is payback!" He glared at the aldermen. "Are you going to let her get away with this?"

"Lyle, sit down." Russ kept his voice even.

"It's not an offer, it's a goddamn stab in the back!"

"Lyle. Sit down."

Lyle thumped into his seat, red-faced.

The mayor stared at his hands for a moment. "Ms. Howe." He looked around the table at the aldermen. His eyes slid over to Russ. "Thank you for presenting your board of trustees' proposal. We will consider it and get back to you."

Howe let herself out. There was a moment of profound silence. Jim wiped his hands over his face.

Harold Collins cleared his throat. "I move we vote—"

"We're not voting on the proposal." Jim pushed the glossy folder away. "We've already agreed to let the public decide if they want to maintain the police department. It's on the ballot."

Bob Miles cut in. "Don't you think our taxpayers have the right to know there's a potential funding source that would allow us to keep the department *and* balance the budget? It's a win-win!"

Garry Greuling stared at him. "Really, Bob? A win-win?"

Miles rubbed the back of his neck. "Well . . . for the public." He looked toward Russ. "Nothing against you, Chief."

"Exactly," the mayor said. "Our entire issue with the police department has been funding. No one at this table has ever suggested Russ Van Alstyne isn't the right man for the job."

"He did say the actions of his officers are his responsibility," Collins pointed out.

Russ stood. Lyle immediately got to his feet as well. "They are,"

Russ said. "I'm the person responsible for the men and women of my department."

Jim Cameron held up his hands. "Stop. Right there. Russ, before you say another word, you have to go home and think it through. Think about it long and hard. Talk to your people. Talk to your wife." He looked at the aldermen. "And we need to consult with our lawyer before we proceed on any of this. Ms. Howe raised a lot of issues that directly affect our legal obligations; election law, contract law, and tax law just to start."

"We could—" Collins began.

"Harold, are you an attorney?"

"No."

"Then I'd like you to hang on to your opinion until we get her offer vetted by counsel." The mayor pushed his chair back and crossed to where Russ was still standing like a pillar of salt. "I'm serious," he said, dropping his voice. "Take a couple days off. Take your wife up to the lake. Think things over. And keep in mind, we could still win this at the ballot box."

"Exactly," Lyle said. "I think we've got a lot of support."

Except, of course, they'd be in the same spot they were now. Understaffed and underfunded. "Sure." Russ forced himself to turn, to shake Jim's hand, to nod toward the aldermen, looking at him with expressions ranging from calculation to concern. "Yeah. I'll think about it."

64. Clare was thinking about the pills. She hadn't had any yet, but she wasn't sure if that was because just knowing they were there was enough to keep the craving away, or if she needed plausible deniability if someone noticed they were missing. She had an excuse already—*I was in a hurry, didn't read the labels, I grabbed both bottles. I put this in my pocket and in the rush of events forgot to return it*. It sounded believable. But no one had asked. The police had seized Audrey Langevoort's Seconal, which had Clare's, Audrey's, and Kent's fingerprints on it. During her interview, Audrey had told them she'd had the same prescription for decades, since before the 1972 murder of Natalie Epstein. But no one had asked about the pain pills, missing or not.

Right now, they were in an acetaminophen bottle in the glove compartment of her car, parked across the road from what had once been the entrance to the lake house. She had shoved them there, ready to slip them back into Audrey Langevoort's bathroom—she hadn't—or to drop them into the medicine disposal bin at the police station—she hadn't—or bury them in the depths of the trash before taking it to the curb. She hadn't done that, either. She and Russ and the baby had arrived at the lake house last night. Maybe—maybe—she would pitch the bottle into the water or open it and pour the pills off the edge of the boat house. But she didn't think so.

She shook her head to focus, and pushed her hair off her forehead with her wrist. Her job this morning was to scrape and repaint the used cabinet doors they had picked up cheap at a salvage store. They had lost most of the kitchen and bedroom and everything upstairs when fire had damaged the house the previous winter; it was not going to be the relaxing getaway they had envisioned for a long time to come. So far this summer, Russ had torn away the ruined roof and second floor, and installed a temporary roof over the still-intact great room—which was also serving as their bedroom, nursery, and, thanks to a propane camp stove, kitchen. Russ was roughing in the cabinets in the actual kitchen, and while normally the sight of her husband doing his carpentry thing lifted her heart, this morning it was more like seeing someone build a house of cards with a shaky hand. He wasn't focused; he kept making mistakes, muttering under his breath, then making another. As Clare watched, he set his level on the boxlike frame. Even from the great room, she could see the bubble slide to the left.

"Goddammit!" Russ snatched the level and threw it into his open toolbox. He glared at the wood and then swung his hammer into the

313

side of the offending one-by-three. He hit it again, and again, until the wood cracked and sagged. Ethan began to wail.

"Russ!" He dropped the hammer to the floor. Clare plucked Ethan out of his playpen and approached her husband, hand outstretched. It wasn't going to be a great weekend if he was teetering on the edge of exploding the whole time.

He took it. "I'm sorry." He shook his head. "I don't know why . . . usually working with my hands settles me."

"C'mon. Let's all sit on the porch for a bit." The screened porch facing Lake Inverary had survived the fire intact. She took one of the two Adirondack chairs and set Ethan on her lap. His crying had died down into a tiny, bearlike snuffling. Russ collapsed into the chair next to her.

They sat in silence for a while. A breeze ruffled the dark water, so that the sunlight broke and turned and flashed in their eyes. A canoe emerged from behind the small island in the middle of the lake, the paddlers' oars rising and dipping in unison.

"There's a poem about Inverary, isn't there?" Russ rubbed his hand on his T-shirt. "Something about building a cabin and beehives.'"

"Innisfree." Clare kissed Ethan's head. "'And I shall have some peace there, for peace comes dropping slow.'"

"Mmm."

They sat awhile longer. Finally, Clare said, "Tell me what it is you're most afraid of."

He sighed. "Being selfish. I don't want to resign. I love my job."

"That's not selfish."

"Yeah, but I don't *need* it. Not like my officers need their jobs. I mean"—he waved a hand around—"we don't even have a mortgage." It was true. They had bought their lakeside getaway with the proceeds from selling the house Russ had owned with his first wife, and the rectory belonged to the church.

"Your officers could find other positions, you know. If the vote went the wrong way. Look at Kevin Flynn."

"Some of them could, sure. Any department would be glad to get

Hadley, and Eric McCrea's really wasting his talents in our small shop."

"But . . ."

"But Eric's hanging on to his wife and kid by a thread. He's still in therapy and taking anger management classes. And Hadley's got kids in school and her grandfather to think about."

That was true. Clare suspected the reason Mr. Hadley was still alive was his granddaughter monitoring his diet.

"So let's say they can find work within commuting distance. Even Paul Urquhart, God help the poor sergeant who winds up with him. But Noble Entwhistle? Or Lyle, who's sixty? Or the part-time officers? They're just shit out of luck, excuse my French. Lyle has to take early retirement and Noble gets a job as a mall cop. Maybe. Tim and Duane—I don't know what'll fit around their part-time EMT stints. Jacking deer and collecting recyclable bottles."

"So if you resign, and everyone else gets to keep their jobs, what's the worst that could happen?"

Russ spread his hands. "I never work again."

"I find that very hard to believe."

"Okay, I never work around *here* again. I get another chief's position or do private security consulting and we have to move away from our friends and family and then *you're* out of a job."

She held up her hand. "You don't get to worry about my possible theoretical future unemployment."

"You asked."

Ethan chose that moment to blow a big, wet raspberry. Russ laughed. "Thanks for the support, kid." He reached for the baby and Clare handed him over. Russ lifted Ethan high and pressed his lips against their son's fat tummy and blew. Ethan squealed in delight. Russ bounced him gently in the air. "Maybe I could just be a stay-at-home dad."

"You'll get no complaint from me." She watched them for a minute. "So, you'd have to leave a job you love, and we might have to move in order for you to find comparable work."

315

Russ lowered Ethan to his chest. The baby began patting his father's chin. "Yeah."

"Which possibility weighs more heavily? That, or what might happen to the rest of the department?"

"What happens to my people. No question."

Clare let him sit with that.

"It's just . . ." He bent his head over Ethan.

"It's just?"

"If I resign, John Opperman wins."

She kept quiet.

"Did I ever tell you what he said to me? When he got arrested?"

She shook her head.

"He said, 'You have no idea the power money can bring to bear.'" Russ laughed, a painful sound. "He was right. I didn't. But I'm finding out now. So he wins. And yes, he's still in prison and I'm walking around free. But he wins, and he knows it, and I know it." He swallowed. "That leaves a taste in my mouth I don't know I'll ever be rid of."

She reached out and took his free hand. Held it tight. After a minute, he released her and stood. "Let's go take a ride down to the end of the lake."

"Now? Why?"

"Because we can get a cell phone signal down at Cooper's Corners. I want to call Jim Cameron and let him know I've decided. He'll have my resignation letter on his desk Tuesday morning."

65. Hadley had been sitting on her front porch swing, looking at her phone, for fifteen minutes. Her thumb twitched, never quite touching the keypad. Should she call or should she not call? On the one hand, she didn't want to sound like she was seeking him out. It had only been two weeks since she had last seen him at the fair, after all. She didn't miss talking with him, and she didn't want him to get the wrong idea. On the other hand, in all the discussion at the sta-

tion, no one had mentioned letting him know. Chief Van Alstyne had been Flynn's first boss. He had shaped Flynn into the cop he was today.

What finally decided her was the realization she could just leave a message. As far as she knew, he was still undercover with the carnival; they had left Washington County far behind and were in some other part of the state by now, welcoming Friday crowds. She hit his number. It rang, and rang, and rang. *Oh, crap,* she thought. *What if he's changed it?*

"Hadley?" He sounded out of breath.

"Uh. Flynn. Hi. I didn't expect to actually reach you." There was an awkward silence. "Are you, uh, busy? With the carnival? Is it okay to talk?" She sounded like a preteen calling a boy for the first time. Now would be the perfect moment for Millers Kill to have its first drive-by shooting, with herself as the victim.

"I'm back in Syracuse. They pulled me off the case."

"What?" She sat up straighter, setting the swing rocking. "Why?"

"I don't know. Some interagency bullshit. I was so freaking close I could taste it. I had a contact, he had introduced me to a couple other guys, they were talking about something big going down at the end of the season, and now, boom. Nothing. An entire summer freaking wasted. Plus I felt like crap when I had to tell Mr. Hill I was leaving."

She couldn't help it, she laughed.

"It's not funny!"

"It's not the case getting taken away from you, it's just—Flynn, only you would feel bad about leaving your fake boss in the lurch."

"The show has a lot of gigs through the beginning of October! It's not easy finding a jointy for one month. And I was good at it." She could hear him sigh. "It doesn't matter now. That's what's so damn frustrating. All that work for nothing."

"I'm sorry." She found she really was. He may have been an awful boyfriend, but he was a good cop, and for that, he deserved better. "Do they want you for another undercover assignment?"

"No. They want me to drive around off-campus housing and pick up drunk university students. I've asked for a meeting with the captain about it. I mean, I want to be a good soldier and all but what I was doing was a lot more important—" He broke off. "Hadley, why are you calling me? Is there more news about the lawsuit?"

Now they had come to what she wanted to tell him, she didn't know what to say. "No. It's the chief."

"Oh, God. He wasn't—"

"No, no, no, he's fine. Perfectly healthy. But Flynn . . . he's resigning."

"What?"

"To hopefully save the department. We had a meeting about it this afternoon." Picturing the chief standing in his usual spot made her throat feel tight. "He cut a deal. He resigns, and the Algonquin Waters pays the town enough money to keep the force going."

"I can't believe it." There was a long pause. Finally, Flynn said, "Do you think . . . could it have had something to do with the lawsuit?"

"God, I hope not." She had wondered the same thing herself, but had been too much of a coward to bring it up during the question-and-answer period after the chief's announcement.

"When is he leaving?"

"Not until after the election."

"They're still having the question on the ballot? Why?"

"Some legal thing. The town's going to send out information to all the voters, letting them know what's changed. We just have to wait and see if they pick the staties anyway. In which case, we're all out of a job."

"God. I can't imagine the department without him."

"I know." She braced her bare feet against the wooden porch railing.

"Maybe I should come over there."

"For what?"

"I don't know," he snapped. "To see if I can do something. Maybe if I plead guilty to the drug thing—"

"It's a civil suit, Flynn, you don't plead guilty."

"You know what I mean."

Yes. She did. Her neighbor across the street came out of her side door with her dog, and set off toward the old cemetery. "Listen. I thought of doing the same thing myself. Like, if I walked away, maybe the trouble would walk away with me. But I don't think there's anything either of us can really do. It's about money, Flynn, and they have it and we don't."

He snorted. "That's for sure."

There was a long pause. The fading end-of-the-day shadows merged with the violet twilight. It was getting dark earlier these days. School had started back up. Summer was over.

"Anyway." She ran her hand through her hair. "I thought you ought to know."

"Yeah. Thank you."

"Good luck with talking to your captain. I hope you get a better assignment."

"Thanks."

She waited. For what, she didn't know. It wasn't like he was going to start apologizing. "Okay, well—"

"Look, can I call you? After the election? Just to, you know, find out what's going on?"

She blinked. "Okay. Sure."

"Good. I'll talk to you in November. Thanks again for letting me know."

"You're welcome."

"Bye, I guess."

"Bye."

She sat out for some time on the porch swing, rocking to and fro. Some evenings, it made her feel comfortable. Cocooned. Tonight . . . she watched her neighbor bring the dog back in. They waved across the street. Tonight it felt like an unmoored boat, swinging with the tide, lost at sea.

SATURDAY, NOVEMBER 4, PRESENT DAY

66. Clare sat in her kitchen, introducing Ethan to the wonderful world of squash, listening to her husband lose it over the phone.

"—then they asked for a goddamn ten-point transition plan, and I told them I couldn't plan the damn transition without knowing who the hell is going to step into my shoes. They're *still* refusing to look for a new chief. Absolutely not. What if the town votes out the department anyway? How could they ask someone to hand in his resignation if the job might not be there blah blah blah blah."

"Mmm." Ethan liked the squash. She had begun weaning him a month ago, when he hit the half-year mark, and now he was off breast milk completely, he'd developed a prodigious appetite for baby food. Unfortunately, in addition to eating, he also liked to throw it, stick it up his nose, and rub it into his hair.

"So I said they might want to think about the fact *my* resignation takes place on November eighth unless the referendum passes, in which case I get the joy of laying off everyone and shuttering a department I've given the last ten years of my life to."

"I'm sure the referendum will fail, love." It had damn well better. It felt as if every free moment either of them had had over the past two months was swallowed whole by meetings and town halls and knocking on doors and mailing out leaflets. They had spent their first anniversary apart; she on a phone bank Mrs. Marshall had set up, Russ talking to the Tri-Town Area Republicans.

"I told 'em Lyle would have to step in as acting chief. They accepted my resignation; I'm not changing it now and I'm not hanging around breaking in some newbie for free. If they want me to run a transition they can damn well pay me a consulting fee."

"Russ, the money's not going to be a prob—"

"It's not about the damn money, Clare!" There was a pause. "I'm sorry."

She returned the spoon to the mashed squash with enough force to send the jar sliding across Ethan's high chair tray. "I'm not the person you're mad at."

"I know. I know they're just making me so crazy. 'If Lyle's the acting chief, won't that leave the force shorthanded?' Why yes, it will, so maybe you ought to loosen the purse strings some, you cheap bastards, and give us the money for another officer!" He made an inarticulate noise. "Which they won't do, of course, because—"

"What if the referendum passes?"

"Got it in one. God, Clare, I am *this* close to just quitting right now."

Clare put the spoon down and shifted the phone to her other ear. Ethan, taking advantage of the single hands-free moment, wrapped his chubby fingers around the jar of squash and heaved it over the side of the tray.

"Oh, for God's sake!" Clare jumped up. The glass hadn't shattered, but the kitchen floor and half of one cabinet were now decorated with a spray of pureed squash. Ethan, startled by her loud exclamation, began to cry.

"What is it? Is the baby okay? Clare?"

She gritted her teeth. "We're all okay. Ethan just chucked a jar of baby food all over the floor." She moved to the counter to grab some paper towels. Ethan twisted in his seat, reaching for her, crying even louder. "Are you going to be home soon?" She bent over and began wiping up the mess.

"I'll try. Did you at least finish up your sermon?"

She tossed one soppy paper towel into the garbage and tore off another. Ethan's cries were taking on a rhythmic quality, like a dental drill to the jaw. "Not finished, so much as I gave up on it. It may be the worst All Saints' Day sermon in the history of Christianity, and I don't care." She laughed, because if she didn't, she might start to cry. "I have to go now, I need to see to the baby."

"Okay. I love you."

"Love you, too." It took five swipes to clean up the squash, and she knew she ought to go over everything with a wet sponge, but she just didn't have the energy. She unbuckled Ethan and cuddled him close, rubbing his back and shushing him. He knotted a squash-covered hand in her hair and hung on as his sobs slowed down to whimpers. Her phone rang again.

"Hi, Reverend Fergusson? This is Washington County Hospital admissions. We've had an admission to the intensive care unit for a stroke and the family is asking for you. Mae Bristol, one of your parishioners?"

Clare's brain stuttered to a stop. The baby. And no childcare. Twenty minutes to get to Margy's and twenty minutes to the hospital from there. Elizabeth de Groot was away for the weekend. Could she call the Presbyterian minister? If it was a normal hospital call—but Mae Bristol was part of her congregation. Her mouth made the decision before her mind could. "Tell them I'll be there as soon as I can."

She called Russ. "I need you to come home and take care of Ethan right now."

"What? Clare, I can't do that. I'm just about to start the shift-change briefing."

"Have Lyle do it. I mean it, Russ, I've got a parishioner in the ICU and the family is asking for me."

Silence on the other end of the phone. Finally, he said, "Can you wait half an hour?"

"I don't know, does Mae Bristol have half an hour?"

He let out a puff of air. "Okay. Bring Ethan here."

"What?"

"Bring him here. I don't mind if he's in the room during the briefing. Christ knows, we could all use something to smile about."

"But—"

"You literally have to drive by the station to get to the hospital. It'll add on two or three minutes, tops."

"Okay, I'll be there as soon as I can." This was fine. It probably wouldn't take her as long as it would if she had to wait for Russ to get home. She grabbed Ethan's diaper bag and tossed the bottle she had made up for later inside. She set him in his playpen in the living room as she dashed upstairs, his indignant shrieks following her. She didn't bother changing her jeans, just pulled off her shirt and wiggled into a black clerical blouse. She looked in the mirror to snap on her collar, and saw her hair was half down and crusted with drying squash. She swore, grabbed a brush, and frantically yanked it into a ponytail.

Downstairs, she plucked her travel kit off a shelf and scooped her son out of the playpen, snatching his coat off the stand on the way out the door. Car door, infant seat, buckle, tug. Diaper bag, yes. Travel kit, yes. She forced herself to reverse carefully and drive only five or ten miles over the speed limit to the police station.

She drove too fast into the department's lot and slewed over two spaces as she parked. Car door, infant seat, squeeze, unbuckle. She slung the diaper bag over her shoulder, picked up Ethan and held his coat against his back as she carried him up the stairs. Past reception, down the hall, she nodded to Harlene at dispatch and rounded the corner into the briefing room without stopping. Only to see Lyle MacAuley, looking grim, several officers, their faces toward the floor, and no Russ.

"He's—" Lyle began, but she spun on her heel and strode back toward his office. Harlene, out of the dispatch seat, stepped in her way.

She held out her arms. "Let me take him for a bit, poor little thing."

Clare looked past her toward Russ's closed door. "Harlene, it's not your job."

Harlene held a finger to her lips. In the quiet, Clare could hear sounds coming through the door. Russ's voice, words inaudible, rising and falling in a soothing cadence. And someone else, crying. She stared at Harlene.

"Noble took a bit of a turn." The dispatcher's cheeks reddened. "He's scared. We all are, I guess." She held out her arms again. "Let me take him, Clare. It'll do us both some good."

Clare handed Ethan over. She set the diaper bag on the dispatch seat.

"Everything I need there?"

Clare nodded. "I'm not breastfeeding anymore, so there's a bottle.

Just in case." She tried to think of something to say. "Harlene . . . I'm sorry."

"T'ain't your fault." She took Ethan's arm and made him wave bye-bye. "You go on to the hospital. We'll be fine here."

In the car, Clare mechanically reversed, drove, signaled, turned, stopped and started. At some point she realized tears were flooding her eyes. She went past the hospital entrance and around to the chaplain's parking spot near the ER. She parked the car and turned off the ignition. She was crying in earnest now, mouth open, shoulders shaking. She needed to stop. She needed to get hold of herself. People were relying on her.

She unscrewed the top of the water bottle she kept in the car and took a gulp, then poured a little into her palm and splashed it on her face. She took another swallow. Leaned over the console and popped open the glove compartment, where the travel package of tissues lived. She pushed the spare hairbrush aside. Her hand closed over a bottle of pain pills.

Oh. Yes.

Just like when she took them from Audrey Langevoort's bathroom, her body made decisions without her input. It was Clare twisting off the top and shaking a pill into her hand, yes, but it wasn't *her*. It was a more selfish Clare, or maybe a smarter Clare. She laid the pill on her tongue and washed it down with water. Not unlike Communion. *Take, and eat.*

By the time she stepped off the elevator at the ICU nurses' station, she felt wonderful. Focused, peaceful, with a kind of warm hum through her body. She could deal with Mae Bristol's frightened family, and with the referendum, and with Ethan, and with everything. This was what she had needed all along, not day care, not meditation, just a tiny chemical adjustment. She breathed in. *Quiet mind. Calm mind.* She smiled.

NOVEMBER 1952

67.   Harry McNeil didn't usually stop at the Dew Drop Inn, the Cossayuharie bar that edged up against the dry town of Millers Kill. But it had been a long drive from New York, and he was tired and hungry and well into the deep blue sadness that always followed his monthly weekend in the city. He wanted a beer and a burger and to be left alone, which wasn't a problem at the Dew Drop, where most of the regulars pretended they didn't see him.

So of course, of *course* a fight spilled out of the front door before he'd turned the ignition off in his Special 68. For a moment, he weighed the idea of cranking the car back up and driving away, but even though the Dew Drop wasn't technically in his jurisdiction, it was likely the two idiots pounding each other in the parking lot were.

He slid his baton from its place beneath the seat and stepped out of his car. He knew some cops who liked to keep a gun in their vehicles; to Harry that was looking for trouble. Two feet of iron-hard oak— now that could stop almost any problem before it started.

Neither of the two men fighting seemed to have an advantage, which was probably why no one in the small crowd squeezing through the door had put a stop to it. The only light outside came from a single metal lamp hanging over the bar's entrance, making it hard for Harry to ID the pair. One was tall and lean, the other short and muscular, and both looked to be Dutch-boy blond. Then the taller one caught the shorter with a hard cut to the jaw and his opponent reeled back, almost falling onto the packed dirt, and Harry could see it was Jack Liddle.

"That's enough," he roared. "Police! Put your hands down." Before he had a chance to get close enough to clip either man with his baton, Jack launched himself toward the taller man, hitting him square in the gut, sending them both sprawling.

"I said that's *enough*!" Harry grabbed Jack's collar and hauled him away, still trying to punch his opponent. He tossed Jack ass over tea-kettle and jabbed him hard in the breastbone with the baton. The boy collapsed, breathless.

Harry swung around, ready to give the other guy what for, but the tall man held up his hands. "I don't want a fight," he said. "I told him, I don't want a fight." He lurched to his feet, brushing the dirt off his suit pants. "Oh, hell. If I tore these, my wife's going to kill me." He twisted around, trying to get a look at his backside.

Harry relaxed a fraction. He recognized the fellow now. Walt Van Alstyne. A little too fond of the juice, true, but Harry'd never known him to get aggressive. Walt was more likely to buy the bar a round when he was sauced than to start a fight.

"All right, you all." Harry turned toward the looky-loos. "The show's over. It's cold out, get back inside." Van Alstyne made to follow the crowd, but Harry caught his sleeve. "Not you, Walt. I think you ought to head home."

"I tell you, I didn't start anything!" He rubbed his midsection. "I don't even know why Jack'd try to pull my cork."

"You gotta treat her better." Jack's voice was still hitched up by the blow Harry had delivered to his breath box. "No more hanging around bars all the time, Walt. I mean it!"

"I treat my wife fine, not that it's any business of yours, Jack Liddle!"

Harry took Van Alstyne's elbow firmly. "Where's your coat, Walt?"

One of the fellows had held back, hovering at the bar's door. "I'll get it!" he yelled, disappearing inside.

"Which one is your car?" The younger man pointed out an aging Studebaker. "Fine," Harry said. "Can you make it okay?"

"I only had a few drinks. I wasn't even—I don't know what Jack was—"

"Right, right."

The helpful drinking buddy dashed out, a wool coat in hand. He gave it to Van Alstyne, along with a slap on the arm. "Congratulations!"

"Thank you!" Van Alstyne struggled into his coat. "I'm a dad!" he announced.

"Good for you." Harry steered him to the vehicle. "In you go. Slow and steady and you'll get home fine, Walt. G'night." He watched as Van Alstyne pulled out of the lot, wavering a bit over the centerline before straightening her out. Then he turned toward Jack, still sitting in the dirt. "You want to tell me what that was all about?"

Jack wiped a trickle of blood from his lip. "Margy Van Alstyne had her baby."

Harry thought back to the pretty brunette he had met last summer. Yeah, that sounded about right, the size she was then. Jack had acted right surprised about her pregnancy. An unpleasant possibility blew into his brain. "Have you been fishing in some other man's pond, son?"

"No, no, God, no. Margy would never . . ." Jack braced his arms and struggled to his feet. Up close, Harry could smell the alcohol on him. "He doesn't deserve her. He goes out and gets drunk every week, two or three times, while she's at home waiting for him . . ." Jack staggered, as if overcome by the thought of Margy waiting by the window. "She's so . . ." He waved his hands, then looked Harry in the eye. "I thought sooner or later, she'd see. What he is. But now they've got a baby." His voice broke a little. "And she'll never leave him now. Never never never."

He staggered again. Harry caught his arm. "What is Mrs. Van Alstyne to you, son?"

"Nothing. We were friends. All through school. Best friends." He smiled beatifically. "She was salutatorian."

Harry was impressed. He wasn't sure he could pronounce that word sober. "What about her husband? Does he beat her? Is he not supporting her?" Harry thought Van Alstyne had a desk job at the Allen Mill.

Jack shook his head. "No. I mean, yes. He supports her. He doesn't hit her. I don't think. God, I hope not."

Harry shook the boy gently. "Then whatever's going on at home is between man and wife. She's married and made a mother, son. Time to forget her and move on."

"Why didn't she *wait* for me?" Jack's voice was loud enough to be heard above the noise coming from the bar. Harry steered him toward his Olds. No need to let the boy embarrass himself further. "We wrote the whole time I was in the air force. I wanted to do something good, something she could be proud of, so I went to the police academy and while I was there she married Walt Van Alstyne!"

Since Van Alstyne was tall, good-looking, and a genuine war hero, Harry wasn't going to find fault with the girl's choice.

"Now I don't even have that."

"What do you mean?"

"I quit." Jack jerked his head sideways. "The hell with being stuck in that damn troop ticketing cars and pretending to laugh along when they call me hillbilly." He looked at Harry, then dropped his eyes. "Nobody cared over there. Nobody wants me to use my *brain*. I didn't expect to make detective the first year!"

Harry had an idea that was a direct quote.

"I just wanted to make a difference. That's all I wanted to do. To help folks. To . . . take care of things."

Harry cupped his hand over Jack's head and steered him into the front seat of the Olds. Jack blinked up at him. "Are you going to arrest me?"

"No." Harry paused, leaning off the door. "I'm driving you home. Tomorrow morning, when you've sobered up, I want you to come see me."

"Why?"

Harry sighed. Somehow, Jack Liddle had become his responsibility. Like the farms and the shops and the men and women who lived in his town. Who was going to take care of them if he didn't? "I want you for the MKPD, Jack. I think . . ." The boy looked up at him, dazzled. Harry sighed again. "I think you'll fit in just fine."

NOVEMBER 1972

68. "Thanks for the ride." Russell tossed his duffel bag in the backseat and swung into the car. Through the windshield, Jack could see Margy's ghostly outline in the window. He shifted into reverse and backed out of her drive.

"What did you do with your motorcycle?"

"Sold it." Russell ran his hand over his face. "Gave the money to my mom."

"Mmm. How's she taking it?"

The boy flipped his hand open. "About as well as you'd expect. I'm not sure if she's more upset over the idea I might kill someone, or over the idea I might get killed."

"Seeing as how she became a peace activist after you got drafted, I suspect it's the latter."

Russell looked at him sideways. "You know I—" He paused.

"What?"

"Never mind."

They drove out Old Route 100 in silence. They had had an early snow yesterday, dry and light, and the rolling fields were lapped with white in their hollows and along their stone walls. "Oh. I almost forgot. Happy birthday. One day late."

Russell frowned. "Did my mom tell you?"

Jack snorted. "You forget I've known your mother since we were in grade school together. I was around when you were born." He turned onto Route 9. "And your birth date was on your arrest sheet." Jack didn't need that to remember the day, but no need for the boy to know that.

"Thank you for writing that letter. To the recruiter. It made a big difference."

"The army's lucky to get you. Most young men are running the other way as fast as they can." They crossed the war memorial bridge, and the town opened up around them. "You're sure about this, right? It's not just because . . ."

"Because I was a suspect in a murder?" Russell smiled in a way that made him look much older than his years. "Mom says as soon as somebody else gets into trouble, everybody will stop talking about me."

"She's got a point." Jack rolled to a stop, then turned right onto Main.

"Maybe. Me, I think until you can actually *prove* I didn't do it, there'll always be people talking. Because I'm a baby killer, you know."

"Cut that out." Jack's voice was sharp. "I'd take anyone to the curb who said that about you or any of the boys who've come back from Vietnam. I'm not going to let you say it about yourself."

Russell rubbed his hands along his jeans. "Sorry." He looked out the window as they passed the police station. "That's not the real reason, anyway."

Jack turned onto Church Street. The small park facing St. Alban's was leafless, the bleak sunlight revealing how badly the gazebo at its center needed painting.

"Look around." Russell waved his hand. "What's my future? A job at the mill? Working for a dairy farmer? I'm sick of living in a place where the old folks still call me Erasmus Campbell's great-grandson. That's not normal."

"He was a mighty colorful man." Campbell had run off to fight in the Civil War at the age of fifteen, traveled throughout the young United States, and scandalized his hometown when he returned, married a much younger woman, and started producing little Campbells while in his fifties.

"Having kids when you're old enough to be a grandfather isn't colorful. It's gross."

They swung onto Route 57.

"I get that it's different for your generation. My mom never wanted to be anywhere but Millers Kill. You were born here and you've lived here your whole life. People my age, we want to live."

Natalie Epstein had wanted to live. Jack felt a stab of guilt, like a pinched nerve in the middle of his heart. He suspected he always would, when he thought of her. "I'm sorry your homecoming was so rough. That's not what anyone wanted for you."

Russell shrugged. "It was good to see my mom. Good to know she has a life here without me around. I love my mom, don't get me wrong—"

"I understand." Jack bumped the car over the old train tracks. "You worried she didn't have anyone to take care of her, without you or your dad around." He turned and cut through a half-built development, future housing for GE's bright young men and their wives. Right now, it was a field of frozen mud and yawning foundations. "She's a strong woman. Don't worry about her."

330

Russell nodded.

"So where are you headed?"

"From Glens Falls to New York, New York to Fort Bragg. Then I get my orders for Fort Leonard Wood."

"Where's that?"

"Missouri. It's the army's training ground for MPs."

Jack jerked to a stop before a red light. "MPs. Military police." He swiveled to face Russell.

The boy looked almost shy. "Yeah."

"Huh. That's . . . unexpected." Someone honked behind him, and he almost reached for his magnetic emergency light. Instead, he depressed the gas and drove forward. "You didn't exactly see the bright side of the profession this summer."

"It was interesting. Looking at people, trying to figure them out. Putting pieces together."

"Or not." Jack's voice was more sardonic than he had intended. He tried a lighter tone. "It's not detective work at first, you know. It'll be a whole lot of traffic patrols and checking IDs and escort duty." He slowed down, then gave the car some juice as the light ahead changed to green. Shoppers were out in Glens Falls, bundled up against the cold.

"I know. I just like . . ." The boy paused. Jack could hear him turning words over in his head. "I like the purposefulness of it. It's like being in the army. It's real. It means something. And . . ." He paused again. "I like the idea of doing good." He ducked his head. "Not like a goody-goody. I like the idea of doing something that matters. That can make things better and keep people safer."

Jack pulled into the POLICE PARKING space in front of the bus station and turned off the car. They both got out. Russell retrieved his duffel from the backseat. They shook hands.

"Thanks, Chief Liddle. For everything."

"Think of us when you get tired of army life. We could always use a smart young man like you." Jack smiled a little. "Who wants to make things better."

69. "Clare. They've got the results."

Clare roused herself, wincing as she straightened. She had dozed off in some uncomfortable places before, but a plastic chair in the town hall meeting room was definitely in the top ten least pleasant. She scrubbed her face and focused on Hadley Knox. "What time is it?"

"A little after one."

Clare groaned. "Don't you have to be at work tomorrow? Today?"

Hadley's mouth set in a line. "Depends on what the election clerks have to tell us, doesn't it?"

The jogging stroller next to Clare was empty. "The chief has Ethan." Hadley thumbed toward the windowed end of the room. Russ was in close conference with Lyle MacAuley, the baby balanced against his shoulder. He'd been arguing most of the past week with his deputy chief, who wanted to quit in solidarity. "Has he talked Lyle off the ledge, yet?"

"The dep's agreed to stay through the transition. After that . . . I guess we'll see."

The town had treated Russ's resignation as conditional, while the mayor and board of aldermen did their best to update every voter in the three-town system. There had been meetings, a mailing, e-mails, handouts at the library and the schools, all leading up to today. Yesterday, now. "Where are Hudson and Genny?"

"I sent them home with Granddad. Who knew it took this long to count votes?" The television set on a stand near the aldermen's platform had long ago called the election for the senate and the house, and given strong odds on their New York state assemblyman. As usual, it wasn't the person Clare had voted for.

The meeting room held what Clare thought of as the cop contingent, less Margy and Jack Liddle, who had excused themselves early in the evening. "It's a lose-lose proposition," Margy had told Clare out of earshot of her son. "I can't stand to watch." The two aldermen running for reelection and their opponents were still around, along with a handful of family members. For some reason, the probate judge candidate was still here, despite running unopposed. Maybe he thought the write-ins would beat him?

The election clerk came in, flanked by two volunteers who looked as tired as Clare felt. The clerk looked at the motley gathering. "I'll skip the state- and district-wide results, shall I?" She consulted the paper in her hand. "For the board of aldermen: Garry Greuling and Ronald Tucker. For judge of probate, Peter Eliot. For question one, dissolution of the police department: yes, one thousand two hundred forty-five; no, three thousand eight hundred twenty-nine."

Hadley let out a huff of air that might have been relief or sorrow. Clare turned toward Russ. Behind her she could hear sounds of happiness and disappointment, all muffled with the fatigue that layered itself over the room. She crossed the floor, keeping her eyes on her husband. He looked . . . tired, in a way that had nothing to do with the hour.

"I still think we should sue," Lyle was saying. "We never got a good answer on whether this is legal or not."

Russ held up his hand. "We've got enough going on the lawsuit front. Let it be."

Clare tilted her head back. "How are you doing?"

"This was the outcome I wanted. The department is still here. And fully funded."

She nodded. When he figured out how he felt, he would tell her. In the meanwhile . . . "You want me to take him?"

"No." He pressed a kiss to the side of Ethan's face. "He's my emotional support baby."

Lyle snorted.

Hadley joined them. "Chief." She worried her lower lip. Took a breath. "I'd like to submit my resignation—"

"Denied," he said.

"But, Chief! If it wasn't for that damn lawsuit—"

"Knox. Hadley." Russ shook his head. "Asking for my resignation had nothing to do with you, your ex, your reputation, or anything else you're worried might be a failing." He rested his hand on her shoulder. "You're a good cop. I want you to stay on the job and keep being a good cop."

She nodded. Her chin quivered. "Yes, Chief. Thank you—" Her voice broke. "—for giving me the chance." She spun around and quick-walked toward the door, wiping at her face.

"Keep an eye out for her, Lyle."

"I will."

Russ's mouth turned up in a half-smile. "And take good care of my department. Okay?"

"Goddammit." Lyle fished a tissue out of his pocket and blew his nose. "You're not going to get me to cry, you sonuvabitch."

They had left their car at home. They walked along the cracked and whole sidewalks, past the dark windows of the Main Street shops, Russ pushing Ethan's stroller. The temperature outside AllBanc read thirty-two degrees. Another winter on the way.

"Penny for your thoughts?"

Russ gave her a look. "Save it. We'll need it."

She rolled her eyes. "We've got my salary and your army pension. We'll be fine." She didn't add *until you get another job*. Russ had avoided every conversation on that subject.

They turned onto Church Street. A burst of red and white caused them both to stop. An MKPD car flashed passed them, light bar whirling. "Huh." Russ pushed the stroller forward. Clare fell into step beside him. "Must be an accident. Yeah, there he goes toward Route 57. Maybe the Algonquin Waters has burned down."

Clare pursed her lips. Tried out and rejected the first responses that came to mind. Finally she said, "Who was it?"

"Eric. If it was Paul, he would have been blaring the sirens despite the empty streets." He shook his head. "Well. He's not my problem anymore." He stopped again. Stood still beneath the old Rexall sign.

Clare put her hand on his arm. "Russ?" She loosened his grip on Ethan's stroller and took his hand in hers. His skin was cold. "Love?"

He tilted his head back. "I just wanted to take care of my town. When I took this job, I knew it wasn't going to be, I don't know,

glamorous and exciting." He looked down at her. "It did turn out to be more exciting than I planned."

She smiled a little.

"Did I do the right thing, Clare? I wanted to take care of my people and do right by the town. Should I have waited? Seen how the vote went?"

"I don't know." She wrapped her arms around him. "Maybe it's like jumping in front of a gun. Is it the best choice? Maybe not. But at least you're the only one who gets hurt."

He rubbed over the spot where, beneath his coat and shirt, he carried a scar from the bullet that nearly ended his life. "Every day since I was twenty-one I've gotten up in the morning and I've been a cop. Who am I going to be when I get up tomorrow morning?"

She stepped back. Took his hand and set it on the stroller handle. "I don't know that, either. Let's go home. Get up in the morning. And start figuring out the rest of our lives."

EPILOGUE

Russ was wiping down Ethan and his surroundings following lunch when he heard a knock on the kitchen door. He was still trying to figure out how, after he had personally shoveled the best part of a jar of organic lamb stew—which looked like cat food, although he wasn't about to tell Clare that—into his son's open mouth, there seemed to be another jar's worth of food smeared on Ethan's face, in his hair, across the high chair tray, and spattered on the floor. At least Oscar took care of that last part.

He wiped his hands on a dish towel and pulled the lacy curtain aside. Hadley Knox, in uniform. He unlocked and opened the door. "Hey. I'm surprised to see you in the middle of a shift. Is everything okay at the station?" He kicked himself as soon as the words were out of his mouth. *Not my job anymore.*

She stepped inside, bringing a gust of damp, cold air with her. "I'm not sure how to answer that. It's the same, I guess?" She shuffled from foot to foot.

"You on your lunch break?" She nodded. "Take off your coat, then. Want a cup of coffee? It's Clare's fancy stuff, much better than anything you'll get at the shop."

"Thanks, I'm fine." She peeled off her parka, but didn't look any more relaxed.

He gave Ethan one last swipe and tossed the cloth into the sink. "What's up?"

"It's probably nothing. I don't know." She sat in one of the kitchen chairs and braced her hands on the table.

Russ unlatched the tray and pulled it away, then unbuckled Ethan. "Here." He hoisted the infant up and out and handed him unceremoniously to Knox. She huffed a laugh. "I've noticed it's hard to get too self-conscious when you've got a baby on your lap." He sat across from her. "What's going on?"

"It's Flynn. Kevin."

"Okay. Is it something about the lawsuit?" That was one facet of the job he was happy to leave behind.

She shook her head. "So, we were talking around Labor Day, after you had, you know, told us about the deal you cut. Just passing it on to Flynn. He told me he'd call me after the election. To see how everybody was, you know?"

Russ nodded.

"And I haven't heard from him." Knox folded her arms more closely around Ethan and dropped a kiss on his fuzzy head.

"It's only been six days."

"I know, Chief, but this is Kevin Flynn we're talking about. He's *reliable*. Old Faithful. If the geyser doesn't come up, something's wrong like Horton the Elephant. 'He meant what he said, and he said what he meant.'"

"Have you tried reaching him?"

"His cell phone went straight to voice mail. His apartment phone, too." Her cheeks pinked up a little. "I called his folks, they haven't heard from him since the beginning of October."

"He could still be undercover." He hoped not, for Kevin's sake. That sort of work, even when it wasn't innately dangerous, wore hard on a person's heart and mind. After his long stint over the summer, he ought to be riding a desk for a while, getting his equilibrium back.

"No. Or at least, not on the same investigation. He was pulled off back in September. I don't know what he's doing now, if he's got another assignment, or he's away on TDY, or what. That's why I came to you." She shifted Ethan to one side and leaned forward. "Chief, can you call the Syracuse PD? The brass will talk to you. You can find out the basics, even if they can't tell you exactly what he's up to."

He pinched the bridge of his nose. "I'm not the MKPD chief anymore. I don't have any authority to ask any questions."

Her face took on a crafty look. "But *they* don't know that yet, do they?"

Russ laughed a little. "You sound like my wife when you say that."

"Please, Chief? I'm just . . . I'm worried. It really isn't like him to say he'll do something and then not." An expression flashed across her face, too fast for Russ to decipher. "Most of the time," she amended.

"All right." What the hell. It was a little thing, to set Knox's mind at ease. And if Syracuse brushed him off, well, he'd be getting a lot of that in the future, wouldn't he? Might as well get used to it.

It only took a minute to find the number. Knox held Ethan while he waited for the connection. He stepped into the living room, in case the baby decided to get vocal while he was talking. Recruits were getting younger, but no one would believe his son was fresh out of the academy.

"This is Chief Russ Van Alstyne, from Millers Kill. Can you put me through to Chief Iacocca? Thank you." One hoop through. The Syracuse chief picked up. "Ray? Russ Van Alstyne, from Millers Kill. I'm calling about one of my guys you hired away from me. Kevin Flynn."

He listened to what Ray Iacocca had to say. He assured him everything was fine. He thanked him for his time. He hung up. He walked back into the kitchen.

"What did they say? Did you get through? Was there a problem?"

"No. As far as they're concerned, I'm still heading up the force here." He reached for Ethan, and Knox surrendered the baby to him.

"So what did they say? Is he working undercover?"

He held his son tight against his heart. "Kevin went out on unpaid personal leave almost a month ago. He said there was a family emergency."

Knox stood up. "But I called his family."

"I know."

"I mean . . ." She pressed her hands against her face. "Even if they knew about the, you know, my past and the tapes and everything. Even if they knew, I think they'd say 'Kevin doesn't want to talk to you' or something. They wouldn't lie about not speaking to him."

"No, I don't think they would."

"Then where is he? A person just doesn't just vanish."

But of course, they did. He thought of Carmella Marino, who had died nameless and unknown and remained that way for over fifty years. There were cold cases all over the country whose victims were only known by a number.

"He was worried about the lawsuit," Knox whispered. "He asked me if it might have been the reason why the board pressured you to resign . . . Oh, God, you don't think he—"

"No." His voice was firm. "I don't."

"Then where's Flynn, Chief? Where is he?"

Russ shook his head helplessly. "I don't know, Knox. I don't know."

ACKNOWLEDGMENTS

The first person I need to thank is you, dear reader. Six years is an eternity between publishing books in crime fiction, and I'm deeply grateful that you've stuck with me long enough to hold this novel in your hands.

Likewise, I owe so much to my publisher, St. Martin's Press, and my literary agent at the Jane Rotrosen Agency for their unwavering support. Pete Wolverton, my editor, and Meg Ruley, my agent, were heroic in their ability to wait patiently when I couldn't write and to gently—but firmly!—nudge me when I could.

I need to thank Luci Zahray, not only for first discovering me, but also for her technical expertise, which she shared for this book.

Rhys Bowen, Lucy Burdette, Deborah Crombie, Hallie Ephron, Jenn McKinlay, and Hank Phillippi Ryan, my sisters at the Jungle Red Writers blog, continue to uphold, inspire, and encourage me. I'm so lucky to be part of this sorority.

Three people who always worked to make my writing better are missing now. My husband, Ross Hugo-Vidal, died in 2017 after a year-long fight with cancer. Our friend Timothy LaMar, who made sure the guns and ammo were always correct, passed away a month later, and my mother, Lois Fleming, who was my best first reader, died unexpectedly eight months after that. My life is much diminished without them; I can only hope this book is not.